Knot For Real

By Anida Clarmen

Knot For Real, Second Nature Series, Book 1

First published 2026 by Romantical Publishers

ISBN: 978-1-7646585-1-5 (paperback)

Cover design by Anida Clarmen

First Edition

I dedicate this book to anyone who was ever made to feel like they weren't good enough or didn't deserve to be loved. They were the assholes. You are a wonder.

Welcome To My Omegaverse

The world of *Knot For Real* is not quite the one you know.

It looks familiar enough on the surface, cities, coffee shops, lawyers in good suits, men who can't figure out what to order. But underneath all of that runs something older. Something biology never quite managed to explain away.

In this world, every person is born with what they call a second nature. It emerges in your early teens, quietly at first, a shift in how you smell to others, how others smell to you, a pull in your chest toward certain people and places. By the time you're grown, it has shaped you in ways you might not even recognise until something, or someone, cracks you open enough to look.

There are three designations: **alpha**, **beta**, and **omega**.

Alphas are built for strength and dominance. They are territorial and protective, wired to lead and to provide. Their biology has given them certain physical advantages, including a knot — an anatomical feature that, in moments of intimacy, binds them to a partner. Alphas form packs with one another, drawn together by trust and shared purpose. But a pack without an omega at its centre can feel, for all its power, incomplete.

Betas are the quiet majority. No intense compulsions, no perfume, no heat. They live close to what you might recognise as ordinary human experience, choosing partners by preference rather than pull, building lives on decision rather than instinct. Betas can be loved, and can love deeply. Their second natures are simply quieter. For now.

Omegas are rarer, and the world has a great deal of opinions about them. The common understanding is that omegas are small and soft and built for surrender. Yielding, fragile, decorative. Neat in their categories. The reality, as any omega will tell you, is considerably more complicated than that.

Omegas experience **heat cycles**, periods of intense physical and emotional need that arrive whether they are convenient or not. Heats can be managed with suppressants, though this comes with costs that medicine is only beginning to understand. An omega in heat without someone to care for them is in genuine pain. That is not a metaphor.

What marks an omega most distinctly is their **scent**. Every omega has one, warm and individual and impossible to ignore. When an omega is distressed or aroused, their scent intensifies in what is called a **perfume**: a concentrated signal, unconscious and involuntary, that reaches the people nearest to them.

Sometimes, an alpha encounters an omega and something shifts. The scent becomes more than pleasant. It becomes necessary. This is called **scent sensitivity**, and it is uncommon enough to mean something. Scent-sensitive pairs are called mates. Their responses to one another are not quite rational, not quite voluntary, a recognition that operates below the level of language or decision.

When an omega and their pack choose to fully commit, they **bond**. The bonding bite is not merely physical. The best way anyone has found to describe it is this: your soul makes room for someone else's. You do not lose yourself in the bond. But you are never entirely alone inside yourself again.

The 'second nature', in all its forms, is not about control. It was never meant to be a hierarchy, whatever society has made of it. It is older than that and stranger than that. At its root, the second nature is a system of protection, a deep, instinctual self that has been watching for threats you have not yet named, waiting for you to be ready to listen.

Some listen better than others.

Content Warning

A note before you begin.

Knot For Real is an explicit adult romance intended for readers eighteen and over. It contains content that some readers may find difficult or distressing.

A full list of content warnings can be found at the back of this book.

If you would like to check them before reading, flip to the final pages. If you would like to go in without knowing, that choice is entirely yours, the story will still be there waiting.

Either way, please take care of yourself.

- Anida Clarmen

Playlist

Here are just a few of the songs I was listening to when I wrote this book.

Not Alone - Ben Taylor *(Listening)*
Messy - Lola Young *(Messy)*
Sex & Candy - Marcy Playground *(Marcy Playground)*
Stronger Than That - Bahamas *(Bahamas Is Afie)*
The Bare Minimum - Garrett Adair *(The Bare Minimum)*
This Feeling - Alabama Shakes *(Sound & Color)*
Heartbreak Warfare - John Mayer *(Battle Studies)*
Like You Mean It - Steven Rodriguez *(Like You Mean It)*
Cage - Newton Faulkner *(Interference (Of Light))*
Loved by You - KIRBY *(Loved by You)*

Follow Me

AnidaClarmen.com[1]

1. http://anidaclarmen.com

Chapter 1. Melanie

'I hope you have a great rest of your day.' I smile through my teeth.

It isn't technically a lie. It's just, I'm pretty sure the little omega in front of me will have a fantastic day no matter what I hope for her. At least once a week one of her alphas brings her here to buy to her heart's content. Mostly it's books but occasionally something from the gift section or some art. Always a hot chocolate. Today she was with her whole pack. Four great big hulking alphas whose only wish is to see her happy. So, yeah, I assume she's gonna have a great day.

'Thanks, Melanie. You always pick the best books.' She smiles up at me. She's easy to pick for, she wants romances, fantasy, nothing too scary. Occasionally poetry so that her alphas can read it to her as she falls asleep. Yeah, her day is going to be fine.

'No worries Steph. Come back again soon.' That is a sincere wish. Steph and her friends were the majority of my business. The other chunk was made up of people looking for gifts and betas who liked to read. Plus the regular coffee crowd, but the margin for profit on them was not high.

I sigh once she's left and start making a mocha for myself since the store is in a lull. I designed Second Nature to cater to omegas and so I filled it with everything they loved. Books, new and second-hand, stacks of vinyl in one corner along with band shirts already washed into softness. The drinks came in large thick ceramic mugs. The gifts section up the front was made up of things by local artists or things I found second hand. Sweet trinkets, candles, soft blankets, hand-knitted beanies, and so forth.

Since they usually browse for hours I'd learned to make strong coffee for their alphas while they waited. And my coffee and food was good enough, I had regulars who came just to eat. But this store wasn't for them. It was for the omegas and it was their joy that kept me going even if some days it felt hard. And today was very hard.

I had half a dozen compliments from omegas like Steph today. They came in with their alphas to pick out 'just because' gifts. Every time they said essentially the same thing. 'This was their favourite store ever.' And that they didn't know how I did it, it was so perfectly comforting and practically every item was something they wanted. Their alphas always tip heavily when they say things like that so I try to accept their gratitude gracefully. But some days I just couldn't.

That's probably why I was thinking unkindly to sweet little Steph. I was in a mood. And she didn't make it better when she'd said, 'I've never met a beta with such a great taste.'

I wanted to scream at her.

'And you still haven't because I'm a bloody omega.' But I didn't. It was better that no one knew and no one guessed.

Thanks to the extra strong suppressants my doctor prescribed me, no one had guessed at my secret in a long time. The store was eight years old now and the last time someone hinted I might be something other than a beta was in my first year so... seven years. It had been seven years since anyone had wondered if I was an omega.

I don't know why that thought made me so sad but it did.

It was by choice, obviously. No one spent the amount of money I did on scent neutralizers and suppressants by accident. No one put on the restrictive and padded slick-proof underwear for fun. I deliberately hid my status. But it annoyed me nonetheless because I knew the real reason no one guessed was that I didn't look like your standard omega.

Sure I was short but I was also thick. Omegas were known for the lithe elegant frames and that was not me. I was chunky, to say the least. My thighs were massive, my bum was round, my breasts so large they knocked me up a couple of t-shirt sizes. My arms were soft and squishy. On a good day, I would call myself Rubenesque. On a bad day, like today, I'd probably describe myself as a couple of beach balls strapped together with some legs.

I swivel off the steaming wand as I contemplate my distorted reflection in the shiny metal of the coffee machine.

I was pretty, I didn't doubt that. I have chubbier cheeks than would be considered in vogue but I have long lashes, crystal blue eyes, and plump naturally rosy lips. And I spent way too much time on my curls. Every morning I reset them, pin them off my face, and use essential oils to make them waft soft lavender or sweet vanilla around me all day. Sometimes cinnamon if I was feeling spicy. I love sweet scents, just like any omega.

But am I even an omega at this point?

That was a mean thought. I stick out my tongue at my reflection in the machine. Of course, I was an omega. I was just built differently. And not just physically.

I was too independent to ever be considered a real omega. I didn't need anyone to look after me. I did it all by myself.

I scoot onto the stool I keep behind the counter for moments like this to give my feet a break while I sip my drink and relax a little.

Once upon a time, did I think I needed other people? Yes, of course. Even better, once upon a time, I thought I had other people. Other people who would look after me. I'd be a part of their pack, their center. They'd cherish me like I cherished them. But it didn't work out. And it broke me.

Chapter 2. John

Today had been long and boring but it was about to get better. I was taking an extra afternoon break to go get coffee for the office which means I am about to see Melanie.

It was getting really hard to convince myself that I wasn't a stalker. For the last six months I'd been stopping by Melanie's shop more and more. I had the perfect excuse, I had to get presents for the omegas we'd been courting. She asked all kinds of questions I didn't know the answers to and yet somehow she always picked out just the right gifts.

Last week the omega we'd been courting had sobbed about how she couldn't believe she wasn't falling for the alphas who had bought her the best presents ever. We soothed her as best we could and assured her we weren't mad. In fact, I felt relieved, she was a dear thing but none of us had been feeling a match either.

That was our fifth courting that hadn't worked out in six months and so as a pack, we'd agreed to take a break from it all. I know that at least two of the others wanted to give up entirely. Sam and Mick had both made that abundantly clear.

Sam was happy, focused on work and having flings with betas. Mick was always happier alone. It was only me and George who wanted an omega. For me, it was about the connection for all of us, for us to have someone to rally around, to support, to love, someone to be our center. For George, I think it was just a checklist thing. Like, finish university, check. Find a pack, check. Become wildly successful, check. Get an omega...no check. Yet.

Not that he wouldn't love whomever we found. And I didn't doubt that if we found an omega the other two would pull their heads out of their arses and get on board. Eventually. But for now, we needed a break.

Three months, no omegas. That was what we'd all agreed. George had some big something going on at work so it was a good time to take a break. Sam would get back to dating his many betas. Mick would probably use all the downtime to start a new project of god only knows what.

Last time it was brewing beer, he'd changed something in the process that made it brew faster and sold the idea to a brew house for more than most people make in a year. The time before he'd come up with an idea for a new way to track people's purchasing habits in malls to better improve customer experience. The time before that had something to do with cheese and the time before that he'd learned to knit. The knitting was the only thing that hadn't turned an insane amount of profit. And it was the only one he'd persisted in.

Me, I was apparently going to use this time to stalk a sweet beta simply because I enjoyed her company. Not that I was really stalking her, just frequenting her place of business more often than strictly necessary.

Her store was halfway between my work and our pack house. I'd come in here for the first time a little over a year ago when my colleagues had taken me out for some first-week-on-the-job beers. On my way home I'd seen the cafe lights on and had burst in asking for a bathroom. She waved to the back and I hurried towards the sign faster than could ever be considered appropriate.

Once I relieved myself, I'd come out ready to make a purchase and she'd waved me off. I'd insisted but she explained she was technically closed. I blame it on the beers but it had taken me longer than I care to admit to realise that I was making her uncomfortable. Eventually I noticed how she scooted right to the back of the space behind the counter and how her eyes were darting to the exits. Then I freaked out on her behalf and ran from the building. Not a great first impression.

It was even worse when she made eye contact with me through the glass door, as she locked it and pulled the blinds and I realised I was standing across the road staring at her like a freak.

I went back the next day to apologize and she'd kindly laughed it off and told me to buy an extra large coffee to make it up to her and that was it. I was hooked.

There were coffee places closer to my work but hers was the best. Everyone from the office agreed, if you had the time you would come here. I stopped by every day on the way to work and usually a couple of times during the week to do a run for the office like I was now.

Slowly, Melanie and I became friends. Not friend friends. Just polite chit-chat friends. We'd share some small talk, her smiling and giggling, me teasing her to get her to giggle. It sounds like bells.

So when at the end of last year George announced he was signing us up for a dating service and putting me in charge of courting gifts I hadn't hesitated to come to Melanie for help. And that's when I started to get to know her for real. And wow.

She was funny and kind and the way her dimples popped made me swoon. And she had amazing taste. The omegas we courted loved her choices. They just hadn't loved us.

On paper, we were not a hard sell. An older, well-established, and well-funded pack. I worked as a tech consultant. Sam was a lawyer. George was the CEO of his own company. Which owned several other companies. And Mick was whatever he chose to be that week. We were all fit and healthy and while I'm no great judge of beauty I know none of us were bad to look at. And if I'd had any doubt, the many omegas wanting to meet us would have squashed them. The problem was they eventually met us and none of us were naturally personable.

I was a hardcore nerd. Unless you enjoy discussing data analytics and code or corny-as-shit action movies, I am not your guy. George comes in a close second with his conversations about environmental sustainability. Sam only knows how to argue which he blames on being a lawyer and I blame him for being an arse. And Mick, well he just doesn't talk much at all.

So every time we met an omega we'd try but with no natural spark, it just didn't work. Which is why we were taking a break from courting. To regroup and reenergize. It also meant that I was now free to ask Melanie out. I think I'd been crushing on her since the beginning but when we began talking more and I'd seen how quick witted she was I'd started to develop a full fascination with the woman.

I finally arrive at the front of the store just in time to see her poke her tongue out at the coffee machine. I want to laugh. What has the machine done to warrant such mockery? But as I watch, her expression turns sad. She slides onto the stool she takes her breaks on and stares into her coffee. My stomach swoops within me. I don't know what is wrong but I know I want to make it better.

KNOT FOR REAL

Chapter 3. Melanie

'Hey, do you have a bathroom?' My sadness flees me at the sight of one of my favourite customers. The stunning alpha shocked me into silence the first time he stormed into my shop because wow. Just wow.

His mop of curly hair with ringlets tighter than my own. His thick-framed, wanna-be Clark Kent glasses. The cute way he almost always wears a t-shirt under his work jackets. The one time he'd come in with a button-up shirt on and the sleeves rolled up, I'd swooned internally. Even when he'd first stormed in clearly tipsy it was lust more than fear that surged through my blood.

When he showed up the next day apologizing for distressing me, my omega instincts had gone wild for a bit. Without giving my brain permission it started daydreaming about romantic dates, long lunches, and other less PG scenarios.

My crush lasted longer than I care to admit considering he showed zero interest in me. It wasn't until six months ago when he asked me to help pick out some gifts for his new omega that my stupid heart finally got the message. Mostly.

'Hi, John.' I smile. 'Straight down the back on the left.'

'Thanks.' He winks at me. Like seriously actually winks, and yet somehow on him, the corny things work. Like this stupid little script, we've been running whenever he comes in and I'm not busy. He charges in like it's that first night all over again when he was just an incredibly hot drunk looking for the bathroom.

'What can I get you?' I ask him as he leans on my counter. Today beneath the blazer he has on a vintage The Goonies t-shirt clinging to his broad chest so tight it seems downright indecent.

'It's a big order, the whole office I'm afraid.' He slides a piece of paper with everyone's order on it across to me. I try not to sigh but it slips out. I'm tired. It's already been a long day and I'm in a mood.

'I'm on it.' I mumble, readying myself to slide off my stool and get to work.

'Hang on a minute.' John smirks, reaching across to touch my hand and still my movement. 'Sit, finish your drink. No offense but it does seem like you might need the break and I'm in no rush to get back to the office.'

'You say no offense and yet, telling someone they look tired...' He laughs as I let my voice trail off. By the goddess, he has a great laugh.

'Come on. You look like you're enjoying your break, I can wait a minute. Tell me about your life?' He asks this question all the time and yet it still makes me uncomfortable. I never have anything new to say.

'Pretty good, my reread this month is an Austen. Emma, my favourite. So that's excellent. Otherwise, everything is the same. Work is steady.'

'You know you can reread more than one book a month. This torture is of your own infliction.' He teases me leaning in to whisper the last as if it were a secret.

'It's not torture it's discipline. Otherwise, I think I'd just lie around reading my comfort books on repeat all year round. It's important to push yourself.' I point my finger at him as if I'm scolding him.

'You call it discipline, I call it torture.' He shrugs.

'I guess it just depends on if you can find a way to enjoy a little pain.' As soon as the words slip out, my cheeks warm. Oh my god did I just make a BDSM joke? I guess I did. Well, excuse me I think I'll just go die in a hole. I stare into what's left of my Mocha. Not enough to drown in but maybe I could just choke on it.

My brain suddenly scrambles with the image of John standing above me as I choke on his dick. The head sliding across my lips, along my tongue, as he gently pushes himself into my throat, stroking my cheek to catch my lone tear as his hand slips down to wrap around my throat.

My blush deepens. Where the hell did that come from? A side effect of my suppressants is meant to be not having those kinds of thoughts. Thank the goddess for slick-proof underwear and extra strength scent neutralizer. I jump to my feet skirting away behind the coffee machine just in case. A little distance and the stench of coffee should help dispel any hint of scent that escaped me. I don't dare look at John. I just grab the list and start making a plan for how to tackle the sixteen coffees he's ordering. Cold ones first. Then the hot ones. I'll need 10 shots of coffee, the rest are chocolate or caramel. I've got this.

I sneak a glance at John. Nope. Bad idea. He has a strange expression on his face, somewhere between he's seen a ghost and he's hungry. So eyes down. Make coffee. Pretend I am not an idiot.

I've got this.

I do not have this. My hands shake as I fill the cradle and try to get it into the machine to make the first of the shots. Goddess, he must think I'm an idiot. He hasn't said anything. Why hasn't he said anything? Because there is no appropriate response to a BDSM joke in a cute little coffee bookstore for omegas, you idiot.

John clears his throat. Should I look at him?

'So how's Whisper?' My dog? He's asking about my dog. Okay. That's good. We're gonna skate straight past the sex joke. Awesome.

'Whisper is still perfect.' I smile awkwardly as I start setting aside cups with shots. I'll load him up with reusable travel mugs and he'll bring them back for me to wash and reuse. Have I lost a few cups over the years, yes. But a negligible amount and otherwise I'd refuse to do takeaways.

'You say perfect and yet the only time I met Whisper he licked my shoe and then fell over while standing still.' I can hear the teasing in his voice. Wow he really is willing to blow straight past my inappropriate comment. My shoulders slump with relief.

'Like I said, he is perfect. Just as he was that day. This morning he got stuck in a blanket and fell off the couch. Perfection.' I smile. My dog is one of my favourite things in the entire world. He's a mutt, he looks like five dogs rolled up in one. And he pretty much sleeps 90 per cent of the time, unless I'm walking him or I have food, he's asleep. He is the best.

'I'm surprised you're willing to leave him at home alone. Has he ever almost drowned in his water bowl?'

'Don't be mean.' I tease back. 'And no. Besides he's just upstairs, if I hear any strange sounds I can just go up and check on him?'

'You live here?' Confusion clouds John's voice so I look up from where I'm making coffee art no one will ever see.

'Yeah, this is my place. I live upstairs.' I don't know why he's so surprised. It's not uncommon for people to live above their shops but his face suggests this is groundbreaking information.

'I didn't know.' His voice seems distant.

'Why would you?' I definitely don't advertise the fact. It doesn't matter that no one knows I'm an omega, a woman living alone, even a beta, is still a target.

'I don't know.' He mumbles. As the moment stretches the silence becomes uncomfortable. Well not silence, I'm making coffee. But the lack of talking is very awkward. He seems bothered. Although, why would he be bothered by the fact that I live here? I've got no clue. But he wouldn't be alone.

My parents hate that I live here. They love to bring up how dangerous it is for me to live alone. But they also definitely don't want me in their house.

Even when I wasn't having meltdowns it always seemed like nothing I ever did was quite right. When I'd first tried my hand at cooking, the food hadn't been good enough. Then I hadn't made enough. Then I'd made too much. Then I'd left too many dishes. Then I'd done the cleaning which was rude because other people deserve the chance to contribute. And then I stopped cooking and I'd been a bitch. A bad omega. Unable to do the basics of nesting and making a home. A home I had to go back to this weekend.

'I lied.' The words slip from my lips as I start adding whipped cream to four of the drinks.

'You lied? You don't live here?' He asks.

'No I definitely live here, there's a massive pile of laundry in the middle of my living room to prove it.' I laugh. 'I lied before when I said everything's the same. I forgot I'm going to see my family on Sunday.'

'Oh well, that's fun.' The snort that flies out of me is beyond unladylike. 'Not fun?'

His question hangs in the air. No, visiting my family was definitely not fun. My perfect omega sister with her bonded pack, my parents goo goo-eyed over her and her packs and all their accomplishments. And me. Sitting at the end of the table trying to eat under the scrutiny of my mother's gaze. If I could avoid it I would. But I can't, so I shrug.

'It'll be fine. What's the worst that can happen?'

KNOT FOR REAL

Chapter 4. John

'You know those are famous last words, right?' I try to laugh but it comes out as a strange croak. More things I don't know about her. And they are really starting to bug me. How could I not know that she lives here?

And she clearly doesn't get on with her family. That one surprises me. Partly because betas usually don't have much animosity with their parents. Omegas and alphas on the other hand, extra hormonal teen years coupled with strong personalities and undeniable natures, parents and their children often had problems. But it was less common for betas. And if I'd had to guess I would have assumed Melanie had a great childhood, purely because of how sweet she is. But maybe not.

'Well it's only Thursday, I still have time to catch a cold or sprain an ankle or... is the plague still a thing?' Her smile is bright but definitely not genuine.

'Do you have anything fun happening next week? That's how I get through the hard things by focusing on the fun things that come after. Like what do you have planned for next week?' She blows a stray curl back from her cheek as she pours frothed milk into the remaining cups. The curl falls back down clearly bothering her. I grip my thigh to stop from reaching out to push it back for her.

'Next Wednesday I have a doctor's appointment.' Her smirk says it all. She thinks this is funny.

'Okay and after that?' I press.

'Just more work I'm afraid. As far as the eye can see.'

'You have to have something you're looking forward to? Come on, it can be anything?' She ponders my question as she loads up the drinks in the special reusable drink caddies she loans out. Does this girl really have nothing she could look forward to? The thought breaks my heart.

Suddenly her face flares red and she giggles. Then she pales and begins rearranging the perfectly balanced drink caddies.

'What was that?' I'm pretty sure I'd give every cent in my bank account to know what thought just slid through her mind.

'Hmm? What?' She feigns ignorance even though I know she knows I noticed.

'What did you think of?' I press.

'Think of?'

'Yes, what did you think that made you blush so prettily?' I lean into the flirt. And boy have I been missing out. Simply calling her blush pretty earns me another deeper shade of pink dusting her cheeks as she bites her lip. God, she is adorable. I'm tempted to start explaining to her just how charming I find her and her curvy soft delicious body.

'I didn't blush.' She hedges. Adorable.

'No, of course not, it's just warm in here, right?' I ask to let her fluster pass. As adorable as she is I have to keep reminding myself, this is her place of work. She works in hospitality, it's literally her job to be nice to customers whether she wants to or not. So I can't cross any lines. No matter how much I want to.

'Yeah, it's warm.' She mumbles as she rings up all the various drinks and I fish the company card out of my wallet ready to pay. 'Sandra.'

'Sandra?' I repeated the name back to her as a question. Who is Sandra?

'Yes, my friend. She's coming over Sunday night, I can look forward to that.'

‘Tell me about her?’

‘She’s been my best friend since pre-school. Her pack is expecting a child soon so we haven’t seen as much of each other lately, so, I’m pretty excited. We’ll spend the evening just sitting and snacking, maybe take Whisper for a walk.’

‘That sounds awesome. Definitely something to look forward to.’

‘Yeah.’ Her sigh is sad. Resigned. I hate it. ‘Anything I can do to cheer you up?’

‘No, today was just long. I’m tired. I feel like I need a month off.’

‘I know the feeling. And I see the hours you work, I’m impressed.
’

‘Thanks. That’s a nice thing to say.’ She looks sad again. Damn it.

‘I think I’m going to punch Mick in the face when I get home.’ I don’t know why I say it. But it works. She snorts again and I feel like a hero. Take that sadness.

‘Which packmate is Mick again? The lawyer or the inventor?’

‘The inventor.’

‘There’s just three of you right?’

‘Four, all alphas.’ I shrug. Four is a large number of alphas and without a beta in the mix or an omega to center us, most people have questions as to how we don’t kill each other.

‘You’ve been together long?’ Though apparently not Mel.

‘Six years in August. Probably six years too long if I’m being honest.’ I tease.

‘Is that why you’re punching Mick in the face?’ She asks.

‘No. You see me and Mick, we’re fans of a good prank. Sam and George, not so much. And I think Mick went too far.’

‘What did he do?’ Her intrigue feels like victory in my veins.

‘He pranked Sam. Our other brother. Plastic wrap pulled tight, under the toilet seat, massive mess.’ I shake my head as I think about it.

‘Okay but what does that have to do with you?’ She questions.

'Mick framed me, left the leftover wrap in my bedroom. Sam tackled me and got in quite a few decent shots so I think it's only fair that I pass them on to Mick.'

'Seems a bit basic to me.' She shrugs.

'Basic?' I'm offended, no one has ever called me basic.

'Yeah, you say you like a prank war?'

'Yeah...' I let my voice trail off, intrigued by where she's going.

'So obviously you should prank him back but since he got Sam involved you should get Sam to help you. You two should prank him together. It would be more fun.'

'It's a shame, but you're right.' I concede.

'Of course I am. But why is that a shame?'

'I was looking forward to punching Mick in the face.' She laughs again and I feel like a golden hero.

'Well, you can still come up with another reason to swing at him. I just don't think this is it.' She teases as she slides the coffees towards me.

'Very true.' I acquiesce.

'Well I guess you better get going, otherwise, the coffee will be cold by the time you get back and I don't need anyone spreading rumours I don't make my coffee hot enough.'

'Of course not.' I lift the coffee caddies from the counter.

'Can I ask you a favor?' She calls as she rounds the bench and crosses the room to open the door for me.

'Yes, anything.' Was that too enthusiastic?

'Do you think you could get those coffee cups back by tomorrow? Even if you just leave them at the front door here on your way home. I'm running low.'

'Yeah, no problem.' I smile as I pass her and head out into the street. And there it is again. The faintest hint of strawberries. Even though I don't think she serves anything strawberry-flavoured here. It's a shame, it's one of my favourite flavours. And there's something about this particular strawberry scent. It's so sweet, it reminds me of these candies I used to get when I was young. They had a dumb strawberry pattern on the wrapper with a green twist on the end. God I missed them.

I smelled it before when she was still relaxing and sitting on her stool. When I'd pointed out that she was the one inflicting pain on herself she'd told me you just had to find a way to enjoy it. There was no way she knew that was my thing, right? But the way she'd said it with her dimples popping and her eyes flashing, maybe I was wrong.

I start my walk back to work with less enthusiasm than I had had coming here. Did Melanie like a little rough tease? She didn't seem like the type. But what did I know? Maybe she likes to be restrained? Maybe she likes being pinned down and tortured with soft touches and firm spanks, never knowing which was coming next.

Fuck. I was in desperate need of a second to adjust myself but both my hands were taken up with the stupid coffee cup caddies. What was wrong with me?

I knew what was wrong with me. I had a thing for Melanie.

Chapter 5. Melanie

Four hours. I just had to get through four hours.

Chatting to John on Thursday turned out to be the highlight of my week. Friday, Mindy, my very occasional part time waitress had to leave suddenly because her kid had gotten into a fight at school and no one else from her pack was available. It was very understandable but it left me short-handed. So rather than sorting the stock while she was covering the counter I'd had to do it all myself after closing.

Saturday had been better. We stayed open for our monthly poetry reading. It was fun. But we didn't close till nine which meant a fourteen-hour day for me. And even though I slept in today, I'm exhausted. And now I was walking into the lion's den.

Actually no, that is incorrect, they aren't lions. More like vipers or some kind of snake. My old therapist would have told me to imagine them as something less intimidating and scary but I wanted to be scared. Scared was prepared. And for my family, it was best to have your guard up. I wish John was with me.

That's weird. I haven't seen him since his on-the-way-to-work-coffee Friday morning, so I'm surprised he's on my mind. Plus, John is lovely but what could he or anyone do when it came to my family? I just want to get it over with already. But alas I was still on the doorstep.

I could hear my family inside all laughing and talking. Maybe they hadn't heard the bell? If they have and I ring again I'll get in trouble for being annoying. Best to wait. Then again if they haven't heard it and one of them catches me out here, the mocking will never cease.

I wait a few more breaths. No signs of movement toward me from inside. Just a peal of laughter that belongs to my sister coming from deep within the house. I ring the doorbell again.

'Oh my god, alright, I'm coming.' I hear my sister's voice yelling loudly. 'She can't wait two seconds.'

The last is not directed at me but it finds its audience. I can hear the chortling deep laugh of her alphas and my mother's cackle. It's my own fault, I fell for the bait.

'Hey, big sis.' Lucy chimes as she swings the front door open. She looks effortlessly chic in a pale blue sweater and black denim jeans. Damn it. Last time I was here for lunch everyone had dressed more formally and I'd been ridiculed, so today I'd put on my nicest sundress. 'You look ... nice.'

'Thanks.' Her tone tells me that she does not in fact think I look nice, but what else could I say? She spins on her heel taking off toward the kitchen while I kick off my sandals by the door and follow her at a slower pace.

In the many years since I left home, my parents' house hasn't changed. Cream walls, pale wood furniture, a hint of beachy blue here and there. It was exactly as my sister had done it shortly after she'd been designated an omega. I'd wanted to add my touches when my designation came through but it had been met with a lot less enthusiasm. Apparently, my colour choices were too intense and overbearing. But mum loves pastels. Personally, I feel like I'm in an asylum with all the colours purposefully pale to keep me calm. But to each their own.

I follow Lucy into the kitchen which is also five different shades of cream. White appliances with light granite counters on pale wood cabinets. The space was relatively small, made more so by the three giant looming alphas who turned their gazes on me. All three of them were wearing khaki pants and pale blue button-downs. They look like they'd dressed to match the house. In all honesty, if it wasn't for their slightly different hair colours I'm not sure I could tell them apart.

'Hey.' I mumble weakly as I enter and loiter by the door, my sister sits by her alphas on one of the stools along the breakfast bar.

'There you are.' My mum smiles from her place stirring a pot on the stove. 'I was just saying it's a good thing your sister was here on time. Why are you so late?'

'I thought you said twelve-thirty for lunch?'

'Yes twelve thirty for lunch but your sister came early to help.'

'I didn't know you wanted help.' I explain, remembering the last lunch we had when I did come early to help and she yelled at me that I was under foot and in her way.

'Nevermind. The boys have been regaling me with stories from their new start-up.'

'Sounds fun.' I murmur.

'You wouldn't understand.' Mark chuckles from behind Lucy's right shoulder.

'Yeah unless you've ever run your own business you wouldn't get it.' Josh nods in agreement to his packmate.

'Unless you're as devastatingly smart as your mother, that is.' Matt adds for good measure. And there it is. My sister's pack mates have perfectly executed their usual little routine. Insult me, mock me, compliment mum so I can't complain.

'I do run my own business.' I point out. I know there's no point in defending myself but it would be pathetic not to try.

'You mean your coffee shop?' My sister snorts with derision. 'That's not what they're talking about. They're talking about like an actual company.'

'And it sounds like it's doing well?' My mum chimes from her place by the stove.

'In a couple of weeks, we have a meeting with the investor we've been waiting for. If we can get him on board, the sky's the limit.' Mark winks at mum. Unlike when John does it, it doesn't seem like a cute gesture. Instead I feel a little nauseous.

'Oh, you'll have no trouble with the investor. Three charming boys like you.' Mum smiles over at them. Yep definitely feeling nauseous. 'Unlike poor Mellon over here.'

'Mum.' I can't help the whine in my voice. I hate it when she calls me that. It was the nickname the bullies in my school gave me and the fact that she thought it was cute meant she didn't see the harm in using it. No matter how many times I ask her not to.

'Oh shush you. They already know the story, they're the ones who got you the meeting with the bank that did give you the loan.' She charges on, mistaking my distress over the nickname for something else. 'We were so grateful. Mellon had already been to like eight different banks for her little cafe when you helped her out. I get their reticence though, she doesn't really look the part. And all the pretty coloured pie charts in the world don't help.'

'They were forecasts and projections mum. My five-year plan for the store.' I don't know why I bother, but calling the company plan I spent several months perfecting 'pretty coloured pie charts' makes me sound like a toddler with crayons.

'Never mind that dear. Let's all sit up for lunch. The boys already set the table for me.' She croons with pride as she loads the food up into serving dishes to take to the table. The boys grab the dishes and head towards the dining room, my sister in tow. 'Hang on a second.' My mum calls as I go to follow them. She unties her apron and pops it on the counter next to the stove before coming towards me. 'I made the salads especially for you, and the fish. It's very lean.'

'Thanks.' I mumble to my shoes. Mum slides past me, wine in hand, and pats my belly with a raised eyebrow as if I didn't already get what she was referring to. I get it.

I wasn't proud of it but the stress of knowing that I was coming here this weekend and what mum would say had caused me to miss several meals this week. In fact I'd been drinking black coffee all week except for that one mocha. Not that I thought it would help it was more just a habit whenever I knew I was going to see her. Just in case she asked me to recite what I'd eaten that week so she could help me figure out what to cut out.

'What are you doing loitering in the kitchen?' My dad's voice booms from behind me as he emerges from his study, swinging by the fridge for a beer. 'Mum texted lunch is on. You're always hungry.'

'Hi Dad.' I nod as he charges straight past me to the dining room to a loud round of hellos from Lucy's pack. They all adore each other.

Okay, deep breath. I can do this. It's only three hours and forty-five minutes to go.

Chapter 6. Sam

'Do you want to die?' I call across the gym to John. Everyone knows I'm down here Sunday nights for a long run and yet he is on the treadmill.

'Sorry, I wasn't keeping an eye on the time.' He jumps off the machine with a smile, mounts the bicycle and gets to pedaling instead. I jump on and pick the hill run that makes me feel like my lungs are going to fall out of my chest.

I know I have no more right over the space than him but I'm still annoyed by his presence. Normally I have the basement gym all to myself, although I designed it with everyone in mind. Besides the bike and the treadmill, there's a rowing machine and then a bunch of free weights. In the back corner there's a Smith machine and on the other side is a punching bag as per Mick's request.

'What are you doing down here?' I ask John. The few times I'd seen him down here he was in the sauna or plunge pool in the courtyard, he was a long walks guy, and hiking kind of guy, not a gym guy.

'Just needed to burn off some energy.' He mumbles as he pedals faster.

'Say more.' I demand.

'How was your date last night?' John avoids my question with his own. I want to call him on it but damn it, it's going to work. There's a reason I'm in the mood to run till my lungs explode and it's not because last night went well.

It went exactly the way I'm starting to expect these things to go. I like dating betas because they don't need me. We can just have fun, and enjoy ourselves. And yet eventually it gets to this point where they're asking about commitment and if they can meet my pack. I know the other guys aren't going to be interested so I always decline and that's usually when they dump me. Or just stop calling. Or call me an alphahole and throw a drink in my face as I experienced last night.

I can take a lashing out. What's bugging me is the consistency with which this is happening. It used to be after five or six months, now sometimes it was within weeks. Last night was a first date. But I'd still prefer to be upfront and honest about what I want.

I have no interest in a long term relationship. I had to drag myself to each of our meetings with the prospective omegas. Listening to them lay out their hopes, dreams and expectations was painful. I'd had enough of that.

My parents had been good people but they were tough love types. And every time I met their expectations, they just came up with something new. Nothing was ever good enough. And the whole way along they always reminded me that I owed all my success to them and I had to work hard. After all, I owed them more than just my life.

'Shouldn't you be off reading a book or watching some crap?' I demand of John who's now pedalling so leisurely next to me he might as well not be on the bike at all.

'I told you I need to burn some energy off.' He shrugs his shoulders in response.

'You tell me yours and I'll tell you mine.' I offer. He climbs off the bike, coming to rest across the side of my treadmill like a teenage girl caught in a daydream. I push his face away but he immediately resumes the position and I can't help but smile.

He's always been the sweet one in our pack. Mick's the strong and silent type. George is the bossy know-it-all. I'm the arsehole. It still surprises me that these three had wanted me for the pack. They'd already been together a year when we met.

'You've dated a lot of betas?' His question surprises me.

'I've dated a few betas.' I hedge unsure of where his question could be going.

'What do you say?'

'Like in general?'

'No what do you say to get them to go out with you?' I pause my run.

'You want to ask someone out?' I think if the sky had suddenly turned green I would have been less surprised.

'Yeah, I mean, no. Maybe. I was just thinking about it and... what do you say?' The urge to tease is strong. But I resist.

'I guess it depends on the situation. How well you know them, how much rapport you have, why you want to go out with them?'

'Why I want to go out with them?' His confusion is obvious.

'Yeah, like if it's just for sex you'd ask them to meet you at a bar, but if you're interested in more, then ask for a dinner or a movie or something you think they'd like.' He looks at me like gospel is dripping from my lips rather than the most basic dating advice in the entire world. 'What's this all about anyway?'

John meanders over to the Smith machine and begins setting it up for chest presses so I abandon my run and follow him over. This was clearly going to be an awkward conversation, having something to do with our hands would make it easier.

Not that we hadn't talked about sex before. We were both alphas after all. But I'd never really known him to date. And since we'd moved to this place about a year ago he'd gone from not interested to seemingly disgusted by the thought.

John gets into position on the bench having set his weights so I stand behind the bench ready to spot him.

'There's a girl.' He breathes out on his first rep.

'Okay.' I mumble. I figured there was someone.

'A beta.' That at least explained his sudden interest in my dating life.

'What's their name?' Seems like an appropriate question.

'Melanie.' He sighs her name as shelves the bar. Melanie. It's a good name. I've also heard her name at least a couple of times a week for the last year.

'From the bookstore?' I ask as he sits up.

'Yeah.' He hedges as I slide into position and adjust my grip.

'Why now?' I push for him to keep talking before I lift the bar off its hooks and take the weight to begin my reps, it's a bit light for me so I push hard and fast.

'Well, we're not doing the courting thing anymore so now I can.' John murmurs and then lapses into silence. I finish my set and sit up as I try to process this.

'So you've liked her this whole time?' I've heard him talk about the bookstore owner but I'd never gotten the vibe he was into her.

'Yeah. Well no. At first I just liked her as a person. But then when I got to know her better, buying all those gifts and talking to her more, I started to like her like her.'

'But you've known this girl for a year and you want to ask her out now?' I point out skating past his teenage romance antics.

'Yeah. Is that a problem?'

'Maybe. If it's been a year and she's never hinted at you asking her out she might not feel that way about you.' I hedge. He looks so sad I feel bad. 'Have you tried feeling her out, seeing if she'd be open to being asked out on a date?'

'No. How do you do that?' I try not to roll my eyes at his question.

'You have a chat. You bring up dating. You see what her opinions are. What her body language is like.' I offer with a shrug.

'Can you do it for me?'

'What? No.' This time I do roll my eyes as I stand and he takes my place.

'Tomorrow morning, come with me. You can ask her the questions. You can find out if she'd be open to dating.' He seems proud of his plan but there's no way.

'It works better if the guy who wants to ask her out asks the questions.' I explain.

'Please?' He begs. I'm unmoved. I don't have any interest in detouring tomorrow morning for some girl who's making John go all mooney-eyed. 'You owe me!'

'I owe you?' I snort as he starts his next set.

'Yeah for beating me up the other night.' He puffs out.

'You cling-wrapped my toilet. The mess was feral.' I grump. I'd cleaned it up as best as I could but I'd still had to explain to our regular cleaner that I hadn't simply decided that close enough was good enough and stopped aiming.

'Nope, that was Mick. Mick did that. He left the stuff in my room so you'd blame me.' John sits up and folds his arms over his chest to look intimidating. It doesn't work.

'Oh shit, sorry.' I feel guilty. I know I got in quite a few good swings.

'So come tomorrow? Meet her? Help me?' He returns to begging.

'Fine.' I growl as I swat at him to stand up.

'Which leads me to point number two. And Melanie's idea. I think we need to team up.' He reaches his arm out to rest on my shoulder as he gestures between us.

'Team up?' I'm confused.

'Mick got one over both of us. So we take him down together.'

'Oh, I am in.' I high five John. The guy was cheesy but I love him. I have a feeling I was going to like Melanie too if she was the type to come up with revenge plots.

KNOT FOR REAL

Chapter 7. Melanie

'Red or white?' Sandra asks as she holds up two wine bottles on my doorstep.

'What do you mean 'or'?' I tease as I let her in. I'm not much of a drinker but it's fun to joke. She deposits the wine on the kitchen counter before turning to me.

'Are you okay?' She asks, pulling me into a hug.

'I'm fine.' I assure her as I pull back and move to get us some wine glasses.

'How bad was it?' She asks, making herself at home on the couch. I bring the glasses and the chilled white wine over to the coffee table.

'It honestly wasn't even bad. Just usual.' I sit beside her.

'Lucy was in fine form, I bet.' Sandra snarks along with a large sip of her wine.

'Same old, same old.' I shrug. Seriously there was nothing that my parents or sister did or said today that I hadn't heard a hundred times before.

'And how were the three ass-keteers?' She queries.

'They were fine.' I shrug. My brothers in law were the assholes they always are.

'Uh huh.' She rolls her eyes in disbelief. 'I should have brought whiskey.'

'You should always bring whiskey.' I tease. I might not like wine and I might not be much of a drinker but a really good whiskey on a cold night was one of my favourite things in the world. I blame my grandma. When I was little I would stay with her in the winter. She had a ritual of making warm honey and vanilla milk with cinnamon and a hint of lavender. When I got older it also included a tablespoon of whiskey. Just the thought has me drooling. 'What I need is a distraction.'

'Ooh, what kind of a distraction?' Sandra coos already refilling her wine glass.

'Tell me about you. I haven't seen you in more than a month.What's happening?'

'Well, Jules is pregnant as you know. Which has made her a little more intense and needy than normal. And not just for the guys. The other night she said she felt like she was going to die if we didn't hang out and have girl time. All she seems to want is to have her hair brushed and her feet massaged.'

'Who doesn't?' I ask.

'Me. Feet massages yes, the hair brushing I just don't get.' Sandra responds.

'Sounds like heaven to me.' I chime back. To be fair most of Jules' and Sandra's life sounded like heaven. Sandra fell in love with her college boyfriend David. Everyone warned them that him as an alpha and her as a beta was destined to fail and when David had first met his pack she'd worried everyone was right. But the other guys had adored her almost instantly.

There had been another tense moment when the pack met Jules. They'd been scent sensitive and it had been a whirlwind of emotions and drama. But as it turned out Jules had wanted Sandra in the pack as well. She said she'd hate to be the only girl and the two of them had become fast friends. If I didn't love Sandra so much I'd probably be mad at her for how well her life seemed to be working out.

'So tell me...' Sandra poked me with her foot from the other end of the couch.

'Hmm?' I yawn as Whisper emerges from the bedroom and comes over to say hi.

'Hello, my sweet boy.' Sandra coos at him as she helps him up onto the couch.

'You tired too, cutie?' I ask him as he yawns and curls up between us so we can both reach him for pats.

'Of course he is, you both are. You work too much. When are you taking a holiday?'

'When there's magically someone else who can run the store for me, an abundance of money in my bank account and somewhere to go.' I snap back.

'You need a break.' She insists.

'There's nowhere I'd want to go anyway. Not unless I can take Whisper.' I respond, dropping kisses on my fluff ball's head.

'Did you at least get a bit of a break for your heat?' Oh shit, oh shit, oh shit. Sandra had been caught up in the Jules pregnancy drama for the last few months so she had no idea I'd skipped my heat. Again.

Everyone, myself included, knows it is dangerous to skip your heats too often. You can with suppressants but it's considered bad form. Some doctors won't let you, they say suppressants are only for delaying not skipping. Thankfully my doctor let me skip most of the time. But even he insisted I go through one a year. Still, that was better than the three to four heats most omegas had to suffer.

I'd been scheduled to have my heat two months back but I'd decided to push it back. Again. I hadn't lied to Sandra but she was busy and I didn't feel the need to reach out just to worry her when there was nothing she could do to help anyway.

'Nope, no break.' I mumble.

'Is the shop at least going well?'

'Yeah actually, it's been a great few months. We've got this new line of hand-knitted scarves and beanies that I'm having to put a waitlist on. They only make a few each month. And they're going to start doing socks.'

'Ooh. Any chance I can get to the top of the knitted socks list? I think Jules would cry with joy. Then again she cried with joy the other day when I made her a chai.'

'She's a pregnant omega. Cut her a break.' I smack Sandra playfully in the arm.

'Oh, I'm not complaining. It's adorable and somehow even though I know it's just the hormones, it still makes me feel like a hero when I'm the only one she wants to cuddle, or I bring her the present that she loves the most.'

'Jules is so lucky.' I lament.

'You could be that lucky.' It takes me a second to realise what she's suggesting.

'Please don't start.' I groan.

'Won't you at least consider it? You could try online dating. Or a scent-matching program? Or hell just go get drunk in a bar and find someone to fuck.'

'Language.' I scold her reaching down to cover Whisper's ears. But it's too late. He's already growling at her. Goddess only knows why he is always so offended by swear words, but call it the quirks of a rescue dog. You could say fudge or fork, ship or shirt, but if you said the actual swear words, Whisper was mad.

'Sorry Whisper. I meant fudge. Your mum needs to get fudged.' That appeases him enough that he stops growling.

'Good boy.' I soothe him with pats behind the ears so that he settles again. 'It's okay. She didn't mean to say the bad word.'

'Your dog's insane.' She teases me as I settle back at the other end of the couch.

'No, he's perfect.' I reply on impulse.

'Please just think about it, Mel. I hate to think of you alone forever.'

'I'm not alone, I have Whisper.'

'You know what I mean.'

'I just can't go through all of it again.' I shudder at the memory.

'What happened was horrible, but I do think it's a once-in-a-lifetime shit show.'

'Even if I did agree, who do you think is out there that's going to want a soon-to-be thirty-two-year-old broken omega with horrible nesting instincts who has no idea how to even be an omega anymore? Not to mention a sickly sweet scent and a body shaped like a bunch of marshmallows stacked together.'

'Oh god. What did your mum say this time?' She groans,

'Literally nothing. She just pointed out the healthier options for me.' I shrug.

'And?' Damn she knew my mother and me too well.

'And offered to buy me a whole new wardrobe in my target size for inspiration.'

'There it is. I know you're going to say no but have you considered lifting your 'no bitch slapping my mum rule'?' She asks, her eyes full of mischief.

'No.' I smile at her.

'Okay well I know you're firmly against actual poisoning but have you considered laxatives, just for fun.'

'I'm not going to let you drug my mother no matter the drug.' I point out.

'I know, but it's fun to daydream.' Her voice turns misty as she stares off imagining whatever pain she thinks she wants to inflict.

'Thanks for coming over.' I reach for her hand and squeeze.

'Anytime sweetness. Now where is the backgammon board, I feel like having my ass handed to me. And I'm ordering pizza since I know you will have only had like five mouthfuls of lunch.' She's right. So I grab the board and set it up on the coffee table in front of us while she orders us some pizza.

KNOT FOR REAL

I don't think I'll last long. Between the long work week, the long lunch with my parents, and the long list of things I know I still need to get done around the house my exhaustion is chasing me. For now, the dirty laundry pile is at least next to the washing machine. The clean pile is on the chair in the corner of my room. And all my dirty dishes are at least stacked in the dishwasher instead of in the sink. Baby steps.

Chapter 8. John

I don't regret much in life but I do regret inviting Sam to come and meet Melanie. What was I thinking? Well, I know what I was thinking. It was, Sam is good at getting dates, maybe he can help me get one. What I hadn't thought about was the fact that Sam is an arsehole. Particularly first thing in the morning.

He's grumbled and groaned since we left the house. But everything was going according to the plan we'd decided on last night. We're going to get there right at seven when she opens, before the crowds start rolling in and that way we could linger over our coffees and he could find a way to casually ask her if she was available for dates.

I was pretty sure she was single. There was never anyone around, she never mentioned anyone but that didn't mean that she was interested in dating either.

'You know the birds aren't even up yet.' Sam grumbles beside me.

'You said you still wanted to make it to the office by nine so we have to come early.'

'You're buying me the biggest coffee she serves when we get there.'

'I know and I will, I promise.' He wasn't normally this bad in the morning but we'd stayed up pretty late plotting our revenge against Mick. The man was generally unbothered which is why pranking him had always presented a challenge. Mess didn't bother him. Noise didn't bother him. I'd once shaved his eyebrows off while he slept, he didn't even flinch. He had the soul of a laid back surfer, even if he looked like a beast.

So far the winning idea was a shaving cream water bomb followed by a confetti cannon. It was something Sam had found online. He'd been way more into the prank planning than I ever would have thought. It was nice to spend some proper time with him. Just one more thing to thank Melanie for.

'Are we there yet?' Sam whinges.

'Are you five?' I shoot back.

'No, I'm uncaffeinated.'

'Well you can relax, it's just this next block.' I lead the way, crossing the street to Second Nature. The open sign is already on. I hold the door open for a customer to exit as we go in. Sam said I should act as I always do so he'd be able to figure out if she had any interest. Here goes nothing. 'Hey, do you have a bathroom?'

'Down the back on the...' Her voice trails off as she properly looks my way and spots Sam behind me. Okay now I had another reason to regret getting Sam to come with me. Because if her dropped jaw was any indication, she found him attractive. And I hadn't thought about that. I mean I wouldn't have a problem if she wanted to date Sam. But if she wanted to date Sam and didn't want to date me I think I would struggle. Then again if the two of them were dating I'd at least probably get to see her a lot more and away from the cafe. This could work.

'Melanie, this is my packmate Sam.' I gesture between them. Melanie's frozen behind the counter damp cloth in hand. Sam is paused part way through the door.

'Hi.' Sam is the first to recover, walking towards the counter. 'I'm Sam.'

She nods but doesn't say anything. Okay not the sparks flying I had started to hope for but I'll take what I can get.

'Can we get a large long black and my regular to have here?' I order from a pace behind Sam.

'Yeah, sure, no problem. Peppermint hot chocolate, extra whipped cream, extra sprinkles, right?' Melanie's gaze finally wanders over to me, her smile creasing dimples into her cheeks.

'Oh god. You drink that crap?' Sam demands of me as he glances between the two of us.

'God no. Melanie here thinks it's funny to call out ridiculous drink orders for me, particularly when we have an audience.' I smile at her.

'Calling out pumpkin spiced matcha latte, no cinnamon was probably my favourite. The woman waiting next to you made the best face.' She chimes throwing down her damp rag to get started on the coffees. 'What are you doing here so early?'

'Oh Sam wanted to try the coffee I'm always on about and he has to get down town so we came early.' It's not a lie, he did want to try the coffee and it was better than telling her the truth. That I'm slowly becoming obsessed with her and dragging my pack mate into it with me.

'Well I hope it lives up to the hype.' Melanie smiles.

'I'm sure it will.' Sam smiles in return. I shove him towards a corner table, desperate to ask him what he thinks. Does she like me? Does he like her? Does she like him?

I sit at one of the tables along the padded bench in the window and let Sam take the armchair opposite me. It's always been my favourite spot because you look back onto the store and Melanie. Her curls aren't pinned back off her face like normal today. Instead she has them up in some kind of high ponytail thing so that they burst into a little cloud on her head and topple down. She normally only wears it like this when she's really busy.

'Okay well I've confirmed one thing.' Sam cuts into my reverie.

'What's that?' I ask, dragging my gaze back to him.

'You definitely have a crush on her.' He smirks.

'I could have told you that.' I shrug unashamed. I'd figured that out a while ago and in all honesty I would have done something ages ago if not for all the omega courting crap we'd been going through.

'Here you go.' Melanie chimes sliding the coffee in front of us. 'One long black and one unicorn milkshake extra rainbow.'

'Thanks.' I smile as she places my latte in front of me.

'Thanks.' Sam nods at her before taking a sip. 'Damn.'

'I told you.' I smirk.

'Do you put crack in here? It's amazing.' Sam takes another longer sip.

'That's very high praise from Sam, he's a coffee snob.' I offer.

'I'm not giving away my trade secrets.' Melanie shrugs. 'Businesses like mine make their money off repeat customers.'

'Well I'll be coming back for sure.' Sam smiles up at her.

'Then my work here is done.' She dramatically dusts her hands in the air before wandering back behind the counter.

'I thought you were going to ask questions.' I whisper to Sam once she's gone.

'Relax, I met her like thirty seconds ago. You need to warm up to 'hey are you interested in dating' or you just come off like a creep.' He had a point but I didn't like it. Something had flipped in me last week. Thursday when we'd been chatting it was like I'd gone from interested in her, to needing her. It was almost painful how I wanted to just be in her space. There wasn't any good reason, but I was becoming desperate.

'I told you it was drab.' A high pitched whiny voice calls out as a woman comes into the cafe. I hate her. She's ugly. Not physically. I guess technically she was quite pretty, but her voice and her scathing comment has me seething under my breath.

'Down dude.' Sam steadies my hand where it grips the table.

'You were right babe.' Douchebag number one laughs as he follows her in. I say douchebag number one because there are in fact three douchebags following her in. They're all wearing identical suits cut slightly too tight.

'Lucy?' Melanie exclaims. Okay, so she knew the mean girl even if she wasn't expecting her to be here.

'Hey big sis. You were going on and on about how proud you were of your little cafe. We thought we'd stop by while we were in the area. So we could...check it out.' As she speaks, her gaze turns to the space. The grimace on her face would have been more appropriate for standing waist deep in garbage then the gorgeous cafe she was in. 'It's cute.'

'Cool it.' Sam grunts at me.

'What?' I'd forgotten he was here. I was using every part of my will power not to stand up and run across the room and intercede. The douchebags wander along the nearest shelves with looks of disdain and disbelief that are too dramatic to be anything but purposefully insulting.

'You're growling.' Sam mutters under his breath. 'Cool it, she's not in any danger and if she is, we'll get up, I promise.'

'Fine.' I mutter.

'So BIG sis, got anything healthy on the menu?'

Chapter 9. Melanie

Why today? Why now? While John and Sam sit in the corner to witness my shame. I have been here for eight years, and not once has my sister come here.

'There's fruit and yoghurt, with homemade muesli.' I answer. I want her to leave, to take the three ass-keteers, as Sandra likes to call them, and get out. The idiots in question are perusing the books at the front of my display scoffing at the titles. I could have told them, those books weren't for them. Hell, nothing in this store is for them. It's designed for omegas. I'm sure if my sister wasn't so intent on being malicious even she would find things here she wants.

'Full fat yoghurt, I assume?' She condescends while staring into my fridge display.

'Yes.' I do not prescribe to the idea that fat free dairy products are better for you. If you take out the fat all you're left with is the sugar which gives you horrible spikes and just makes you hungrier later but I wasn't going to try and explain that. I was focused on staying calm. No one could make me cringe into myself quite like my sister. I knew if she pushed hard enough I'd whine in that distinct way that would reveal me as an omega. And I was determined, if nothing else, to at least keep my secret today.

'They don't look very fresh.' She gestures at the fruit.

'Fresh sliced this morning.' I speak through my teeth.

'Oh, did you cut them yourself?' Her voice is so condescending it makes me want to scream and throw things against the wall.

'Yes.' I grunt out.

'How sweet. Well I guess we'll just take four long blacks to go.' I am about to make four coffees quicker than anyone has ever made coffee before. I pull out four of my reusable takeaway cups already mentally saying goodbye to them. If I had to place a bet on four people who would not honour a trust based system it was the four people currently laughing at my gifts section.

I know my sister actually does like the candles she rolls her eyes at. And the jewelry she scoffs at had made me think of her when I'd first picked it out. It was exactly the kind of thing she loved to wear. But she is in full mocking mode so I could have had her favourite snack, her favourite scented candle and her dream jewelry laid out in front of her and she wouldn't have been able to say a nice word.

She wasn't always like this. She'd always tended slightly more towards the judgemental than me, but when we'd been younger we'd been allies of sorts. After her designation came through there'd been some distance but that's just what it was like with teenage girls. She'd never been properly mean to me till shortly after I got my omega designation. And when she'd bonded with her pack, well after that she'd become down right vicious.

'Here you go.' I call setting the coffees on the counter for them. 'Four long blacks to go.'

'Oh look at that. You made them so quick. Good job.' The words coming out of her mouth may have technically been nice but the way she said them was not dissimilar to how you might praise a toddler for showing you the contents of their toilet.

'Just the coffees then?' I ask, desperate for them to be on their way.

'Yeah, there's nothing else here we'd want.' Lucy snarks. The chuckle gallery behind her begins filling out. 'See you later big sis.'

She calls the last out as she blows a kiss from the door and leaves. I'd never ask them to pay but I can't help but be a little surprised they didn't at least make a show of offering. Bragging about how much money they make is a favourite pastime of theirs.

I look over at John and Sam. Their heads bent towards each other while they have what seems to be an intense whispered conversation. At least hopefully they didn't notice too much of that interaction.

I look past them and out the window to my sister and her pack now howling with laughter a few paces away from my store. They're loitering near the bus stop sign which seems strange. They are definitely more rideshare people. But as I watch I realise they're not waiting at the bus stop. They're ceremoniously dumping the coffee I made into the trash can. Each of the guys in turn make gagging noises while Lucy drops each cup in from up high.

I continue to stare as they wander away, falling over each other laughing. I bite my lip as hard as I can to try and bring myself back into my body. I wiggle my fingers and my toes. Deep breath. You're okay.

But holding back the hurt is only helping me feel my rage. Those four keep cups were practically brand new. They needed to be used for a minimum of six months to offset their carbon footprint. How dare they. I'm out from behind the counter before I know what I'm doing.

I head to the garbage bin which thankfully is empty except for two candy wrappers and the four coffee cups. I fish them out, shaking off the mess. Now what? They've been in the trash so even if I sent them through the steriliser half a dozen times I still don't know if I'd feel right using them for customers.

Put them in the courtyard, we need more seedling pots anyway, my brain supplies. I turn back to the cafe but before I take a step I see Sam and John. They're both staring at me through the picture window and I realise how crazy I must look. Red faced and blotchy with anger, fishing coffee cups out of the bin. At least John already probably guessed I'm a bit unstable, Sam was learning it for the first time.

I head into the cafe and walk straight past them, down the outer aisle to the door that says staff only. People assume it's a break room but it's actually a little courtyard. It was a smelly disgusting bit of concrete when I'd bought it and for years now I'd been using my spare time and energy to clean it up. My goal was eventually to turn it into a little garden oasis to add extra space where people could sit and read or have a coffee. I hadn't gotten there yet. But I would.

I put the reusable coffee mugs down on the ground next to some potting mix. I'd deal with them later. I head back inside and straight behind the counter to the kitchen so I can scrub up. Any minute now the morning rush is going to start and I'm going to focus on that. Not my desire to break down. Not the fact that John and Sam witnessed my embarrassment. I'm going to focus on what I am good at, my work.

Chapter 10. Sam

I am so late for work at this point it's actually funny. I'd called my secretary and she'd assured me that my first meeting wasn't till eleven, so it's not like I was letting anyone down. But still. This was not like me.

I love my job. I was almost always the first one in and the last one out. I know most people didn't consider being a lawyer a noble profession but I loved it. I helped people through difficult situations. I helped those who deserved it get second chances and those who didn't get off the streets. It was good work and I was good at it.

So the fact that I was still lingering in a cafe at nine thirty when my work day normally started an hour earlier was weird. But I knew why. Her name was Melanie.

I'd convinced John to go ahead to work, he was on a big project of some kind at the moment. Something about encryption that I did not understand. Plus, as I'd explained to him, it would probably be easier for me to chat to her once the rush had passed without him next to me. Plus the boy needed to calm down.

I thought he was in serious risk of breaking the table when Melanie's sister and the douchebags came in. I got it. I didn't like it either. I had thought of several less than polite things I could say to put those arseholes back in line. But I also did not see it as our place to step in. John disagreed.

Watching Melanie storm outside to retrieve her coffee cups, red faced with rage had been a thing of beauty. I saw embarrassment flicker across her face but all I'd felt was impressed. Impressed at the way she'd handled them professionally even if I could tell she was hurting underneath. The girl was stunning.

And not just in spirit. Damn the girl was beautiful.

Her pretty dark shiny curls piled on her head like a halo. Her crystal blue eyes. The dimples in her cheeks. Her plump rosy lips. And I'm not trying to be a dick here but her plump other things were drawing my attention to. Her shirt was high collared but I imagine that without it I would have been treated to some gorgeous cleavage. And her ass. My mouth watered.

When she'd bent over into the trash can to retrieve those cups and her skirt had pulled tight over her rear end I thought I was going to faint. As it was I'd had to adjust myself as subtly as possible because my brain had very quickly supplied a rendering of her in the same position, bent over, just minus the clothes.

She was wearing some kind of pencil skirt made from a stretchy material that clung lovingly to her thighs and left little to the imagination. When she turned to the side I could see the little puff of her belly as it curved away from the tops of her thighs. I knew what would be tucked into the little valley below. I was trying hard not to think about it.

I swear to god I'm not this much of a horndog but the girl is my type. My brain keeps supplying thoughts of digging my hands into her soft hips as I pound into her from behind. What it would feel like to bury my face against her chest simply to snuggle against all that soft deliciousness. She has strength and fire and she is all kinds of luscious. I'm intrigued. But I'm also not here for myself.

Not that I think John would be bothered if I said I wanted to date her too, but he asked me here as a wingman and I took that seriously. Now I needed a reason to strike up a proper conversation. There was only one person left in line and hopefully after that she'd get a break.

Not only so I could talk to her but because the girl needed a break. She'd been on her feet and moving for almost two hours straight. All the while chatting with everyone that came in. Full of bubbly laughter and sweet comments that had every single customer feeling like the center of her attention. She was gifted. And I wasn't the only one who'd noticed.

A few regular customers, three guys in particular and two women, seemed to linger over their coffee pickups longer than strictly necessary. But while she received their attention politely she didn't flirt back with anyone. Which was both good and bad. Good because it meant as far as I could tell she wasn't interested in anyone else but bad because it could mean she wasn't interested in dating. Which would probably explain why there was clearly a queue of people eager but who hadn't made a move. But none of them seemed to really notice her. They all enjoyed her smiles and her laughs but did any of them notice how exhausted the poor girl was.

Whenever she wasn't looking at someone, whenever she couldn't feel eyes on her, her face lapsed into a kind of tired resignation. The corners of her mouth turned down and it was like her whole face would droop. But then sure enough someone would call for her attention and it was like watching someone plug in a light bulb.

Okay so maybe I'd been paying too much attention for a wingman but I'd run out of emails I could answer from my phone a good twenty minutes ago so now it was simply a prop to hold in front of me so that no one thought I was just an insane man sitting in a coffee shop staring at its owner.

'Can I get you anything else?' She asks as she approaches to clear my mug. I've already had two large coffees, a third would be pushing my caffeine tolerance this early in the day.

'No thanks. As good as it is, I don't want to get the shakes.'

'Do you need something to eat? I know I always do better if I put something in my belly before I mainline caffeine.'

'That's not a bad idea.' I chime as I stand to follow her back towards the display fridge.

'The fruit and yoghurt bowls are nice and healthy, sweetened with local honey. Otherwise the muffins are all delicious.' She offers

'What's your favourite?' I ask. A little flirty but still it's an honest question.

'I'm partial to the breakfast wrap. Egg, bacon, cheese with fresh baby spinach and homemade aioli.'

'That's definitely the one, can I get it to go?'

'Sure, should I warm it up?'

'Yeah.' She slides the wrap into the sandwich press before mindlessly cleaning the space around her while she waits. 'Your shop is great.'

'Thanks.' She lapses back into silence as she wipes down the counters around her. Damn I need to get her talking and I'm getting nothing. Considering how much she'd bantered with every single alphahole that came in during the morning rush it was downright insulting.

'How long have you been here?'

'Eight years at the end of next month.' She throws a smile over her shoulder at me.

'Sounds like a celebration is in order.' I persist.

'If by celebration you mean an hour long bath and like ten hours of uninterrupted sleep then yes, I agree.' She turns towards me leaning against the counter in front of me.

'Not much of a party person?'

'I can party when required but I'm much more the quiet night in type.' Noted.

'So is that what you like when you go on dates, a quiet night in, pizza and a movie?' I was more of a head out and party guy but staying in felt really appealing right now.

'Not really.' She shrugs.

'What do you like then?'

'I guess I don't really know. I don't date much.' She shrugs. Well that answers that question. Considering how many patrons I watched press right up against the rules of propriety while talking to her today, it seemed likely she wasn't interested in dating. Damn. Double damn. Damn for John. But also damn for me. It had only been a few hours but I had gotten my hopes up.

Chapter 11. Melanie

What was up with John and his pack mate? Like I know being an omega I am designed to find all alphas attractive on some level. But these two?

It's like someone took the imaginary boyfriends I had as a teenager and turned them into real people. John was my bookish library boyfriend, the sweet one who wanted to see me happy. Sam was the jock. All hard lines and competitive spirit.

The embarrassment from my sister and her pack's antics earlier finally passed and now all I feel is annoyed. Angry almost. She didn't need to ever come here and she definitely didn't need to carry on like that. And unfortunately some of that annoyance has been slipping into my interactions all morning.

I haven't been as nice or as welcoming as I could be. I nearly snapped at a woman an hour ago who was lingering over her coffee pick up asking about how I spend my free time while I had five people waiting at the cash register. What free time lady? If I ever get some I'll let you know.

It's like Sam asking about what I do on dates. What dates? No one has asked me out in years. I contemplate letting his breakfast wrap burn. I feel like it would make me feel better but only for a second or two. Then I'd feel worse.

'Here you go.' I say as I lift the wrap into a take away brown paper bag and hand it over. 'John fixed up for the coffees before so it's just the second long black and the wrap. Anything else?'

'What would you suggest?' Getting away from me because my temper is getting thin.

'Do you two need more omega presents?' I ask.

'No that didn't work out.' Well damn. Now I feel like a bitch. John got a present only two weeks ago so the break up is obviously fresh and still sore.

'I'm sorry.'

'I'm not.' Okay, maybe it's not painful.

'You're not sorry you lost your omega?'

'Lost implies having. We've courted a few omegas over the past six months but none of them were ours. They were suggested scent matches. But none of them worked out.' He shrugs clearly unbothered.

'Oh. When John kept coming in for more gifts, and they were always the same kinds of things, I just assumed you had an omega who really liked books and candles.'

'No such luck. Or maybe we are lucky, I don't know.'

'What do you mean?' I'm more curious than I should be.

'Omegas are a lot of work. Their emotions are always so high, I don't know if I'm built for that. Or if any of us are considering how well it's worked out so far.' This wasn't the first time I'd heard thoughts like these.

'Have you not liked any of them?' I ask.

'They're all lovely in their own way, the problem is more that they don't like us.'

'Are they blind?' I blurt out. Oh that's embarrassing.

'Good to know you think we're attractive, but I meant more than just our pretty faces.' He's clearly enjoying my fumble.

'I didn't say you were pretty.' I snap back.

'But you thought it, and you're right. Well at least John and I are pretty. George is more potato with eyes and Mick... he's intimidating.'

'So you think Mick scares them off?' I ask.

'No I think we all do. We're not the best talkers, we're not soft and inviting. We just don't naturally make a good environment for an omega.' He says it so matter of factly that it bothers me.

'I don't believe that. I mean I do. I believe you. But don't they always say that if you meet the right omega it all just works out in the end?' I offer.

'I think they have to say that or no one would be willing to try.' He rolls his eyes.

'True.' He's more jaded than I would have expected being so handsome and easygoing. I wouldn't have thought he'd missed out on much love. 'What are you looking for in an omega anyway?'

'I don't know. The omega thing wasn't my idea.' He speaks emphatically. Yeah, I was getting the impression he didn't like omegas.

'Do you date, like in general?' I shouldn't care.

'Sometimes.'

'Well what do you look for then?' I push. I really shouldn't care.

'Fun I guess. But I think it has to be more with an omega.' His tone is reflective and I'm beyond intrigued.

'What do you mean?'

'Everyone always describes that spark you're supposed to feel, right? I'm not talking about a scent sympathetic bond or any of that crap.' I nod my agreement. Being bound to a group of people no matter what because of your scents, that's scary. 'But there's still supposed to be something.'

'Joy.' I mumble under my breath.

'What?' Oh well. I was in it now.

'I always thought it was joy. Not happiness, that's what you build together. But the spark, the electricity, I've always thought of it as joy. The spark of happiness that comes from deep in your belly and you don't know why.' Why am I still talking?

'Yeah that. The joy. Well we haven't found that yet.'

'So you're still looking?' I could hear the hope in my voice, I prayed he didn't.

'No we've decided to take a break. I'm hoping permanently.'

'Oh.' And there goes the hope.

'Which is good, leaves us open to date who we want.'

'Just not an omega.' I add.

'Hopefully not.' He chuckles. Ah the final nail in the coffin. Awesome.

'That will be fifteen fifty.' I say and he taps his card casually against the reader. Can he tell I'm spiraling? I doubt it. I couldn't help it, while we talked a part of me I thought I had long since drowned felt hopeful.

'Hey before I go, what's the strawberry flavour?'

'Huh?'

'I keep smelling whiffs of something sweet like strawberries, it smells delicious.'

'Ahh could be the muffins.' I hedge. 'Do you want one to go?'

'Nah. Next time.' He waves as he leaves. God damn my stupid romantic heart getting all riled up over a stupid chat about dating. Time to go upstairs and apply another layer of descenter.

KNOT FOR REAL

Chapter 12. George

What a long fucking day. Actually it was a long fucking week, month, and year. I felt tired in my bones. It was lucky that at this point I was so proficient I could do my job on autopilot because I was barely functioning in the office today.

Luckily being a Monday I finish at five, no matter what. Tonight was pack dinner. I'd had to video call in from Paris once but I'd never actually missed it. As the pack's head alpha it was my job to set the example, to keep my pack together and I had no idea what I was doing. Hence Monday night was pack dinner.

None of us were naturally gifted cooks, yet we each took turns and all sat down to dinner on Monday. We all ate together during the week when we could but it was rarely all of us and even more rarely home cooked.

I'm surprised to hear noise coming from the kitchen as I come in. It's only just gone six thirty, should have just been Mick in there cooking. But I can very clearly hear Sam and John's voices ringing out as well. Nothing in my brain could have prepared me for what I see.

Mick is in the kitchen barefoot and bare chested with wet hair. John's standing on the dining table while pushing a mop against the ceiling. Sam's on his hands and knees collecting paper confetti into a garbage bag.

'Next time we definitely need to consider blowback.' John calls down to Sam.

'Also, timing. If the bastard didn't have to cook us dinner I'd be making him help since he made most of the mess.' Sam grumbles from his hands and knees.

'Not my fault. You two were snickering, you gave yourselves away.' Mick snarks.

'We still got quite a bit of cream in your hair.' Sam defends.

'Not as much as got on the roof.' Mick laughs.

'What's all this?' I call out as I enter. John turns from his precarious position on the dining room table.

'Damn it, I thought we could get it cleaned up before you got home.' John sighs while returning to his ceiling mopping.

'Worried bossman will be mad at you?' Mick snickers.

'No.' John snaps back while shooting me a furtive glance. Was he worried I'd be mad? I'm not. Messes happen, as long as they get cleaned up I don't give a shit.

'How did you get cream on the roof?' I ask the question most present in my mind.

'Prank gone wrong.' Mick chuckles as he tears lettuce for a salad.

'The prank went fine, thank you very much.' Sam mutters as he gets the last of the confetti into the bag and moves to dump it into the bin. 'We just didn't expect you to punch a water balloon full of cream into the ceiling.'

'Not my fault.' Mick grunts as Sam helps John climb down from the table.

I'm shocked. I'm shocked, silent, is what I am.

It's not that we don't get on, we do. We've been together for six years. John and I met first, after I'd bought a company he was working for. Mick joined soon after when I bought some tech from him. Sam joined less than a year later, when he helped one of my staff members through some legal problems. We'd seen each other through highs and lows. We were all close.

But tonight there was a camaraderie in the air that I'd never felt before. All I'd ever wanted was to make this pack as cohesive and supportive as possible. It's why we had our Monday night dinners, our pack holidays and I scheduled check-ins with the guys. But in all the time we'd been together it had never felt like this. As much as I wanted it to be, I don't think it was my structured bonding time suddenly taking effect.

The energy was rolling off Sam and John, but Mick was affected a little as well. There was a bounce in the way they talked to each other and something less tangible. Something in the air that now floated between them. And I wanted it.

'How long till dinner?' I ask Mick.

'It's ready whenever. But it will keep if you wanna go get changed.' I do, I really do. But I'm not about to leave this room till we get to the bottom of this shift. I settle for removing my jacket and rolling up my sleeves. My tie was long gone.

'Nah, let's eat.' I say as I head to the fridge and grab a beer. 'Anyone else?'

'Me.'

'Two.'

'Three.' I didn't really need to ask, the guys were always up for a beer. Particularly since Mick had made that deal with the brew house which now meant we had a near constant supply of local craft beer in the fridge. I grab enough cans for everyone while Sam sets the table and John grabs glasses.

I would have happily drunk my beer from the can. In fact, having spent my day in fancy office buildings feeling like the stuffed shirt I have become, I would relish it. But Mick had become a beer snob during his research and now insisted that we pour out our beers so the gas burned off so as to avoid indigestion. I knew he was right, because he was Mick, but I'd still rather drink it from the can sometimes.

'Incoming.' Mick calls as he brings the lasagna towards the table.

'Come in for landing, over.' John speaks into an imaginary walkie talkie on his shoulder.

'Houston, we have lasagna.' Sam joins in.

'Let me just grab the salad and the garlic bread, you guys start serving up.' Mick calls as he hurries back towards the kitchen. Sam cuts the largest slice of lasagna possible and lifts it onto his plate.

'Save some for the rest of us.' John teases as he reaches for his own slightly more proportional, but not by much, piece of lasagna.

'I made two lasagnas, there will be plenty. And hopefully leftovers.' Mick grunts as he sits down at the table pouring his beer before filling his plate.

'Cheers.' Sam calls raising his own beer in the air until we all follow suit.

'Cheers.' We all chime again as one.

'Damn this is good.' John announces around a mouth full of food. Mick asks about my day. I in turn ask about his and Sam's and John's. We chat about group plans for the week and the coming weekend. It is all completely normal. And yet it's different.

There are no awkward pauses. I don't have to run through my mental checklist to make sure we've covered everything. Sam and John are teasing each other more and more. None of this is abnormal, it just feels seamless and perfect.

'What's for dessert?' John asks Mick, patting his stomach.

'Oh I have been craving something strawberry all day.' Sam chimes in.

'Me too.' John nods.

'Since coffee this morning I keep daydreaming about a strawberry tart, you know like custard with strawberries.' Sam elaborates.

'I can't stop thinking about jam-filled donuts, cinnamon with hot strawberry goodness just leaking out.' John counters. God both options sound amazing.

'Quit it. You're making me hungry.' I scold them. 'And we all literally just finished devouring a banquet. Thank you Mick.'

'Thank you Mick.' John and Sam sing out in unison.

'Now that you've mentioned it I also want something sweet. And I've got nothing planned. I figured I'd carb load you guys into a coma with the lasagna.' Mick shrugs.

'How about we order something in?' Normally I'd be loath to do it on a family dinner but the thought of us all just heading off to our separate rooms is abhorrent.

'Hell yes.' Sam already has his phone in his hand.

'Oh no you don't.' John counters by pulling out his own phone like a gun from a holster. 'I want a say in what we get.'

Mick rolls his eyes while the two of us stand and start shifting the plates into the kitchen. We used to have a rule that whoever cooked didn't have to clean but after John's french cuisine experiment that had changed. Now whoever cooked had to clean. That being said no one ever cleaned up on their own. I rinse the plates while Mick starts stacking the dishwasher, leaving the pans to soak.

'Hey why don't you go get that monkey suit off and grab us a deck of cards. I feel like kicking some little boy but this evening.' Mick smirks, nodding at the other guys.

We were slightly older than the other two. I was the oldest at forty two, but Mick came a close second with his fortieth birthday just around the corner. Sam felt significantly younger at thirty six and John was our baby having only just turned thirty three.

'What's with those two tonight?' Mick nodded towards John and Sam who were now bickering vehemently over what they were ordering in for dessert.

'I'm not sure but I know I want some.' I smirk while Mick nods.

KNOT FOR REAL

Chapter 13. Melanie

Something is very wrong. It's early. But not get up with cows, get started on food prep early. This is I've been up all night early. I keep my room pitch black and there's no clock, but if I had to guess I'd say it's two maybe three in the morning. And there are people in my house.

Well in the shop. I can hear them downstairs. They're directly below me and they're smashing everything they can reach. Fear freezes me. Am I imagining it? I'm exhausted after all.

At another loud smash Whisper howls next to me. I dive on him to get him to quiet down. I hit my arm as I fall awkwardly on the edge of the bed. Ouch. Okay so not a dream.

Do they know I'm up here? Do I need to protect myself? I doubt it. I'm probably best off just staying quiet.

I can hear muffled voices. They don't sound angry. They don't even sound particularly urgent or scared. If anything they sound happy. Like they're having a good time. Why is that scarier? I pull the blanket up and over my head so that me and Whisper are completely covered.

I know we're not safe. I know whoever is downstairs could come up here any moment and find me. But it feels safe. In the warmth of my soft blankets with Whispers breath against my side.

I listen to the crashes and bangs coming from downstairs. Each one feels like a knife in my ear. I know my things, my store, my books, my trinkets, it's all being destroyed. But I don't move. I wait.

The noises stop eventually. Not abruptly, they just kind of fade away. I brace for the sound of sirens but I know they're not coming. This is mostly a commercial area. I'm one of only a couple residences on this street and the only one occupied regularly. It's part of the reason I love this place. The whole block feels abandoned at night. I have peace and quiet. I feel safe. Just not tonight.

I emerge from my bed slowly. I'm pretty sure it's been half an hour, maybe longer since I heard the first crash or tear. I find my phone in the kitchen and pocket it, while I grab my baseball bat. Whisper emerges from my bedroom behind me and follows me downstairs. I appreciate it because I don't really want to be alone right now but I also worry because I don't know what we're walking into.

'Be careful okay?' I whisper as we sneak down the stairs. I swear he nods. I swear he understands a thousand more things than anyone else is aware but I never share that thought out loud.

It's worse than I thought it would be. The front window has been smashed in. There is glass everywhere, across all the tables, across the bench seats and the arm chairs. All the wooden shelves that stock the gifts, the jewelry, the candles, they've all been knocked over. Some things are clearly broken, some of it is just dumped on the floor. To the left I can see my book display has been toppled, some of the books ripped open, their pages torn and scattered.

The coffee machine, the cafe area in general seems untouched. I don't keep any money on the premises so they didn't get any cash. Some of the jewelry maybe. But more than anything it looks like they just came here to smash.

I pull my phone from my pocket and call the police. The woman on the phone is calm and lovely. She has to repeat more than half of her questions because I can't focus but by the time I'm hanging up on her, there are police pulling up.

One of them suggests I go upstairs and get changed and it's at that point that I realise I'm standing barefoot in sleep shorts and a camisole. I hightail it up the stairs grabbing jeans and boots and a sweater. Spraying on a liberal amount of scent neutraliser out of habit.

When I get downstairs again they've taken their photos. They take my statement. I'm fuzzy on the times but I tell them what I heard. They applaud me for staying upstairs and not trying to confront the intruders. Which I appreciate. What I don't appreciate is how they keep suggesting I call someone. Who would I call?

I'll tell Sandra once the day has actually started but calling her at this hour would freak her out. Calling my parents would stress me out. For a moment I wish I had John's number. I feel like his cheesy sense of humour would help me right now. Or his intense pack mate Sam who I met yesterday. He'd know what to do, what questions to ask. But I don't have their numbers. I don't have anyone to call.

The police have been here an hour when they announce there's nothing left they can do. They have their photos. They have my story. That's it. Light is starting to filter through the streets and it makes the disaster which is my shop look even worse.

As soon as they leave all I want to do is sit down and weep. But I can't.

I take Whisper outside for his relief and then fill his food and water bowls and settle him upstairs. Then I grab a broom, the dust pan and the vacuum. I have work to do, and a lot of it.

I right the fallen book shelves with great difficulty. Then I start sorting everything into two piles, things that are broken beyond repair and things that can be saved. I just hope I end up in the second pile.

All the lovely knitted stuff goes into a bag to be washed and repaired. Once all the bigger items are off the floor I get the broom and start sweeping. The window glass shattered into fine pieces like it's supposed to so it's not dangerous but there sure is a lot of it.

I knock the edges of the windows still trying to hold on out into the street and then sweep those up as well. I vacuum the soft seats and all of the cushions knowing I'll have to do it again later when I'm less tired and more focused. Some of this stuff will probably just have to be discarded for safety. But I'll save what I can.

With all the glass swept away it looks almost normal. The space is not what it was but it's not the disaster zone it was a couple of hours ago.

I want to cry. I want to cry and sob and whine and scream but I can't. I'm too tired to cry. I don't cry anymore anyway. I whine sometimes, it can't be helped. And I often lay around with the emptiness and the ache in my chest that makes me think I want to cry. But the tears, the actual tears never come. Even though I'm heart broken and exhausted it just doesn't seem like enough. Not anymore.

I haven't cried since I lost my pack. I cried for three days. Then my mum told me the truth. And I never cried again.

As I sit down, I know it's a mistake. I'm not getting up again in a hurry. But I need to get off my feet and think. Where I used to have a front window there is now a hole. So I need to fix that. And there is the insurance company to call. I'd need the police report number, I hope I've written that down somewhere. And I'll need to check my bank account, see how much cash flow I have at the moment. Could I afford to close for a few days? Probably not, but I might have to. I hope not.

I need to write a list. I have no idea what order I need to do these things. I should probably take more photos, and call the insurance company first. But not right this second. Right now I just need to sit down for a few minutes and rest.

Just let my eyes close and...

Chapter 14. John

At this rate I was going to be at Second Nature before Melanie even opened. Pathetic? Maybe. But I was excited.

After we'd finished our dinner last night, I'd pulled Sam aside to quiz him about Melanie. In the rush of getting home from work and trying to pull off our prank I didn't have the chance to ask him what had happened after I left. And I didn't want to ask in front of Mick and George.

I know we are all pack and all equal. That's how George wanted it to be. But they were older and more experienced and admitting that I was having trouble just asking a girl out was pretty embarrassing. They probably wouldn't care about my crush on a beta but still. I just didn't want them to know. Yet.

Especially when Sam wasn't sure if I had a chance. He said he'd guess she was a romantic at heart but that she just didn't seem to be giving off interest in dating energy at the minute. But he wasn't sure. And I could work with that. I could take it slow. He seems sure she's single, which is great. But he also said that I'm not the only customer interested, which is bad.

Hence why I'm going to get there early. I know that the extra hour isn't going to make the difference but still. Sam suggested I ask her for book recommendations. That it would give me an idea of what she thought of me.

I finally reach her block. Something is wrong. It's like the glass is too clean. The painted trim on it has been scrubbed off? No wait, the glass is gone. Why is the glass gone?

My feet slow as I try to figure out what I'm seeing. The whole front glass wall that acts as the giant picture window into Melanie's store is completely gone. The shelves to the left where you can normally see all her specially picked out gifts and art are empty. There's no lights on in the cafe. The book display table is empty. But the chair in front of it is not.

My heart stops. And then I'm running.

I leap through the hole that should have been her window, vaulting over the cushioned bench seat in my way. I fall to my knees as I slide next to her and grab her hand. Her cold hand. She's so pale, her head tilted to the side. Her hair strewn around her where she's slumped. Oh god.

'Melanie?' I croak as I squeeze her fingers.

'Hmm?' Oh thank god. Her forehead scrunches as if she doesn't want to open her eyes.

'Melanie, are you okay?' I beg, clasping her cold fingers between my two hands kneeling next to her on the floor.

'John.' She whispers. A soft smile slides across her face as she says my name, easing her distress. My name did that. I could die happy. Her eyes flicker open as she beams at me.

'You're okay?' I ask again. She blinks. She's waking up I realise. Whatever happened, she was so tired she fell asleep in this chair in the middle of her store.

'John? How did you... I didn't open the door yet. How did you get in?' Her expression is so confused and adorable I want to kiss her. I barely resist. I find my hand pushing the curls back from her face. She's okay.

'I came in through the window.' I tell her.

'What?' She looks past me to the giant hole at the front of her shop. 'Oh yeah.'

'What happened?' I ask as she sits up, leaning forward to rest her elbows on her knees, her face in her hands. She scrubs at her face before running her fingers through her hair and pulling it back into a bun.

'Intruders.' She offers as she goes to stand but immediately sits back down. She's weak I realise. From lack of sleep and probably lack of food. She needs to eat. I need to feed her. Wait... what did she just say?

'Intruders?' I barely recognise the growl that emerges from my throat.

'Yeah.' Melanie mumbles almost to herself seemingly unaware of the rage now flowing through my veins. 'Cops reckon at least two, probably three of them. They did a lot of damage.'

'There were intruders in here last night?'

'This morning technically.' She nods slowly.

'Where were you?' I speak through my teeth, unable to breathe.

'Upstairs, sleeping. Hey, are you okay?'

Melanie has finally looked at my face and I don't know what she sees, but no. No, I am not okay. I am seconds away from pulling my own hair out or screaming at the universe or maybe wrapping this sweet girl in blankets and hiding her away from the world so nothing bad can ever happen again.

Her beautiful store that she fills up with sweet things and her own sweetness has been vandalised and I am very very far from okay. And while that was happening she was upstairs. Asleep. Vulnerable and unprotected and some assholes decided that they could come into the space and trash it for god knows what reason. This wasn't just her store, this was her home. And even if it was just her store, it's her store. How dare they.

'I haven't fired the machine up yet but it should only take a few minutes if you want a coffee?' She offers as she tries to stand again. This time she makes it all the way to her feet. Before I reach out and gently push her back into the chair.

'No. Sit.' Not my smoothest move but I need a second to calm down and the only way I'm going to do that is if she's sitting and she looks safe and comfortable. 'We should call the cops.'

'They've already been. They took some photos, took my statement. There's not a lot they can do. Random break in and all.' I nod. She's right. There's not a lot that the cops would do for just a random break in, in a random store. But I knew someone who could change that. In fact I knew three someones, all of whom would be very helpful in this situation.

Chapter 15. Melanie

Could I be a bigger mess right now? No, probably not.

I feel dead on my feet and I know I must look it, because John just sent me upstairs to take a shower. Normally I hate being bossed around but right now it feels like exactly what I want. Anything to get away from the parade of regulars calling out their concern despite the makeshift 'closed until further notice' sign I've put out front.

Everyone stopping by for their morning coffees seem as distressed by the break in as I am. Maybe more. Several regulars, on their way to work, assured me that if there was anything they could do I should let them know and that they'd be back the second I reopened. Their warm assurances were nice. It was the omega meltdowns that were getting to me.

Tuesday morning was book club and several of the regular omegas who come early to browse first, upon seeing the store destroyed, had fallen into fits of crying and whining. I got it. I really did. This place was their comfort space, the same as it's mine. And it was violated.

That's what it felt like. Like the space was dirty. Tarnished. The once cozy corner of happiness my shop represented to me was now long gone. And I didn't know how to get it back.

The shower made me feel more sane. I didn't feel like I had time to wash my hair so I'd pulled it up into my old lady shower cap but I'd been less than diligent in keeping the water off it, so my hair was still slightly damp. I finger tightened some of the curls with some vanilla oil and left them down to dry.

I'd also taken a moment to eat a banana so I could take my medication on time. Suppressants had to be taken at the exact same time everyday. Even ten minutes late could mess with you, and I was an hour off, which was worrying. Now dressed and doused in scent canceller with my slick-proof underwear, fresh jeans and a clean shirt on, I felt human. I also felt like I needed a week's worth of sleep, but I felt better.

'Melanie?' John's voice calls from downstairs.

'Coming down.' I call back pausing to scratch Whisper's head as I hurry down to find John waiting at the bottom of the stairs, phone in hand.

'Would you mind talking to my packmate for a second? He wants to help.'

'Ah, okay. I'm not sure what he can do.' I mumble the last as I accept the phone.

'I can do more than you can imagine.' Holy shit. The deep timber of the voice on the phone has my knees weakening. John's still standing next to me and the combination of his proximity and the voice on the phone, and I'm just so tired.

'Eek.' The sound that slips from my throat is a whine. I know it's a whine. I can feel the way it rattles in my throat. I swallow the sound and cough. 'Eck. Sorry. Something in my throat.'

There's silence on the other end of the phone. John is still just standing there, right next to me. Staring. Shit. Does he know I just whined?

'You okay?' He mouths and I nod. There's a slight growl through the phone but maybe that's just static.

'Who's your insurance company?' Okay, I wasn't expecting that question.

'Huh?' I grunt back.

'I assume you have insurance for the business, who is it with?'

'Ahhh.' I'm hesitant to tell the disembodied voice what he wants to know. I mean I want to tell him. I want to answer his question. I can tell even my few seconds of silence, my hesitation, it's bothering him and I want to tell him. But should I? I look at John and he nods, pushing one of my damp curls back from my cheek. 'Matthews and Sons.'

'Good girl.' Well shit. I wore slick-proof underwear out of habit, more than need these days, but thank god. I feel the need to squirm as a quiver racks my body. 'Hand the phone back to John.'

'Do you need anything else?' I should hand the phone straight back. I shouldn't be lingering.

'No sweetheart. I have your address and the insurance company. That's all I need.' My hand wobbles as I hand the phone back to John. If you had asked me even ten minutes ago if I had a thing for endearments I would have said goddess no. I hated them. A boyfriend in high school called me cupcake and I laughed straight into his face. But I was wrong.

My brain replays his voice again. *Sweetheart. Good girl. I can do more than you can imagine.* The same shiver as before rocks me. I need to sit down.

I cross the room and sit in the armchair I'd fallen asleep in and watch John pace on the phone. I should probably pay attention to whatever it is he's doing but I can't. I need coffee.

Coffee.

The thought inspires me and I'm across the room and firing up the machine before I make the conscious decision to do it. Once I get some caffeine in my blood I'll start to feel normal. And with the residual sleepiness gone I'll stop being a puddle of whines and shivers or whatever that was. Some food as well. A banana is not enough to get me through the day I'm having. I should cook something. Offer John some as well. I look over to him where he's hung up the phone and is now texting furiously.

'Coffee?' I call out to him. He looks up and a scowl folds into his brow.

'I should be making you a coffee.'

'You trying to take my job?' I tease.

'No, but I think I would feel better if I could get you to sit down for five minutes consecutively.' He grumbles as he crosses the room to lean against my counter.

'I can't.' I shrug.

'What if...' Whatever he was going to say is drowned out by the wail from the street, made all the louder by the lack of glass. Oh no. Steph. She's already in the arms of one of her alphas as she starts sobbing out her question.

'What, *sniff,* happened?' Oh goddess, I did not want to explain again.

'There was a break in.' John talks calmly as he crosses the room so he can speak more easily through the hole that was my picture window. 'We'll get it all fixed up but Second Nature might be closed for a while.'

'I'll reopen tomorrow.' I call towards Steph and her alpha.

'You will?' John and Steph ask in tandem. Steph is elated but John seems annoyed.

'It might be awhile before the store is back operating in full but I'll try and get at least the coffee shop back in working order by tomorrow.' I explain.

'Oh thank you Melly.' I try not to flinch. That was the second time she's called me that and I hate it even more this time.

'No worries Steph. I know it's not as good as mine but there's a coffee shop two blocks that way that makes a pretty decent hot chocolate.' I point in the direction of Phillip's place. He's nice enough, and our vibes are very different so we're not in competition. I know for a fact I won't be losing any of my regular omega clientele to him because he refuses to have whipped cream.

'Thanks Melanie.' Her gruff alpha grunts as he nods over Steph's head and begins wandering in the direction I pointed. Hmm. I guess he's just going to carry her like a reverse back pack.

'You're reopening tomorrow?' John demands.

'Yeah.' I shrug. I'd checked my bank account earlier, there would be no closed days for me.

'Can't you take a week?' I wish.

'Honestly?' He nods, so I take a deep breath, financial issues made me itchy and uncomfortable. 'I can't afford to.'

'Damn.' His expletive is directed at the ground in front of me but I still feel it in my stomach. The embarrassment that I didn't earn more. The shop did well but I was still paying off the mortgage on the building and I swear it never seemed to actually go down.

'I'll spend the day cleaning and sorting everything, I can get more stock from out back and reorder what needs replacing. It'll be fine. I just need to figure out what to do about the giant hole and I'll be good to go.' I gesture at the gap in the wall.

'Actually I have a solution for the hole in the wall. And it just pulled up.'

Chapter 16. Mick

So this was Second Nature? John has been raving about the place for a year. Well not so much the place. It was always Melanie this and Melanie that. I thought it was cute he had a crush. Even if he didn't realise it. Or I guess he did now.

I overheard part of his conversation with Sam last night and gathered that John was finally ready to make his move. I was excited for my brothers. Not just John. Sam was clearly a little smitten himself and I was more than happy to sit back and watch this all play out. But I'd be lying if I said I wasn't curious about the girl.

That's why when John called asking what I knew about getting a window fixed, I offered to come over and take the measurements and board it up myself. I could have just given him the run down on what needed to be done. Call a handyman to put up plywood. Call a window repair guy. Easy. But that's not nearly as fun as coming and checking out the drama myself. And it was already dramatic.

As I pulled into a space in front of the store an omega in the street seemed to be having a borderline panic attack at the fact that the shop wasn't open. Sweet thing. I'd always found the dramatics of omegas adorable. Sometimes heart wrenching. The way they cared so deeply, felt so much. As someone who also felt deeply but just could never seem to show it, watching them was soothing.

I climb out of my truck and round it to let down the tailgate. I swung by the hardware store on the way, grabbed a half dozen boards of plywood. Should be more than enough to get the hole patched. It wouldn't be pretty but pretty wasn't my style. While I was here I would grab measurements and send them over to George so he could arrange to have the window properly replaced. Then I'd head home and get back to searching for my next project.

I technically didn't need to work anymore. Hell, with our pack investments none of us did. But I also had my own money on top of that and it was plentiful thanks to a couple of patents. But having been raised the son of two carpenters I wasn't comfortable just lazing around.

Weirdly my dad was. I'd paid off his and mum's mortgage a decade or so back when an app I'd developed had gone viral. They'd immediately retired and started just doing woodwork in the garage for fun. Mum sold a few pieces. Turns out she was where I got my work ethic from. As far as dad was concerned his only job now was to love his wife and keep tabs on his kids. Unfortunately with my sister, Susie, bonded with children and settled in another state, most of his interference was directed at me. So I made sure there was nothing to interfere with.

I slide the plywood out of the bed and rest them against the side of the truck. Flipping the tailgate back up, I decide to come back for my toolbox. I grip the stack and carry it up, resting it against the wall in the alcove by the door. I try the handle but the door is locked. Kind of ironic since there is a giant hole at the front of the shop.

'Sorry.' A sweet voice calls and I turn.

Well damn.

On the other side of the glass door frantically fighting the locks is an adorable bundle of dark curly hair framing a creamy complexion. She looks up at me as she slides the bolt lock open. And keeps looking up, and up till she finds my eyes. God but she was short.

I know I'm part giant, everyone comments on it. When you're closer to seven foot than six, people notice. And when you're also three feet wide and built like a lumberjack you also got that pointed out. A lot. But never had I felt as giant as I did right now.

'Sorry.' She mutters again as she finally gets the door open. 'Everyone else has just used the hole.'

'I'm not that rude.' I shrug as she steps back to let me in. Her store is adorable even disheveled and I feel a sudden wave of anger at the destruction that's been wrought upon the space.

'Thanks for coming.' John's voice comes from the other side of the room. 'Melanie this is Mick. My other packmate.'

'It's nice to meet you.' She reaches out her tiny hand and I take it, trying not to laugh at the size difference.

'Wait till you get to know me.' I drawl. 'No one ever uses the word nice to describe me.'

'Well then they're not paying attention.' She counters. Oh I like this girl. She's got spunk.

'I was just explaining to Melanie that you could put some boards up to cover the hole for now.' John interjects.

'Yeah and I'm going to take measurements for George as well so he can get some window guys onto the job.'

'I appreciate the help. But really, you don't have to. I can call the window guys myself and I'm sure I can figure out how to put some plywood up.' I try not to snort. I believe she could call the window repair men but hanging plywood wasn't easy. It was a two person job. The thought of her doing it by herself annoyed me. 'Just let me know what I owe you for the plywood.'

'Nothing.' I didn't need to catch John shaking his head behind her to know the answer he would want me to give. 'It's left over from another project.'

'Even so it must have cost something.'

'Yeah but at this point you're saving me from having to pay to get it disposed of so you're doing me a favour.' That was an outright lie and I didn't like it. I think she can tell too because her eyes narrow. 'I'll tell you what. I haven't had nearly enough caffeine yet, you can pay me in coffee.'

'Okay, but please, I don't want you wasting your time here today. I'll make you a coffee but then you can just go and I'll handle the rest.' I feel a scowl cross my face. Why would she want to do all this alone when we were here and could help?

'I'll tell you what, if you can move one of those boards into the right position on your own I'll take off and leave you to it.' I expect her shoulders to slump. For her to admit defeat and say she'd planned to call a handyman. I wasn't expecting her to immediately bend her knees and drop her shoulder against the plywood, reach out her hands to each side and grip. By the time she lifted the sheet of plywood off the ground and began shuffling it over towards the corner where it needed to go my mouth was hanging open near my collar.

'Stop. Melanie.' John steps into her path. 'Please.'

'I can do it on my own.' She snips.

'I know you can but... Mick's between jobs right now. He needs a project. Please let him help you. Gives him something to do today.' She looks back towards me and I rearrange my face from shocked and impressed to what I hope is a pleasant nice guy face. Or as nice as my face gets. What John is saying is true, just not in the strict sense. I had plenty I could do with my day but suddenly I wanted nothing more than to stay here and fix this sweet girl's broken windows. And anything else that was broken for that matter.

'Okay fine.' Melanie shrugs letting John take the board of wood from her. 'But I'm making you both coffee. And breakfast.'

She storms off to what I assume is the kitchen as I hear the distinct sounds of a metal bowl hitting the counter. I step forward to take the plywood from John. Honestly Melanie looked more comfortable holding it than he does. Not to mention he's staring at the doorway she disappeared through like a lost dog.

'Okay?' I ask and he looks at me, his eyes wide with fear and frustration and shakes his head. I look to the door where Melanie just disappeared and whisper. 'I get it.'

KNOT FOR REAL

Chapter 17. Melanie

I am so pathetic, two, count them, two alphas are currently clearly skipping work to try and help me. I should be calling people and organising things and I'm not. I'd initially come back here to whip up a frittata. But once it was baking I headed back out to make coffees and see if I could help.

What happened instead?

As I finished making the coffees the sight of two shirtless sweaty alphas was burned permanently onto my eyeballs and caused me to actually fall to the floor in distress. Luckily neither of them noticed because at the time John was steadying a piece of plywood while Mick hammered in nails around the edges, both of their backs to me. Oh goddess, their backs.

Perfection, both of them. But in different ways. Mick had bulging muscles, full of strength that had clearly not been made in the gym alone. The muscles were too big, too functional. And yet he looked soft, cuddly almost. John had a kind of tight muscle, leaner but more visible. Like someone had carved the space between each muscle to make it stand out. Oh god, was I drooling?

I made the coffees, Mick surprising me with his request for a caramel latte with whipped cream. But then John ditched his button down work shirt so as not to ruin it and Mick had removed his shirt due to the heat. And wow was it hot.

When Mick casually reached over and plucked another piece of plywood from his pile like it was a feather and not a giant heavy chunk of wood, my brain had chosen to imagine me in the place of the wood board. What it would be like to have his fingers wrap around my waist and lift me up and spin me around. Put me exactly where he wanted me, against a wall. And then hold me in place as he hammered into me. In my mind it was not his actual hammer he was using to nail me.

Which was why I was now making my famous potato zucchini and cheddar hashbrowns. As an excuse to get out of that room until the shirts went back on because the way things were going I was going to whine again or faint or something.

It wasn't my fault. It was just that they were crazy attractive. Mick probably wasn't technically handsome. Too intimidating. He looked like a cross between a Canadian lumberjack and the head of a biker gang. I'd never thought beards were attractive before but on him it looked good. And soft. Would it be soft? I kind of wanted to touch it.

Seriously, what was with this pack? George was now the only one I hadn't met in person but his voice alone had me whining out loud. And the other three? Well now I not only had my nerdy library boyfriend, and the arrogant jock, I also had the bad boy on the motorbike that your mother warns you against. And my brain having cast them in those roles was now imagining what it would be like to make love against the bookshelves of a library, the cold metal of the bleachers after a game or on the back of a motorbike. Can you even have sex on a motorbike or would it fall over? My brain tried to figure out a position that would work and I groaned out loud. I needed to calm down.

Lifting the last of the hashbrowns out of the fryer and onto the cooling racks I lean my hips back against the bench and close my eyes to take a deep breath.

I'm overwhelmed. I think my brain is having filthy fantasies just to distract me from everything else. Between lunch with my family, my sister's visit to the shop and now the break in, on top of my general lack of sleep and exhaustion. It had been potentially the longest three days of my life and the third day had only just started.

'You okay?' The smokey voice floats gently from the doorway and I brace myself before I open my eyes. Thankfully Mick has put his shirt back on. Which is also a shame.

'I'm fine.' I huff out turning back to the stove. 'Where's John?'

'Vacuuming.' Sure enough as he says it I can hear the vacuum start up out in the store. God they're so nice. The least I can do is feed them. I bend over to get the frittata out of the oven. When I turn back to Mick he seems redder. Must be the bloody heat of the kitchen. Great, now I'm boiling the guys trying to help me.

'You don't have to be.' He mumbles.

'I don't have to be what?' I ask, slicing into the dish so it's ready to serve.

'Fine. You don't have to be fine. If I was in your shoes I think I'd be not fine.' He smiles at me and I feel the urge to laugh. The giant lumberjack is trying to comfort me. Him and John have just spent their morning fixing the hole in my cafe. And now sweet guys that they are, he's trying to make me feel better about my disaster of a life.

'And how would that help?' I try not to roll my eyes.

'Doesn't have to help. Just know, you can feel your feelings. We won't run away.' I imagine letting them see everything that I actually feel. I imagine that I scream and cry and they're still both here.

Suddenly I can't breathe.

I try to pull air into my lungs but they won't work. I fall to the floor, the rubber of the non slip mats softening the impact on my knees as I fall forward, my hands slapping onto the tile. I can't breathe. I'm choking on air.

'Shit.' I can hear Mick's voice against my ear as I'm hauled into his lap. It's too bright in here. And it smells wrong, like cleaning products and food. I don't want that. I want dark, I want calm, I want... lavender. I can smell lavender.

I bury my face into the smell, inhaling deeply. Oh my goddess it's so good. It smells warm and hot, almost spicy. This is the plant itself. In summer. The heat of the sun warming the flower. The fresh oils soaking into you as every muscle softens.

With my face buried in the smell, it's dark and it's safe. I can breathe again. I shudder as I drag the scent and the air into my lungs. Better. I feel better. I cling to the soft cotton in my hands. Wait, why is there soft cotton in my hands? There is a wall of muscle around me. Arms. The cotton is a shirt. Shit.

I scramble backwards as fast as I can. I'd curled into Mick's chest. He'd been trying to offer me comfort, reassurance, and I'd climbed into his lap and inhaled him like a psychopath. Oh god, he's on the floor. I hope he got down here of his own accord because if I pulled him onto the ground then I'm going to need to flee.

'I'm so sorry.' I moan. 'I don't know what... I... I was...'

'It's okay.' He lifts his hands in front of him like he's trying not to spook me.

'It's not okay. You and John are just trying to help me and I can't even keep my shit together enough to let you, without accosting you.' I slap my hands to cover my face as I sit back on my heels.

'It's okay.'

'It's not.' For the second time today I feel like I'm going to cry even though I know the tears won't come. I can feel my breath starting to allude to me again. I feel shaky, like my body is moving too fast inside of me. Mick growls at me.

Mick growls at me? I freeze. Everything inside me instantly stills.

'Sweetness, I need you to look at me.' I don't want to but he growls again and my eyes are suddenly staring into his. 'Good. You're okay. Everything's okay. You got overwhelmed just for a moment. And you wanted a hug. That's okay.'

A hug? That's what we're calling it when you climb into someone's lap, wrap yourself around them and breathe so deep you almost pass out?

'I didn't mean to.' I mumble by way of explanation.

'I know. Please don't be upset. I promise I'm okay. And we're going to make sure you're okay as well.' I nod. I believe him. He smiles at me as he stands up, and up and up. Seriously, the man's a giant. He reaches out his hand to help me and when I stand I come up to his solar plexes.

'You're very tall.' I comment as I tilt my head back so I can see his face.

'Sorry about that.'

'Maybe I can get some high heels, or a box to stand on.'

'I could make you some stilts?' He offers.

'Perfect.' It's not really a joke but the hint of playfulness relaxes me a little more. I feel slightly better. I kind of wish I could bury my face back in Mick's chest and breathe deep for a bit but just standing next to him is helping.

I hear the vacuum switch off in the other room and remember where we are. Everything I have to deal with. Shaking my hair back from my face and straightening my shoulders I step to the side of Mick to grab the frittata.

'Grab the plates and the hashbrowns and follow me.' I say as I begin walking the frittata out into the cafe. It's dark out here. I mean not really, the lights are on but it feels like night time because I'm so used to the big window at the front letting the sun in all day. I pause. Something about the darkness of the space rattles me.

'It's okay.' Mick's smokey voice drifts over me. 'We'll make it bright again soon.'

KNOT FOR REAL

Chapter 18. Sam

I thought I was prepared. Like mentally I thought I had this. John called me this morning to tell me about the break in and so I'd had most of the morning to process it. But something about seeing plywood covering the front of her store has me seething. Who would do this? Why did they do this? And how were we going to make them pay?

Mick is still here, his old green pick up truck is in front of the store. John's gone back to work, he called me to complain about it the whole way. When Melanie saw that he had five missed calls from his boss she'd apparently kicked him out. A sight I would have paid to see. But right now I just wanted to see her.

On the front door there's a cardboard sign saying 'closed until further notice' but further notice has been scratched off and replaced with the word tomorrow. I sigh.

I push in, jangling the bell as I do and pause. Melanie is wearing jean shorts and a loose button down shirt with a bandanna pulling back her hair. All up and down her delectable thick thighs and calves are streaks of dark green paint so distracting I almost miss the paint brush in her hand.

She is okay. She's better than okay, she's laughing because Mick is lip syncing to whatever is playing over the speaker. Mick can lip sync? And damn, he was going for it. Facial expressions and hip juts and all the while he's continuing to paint the ply wood. Thank god for the drop sheets underneath, they were catching a lot of splatter. She's laughing so hard, tears stream down her cheeks as she holds the back of her paint splattered hand to her mouth to try and stop the sound.

Damn. Between the two of them they'd found some lightness in a horrible day and now I had to be the one to ruin it. I'd called in a favour from a detective a lot higher up than the patrol cops that had come by this morning and she was going to be here any minute to ask some follow up questions.

'Sam?' Her sweet voice full of surprise echoes across the space as she reaches to turn off the music. 'What are you doing here?'

'John didn't tell you I was coming? He said he'd text?'

'No. Wait... maybe. I haven't been checking my phone.' She carefully puts down her brush wiping her hands across her thighs then on her shirt to rid her fingers of paint. God I'm a pig. Watching her fingers grip her own creamy thighs has me half hard in my pants. Watching her then wipe the residual against her breasts has me gasping. I'm about ready to castrate myself but when I look over at Mick he has a similar grimace of shame. At least I'm not a horny arsehole by myself. 'Oh he did send something.'

'Must not have heard it over the music.' Mick offers as she picks up the phone and reads the message aloud.

'Sam will stop by in a little bit with a detective to ask follow up questions.' She looks up at me confused. 'But wait, why?'

'Just to make sure they've got the whole picture.'

'Oh, I was hoping that bit was done.' She winces. 'Cops kind of scare me.'

'You a secret criminal?' I tease.

'No, I guess I'm just always scared I'm going to get in trouble.'

'I can't imagine you getting in trouble sweetness?' Mick grumbles.

'Oh trust me, I got into a lot of trouble growing up.' Her voice is sad.

'Well, Charlotte's not coming here to get you in trouble, she just wants to ask you some more questions. Okay?' She looks at Mick and he smiles and nods at her.

'Okay, I can do this. I'll go wash my hands properly.' She calls the last as she leaves. I can't pretend I don't feel a tweak of jealousy. Mick met her today and already she was looking to him for reassurance. How did that happen?

'I'll get the paint out of the way so you guys can sit in here and I'll go get started out front.' Mick says to me as he starts shifting around his supplies.

'Pause.' I demand and he does. 'Explain?'

'Explain what?' He asks.

'Whatever that just was. You met her like four hours ago.' I grumble.

'So? You met her yesterday.' Shit was that only yesterday?

'So you feel it too?' I ask him. There was no point denying how I was feeling, I'm sure he could see it all over my face, same as I could see it on his.

'Yeah.' And we both know how John feels. This is weird. We've all been pack for six years now and we've never, not once, all had a thing for the same person. Mick and I had been known to share someone from time to time but that was less about feelings and more about fun. But this?

'It makes sense.' I shrug. 'I mean she's gorgeous. And fierce. You should see how hard she works, I know alphas who would crack. As a beta she's doing amazing.'

'About that...' Mick lets his voice trail off.

'Dude I'm not being a 'designation prick', I know anyone can do anything. I just mean she's really impressive. I got tired watching her yesterday.' I defend myself.

'It's not that... she's a beta?' His question hangs in the air.

'Yeah.' I shrug my agreement but his face is clouded. 'Why?'

'I don't know. It's just something about her. I would have guessed she was an omega.' He shakes his head as if ridding himself of the thought.

'If she was an omega don't you think we'd be able to smell her? Even the world's best descenter doesn't cover up a perfume completely.'

'And what makes you think she'd perfume for you?' He quirks his brow.

'Have you seen me?' I gesture at my immaculate suit.

'Yeah.' He shrugs unimpressed.

'How did that omega last month describe me? An underwear ad come to life?' I straighten my tie dramatically.

'He still wasn't interested in us.' Mick points out.

'Well we can blame that on your ugly mug can't we.' I tease.

'Am I interrupting?' A familiar voice calls from the doorway.

'No, thank you for coming, Charlotte.' I instantly swap to work mode. Charlotte is one of the many detectives I've gotten to know over the years. My work wasn't always pretty and when shit hit the fan you wanted someone like Charlotte in your corner.

'Always happy to help a friend of yours.' Charlotte smiles at me as I drop a kiss to her cheek. 'Where is she?'

'Here.' Melanie's sweet voice calls from the coffee machine. She looks nervous but she's smiling. 'Can I get anyone a coffee before we sit down?'

'That would be great actually.' Charlotte responds. 'Can you do a latte?'

'I can do anything.' Melanie beams as she begins rattling around at the machine. 'Mick? Sam?'

'No more for me, sweetness.' Mick responds, gathering his paint trays and brushes. 'I'll be out front. Are you still against my tie dye plan?'

'Vehemently.' She nods with a smile.

'I'll take a long black.' I request. I wish I could call her something cute like Mick. Endearments just roll off his tongue and seem natural. I could never pull off sweetness. As Mick slides past me he pauses and drops his voice.

'Stay close to her. She's hiding it well but she's not coping.' I nod that I hear him as he continues outside to keep working.

I gesture for Charlotte to take a seat away from the wall of wet paint and sit beside her while we wait for Melanie. Charlotte busies herself on her phone so I busy myself watching Melanie as she works. She's smiling as she goes about frothing milk but Mick's right, there's something fragile about her today. Which is more than fair.

'Here we go, one latte and one long black.' Melanie announces as she sets the coffees down and sits opposite us. Her hands are clean now but there are still streaks of green on her legs. And I can't stop staring at them as she sits and her thighs spread. Their soft pillowiness presses against the armrests of her chair and I want to reach across and slide my hand in between to protect her skin. Or maybe to be the thing digging into her thighs. Squeezing her into me. Leaving bruises.

'Wow this is amazing.' Charlotte's look of awe is almost comical. Melanie beams.

'She has secrets but she won't share.' I tease her trying to help her relax.

'Just so you know I'll be back once you reopen.' Charlotte smiles at Melanie.

'Tomorrow.' Melanie states matter of factly making me want to groan.

'So soon?' Charlotte's as surprised as I am.

'Yeah, can't let the bastards keep you down right?' Melanie shrugs.

'Excellent attitude.' Charlotte agrees. 'So Sam asked me here just to check in on your story and what happened. I have the report from the officers this morning but do you think you could walk me through it again?'

'Sure.' Melanie mumbles.

Chapter 19. Melanie

I like Charlotte. Which surprises me. I'm not generally comfortable around police officers. I was too disorientated this morning to get myself into a proper tizzy, but normally any kind of authority figure leaves me feeling nauseated and shaky. But Charlotte is lovely. She's got a rich chocolatey voice and she smiles with every question.

'Who knows you live upstairs?' She asks.

'Just my family. My friend Sandra. I guess John and Sam now. And Mick. But it's not common knowledge.'

'Do you have anything of value upstairs?'

'Not really. My television broke like six or seven months ago and I haven't had the chance to replace it. I have a laptop but it's not worth anything, I assure you.'

'What are you thinking?' Sam asks Charlotte. For the most part he's stayed quiet through our chat except for the occasional grunt and growl. But he's clearly picked up on something now because he's staring at Charlotte intensely and she seems to be choosing her words carefully.

'Melanie I don't want to upset you but I don't think this was a random break in. I think it was... targeted.'

'What?' I gasp.

'Melanie breathe.' It's Sam's hand reaching out to cover mine and it feels warm and lovely but it's so far away. 'MICK!'

I wonder why he's shouting? Oh to get Mick that makes sense. Here he comes. Oh he's going to sit next to me. That's nice.

'Hi Mick.' I mumble.

'Hi sweetness.' He grunts from his chair next to me. 'What's happening?'

'Charlotte doesn't think this was random.' Sam announces. Yep there it is again. The fear. It's in my fingers making them numb. It was scary enough thinking some arseholes just broke into my store. But broke into my store on purpose? To do what?

'Why would you think that?' Mick's smokey voice demands.

'Smash and grabs tend to target tech stores, jewelry stores, places where they can grab big ticket items and take off. But what Melanie's described, the way they lingered to tear things apart. The fact that they didn't even really try and take anything. Not even all the jewelry? I just can't imagine even the dumbest of our criminals thinking this place was a good score.'

'Not valuable enough.' The words slide from my mouth. They feel familiar. There was nothing of value. Nothing anyone wanted. No one wanted me. Wait no that was a different problem. Why was my head so god damn fuzzy?

'Drink this.' I feel the cold glass of water in my hand and lift it to my lips. It feels nice. The cold against my lips. Gliding across my tongue. Caressing the back of my throat. I feel the cold water slip down into my chest and I start coming back to my body.

'Fuck.' I mutter. I know I'm pretty close to my third meltdown of the day but I can't help it. What she's saying makes sense. Why did they pick my store? There's nothing worth much in here. Not compared to other places downtown or even one street over where that Techtropolis place was. Which leads me to another thought. 'No one else around here was broken into?'

'I'm afraid not.' Charlotte nods at me. 'That's the other reason it feels targeted. If it wasn't a smash and grab then it would be teenagers running amuck but in that case you see a cluster of stores or at least a couple of stores and a couple of cars. This was just your place. Hence it feels targeted.'

'Now what?' Mick demands from beside me.

'I have to ask, do you know anyone who might want to hurt you?'

'No.' My response is instant. I don't do much of anything. Other than work. Definitely nothing that would upset anyone.

'Maybe a disgruntled customer?' She presses.

'I can't think of anyone. A woman complained about her coffee being too hot the other week but she was just having a bad day. She's normally very nice.' I'm rambling.

'And only your friends and family know that you live upstairs?'

'Yeah, and I mean, if it was someone that knew me, that knew I was here, they could have come up at any time.'

'What do you mean they could have come up?' It's Mick's voice from beside me.

'The lock on the door to my apartment, it doesn't work. Never has. But since I lock the door down here it doesn't matter.' Mick stands, squeezing my shoulder before bolting out the front door.

'Where is he going?' I ask Sam.

'To get you a new lock.' Sam answers confidently although how he's so certain I don't know.

'Oh. Okay.' That will help make me feel safer. Maybe he can get me one of those satisfying bolt ones that slams into place. That would feel good.

'What happens next?' Sam's asking Charlotte and I take the second to lean back in my chair and observe them. They both look so professional in blazers with buttoned up shirts underneath. They're real adults. Like grown up grown ups. Compared to them, right now, I feel like a toddler.

'I'm not overly concerned. I don't want you to be either. Despite the damage the attack feels more like a sick prank. Not like anyone intended you real harm. So I want you to just get back to your life, re-open the store. I'm going to do a little digging into your life, if that's okay Melanie?' I nod. I don't have any secrets. Wait. Shit. Yes I do.

'What kind of digging?' I only have one secret but if Charlotte finds out I'm an omega then Sam will find out. I guess that's technically okay. I keep it quiet for safety. I don't think he'd go around telling anyone. But then again didn't he say he didn't really like omegas? If he finds out, will he dislike me? I hope not. I know I haven't known him long but the thought of him not liking me makes my insides burn.

'I just want to talk to your employees, your family, any friends you think might be helpful. See if anyone else can think of a reason you might be targeted.' That makes sense. I only have one employee, Mindy, and she wouldn't say anything about my designation, and Sandra won't if I give her a heads up. That just leaves my family.

'Any chance you could not talk to my family? For now? I just want to deal with it myself first. Otherwise they'll probably come barging in here telling me what to do, for my own good. And that would not be good.' I shudder at the thought.

'Of course, I won't talk to anyone you don't want me to. Have you considered staying somewhere else for a day or two? Not that I think you're in danger but just to feel a bit more comfortable.'

'Not necessary.' I try to say it firmly but I can feel my lip wobble. Other than my parents' place I don't have anywhere I could go. I suppose Sandra would take me in but there were already five people in a four bedroom house. One of those people was a pregnant omega. They didn't need another body getting in the way. 'I'll be fine here.'

'Okay, it's your choice. There's no immediate concern for alarm.'

'I'll be fine.' If I keep saying it, it will become true. Right?

KNOT FOR REAL

Chapter 20. Mick

I bought three locks. A standard handle replacement, a chain and a bolt. Is it overkill? Maybe, but I'd also eyed off a reinforced steel security door. So as far as I was concerned this was a compromise.

When I got back to the cafe I was still pretty riled up so I took a moment to finish putting a coat of paint on the exterior. I would never normally paint a temporary plywood wall like this but Melanie had seemed really bothered by the exposed wood. When she'd mentioned having leftover paint from when she'd apparently re-did the whole store by herself, a thought that was still causing me stress, I'd acted like it was the best idea ever. And I'd realised it was when she disappeared to change and came back in those tiny cut off shorts.

Melanie was an enigma. I know she's a beta. John and Sam are both sure of it. And yet all of my instincts are telling me she's an omega. I want to haul her against my chest and purr until she relaxes into a pile of goo. I want to bark at everyone who's ever been mean to her. I want a lot of other less savoury things as well.

I couldn't decide what I was more obsessed with. Her perfect pillowy breasts. Her thick thighs. The high rounded globes of her arse. Or her soft rounded belly. I think it was just all her delicious softness packaged up together. But when she'd climbed into my lap in the kitchen and I'd felt her soft weight settle against me I knew John and Sam weren't going to be the only ones asking this girl out.

As soon as all this break-in shit was over. For now, while she was distressed I considered her off limits.

Which is why I had to keep my mind off the way the sweet curve of her nose had felt buried against my neck. Her lips grazing the soft spot beneath my ear while she sought my smell. I know betas also loved alpha smell but it was in that second, the feel of her surrender as she scented me without reserve... damn it. I was so sure for a second. And I feel pissed she isn't an omega. Or more specifically isn't our omega.

We didn't need an omega. I'd made it very clear when we were discussing taking a break from the scent matching service that I had no interest in ever restarting the program. It felt contrived. I didn't feel the need to have something else connecting us. We were already brothers. Our bonds were strong. Our life was good.

But if it was her?

Not just some nameless faceless omega. If it was Melanie? I'd be okay with that. She'd already made me laugh more today than I think I had all year. And that's when she was having a bad day. Her chiming laughter, her giggling smile, the sad tilt of her lips, the hurt in her eyes. I wanted all of it. I wanted all of her emotions to pour into me and fill me up. To take all my empty barren places and make them whole again.

God I needed to let this go.

She wasn't our omega. She wasn't even an omega. She was a sweet girl who needed our help. Plain and simple. We'd help her get this current mess sorted out, make sure she was safe and then after that we could talk about if she wanted to date any of us. Or preferably all of us.

I run the paint roller over the last panel one more time but there's no excuse to keep lingering out here. The job is done. I grab the bag with the three locks in it in one hand and some of the painting supplies in the other and head in.

'Mick!' Her voice trills with excitement as I enter. Charlotte and Sam are nowhere to be seen and she's busy wiping down her gift display shelves with something that smells like vanilla.

'Still busy working sweetness?' I call setting everything down on the ground.

'You know it.' She grumbles with humour still in her voice. I smile at her, before heading outside to grab the last of the paint supplies off the pavement. It was a wonder we hadn't gotten a complaint in the half hour they'd just been sitting out there.

'I got some locks for your apartment.' I call out as I come back in.

'That's what Sam said you'd be doing.'

'Can I go on up and install them?' She pauses in her movements.

'You don't have to do that, I can do it later.'

'I have all my tools, it will only take me a few minutes.'

'Okay.' She hedges. 'Let me go up first. Just so I can tidy up a little.'

'I couldn't care less how messy your apartment is. I once legitimately used a shovel to move stuff out of the way and get to my bed.' I laugh at the memory.

'Seriously?' She seems more amused than horrified.

'I was at university and new to living on my own. I went wild for a bit.' I shrug. Don't we all go through a gross phase when we're first left to our own devices.

'Fair enough. But still... I... um... I need... to... um... I need to settle Whisper!'

'What is Whisper?' I ask ignoring the obvious fact that, whatever Whisper was, it was also an excuse.

'My dog. Whisper. He's upstairs. Has his own little balcony up there, he just sits and watches the street most of the day.' She says with a moony smile.

'Sounds adorable. You go ahead and settle him and then call for me and I'll come up. Do you want me to keep wiping down the shelves or deal with the paint stuff?' This was a technique my sister told me she used on her toddler, letting him choose between two things even though he didn't have a choice. I was done asking if she wanted help. I was only going to ask which way she wanted to be helped.

'Can you take the paint stuff out to the back courtyard? There's an old sink there you can use. Through the door that says employees only.'

'No problem.' I follow her instructions while I listen to her dash upstairs. I find the 'employees only' door and sure enough it leads to an adorable courtyard. It needs some work but clearly someone has been tidying it up. There are plants ranging from seedlings to fully grown and there is some furniture in the corner which needs some TLC but would look great in time. And from what I'd seen today I was comfortable guessing that she was also trying to renovate this space all by herself in whatever limited spare time she had.

Shaking my head at the thought of how much she must push herself I head over to the old sink. The paint tin is already hammered shut and ready to be stored. I'd let the paint dry in the tray and then she could peel it off another day. It didn't take me long to get the brush clean, the roller resisted but was no match for the twist and slide method my mum had taught me as a teen. And sure enough as soon as I laid the roller to the side so it could dry too I could hear Melanie calling for me.

I was excited to see her space. See her touches in a room, her pops of colour and her sense of style. I was not disappointed.

I thought downstairs had been a vibrant beautiful space but this was something else. Her apartment was small, so I was looking into the combined kitchen and living room. To the left was an alcove with three doors, each of them closed and painted a different colour. To the right was a small balcony over the courtyard that had some fake grass on it, presumably for the dog. The backsplash in her kitchen was bold green, all of her cabinets dark blue. The appliances were black. Her living room was charcoal which only made all the colour stand out more. Her dark brown leather sofa sat in front of a wall of art so eclectic I think it would take a couple hours to take it in.

There was a sketch of a frog dancing with a top hat in a golden frame. Next to it was a beautiful farming landscape done in the style of the realists, except over the top someone had painted an alien ship beaming up a cow. Next to that was a neon print that said 'Be As You Are'. And it expanded from there. All of it different, colourful and interesting.

'Wow'. I mutter.

'You like it?' I turn to find her hunched over a ball of fluff I assume to be her dog. I cross the room and smile as I bend down to greet Whisper.

'I love it.'

KNOT FOR REAL

Chapter 21. Melanie

I was nervous to let Mick come upstairs. Sandra is the only one who's ever seen my apartment. And it's dark. Or I prefer the term warm. But even I have to admit its charm is very The Addams Family. I only put things on the wall if they make me happy so nothing much matches. There are lots of colours but they're all warm jewel tones even if they're dark so the overall feeling is meant to be rich and warm. At least that's what it feels like to me.

'Why did you call him Whisper?' Mick asks me as he scratches the dog behind the ears.

'I didn't, he's a rescue, he came with the name and he'd already gone through so much. I didn't want to give him an identity crisis too.'

'Fair.' He chuckles. Whisper rolls over in his bed to offer his belly for pats to the stranger and Mick smiles at me. I know he didn't buy for one second that I needed to settle my dog. What I needed to do was run upstairs and make sure the door to my room was firmly closed and just generally hide any signs I was an omega. Spray some room descenter. Also to tidy up.

The two day old plates that had been sitting in the sink were now in the dishwasher. The pile of laundry that had been next to the machine was now in it. And the doors to the laundry, bathroom and most importantly the bedroom were all closed. I'd also tidied the coffee table and just generally straightened up. I wasn't unclean but I was messy.

'Shall we get some locks on your door?'

'Locks plural?' I ask.

'Yep three.' He declares as he pours them from the bag onto the floor.

'Three? Seems like overkill.'

'The standard handle lock, a chain for if you ever need to crack the door and a bolt because it makes you feel safe.' He explains.

'Oh I did think about how great a big bolt lock would be. They just feel satisfying.' I smile thinking of the sensation of a dead lock sliding into place.

'Agreed.' He murmurs as he begins digging in his toolbox.

'And if I said you can just leave them and I'll put them on myself so you can get back to your day?' He sighs at my question.

'If you're uncomfortable having me in your space or there's some other issue that I'm not seeing, say the word and I'll go. But if you're really just worried about my day, please don't.' His voice is deep and pleading

'I just don't want you wasting so much time on me. You're all being so nice.' I shrug. I can't explain why but the more time I spend with them the more uncomfortable I get. Not because they were making me uncomfortable but because of how much I love just being in their company.

'We can't be nice guys?' He asks.

'Literally the first thing you said to me was that you're not nice.' I tease.

'True. I guess I need to amend. I'm not nice to everyone.' He smiles and I get the feeling there are dimples hiding beneath his beard.

'Fair. I guess I'm not either.' I nod. I try to be kind to everyone I meet but it's not always easy. He begins sorting through the lock packets, taking all the screws and tossing them to the side. 'What are you doing?'

'Swapping the screws.' He responds, tossing the last few to the side. 'We're going to use these instead.'

'Why?' I ask as he pulls out a packet of screws at least twice as long as the others. They have bigger heads too and I can't explain it but they look meaner than the other ones.

'If you're ever installing locks you should always get screws that go deeper into the wood, makes the locks more secure. With the tiny screws that come with the locks most people could just ram the door open. But with deeper screws with sharp wide teeth it's a lot harder.' There is something very wrong with me because I know he's sharing a helpful handy man tip but my body is reacting to the word screw repeatedly coming out of his mouth.

'Shall I leave you to it then.' I say backing away.

'One second, I got you something.'

'Other than enough locks to make this my own little prison?' I goad him.

'Yes.' He smirks, pulling a lollipop out of his pocket.

'What's this for?' I try to snatch it from him greedily but miss.

'You had a long day. I thought a little treat would be nice. Plus I wanted one.' He pulls another from his pocket.

'What flavour did you get? Would you be open to a trade.' I don't know what flavour I have but I like options.

'Sorry but I got us both the same, I've been craving it all day.' My heart stops as he hands me the ball of sugar on a stick wrapped in a bright pink wrapper. 'Strawberry.'

'Thanks.' I murmur as I take the gift. Shit. I have plenty of descenter on and I know I took my medication this morning. He can't have scented me right? But everyone always describes it the same way, sickly sweet strawberries. 'I'm going to go downstairs and finish wiping down the shelves.'

I flee.

Chapter 22. George

Some people really shouldn't write their ideas down on paper. Like the douchebags in front of me. The Sampson pack was composed of two alphas, two betas and a whole bunch of idiocy. Their grand idea to save the world? Another car share app that gives you points for carpooling. At best it is a software update.

My assistant Jamie is usually better at picking projects for these pitches. Every two weeks, on Tuesday I stay back an hour after work to make time for innovation. But these four are not innovative.

They shouldn't be here trying to sell this to me. They should be at one of the existing car share companies selling it to them as a chance to green wash their company and pretend to care about the environment. I email the suggestion to Jamie as I stand and leave the room.

Is it rude to simply walk out of a meeting while someone else is still talking, yes. But it's an unkindness to keep sitting there when I already know I'm going to pass. I have no problem with a company that only exists to make profit but I do have a problem with a company that exists to make profit and pretends that isn't its main goal. And I have other more important things to be getting on with today. Specifically getting a straight answer from Melanie's insurance company.

This should have been done by now. I submitted a quote for the window repair along with an estimate of what stock was destroyed, thanks to John's efforts. That should be all they needed. But I was getting the run around.

Just before this meeting, out of frustration, I suggested to the idiot I had been dealing with that he might want to mention my name and the company I owned to his higher ups and see if that changed the advice he was given. It worked, which was both disgusting and a relief.

I had three missed calls and two voicemail texts, so I read them as I made my way to my office. One was from the guy I had been dealing with earlier saying that he had sent over the coverage information and that if there were any problems to give him a call. The other was from a woman I assume was his boss assuring me that whatever coverage and support Melanie needed she would get. I really liked this outcome. I did not like the method.

When John called this morning I'd reluctantly agreed to help his friend. I didn't really want to, I had more than enough going on. I was going to get Jamie to handle it. But after speaking to her I felt like I wanted to do it myself.

I sit at my desk and fire up my computer ready to read over the policy and its inclusions when my phone rings again. Another unknown number, and since very few people have my direct line it's probably the insurance company.

'Hello.' I let the power of my alpha flow through my voice. Based on their change in attitude they already knew my reputation. Why not lean into it.

'Sorry.' A sweet voice squeaks into the line and then the call is dead.

Shit. That was Melanie. She would have felt that. I once let a full bark escape me during a strategy meeting and one of the men in the room, a beta, had actually fainted.

I call her back immediately and it rings and rings.

'Hello?' Her voice is so timid I feel a pang in my gut. Shit.

'Melanie, I didn't realise it was you calling.'

'It's okay. I'm sorry. John gave me your number and said it would be okay, but if it's not?' She lets the question hang in the air.

'No it's fine. What do you need?'

'Oh, I um... John said that you'd have contacted the insurance company and I wanted to check in because well...' I waited. Patience was always the best way to get someone to say what they were avoiding. 'I don't know you.'

'No you don't.' I can feel myself smiling.

'And well as nice as John and Mick have been. And Sam, getting the detective down here. It seems wrong to let you just figure things out for me.'

'Good girl.' I hear her breath catch. I'm probably going to be tortured in the afterlife, but it does things to me.

'Pardon?' She whispers.

'Did you want me to say it again?' Now I'm definitely teasing her. 'It's good that you called.'

'Thank you.' My brain imagines her saying those words from her knees. I haven't even seen this woman, yet the way she responds has me spinning out. But I can hear the uncertainty in her voice. As much as I want to play with her, she needs me right now. Which has my blood boiling in a different way.

'That's very responsible of you, to follow up. And not just to let someone else come in and take over. It's your business after all.'

'I hope you don't think... I wasn't trying... I didn't mean to let the guys help me so much today. But they insisted.' She hedges.

'As they should.' I cut across her. 'We aren't cheesy enough to have a pack motto but if we did, or more specifically if late one night after a bit too much to drink we'd discussed it, we would have chosen, 'be kind but fierce'.'

'Be kind but fierce.' She repeats. I want to tell her to say it again. Slower.

'So they were merely doing what they should today in helping you.' I explain.

'Well I do appreciate it. I know you're all busy. That's why I was calling. I was hoping you could tell me where you got to in lodging the claim? I don't want you to waste more time on this. It will be easier for me to just deal with it directly anyway.'

'Your claim has been processed.'

'It has?' The awe in her voice makes me feel like a superhero.

'Yes, I'm looking over the final details now. It seems they'll cover the entirety of the work to be done and the stock that was damaged up to fifteen thousand. What's unclear is what compensation they will give you for business lost during the time it takes to get back up and running fully.'

'They'd cover that?' Ordinarily no. But I didn't think it would be hard to get them to acquiesce.

'If you are willing to trust me to keep talking to them on your behalf I can see what I can do.' And if they didn't see their way to covering Melanie's lost income I could always cover it myself. Or buy the insurance company and change her policy.

'I trust you.' I feel the soft words sink through me and glue me to the seat. Fuck. I expected her to say, sure or thanks. But those three words whispered so gently into my ear. What did a heart attack feel like?

'Good.' I want to groan. Or growl. Actually, I want to purr? I knew many alphas who purred out of habit whenever their partners were near. I'd always thought it weird. But right now I could feel it in my gut. Like it wasn't something you did because you were supposed to but something you did because otherwise your insides would melt.

'Can I ask a favour?' At this point she could ask for my kidney. I'd give it to her.

'You can always ask.' I hedge.

'I was just wondering, what was the quote for the repairs?'

'I got a couple, and submitted the more realistic one.' I try to reassure her.

'How much was it for?'

'Just on two grand, for the materials and installation no later than Tuesday next week.' I recite the basics of the chosen estimate.

'Damn.' I'm surprised to hear the oath slip from her sweet mouth.

'What's wrong?' I ask.

'It's nothing.' Her voice drifts higher.

'I'm going to need you to tell me what's wrong, sweetheart.' I push.

'Nothing's wrong. I had hoped I could use these other guys but they're a bit more expensive.' Her words are slow, almost as if... she's embarrassed?

'Why would you want to use them then?' She seems like the fiscally responsible type so I am surprised.

'They're artists. They live locally. It wouldn't just be a new pane of glass it would be a stained glass window with my logo in it. They use all recycled glass and metals. They melt down old beer bottles and soda cans to do it. I always thought that if I ever replaced the glass I'd use them. But that quote is way too low, even if I added in what I could. I know they'd try and match it but I refuse to ask people to work for less than what they're worth. You know?'

'Yeah. I do.' I'd seen many artists and passionate people in general be asked to do work for less than its value and it had become a pet peeve of mine.

'Maybe I can get a line of credit with my bank, add it to the mortgage? I just worry if I replace the glass now, then the next pane will probably last me a decade and I could never justify replacing something unnecessarily. And I really would prefer to support these guys.' Something in her voice irks me.

'Do you like them?' I snap.

'Brian and Dan? Yeah they're great. When they first moved to the area they'd come in all the time and they really helped me spread the word on my place. They're really good guys and I like what they do.' I let out a sigh of relief. She liked them but I didn't think she was interested in them.

'Well then we'll have to find a way to support them.' I smile into the phone.

'But with the quote that low...' Her voice trails off. 'I'll have to talk to my bank.'

'Would you let me handle it?' I ask.

'You've already done more than enough, I don't want to be a burd...' My growl cuts her off. I feel bad for growling at her. But I couldn't let her finish that sentence. I hate that it even occurred to her to think of herself as a burden.

'I decide when it's enough. Will you let me handle this?' I ask keeping my tone light, even though what I really want is to demand she let me handle this. And then purr till she melts into me. Maybe spank her for calling herself a burden.

'Yes.' She acquiesces and I sigh with relief.

'I'm going to need the details for these artist friends of yours, I assume you've already talked to them about what design you want?'

'Yeah I talked to them earlier today.'

'Good. I'll also need the details of who you bank with, what branch and who you normally talk to, okay?' I would be covering whatever the excess cost was but a chat with her bank to make it look like that wasn't the case would be necessary.

'Sure I can text those over.'

'Can you trust me to do this for you?' I ask.

'Yes.'

'Good girl.'

KNOT FOR REAL

Chapter 23. Melanie

Today was amazing.

Last night I'd been wired and was sure that I was never going to settle. Yet after talking to George, I felt so calm that I drifted off at an embarrassingly early time. As a result I woke early and decided to take Whisper for a long walk.

I discovered Mick out the front of my store painting the words 'still open' in giant, beautiful, cursive letters across the plywood wall. I tried to pause in my plans, to assist him, but he insisted I still go on my walk. By the time I got back he was done.

I begged him inside so I could make him a coffee in thanks and he resisted. Which turned out to be a ruse. He surprised me with two long strands of string bulbs. He hung them from the roof, draping them artistically between the tables. The final effect was stunning, so much so I was definitely keeping them even when I had a window again. But best of all it was a little brighter and happier in the store again.

My day had only gotten better. John and Sam had come in for coffee on the way to work and the three giant alphas sat near my counter eating breakfast while fielding questions about the store from other well meaning customers. Which was incredibly helpful. I refused to let them pay for the coffee or breakfast as a thank you. Especially since Mick wouldn't let me pay for the lights. He swore they were just lying around in his garage but I didn't believe him. But I didn't have time to argue.

Yesterday's book club was rescheduled to today, so my normal mid-morning lull did not exist. And everyone was in a buying mood. Along with their morning coffees several of my regulars bought books. And Steph led the charge after book club, buying books but also one of everything I restocked in the gift store. Today was one of my best days financially in a very long time. I should have known it was too good to be true.

Shortly after the lunch rush, which I had spent furiously making more sandwiches because I under-stocked this morning, my phone vibrated in my back pocket. And then it rang again. And again. By the time I paused and got my phone out I didn't have to check the caller ID to know who it was.

Mum.

I called her back immediately. It was better to get it over with, the longer she stewed the angrier she got. She opened with how embarrassing it was for her to hear through a friend that my store had been broken into. Then she spent some time grilling me on what I had said to the cops and what I had sent to the insurance company. She then explained how much of an imposition it was going to be to have me home.

When I told her I wasn't coming home. No, not even for a few days, she lost it. They were only trying to be supportive. I didn't have to be so obstinate. Why did I always reject their help? Why was I so ungrateful?

I apologised explaining that the store wasn't closing. I assured her I was very grateful. Then she hung up on me because my sister was calling.

It didn't really bother me that she never actually asked how I was. Or if there was something she could do to help. This was the way it always was. And yet today some little part of me wanted to call bullshit.

And now, the doctor's office.

I would have cancelled if it wasn't that I was in desperate need of having my prescription refilled. Like I took my last pill this morning, desperate. Normally I would never leave it to the last minute like this, but my regular doctor recently retired and the transition to a new doctor had caused a delay.

'Melanie Rodgers?' The nurse calls into the waiting room. I stand quickly, I hate to keep doctors waiting. 'Exam room three.'

I head down the hall, let myself in the room and sit down to wait. Why did doctors' offices always have to be such a horrible white colour? I get that they had to be easy to clean but surely they could be a soft peachy colour or at least like a warm white.

'And what are you here for today Ms. Rodgers?' The doctor asks as he enters. Immediately putting the blood pressure cuff around my arm as he glances at my file. My blood pressure would be high. It was always high in the doctor's office.

'I'm just here to get another prescription for my suppressants.' I try for a smile but I'm pretty sure it comes out a grimace as the cuff thing is now strangling my arm.

'And what are you on and how long have you been on it?'

'Shiffalix, ten years.'

'Really?' He looks shocked. 'That's very strong medication. Why are you on it?'

'I had some pretty serious problems with my heats. I used to be on Manstarred but after I lost my pack things got worse, so they changed me across.' It's amazing how a very complicated time in my life can be summed up in a few sentences but there it was. The blood pressure machine beeps next to me. Yep, as I predicted, it was high. The doctor tuts as he writes down the result.

'I'm afraid I can't help you today. Shiffalix isn't available for general use anymore.'

'Oh, okay.' Shit. Shit, shit, shit, shit, shit. 'What else can you prescribe?'

'I see from your charts here that you haven't had a heat in over a year?'

'No, I was going to, a few months back but I had a problem getting the time off.'

'Well, you're going to have to make time. I understand the benefits of being able to skip when you're unbonded but the long term health ramifications aren't worth it.'

'Okay.' I didn't love the way he spoke to me like I was some sort of ignorant child but I didn't disagree. 'Well, what can you prescribe in the meantime?'

'I don't want to prescribe you anything. You should take your heat immediately.'

'But I'm completely out of medication' I stammer through my shock. 'I always take half doses. Won't stopping completely... well doesn't that hurt?'

'It can do, although most doctors agree that the descriptions of the pain seem wildly exaggerated.' He turns to the computer, typing as he speaks.

'Are any of those doctors omegas?' I mutter under my breath.

'What was that?' He asks.

'I was just saying to myself... Now's not a great time. And I'm not sure I can handle it, I have a lot going on.' That was an understatement.

'Look, the pain is definitely tolerable and you can always take over the counter pain meds to help.' His smile is condescending.

'I more meant the timing. Work.' The fact that my store has been broken into.

'You'll make it work. When you're next in we can discuss what else we can do in terms of lifestyle choices and some new weight loss medications. In the meantime you need to take your heat, no excuses.' He frowns at me before turning away to his computer. 'Do you need help getting registered at a heat clinic? I volunteer at several.'

'No thank you.' I mumble to him.

'Well then, let's see, why don't you come back next week after your heat and we can discuss what suppressants I would be willing to prescribe to you, a more appropriate schedule for your heats and what else you need to be doing in terms of diet and exercise. Hmm?' He doesn't actually wait for me to respond, just leaves.

I check in with the front desk on the way out to make sure everything's settled but I don't make the follow up appointment. I walk outside and sit on a bench.

Fuck.

I can go see another doctor but that could take days or even weeks. Which means I took my last pill this morning. I have till midday tomorrow till the medication starts to wear off. Then the cramps would set in. And without any half doses to ease into it I'll be in full heat by tomorrow night.

I would get through it on my own. My very first heat, I'd gone to a clinic at my doctor's recommendation. The heat haze always left your memory slightly foggy, but I remembered some of it. For the next year if anyone so much as uttered the words 'heat clinic' I felt the need to throw up. I'd never gone back.

After that I used suppressants, the milder ones to lessen the intensity of the heats and locked myself away in my room for a few days with plenty of snacks and toys. My heats have never been bad. Not really.

I knew other omegas who talked about the pain like it was the most excruciating thing in the world. I never figured out if I was lucky and mine weren't bad or if I just had a high tolerance for pain. But either way I was fine on my own. Until I'd met my pack.

But I didn't want to think about that. Whenever I did it felt like my own mind was attacking me. Just like someone attacked my store. And soon my own body would be attacking me thanks to Dr. Arsehole. Everything was crashing down around me again. And I felt so alone.

For a day that had started off so well it was now a dumpster fire.

Chapter 24. John

Today was a great day. Not because my stupid work project was finally done, although that was a relief. It was a cool bit of code but securing corporate information was not the kind of work I loved doing.

It also wasn't because Sam and I had finally gotten Mick in the face with a water balloon full of cream last night. Third time's the charm. The second time was an even worse disaster that ended with Sam covered in cream and me with a mouthful of confetti. But we didn't give up and I now had a picture on my phone of Mick's cream smothered face, dusted with confetti, laughing his arse off with both me and Sam locked under each arm in a headlock.

Today was a great day because this afternoon I would have Melanie all to myself. Unlike yesterday when I showed up for my morning coffee and found Mick was already there and helping string lights around her space. Sam arrived ten minutes after me, so we all had breakfast together. Today we'd made it an actual plan to all go together and support her rather than all just showing up randomly. But unlike yesterday when she'd practically been bubbling over with joy at our presence, today she seemed kind of down.

It was a particularly intense morning rush so she hadn't had time to stop and chat with us. Which meant I didn't know what was wrong. But I was pretty sure the ridiculous photo on my phone would go some way to cheering her up.

It was already two thirty so I knew she wouldn't be open much longer and I hurried. It was once again a big order, everyone in the office had wanted something. Many of them also asked me to pass on their sympathies and wishes to Melanie for her shop to be back to its glorious self soon. Everyone was worried about her. But none so much as me.

Or I guess me and my pack.

Mick was more overbearing than I was. This morning he thought he had seen her shiver and had offered her his flannel. She shook her head no and rushed away with a blush on her cheek. Although why she'd be embarrassed by being cold I had yet to figure out. Sam was equally annoying but that was purely for the drool. Watching him watch her was like watching a starving man stare at a buffet.

I round the corner to her block and pause.

'Melanie.' I call. 'What are you doing?'

'Oh John. You startled me.' She scolds as I rush to her side.

'Why do you have a ladder?' I ask.

'I'm just hanging up this to cover the 'still open' sign.' She indicates the fabric in her hand.

'You're worried people will get confused overnight?' I tease steadying the ladder as she climbs up and nails the corner of the piece of fabric on one side.

'No.' She scurries down the ladder, moves it to the other end and begins her ascension again.

'Steady there.' I say as I grab hold of the ladder again. 'This pavement isn't exactly even.'

'I know okay.' She snaps, hammering in the other corner of the fabric. She lets it fall now and I see the words, 'closed until further notice' hastily scribbled across the fabric in some kind of black pen.

'What's going on?' I ask cautiously as she climbs down the ladder. She moves it to the center of the fabric before going up again.

'I need to close for a few days.' She sighs, putting another nail into the center of the fabric before giving the whole thing a gentle tug to check it's secured.

'I thought you wanted to stay open?'

'I do... I mean, I did.' She snaps again, descending and then folding the ladder shut.

'Then why are you closing?' I'm so confused.

'Because I am. I was wrong. I need to take some time off. I can't afford it, but I have to... I don't have any time to come up with another plan. So can you just leave me alone, okay?' She snaps at me.

No. It wasn't okay. Something very clearly wasn't okay. I'd known Melanie for a year. And in the past few days she had been through some very hard things. And in all of that time, in all of those situations she had never once lost her cool. I'd seen her deal with difficult customers and omega meltdowns and not once had she even batted an eye. I'd found her after her store had been vandalised and she'd barely been distraught. Something was wrong.

'What's going on?' I ask, reaching out to push one of her curls off her cheek. I marvel at how soft her hair is, like fairy floss made of silk. Normally it smelled like vanilla or cinnamon. Occasionally lavender. But today there was a sweet strawberry smell coming off her and it had rocketed straight to number one. It was now my favourite. It was possibly the best smell in the whole world.

'Nothings going on.' She shakes her head and as she does, my fingers catch in her curls, tugging slightly. She shivers but she can't be cold, it's warm out and she's wearing a sweater.

'Talk to me.' I urge, resisting my own desire to pull her into my arms and hold her.

'It's nothing.' She shrugs. 'Seriously. I just need to take some time off. It can't wait. I'll be back on Monday. Or hopefully Tuesday at the latest.'

'Why don't you know when you'll be back?'

'I just don't know how long... it changes and... it just depends on some things, okay?'

'Okay.' I don't know what else to say. Clearly something is going on here. She's upset, and not just startled upset. Something is really bothering her. She's still as gorgeous as ever but there are creases around her eyes like she's in pain. 'Are you already closed for the day?'

'Yeah I fired down the machine early. I'm not feeling great.' I could see that. 'Did you want coffee?'

I hide the list from the office in my pocket. I know her well enough to know that if she knows I'm here to order for the office she'll fire back up that machine and push through. And I don't want that. What I want is to take care of her somehow.

'No. Can I get you anything? Did you want help with something? I could get you some food or something?' I offer.

'No it's okay. I'm stocked up on food. I'm just going to go in, lock up and lie down. I'll see you next week.' She looks pale as she raises her hand in what is barely a wave and heads inside.

I feel scared. And itchy. Watching her walk away sad is killing me. And she looks unwell. Her skin was always pale and creamy but just now she'd looked ashen. Like there wasn't enough blood in her body. I don't know what is wrong and I can't make it better. At least I knew three other alphas who could freak out with me.

KNOT FOR REAL

Chapter 25. Melanie

Everything hurts. I can feel my bones being crushed underneath my own muscles. Every breath carves up my chest like the air is made of razor blades. My throat is on fire. My body was shaking.

'Goddess help me.' I beg in my mind.

My heat came on so quickly. This morning I hadn't felt anything other than flushed. And really turned on. When Mick had offered me his flannel I'd wanted to grab it and inhale his lavender smell till I passed out. I'd kept imagining Sam's eyes on me, tracking the sway of my hips until heat was pooling between my legs. I could barely stop shivering whenever I neared any of the sweet alphas. My body wanted them. I wanted them. Thank god it seemed to be only them and not every alpha that came in.

By the time John stopped by this afternoon I'd been cramping. I'd taken as much over the counter pain relief as I could but they weren't helping at all. I hoped that he would just come by tomorrow, see the sign and take it at face value. And so I'd been annoyed and snapped at him. I knew he knew something was wrong but I couldn't tell him. I wouldn't tell him.

It was irrational. These guys, these alphas, they'd shown me nothing but kindness. I just didn't want them to know. At first I kept my omega status quiet because it made it easier to be taken seriously and run a business. Then it just became a habit. But when people didn't know your designation you heard all the complaints. About omega meltdowns and how they were too emotional, too needy. They always needed so much attention. It echoed everything

I'd heard while I was growing up. I was too much, I wanted too much, I was annoying. At least on suppressants my family had found me tolerable.

After I left John on the curb, I set Whisper up with enough food to last him a few days. He wasn't a big eater so I knew I didn't have to worry about him overeating and then going hungry but it still wasn't the best solution. Normally Sandra would dogsit but she hadn't picked up her phone. So I just made sure the balcony door was open so he could get out to the patch of fake grass whenever he needed.

I handled all the logistics last night. I did a grocery run to make sure that there were lots of snacks for during my heat and plenty of food for after when I'd be hungry but weak. Then I fluffed up the makeshift nest I made out of my bed and made sure all my toys were charged, clean and ready. My body didn't seem to crave the stimulation the way it did when I was young but I still needed to take care of myself or the cramps from clenching around nothing could be excruciating. So with everything set up, all I needed to do was flop on my bed and wait.

I wasn't waiting long.

The fever kicked in and then all I could feel was pain. My body twitched and spasmed. I felt the pressure, the desire, flooding my body. I was supposed to have someone. I wasn't supposed to be alone. It hurt.

Even as I settled myself down on one of my toys and I had something to clench onto, still it hurt. These toys had false knots that could expand and lock into you. They were supposed to feel like the real thing. They did not.

Twice I'd spent my heats with others, once at the clinic and once with my pack. And maybe they didn't go well and I might not remember much because of the haze but my body remembered the sensation of being knotted.

The omega body was designed to clench and pull. And even as you orgasmed you could feel it. The space inside you that was never quite full. That was always yearning, always wanting. And then you'd feel their knot. There at the base it was like a firm bubble, I could remember rubbing against it, writhing, needing it inside me. The feel of it sliding in, like having a gentle roll of electricity through your spine. And still the wanting. The need. Until they came inside you. And it expanded. It filled you up. And it always felt the same. Like for the first time in your life you were full. Sated. There was no space inside you. Only warmth and connection. The explosion rocking through my body was not an experience I would ever forget. And these toys were not the same.

They helped with the cramps and the needs. But there was still pain. And it wasn't just my body. My body didn't really know better. It was full, it was fine. It was me. It was my heart.

I wasn't supposed to be alone. That's all I could think, every heat. No one was supposed to be alone. We were supposed to be with people, together, taking care of each other. But me? I was alone. Always so alone. In my store. In my life. It was always just me. And I ached.

I writhed my body on the toy until I felt the release rock through me. My muscles relaxed, I lay down and tried not to let the pain take me too far under.

This is why I avoided my heats. The physical pain was one thing, but the way all my old hurts would come up was unbearable. The way they'd crush me and bind my chest until I could barely breathe.

But I couldn't breathe. I actually couldn't breathe. The razor blades in my chest were in my throat now. I was choking. This wasn't right. This wasn't the right kind of pain.

I open my eyes. It's dark in here. I can't see, but I can feel it and the air is too thick. I try to focus on what feels wrong but there is a noise. No, not a noise. Barking. Whisper's barking at my door, and scratching. His balcony door is open, he doesn't need me. Is he worried about me? Maybe. I should check on him.

I climb out of my nest bed carefully. Even the fabric of my favourite pillows bothers my skin. I need my robe. Where is it? There it is, the hook on the back of the door. Why am I at the door?

Another bark. Oh yes, Whisper.

I slip the robe on and open the door. I expect to see Whisper, what I don't expect is the room full of smoke. I cough. It's thick. It's thick grey smoke. Something's on fire.

We need to get out of here.

I'm moving. Whisper at my ankle. I slam into the door. Why is it so hard to walk? I undo the bolt. The chain is trickier, it takes me two tries. Then I twist the handle. I open the door expecting relief. The smoke is thicker.

We don't have a choice. We have to get downstairs.

I grab Whisper by the collar and pull him down the stairs with me. I can't see where I'm going but I know these steps like the back of my hand. We make it to the bottom and still all I can see is smoke. I push through the curtain, turn the corner and I'm behind the counter. I can see the counter because right in front of it is a giant pile of my books. And they're on fire.

Whisper darts away running through the closed door? Wait, how did he do that? Oh, the glass door has been smashed. Okay. I can hear him barking in the street. I need to get out of here. But the books. They're on fire.

I turn into the kitchen and find the fire extinguisher by the door where it should be. I pull the pin and then aim the nozzle at the fire. The part I can reach goes out instantly. But the spray isn't strong enough.

I round the counter to get closer and try again. More thick white foam shoots from the end of the nozzle and more fire disappears. It's like magic. Squeeze the handle, point the nozzle. No more fire. Bye bye fire.

I slump to the floor in front of the pile of books and foam. There's still so much smoke in the air. It's too hard to breathe. Lower. I need to go lower.

I lie down.

Ouch something's biting me. No wait, nothing is biting me. I'm on fire. The edge of my robe is on fire. And it hurts. I shoot the nozzle at the offending spot near my ankle and squeeze the handle again.

'Take that.' I mumble. Wow that hurts. And I'm so tired. Everything hurts. But I need to do something. What did I need to do?

It smells wrong here. I need something that smells good. Like lavender.

No wait, I need help.

Whisper is still barking in the street. I hope he's okay. There's no one around to help us. But we need help. What should I do?

I roll to lie on my back so I can stare up at the smoke still hovering above me. Something bangs against my thigh. My phone. That's right I put it in the pocket of my robe so if I had to get up at any point I'd have it with me. That way I could call someone if something went wrong. And something did go wrong. And I should call someone. I should call the people who fix everything. But I only have one of their numbers.

KNOT FOR REAL

Chapter 26. George

John is getting on my nerves. We're all still sitting around the dinner table even though it's late. Midnight at least. I ended up getting us pizza for dinner, even as I committed myself mentally to cooking more and ordering in less. But the pizza is long gone. Normally by now we'd all be in bed.

'I'm telling you something was wrong.' John repeats for the hundredth time.

'I know, I believe you.' I groan. We all agreed hours ago that something was in fact wrong. According to Sam and Mick something had felt off when they saw her for coffee this morning. I'd spoken to her around lunchtime but very briefly. Just letting her know that I'd found a way to make the recycled stained glass window work. I thought she'd be happy but she'd rushed me off the phone so quickly I'd been stunned.

John was the last one to speak to her this afternoon. He recounted in detail her irritation, her shivers. How sad and distraught she seemed. He'd gone over it so many times I'd felt like I'd been there myself watching the defeated slump of her shoulders as she hung a makeshift closed sign.

'If there was something we could do she would have told us.' I assure them.

'Mick and I disagree.' John rebuts. This conversation is past repetitive.

'Even if she does need something from us, we can't do anything at this hour.' Sam interjects. He's mostly been silent for the past hour which is kind of scary. He's not known for keeping his opinions to himself. He's just been checking his phone for the time periodically and rolling out his shoulders.

'He's right, we should all just go to bed.' I conclude. I know we should. They know we should. None of us move.

It's been like this all night. The light and laughter that has filled all of us for the past few days is gone. Instead the four of us keep sitting here repeating our conversation, all agreeing that the only sensible option is to go to bed and stop by and see her in the morning, and then none of us move.

'We could go over and check on her right now?' John suggests. Again.

'It's past midnight, that tips us over into the stalker category.' Sam groans.

'Well I can't just keep sitting here.' John isn't actually sitting. He's pacing next to the dining table like someone trying to beat their personal best on their pedometer.

'What is with us?' I don't mean to say the question out loud but I can't help it.

'What do you mean?' John demands.

'I mean Sam only met her, what? Three days ago? Mick saw her for the first time two days ago. I've never even met her in person. Yet I'm half tempted to take your lead and follow you to wake up a woman the rest of us barely know, even though it's well after midnight. This is insane.' I lean forward onto the table and massage my temples.

'If you want to go as well, let's just go.' John demands. He's already tried to leave twice. I let Mick restrain him the second time.

'That's not the point. The point is that this is insane and I don't get it. All of us are going crazy over a poor beta girl just because she's having a hard time. Does that make sense to you?' The room lapses into silence.

'Strawberries.' Mick whispers.

'What did you say?' Sam asks even though I know he heard him.

'Strawberries.' He says again. 'She smells like strawberries.'

'She does?' Having never met her in person I feel the need to demand why no one has ever mentioned this.

'You smell strawberries on her?' John asks.

'Not on her.' Mick shakes his head. 'She smells like strawberries.'

But that can't be. Betas don't have smells. They often cover themselves in perfumes to imitate omegas but Melanie doesn't seem the type. Which would mean...

'I've smelled it too.' Sam nods solemnly.

'I thought it was her hair.' John murmurs.

'Strawberries?' I ask the room at large, it's Mick that responds.

'Not just strawberries. She smells like warm sweet strawberries. Like when you pick a strawberry straight off the vine in summer, and it's warm from the sun.' My mouth waters at his description. But something does not compute.

'John, did she ever say she was a beta?' I demand. He's shaking his head no, a distant expression on his face and he seems to try and dig into his memories.

'No, she never said... but I never smelled... Well, I did. But not really, not until today.' He's stammering. 'I just assumed and she never corrected me.'

'Fuuuccckkk.' It's Sam who says it out loud but I can feel us all think the same thing. If she was an omega. And we were all reacting like this then there was a good chance that she was our omega.

No one really knew what drew a pack together. It was all kind of mystical. Poets, philosophers, religions, they'd all tried to explain it. Science was now taking its best swing with figuring out what made a pack scent sensitive. But the why didn't matter. What we all knew was when a pack came together it was unstoppable.

'We need to go over there. Now.' John demands.

'At this hour? You'll just scare the crap out of her.' Sam snaps back. He was right but I was getting pretty desperate to see this girl in person. The softly spoken girl who responded so sweetly to me. Who sighed when I called her a good girl. The girl who'd told me she trusted me. This might be our omega?

'We can't.' I shake my head just as my phone starts vibrating across the table. It's one in the morning, who the hell is calling me? I flip my phone over and my heart stops. Melanie's name is flashing across my screen. I show it to the others.

'Answer it.' John demands. I slide my phone to the middle of the table and we all lean in as I put it on speaker.

'Melanie?' I ask. There's a moan, then nothing. A dog is barking in the distance, some paper rustling and another crackling sound I can't place. 'MELANIE?'

'Hmm?' She sounds sleepy.

'Are you okay?' I demand.

'Okay...' She mumbles. It's not an answer. She's just parroting back what I said.

'Melanie, where are you?' I demand. I lock eyes with Mick and I can see the fear I feel in his gaze.

'Store.' She mutters. That was good. At least if she was in her store, at home, she was safe. But why was she calling? And why did she sound drunk?

'What's going on?' I demand. Silence.

'Sweetness?' Mick calls out.

'Yes?' Her answer is softer for Mick.

'What's going on?' He asks more gently than I did.

'I'm calling George.' She answers like it's obvious. She sounds completely wasted. Still, I love hearing her say my name.

'Why are you calling George?' Mick sounds far more patient than I feel.

'I need help.' She sighs.

'Okay, how does George help?' Mick prompts.

'You all help.' She pouts. God but she's cute even on a drunk dial.

'Why did you call George to help?' He tries again.

'Because it hurts.' She sulks.

'What does?' Sam demands. His voice so thick I wouldn't have realised it was him if I hadn't seen his lips move. We're all standing now. Waiting for what she says.

'The shop hurts.' She grumbles. I feel us all relax a little. The shop hurting, I can handle that. What I couldn't handle is if she was hurt. But this, this I can fix.

'And why is that?' I ask. Her drunken rambling is adorable. And better yet. She called us. Which means she thinks of us as help. I'm elated. I let amusement and warmth in my tone. 'What's making the shop hurt?'

'It's on fire.' My heart stops. 'So was my leg. And it really hurts.'

All four of us growl and together our roars combine to rattle the table until I can feel it quake under my fingertips.

'Everyone car.' I bark but I hear a grunt that lifts my head. Mick catches my eye. I feel him push back against my order and I understand. 'Then run!'

KNOT FOR REAL

Chapter 27. Mick

Most people would assume John or Sam are the fastest runners in our pack. John has the frame for it and Sam trains all the time, but neither of them can catch me. I've always been fast, way faster than I have a right to be when, as everyone rightfully points out, I'm built like a brick house. And tonight, I have never run faster.

I'm out the door and at the end of the block before the guys have even moved. I spent most of the afternoon in the gym and I still have my sneakers on but even if I didn't I wouldn't have paused. I would have let my feet bleed. Our omega needed us.

And she was ours. I could feel it. The more we sat around the table and I watched us all go crazy, the more it just made sense. Strawberries. She smelled like strawberries. And I was hungry.

I smell the fire before I even reach her block and somehow I go faster.

Oh god. There is so much smoke. Whisper is on the pavement barking but as he sees me approach he sits and settles. I run past him,ready to break the door down but there's nothing to break. The glass is smashed. I barrel through the hole and look around the space.

There is a pile of smouldering books covered in white foam, still billowing smoke. And there in front of the pile, lying on her back, is Melanie. Her robe is draped haphazardly around her. Her eyes are closed. And for a second I can't breathe. She looks dead. She could be dead.

'MELANIE!' The phone in her hand screams and she groans.

'What?' She mumbles but I know they won't have heard her, her voice is barely audible to me. I reach down and scoop her into my arms. She could be hurt but there's too much smoke in here to leave her where she is. I've only been here a few seconds and I'm dizzy. I have to get her out.

I lift her up against my chest and her face turns into me as her hand grips my shirt. The one holding her phone rests between us and I can see the call is still connected.

'I've got her.' I call out so they can hear me. And then carry her through the door and out onto the street. It's filthy and I don't want to put her down but it's safer if she is injured. I lower myself to my knees and then place her carefully against the ground.

'No.' She mumbles, wriggling against the pavement and climbing back up into my arms. I let her wrap her arms around my neck as her phone falls to the ground beside us. Her robe is hanging down one arm, the belt loose, letting it fall open in such a way one leg is entirely uncovered. She looks like a fallen angel.

'Sweetness, can you talk to me?' I beg and she moans.

'Hmm.' She turns in my arms using her grip on my neck to pull us closer. She buries her nose against my neck inhaling deeply. 'Ahh.'

As she groans into my skin she spins within my grip so that her legs can wrap around my waist. Her robe billows around us and I can feel the heat of her through my pants. She grips and pulls at my neck trying to get closer as she begins sliding herself against me.

'Melanie?' My voice shakes. 'Are you in heat?'

I don't know why I bother to ask the question. I can feel her slick soaking the front of my pants. I pull back to try and get a better look at her. She breathes deep and I watch her pupils push the last of the colour from her eye and I know. Melanie isn't here right now. Her omega just took charge. And she's writhing against my lap.

This is crazy. We're in the middle of the street, I'm kneeling on the pavement in front of her still smouldering shop. And yet I can feel myself harden beneath her.

'Mmm.' She moans into my ear. She can feel it as well. She begins to push against me, circling her hips and grinding against me. The smell of strawberries soaks the air around me. I can't resist, as her head tilts on a moan, I lean forward and lick the curve of her neck. Fuck.

She tastes like strawberry syrup. Hot fresh syrup, just made. So hot you risk burning your tongue but you can't wait. You need it. The sticky sweet explosion of sugar. God I want to eat her. My hands grip her shoulders, keeping her in place while she grinds down onto me. Her head has fallen back in pleasure. I bury my face into the swell of her breasts.

'Oh god.' I moan just as I hear the car door slam behind me. The sound brings me slightly back to reality and I can hear the sirens in the distance. 'Shit.'

'What's..?' Sam's words die as he lands on his knees behind her on the pavement. A part of me wants to pick her up and run. She's mine. But Sam raises his hands in front of himself. He's offering his subservience and it settles me.

'She's hurting.' I grunt out as I hold her in place. She's still writhing against me, lost in seeking her pleasure but moaning in distress. I don't know what to do. I can hear George on the phone not far away, and the sirens are getting closer. John is over to one side comforting Whisper. And I'm holding the most precious thing in the universe in my arms and she's hurting. And I don't know what to do.

'Let me help you?' Sam asks, I'm already nodding. Yes, anything. Anything she needs. He scoots in behind her pressing his chest into her back and she moans loudly again. Her head tilts back to rest on his shoulder as he slides his hands to cover mine on her shoulder blades. He softens my grip, moving my hands lower and lower until they dig into her soft pillowy hips. 'Pull her harder against you.'

I do as he suggests and pull her down into my lap. Hard. Her tempo increases, her hips circling so fast it's like she's bouncing. His hands slide up along her torso, grazing her ribs, moving to capture her breasts. She's bowing between us, the material of her robe now barely covering her breasts, it's pulled so taut I can clearly see her nipples. I want to suck on them.

'We've got you baby.' I hear Sam whisper in her ear. 'You can let go.'

He lets his fingers brush against her nipples through the fabric and she freezes. It's like her body pulls too tight and she can't move. I feel her flesh quiver against me and then she's moaning. Sobs wrack her body as she thrashes and rocks against us. She's beautiful as she crests her peak, shuddering against us. I feel my own release explode in my pants but I barely spare it a thought. A tear slips from her eye and I watch as Sam licks it from her cheek.

'Strawberries.' He whispers as his eyes find mine.

'Strawberries.' I agree. I hold Melanie's weight against me with my hands still gently on her hips as she collapses back onto Sam's chest. He shuffles forward tilting her into my arms and my lap. I pull her gently against me, tucking her head beneath my chin as the spasms in her body begin to slow. On instinct I purr as she nuzzles into my neck seeking my smell.

'You did good.' Sam nods at me, pressing the curls away from her face. I raise my brows at him confused. 'You got her out.'

He tilts his head to the building behind us where smoke still flows from the busted door, around the plywood and from the windows upstairs. I actually forgot the building was on fire. John is still sitting a couple of feet away. Whisper in his lap as he soothes the dog who seems shockingly unbothered by everything he's witnessed tonight.

'Here.' George's voice comes from above us. I look up to find a blanket in his outstretched hand. Sam grabs it from him and wraps it around Melanie. It takes teamwork but we get her wrapped up without jostling her too much. She's dozing, I realise as I lift her so that she's no longer straddling me but cradled in my arms. Sam pulls the blanket around her legs, tucking it so that every inch of her is covered.

'Is she okay?' It's John who asks and I look down at her and then back to him as I nod.

'She's okay.' My mind clings to that thought. If she didn't have her phone, if we hadn't gotten here in time, she could have... I can't even think it.

'She's perfect.' George grumbles looking down at the three of us. John's a pace away with the dog, Sam and I are pressing her between us with her wrapped in my arms. We all nod in agreement. She is perfect.

Chapter 28. Sam

I'm in shock. One minute we're sitting around the dining table, I'm trying to wrap my head around the thought that maybe Melanie is an omega. Our omega.

The next second was a mad dash to make sure we didn't lose her forever. I think my heart actually stopped when I saw her limp form in Mick's arms. I feared the worst. What I hadn't expected was to have one of the hottest sexual experiences of my life.

Melanie stretched out between us, writhing against Mick, seeking her pleasure while bathed in the haze of smoke and streetlights would forever be burned into my brain. All of her lush body bouncing and squirming between us.

George directed the scene explaining to the first responders no one else was known to be inside. The fire department took care of the smouldering mess that was Melanie's store. The cops arrived only moments later. I'd told them to contact Charlotte and to let her know that there had been an escalation.

Up until now none of us had been that worried about the fact that someone had targeted Melanie's shop. Between Mick's extra padlocks and Charlotte's insistence that it wasn't anything much to worry about we'd all put it to the side. But now... well now she wouldn't be leaving our sight.

The paramedics were right, other than the burn to her calf she was physically fine. Sort of. She'd been moaning by the time they settled her in the ambulance. When we got to the hospital and explained she was in heat they went into a frenzy of exams.

None of the doctors can talk to us. We aren't family, we aren't pack. We don't even know if she'd want that. Considering how she concealed that she was an omega I was guessing not. Which annoyed me more than I thought it would.

George was graceful about them not sharing information with us as long as they assured him everything necessary was being done. That is until he found out that whomever was listed as her next of kin wasn't picking up. Next thing I knew he didn't just have our pack doctor on the phone but in the building.

Mary Smithson had been in there with Melanie for almost forty-five minutes now and I was getting restless. She was awake. We knew that. But how was she? She'd been in a heat and yet she had fought a fire as she escaped a burning building. That was bad ass and it made my blood run cold just thinking about it.

It's somewhere around five in the morning. Mick procured us coffee but it was useless and weak. George was on his phone handling god only knew what. John was alternating between pacing and running out to the car to check on Whisper.

'Thanks Melanie.' Mary calls back into the room as she shuts the door behind her. Before any of us can speak she's holding a finger to her lips to silence us and gesturing down the hall towards the official waiting room we were supposed to be in.

'She's going to be okay.' Mary speaks as soon as we file into the room.

'I know you can't tell us anything, but anything she needs you get it for her, no matter what.' George demands of his friend and she nods.

'Of course. But I can talk to you. Since you called me down here, I asked for Melanie's permission to share anything I felt was pertinent with you, and she was lucid enough to consent.'

'What's wrong then?' George demands.

'First I want to ask a question.' She pauses awkwardly. 'Are you scent sensitive?'

We all freeze. Until tonight I didn't realise that the strawberry smell was her. But when she'd come apart in my arms, it had floated off her skin. Now it was the only smell I ever wanted in my life ever again.

'Tonight was the first night I met her in person.' George answers slowly. 'Mick and Sam have known her for a few days. But John has known her a whole year...'

'You're not sure.' Mary nods, pulling something from her pocket. 'This might help.'

Mary hands John a pillowcase and he sniffs it. His pupils expand so fast it's like watching someone take drugs. I can smell it from here. Strawberry sweetness.

'Yes.' John nods as he lowers the pillowcase to clutch it to his chest.

'That explains it.' Mary nods as she gestures towards some chairs for us to sit. 'First of all let me assure you that Melanie is going to be fine. The burn on her leg is not deep. Keep it clean and apply topical analgesics and it will heal quickly.'

'Okay.' Mick sounds as uncertain as I feel.

'The problem is Melanie's heat got interrupted tonight. A situation like this, the stress and everything that happened, can pull an omega out of their heat and that's very dangerous. Over the next week she will slip in and out, falling into heat spikes until the heat takes over again. She'll be in pain often and there's no real way of predicting what that experience will be like.'

'Anything she needs.' George repeats.

'Of course.' Mary continues. 'But I'm afraid that's only half of it. And the other problem is why you haven't fully scented her before tonight.'

'Problem?' Mick grunts again.

'Yes. Have you ever heard of Shiffalix?' All of us shake our heads no.

'Is that some kind of cat? Like a sphynx.' John's question makes Mary smile.

'No Shiffalix is a very strong suppressant. One paired with antipsychotics and benzodiazepines. Basically it's like a tranquiliser for omegas.' She explains.

'Oh god.' George looks like the sky is falling but I'm lost.

'Shiffalix is only meant to be used in the most extreme of cases.' Mary explains. 'Even then I would never recommend it for more than a month and only in conjunction with talk therapies.' Mary pauses. 'Melanie's doctor has had her on it for a decade.'

'What? Why?' I demand.

'I honestly don't know.' Mary shrugs. 'She explained the circumstances that led to her taking it at first but I'm not convinced that her issues were severe enough to warrant this medication. In all honesty I'm not sure they were issues at all.'

'What does that mean?' George prompts.

'I have to be careful about how much of what she told me I share with you. She's given me permission but still there are things that I don't feel comfortable saying to you. If you were further along in your relationship...' Her voice trails off.

'What can you tell us?' George asks.

'She had a pack. It seems before their bonding could take place they died in a car crash. It was a few days before her heat and when she went into it she was upset and destroyed some furniture.' Mary rattles off the facts of the story Melanie told her, like they're not devastating.

'So we need to get her off this stuff?' George asks.

'No, that's the reason you can scent her now. She ran out of medication. Her doctor retired, so she went to see someone new. He refused the medication however he did so without giving her any alternative. Stopping a medication like that is negligent. Even without the interruption, it would have made this heat very painful for her.'

'Why would he do that?' John mumbles in confusion.

'Apparently he is of the notion that the pain omegas report is exaggerated. He also said some other things regarding her health that I do not agree with.' Mary took a breath. 'George I plan to write an official complaint against his care. I'm hoping Melanie will sign it in time but your support would be helpful as well.'

'Of course.' George nods.

'I also plan to file one against her previous doctor, he's retired so it won't affect him but it will put an alert against the name of anyone under his care, encouraging their current doctors to review his findings.'

'Anything we can do to help.' George agrees. Personally I felt the most helpful thing would be for us to track down both of these dickheads and see how they liked it when someone messed with their health.

'Where do we go from here?' Mick asks.

'She can stay here in the hospital till her heat passes but I wouldn't encourage that. This is not a pleasant environment. Plus there's plenty of unbonded alphas running around and while everyone who works here would be on some kind of rut blocker...'

She doesn't need to finish that sentence. We all know the stories of omegas falling into their heats and alphas falling into a rut, or worse, taking advantage. The thought of another alpha touching Melanie for any reason has me shaking my head.

'She can't stay here.' I all but shout. I may not have wanted an omega but if we had one I was going to protect her.

'I agree.' Mary pats my arm. 'The problem is I can't release her to you. I trust you'd all take care of her, I really do. But she's unbonded, there are rules.'

'What are her choices?' George demands.

'We're still trying to get a hold of her next of kin. Maxwell and Irene Rodgers. I'm assuming it's her parents.' Mary pauses and bites her lip. 'I will say that when I informed her I would need to release her to them she did not seem... enthused.'

'She doesn't get on with her parents.' John murmurs still clutching the pillowcase.

'What's the alternative?' George demands.

'I can't release her into your care...' Mary starts.

'You said that.' I snap in anger. We were already failing. We just found her and she was going away when she needed us. My alpha didn't like it. Neither did I.

'Let her finish.' George scolds me.

'I can't release her into your care but she does have the option of signing out AMA, against medical advice.' Mary continues ignoring my outburst.

'Then what?' George asks.

'She could choose where she goes. I don't want to let her know she has that option if she's going to be alone. But if you were all taking care of her, on her terms, and I saw her consent while lucid, I would agree.' I liked this option.

'How do we make that happen?' I ask.

'Slow down.' Mary holds her hand out and I realise I'm trying to stand up. 'First we need to allow some more time to contact her registered next of kin. Then we'll go from there. In the meantime I would like to consult with a colleague and go spend some more time with Melanie. Try and get a better understanding of everything going on.'

I sigh. Fine. If we had to wait a little longer I could do that. But she wasn't going anywhere she didn't want to go. And it sounded to me like she didn't want to go with her parents. If the only option left was for us to take her in then so be it.

Chapter 29. John

Whisper is annoyed with me when I check on him for the ninth time. With the windows down, a bowl of water and some food he seems content to sleep the morning away on the back seat of our car. But I have to do something.

Mick once again found us all coffee and this time it was drinkable. Then he started tapping away on his phone, organising something. Sam was on his phone with Detective Charlotte. George organised a cleaning crew to be on stand by to see what could be salvaged from Melanie's building. Then he rescheduled all of his meetings for the next few days and someone was getting a catered lunch but I have no idea how that was related to everything else. And I was just sitting here. Reeling.

A year. I'd known her for a year and I'd never suspected. What was wrong with me? Mick had known her for forty eight hours and figured it out. Sam hadn't been far behind him. Hell George had basically figured it out before he even met her. But me?

I spent the better part of a year obsessed with the girl and I had never even once clued into the fact that there was a reason for that. I just thought she was pretty and smart and kind. I was completely smitten, and apparently too dumb to think, hmm, maybe she feels like she's perfect for me because she's our omega.

'NO! I do not UNDERSTAND.' George yells into his phone before throwing it across the room. It ricochets off a wall shattering into three distinct pieces. 'Fuck.'

'Calm down.' Mick rushes forward to place his hand on George's chest. He's a braver man than me. George looks feral. 'Look at me and breathe.'

George's gaze focuses on Mick and after a few seconds he settles as he comes back to himself. He sits back down in his chair reaching into his pocket for his phone. His eyes dart to the chunks of metal and plastic in the corner of the room.

'Shit.' He murmurs.

'I just texted Jamie.' Sam gestures to his own phone. 'He'll have a new phone sent to wherever we are in a few hours.'

'Thanks.' George mumbles as he leans forward to rest his face in his hands.

'Do we want to know?' Mick asks.

'No. But you need to.' George grumbles as he sits up again. 'That was Melanie's parents. They're just awake, they've spoken to Mary, they have a gist of what's happening. Mary gave them my number. Said I was a friend who wanted to help.'

'And?' Mick asks.

'They're insisting on taking her home.' Sam guesses visibly distressed.

'No.' George groans as he leans back in his chair and tilts his face to the ceiling. 'At first it seemed like her mum wanted her home. But apparently they don't want her in their house if she's in heat. They want to leave her here.'

'Why?' Mick asks.

'Something about a dinner party. I wasn't really listening by that point.' George mumbles towards the roof.

'But that's good news.' Sam insists. 'That means we can take her home.'

'There's something distinctly fucked up about hearing a woman fret about her dinner party while her daughter is lying in hospital.' George grumbles.

'But we can take her home.' Sam repeats.

'Only, if she wants to go with us.' George argues. 'And that's a big if. She barely knows us. Except for John. She might prefer the hospital.'

'Can I talk to you all?' Mary announces her presence with her question.

'Yes of course.' George responds, gesturing for her to take a seat.

'I've spoken with Melanie's parents.' She snips.

'So did George.' Mick snorts while gesturing to the smashed phone on the floor.

'Yeah, that about sums up my thoughts as well.' Mary nods sadly at the broken pieces. 'It clears some things up for me. What I'm about to tell you is very close to overstepping but I have her permission. I just don't think she understands the problem.'

'What is it?' Sam demands.

'The doctor that prescribed Shiffalix was her family doctor. I think he was swayed by her mother's opinions of Melanie's state. Her mother disagreed with the way she nested and the way she sought comfort. The word Melanie kept using was annoying.'

'To describe her mother?' Sam asks.

'No, to describe herself. She thinks that her omega instincts are wrong. That she does nesting incorrectly. She tried to joke about being defective, a broken omega.'

'What the fuck?' It's Mick this time. 'Why would she think that?'

'That will be for you all to figure out. But I chatted to a colleague of mine. A specialist currently doing some research into the long term effects of suppressants.'

'What did they say?' George leans forward in his chair with concern.

'Mostly what I expected. They've never even heard of a case of someone being on Shiffalix for more than a year. They're pretty keen to meet her if Melanie is amenable.' Mary pauses. 'But they mentioned something to check for and...'

'What is it?' Mick asks.

'If I addressed you or your alpha, you would speak to me, either to answer the question or tell me to get lost.' Mary explains. We all nod. 'You and your alpha have grown together, worked in partnership. You've found a way to balance your relationship.'

'For the most part.' George gestures towards his smashed phone.

'We're all overcome sometimes.' The gentle doctor smiles at him. 'My point is that your alphas are as developed as you are. You hear them clearly, they talk to you.'

We all nod. It wasn't always words, sometimes feelings but my alpha always made his needs known. Even if it was inconvenient for me.

'Melanie's omega, well...' Mary's voice falters. 'It's like her omega has been bound and gagged and shoved in a dark closet for the last ten years.'

'Her omega is hurt?' Mick asks while I wince at the mental image.

'Essentially yes. Her omega has never had the chance to grow and develop. When I speak to Melanie I get clear concise sentences. When I direct questions to her omega, I get gestures, one word answers, sometimes silence.'

'How do we help?' George asks. I hate that he's so ready to act. I want to cry. Scream. Rage. But he's already moving forward and the others are nodding.

'Over the next few weeks, off the medication, her omega will start to emerge. Whatever she wants or needs, give into it. Even voicing preferences might be hard for her so lots of encouragement. And lots of affection. I'm not sure I've ever seen a case of touch starvation this bad.'

'Touch starvation?' I ask. I'm surprised when it's Mick who answers.

'When an omega is not given enough physical affection, hugs and skin to skin contact, they get sick. Their immune system weakens and they lose their regulation.'

'And her case is severe.' Mary nods. 'So when you take her home you'll need to spend plenty of time just sitting next to her, touching her. As long as she's comfortable.'

'She's coming with us?' I ask, delighted by that as I am horrified by the rest.

'I explained her options to her and yes she seems to want to go home with you but there are rules.' Mary's voice leaves no room for argument and we all nod.

'Whatever she needs.' George repeats what I'm pretty sure is now his mantra.

'Firstly you'll all be administered rut blockers, mild ones that won't cause long term damage. But they'll take the edge off. You're newly acquainted and scent sensitive, that's a lot and I don't want her omega to go through any more trauma.'

'Of course.' Mick is nodding most vehemently but we're all in agreement.

'Secondly, and this one goes without saying, but when she's in heat, things will get... heated.' Mary smiles awkwardly. 'Just go slow okay?'

'Anything else?' George snatches Sam's phone from him and writes notes.

'Two more things. I'm going to stop by for the first couple of days. I don't want her coming into the clinic, I want her at home resting. Now that she's stopped the suppressants and the withdrawal has started I can't give her anything but painkillers.'

'Do we need any special supplies or medications?' George asks.

'I emailed the list to your assistant.' Mary smiles at him. 'They'll be at your house before you are.'

'What's the last thing?' I ask.

'Transporting her comfortably. I assume you have a space set up for her?'

'The guest room. Just in case.' George nods.

'I've ordered her some clothes and toiletries.' Mick adds.

'Charlotte left Melanie's place an hour ago, she gave me a list of what was in her fridge and the food delivery is on its way to ours.' Sam explains. Well fuck? When did they get all this organised?

'Well then all I need from you all, is each of your shirts?' Mary extends her hand in front of her and waits. It takes us a second but as soon as George starts pulling his shirt over his head we all follow suit.

Chapter 30. Melanie

I am floating on a cloud. And it smells like heaven. There's whiskey. The smell mild, like a very old whiskey aged to soften its flavour and strengthen the drink. Then there's vanilla, hmm. Not the tacky cheap vanilla of a store bought cupcake. This is the full flavour of the real thing. And next to it is cinnamon. It's so strong it's spicy in my nose. They smell so good together. Like a dessert in winter. And next to them is one more, lavender.

I turn over in the warm cloud. I know this smell. Oh yeah. Mick. Wait.

Fuck. I can smell Mick?

My eyes shoot open. It's not a cloud, it's a large bed full of white sheets and fluffy blankets. In one hand is a soft white t-shirt. The one that smells like lavender. Except it's not white. There are marks on it, grey smudges. There's another smell. Smoke.

The fire.

I sit up in the pool of white fluff. The last thing I clearly remember was getting into my nest for my heat. But there are flashes bombarding me. The smoke. Trying to get down the stairs. The pile of burning books. Two arms lifting me to carry me outside. The need to be in those arms. I remember writhing against a firm length and I can feel my face blanch as my body heats. Oh god, what did I do?

The sirens. The kind doctor asking about my suppressants. Her insistence that George would want to know. That they all wanted to know I was okay. They wanted to take me home. Home?

I glance around the pale sparsely furnished room. It looks like a boring hotel. There's some cupboards to the left near a door. At the end of the bed is a dresser with a television on it. To the right is a window that takes up almost the entire wall, covered in creamy curtains. In front of it is a pale blue armchair. And in that chair is a man I've never seen before.

He's leaning back, his legs stretched out in front of him, his ankles crossed as he stares at the ceiling. He has coppery light brown hair, almost red but not quite. He's wearing black jeans and a blue henley that's pulled tight across his chest.

'Um...' As soon as I try to speak, a cough racks my chest. I lean forward as I gag on nothing, my whole body rocking as I cough harder and harder.

'Here.' A deep voice croons from beside me as I feel a glass of water and a handkerchief pressed into my hand. I snatch at the water and gulp it down. The bed next to me dips and I look up into two incredible green eyes. 'Breathe.'

'George?' I sputter. I don't really need to ask. I know that voice but he nods confirmation as I continue coughing more gently, holding the handkerchief to my mouth.

'Mary said you might have a cough for a bit. You inhaled a lot of smoke.' George explains and I nod. I pull the handkerchief away from my mouth and immediately see the light grey splatter across it.

'Ew.' I mutter to myself and I hear George chuckle.

'Do you want me to take that?' he asks.

'Goddess no. It's disgusting.' I shudder at the thought. Oh goddess. Why did I agree to this? Full of painkillers and delirious from my interrupted heat, going home with the four nice alphas sounded amazing. Particularly when the only other options were my parents or staying in hospital.

'How are you feeling?' George asks from beside me. I look up at him. He looks like a lion. His coppery hair is framed by the last bit of daylight coming in through the curtains behind him. His hand is hovering awkwardly between us like he was reaching out to touch my shoulder and stopped. I whine.

I can't help it. I'm hurting and I'm scared and I can feel all of it. I can feel it like I've never felt scared before. There's no actual pain anywhere in my body, but I still feel pain in my chest. I need something.

'Sweetheart.' George catches my attention. 'Can I hug you?'

I don't answer him. I don't nod. I grab him. I grab the arm that was reaching out to me before and I start pulling him toward me. I climb into his lap, wrapping his arm around me. Burying my face in his chest, I squeeze and when he doesn't squeeze back I squeeze again. I whine. Why isn't he holding me tight?

His arms tense and then contract pulling firm around me. Pressing me into his chest until there is pressure everywhere. Suddenly I can breathe again. I inhale deeply against his chest. Mmm. He's the one that smells like whiskey.

What the hell am I doing? I just met this man in person for the first time a few seconds ago and now I've forced my way into his lap for a cuddle. Oh god. I'm pathetic.

I go to pull back but his arms don't loosen.

'George?' I whisper. He releases me and I hate it. 'I'm sorry.'

'Sorry?'

'I shouldn't have jumped on you like that.' I can feel the tears coming. Wait, I can feel actual tears? What the hell? My eyes are watery. I can feel it.

'Oh no. No baby.' George's voice is soothing. He reaches for me and pulls me back into his lap. 'Come here.'

He hauls me back into the cradle of his arms, adjusting so that his back is against the giant pile of pillows with me in his lap. He pulls the blankets towards us and grabs some other scraps of fabric and puts them in my lap. Hmm, all of the smells.

'I'm sorry.' I whisper this time. I can feel tears rolling down my cheeks. His soft cotton shirt beneath my cheek is already damp and the tears just keep coming.

'Nothing to apologise for.' He murmurs. The rumble of his voice beneath me feels good and I snuggle in deeper trying to get closer to the sound. The rumble of his words turns into a vibration in his chest and the sensation makes all my muscles go loose. He's purring. He's purring for me. I cry harder.

'I'm sorry.' I mumble against his chest. I feel him groan beneath me.

'Can you please stop apologizing?' George begs. 'I'll literally give you anything you want in the entire world if you stop saying sorry.'

'I'll think about it.' I mumble into his chest, my tears ebbing.

'Good girl.' He leans down to kiss the top of my head and I relax some more. I can't help it. I'm so tired. All my muscles feel sore. Like the day after a hard workout. There's a deep ache and other sharp pains making themselves known.

'Ow.' I mumble sliding out of George's grasp slightly to pull the blanket back from my leg. The pain spot is covered by a white sterile bandage so I can't see it but it's definitely hurting. 'What happened?'

'Your robe caught on fire and it burned your calf. It's not deep, the doctor doesn't even think it will leave a scar.'

'Mary.' I murmur the doctor's name.

'She'll be here tomorrow to check on you. She said you'd probably be more lucid this evening and that if you needed anything to call her day or night.' He gestures to a phone on the bedside table.

'That's not mine.' I state the obvious. This phone doesn't have any spider web cracks in the glass. I tuck my head back beneath his chin resting my head on his heart.

'Yours got pretty smashed up so I had my assistant bring a new one for you since he was getting me one anyway.' My phone was probably just its regular amount of broken but I didn't want to point this out to him.

'What happened to your phone?' I ask. I start drawing a pattern on his chest with my fingernail. I know it's weird but I can't stop.

'I spoke to your parents.'

'What?' I sit back so I can look at his face again.

'That's what happened to my phone.' He explains. 'I spoke to your parents and...'

He lets his voice trail off and I feel my blood grow cold. Oh goddess. What did they tell him about me? Their pathetic broken daughter.

'What did they say?' I ask, my voice is a lot steadier than I feel.

'Nothing I liked.' He grunts. I'm shaking. Oh goddess, they told him all about me and my horrible heats growing up. How I destroyed their house. And now I was in his house and I was going to go into my heat again. Oh goddess he was probably worried. I was worried. What if I broke his things?

I climb out of his lap and out of the bed. I have to get out of here. I look down, I'm wearing some kind of fancy pajamas in a material so soft they feel like nothing. They're gorgeous but I can't go home like this.

Shit. I can't go home.

My home is gone. Well not gone but full of smoke and fire damage. And shit. Where's Whisper?

I'm panicking. My breaths are coming short again. Oh god I can't do this. I fall to my knees.

'I'm sorry.' I groan out.

Chapter 31. George

I will give my entire fortune not to hear this woman apologise ever again. Every single time it's for things she can't control. When she started crying she apologised. When she wanted a hug she apologised. Why the hell was she apologising for hugs and crying? And why was she apologizing now?

One second she was in my arms feeling like heaven. All her soft curves pressed into me. Her sweet strawberry scent soaking into me. Now she was kneeling on the floor of our guest room and I have no idea why.

'Don't apologise.' I mumble as I lower myself to kneel beside her. Her breaths are short and panicky. 'Just tell me what's going on?'

'Where's Whisper?' She asks between pants.

'Over there.' I point to the corner by the window where John set the dog up with the largest thickest bed we could find. He has water and food in the kitchen but he's shown no interest preferring instead to sit and stare at Melanie. I understand the desire.

'Whisper.' She coos. For the first time since I've met the dog he shows real life and comes barreling over to her to rest his head in her lap. She scratches him behind the ears as he lets his tongue loll out of his mouth.

'I'm not sure I've ever met such a chill dog.' I scratch his belly.

'I prefer to describe him as a stuffed toy that moves occasionally.' She smiles at me, her dimples popping even with her eyes still damp.

Damn. If I wasn't already half gone for this girl I would be now. Whisper, having received his pats, wanders back to his new fancy bed to resume his napping.

Melanie stares at the carpet. Her hands on her knees, her shoulders back. I doubt she's aware but she was in the perfect pose of supplication. And it was doing things to me. I wanted to run my finger from the swell of her breast, up along the side of her neck, pausing to tease the sensitive spot below her ear. Then I'd drag my fingers right to the edge of her chin and tilt her eyes to me as I grasped tight. Let my thumb drift along her lips. I'd watch her eyes dilate as I explained, 'mine'.

The mental image makes me want to weaken. But I can hear the doctor's voice in my head reminding me to take it slow. She needs affection, not desire.

'I should go.' She mumbles to the carpet bringing me back to the present.

'Where?' I ask. Was she hungry? Did she need the bathroom?

'I don't know.' She mumbles as if she's trying to solve a problem in her mind. It makes me want to smile but her concentration tells me this is a real problem for her. And so I tentatively reach out to push her curls back over her shoulder.

'If you don't know where you're going, why are you going somewhere?' I ask. Whatever it was she needed I would get it. I wanted her back in bed and resting.

'I need to leave.' I freeze. 'Before my heat comes.'

'What?' I can feel anger and fear flooding my limbs but I keep my voice steady.

'What if I ruin something?' She mumbles.

'What are you talking about?'

'You talked to my parents?' I nod. 'Then they must have told you. I wrecked their house. I pulled up the carpet and painted the walls. I don't even remember doing it.'

'That happens.' I blink as I try to process this. When she was young and in her heat she must have not liked the space she was in. It was not uncommon.

'Did you hear me?' She demands. 'If I stay here I'll destroy your pretty room.'

She gestures to the space around us. It's not particularly pretty. Technically it's our guest room but as she is our first guest it isn't decorated. The rest of the house is more our style but this room is kind of barren. I hadn't liked putting her in here but the only other free space is the omega suite and that felt presumptuous.

The building layout was strange as it was technically two townhouses that we'd knocked the dividing walls out of to create one big residence. The basement held the garage, Mick's workshop, the gym and the courtyard that led to the small back yard. The entry level was kitchen, dining, living room, laundry, the joint office and this guest room. It also had a small balcony with stairs down the side to go into the yard. The next level up had our bedrooms, each with an ensuite and my study. Then there was upstairs.

Our third level had another living space none of us used and the omega suite. Since we hadn't had an omega when we'd been designing the place, only the basics had gone in, a walk-in wardrobe, a bathroom and a nest room were all attached to the large bedroom no one had even set foot in since we moved here. But as far as I was concerned it was already her space. As was this room.

'What do you want to do to the room?' I ask Melanie who's still sitting on her knees, her eyes imploring me to understand.

'What do I want to do?' She repeats my question. I want to kiss the confusion straight off her face.

'Yes if you could do anything in here what would you want to do?' She keeps staring at me like I've lost my mind so I shift off my knees to lean against the bed frame and stare out at the room. Then I gesture for her to do the same. She does so slowly. 'Mick said you like dark colours?'

'Yes.' She agrees slowly like she's worried I'm trying to trick her.

'What colour would you paint it?' I ask.

'It doesn't need painting.' She shakes her head. 'It's lovely.'

Her nose crinkles so I know she's lying. I kind of want to call her on it but instead I reach out and tap the end of her nose so that it relaxes again. Her eyes focus on me and I move my hand to rest against her cheek and hold her still.

'I didn't say it needed painting, I asked what colour would you paint it. If it could be any colour in the whole world.'

'Black.' She speaks so softly I would have missed the word if I hadn't read it on her lips.

'Black?' I'm surprised but delighted. 'Black would be cool.'

'But like a dark blue, so dark it's almost black but not really.' She turns from my grasp to gesture at the room. 'You know, like the night sky when it's lit up by stars. You could even paint little stars or clouds just one shade different so the pattern would be barely there. And then you could cover the bed in rich blues and greens and golds and it would be like floating in the ocean at night.'

'It sounds stunning.' I tell her and she smiles. We both lean back against the bed and stare out to the room we lapse into silence. I'm still imagining everything she described, lost in the image when she speaks again.

'I can't stay here.' She whispers.

'Why not?' I ask just as softly.

'You shouldn't have to put up with me when I'm like this. Mary told me what was going to happen. The heat spikes.' I feel her shrug her shoulders. 'It's going to be a lot and I don't want to inflict it on you guys. I can go somewhere else.'

'That's not what we want.' I sigh. I sound calmer than I feel but somehow I know right now that's what she needs. 'We want you to stay here.'

'Why?' She asks.

'Because we like you.' Her snort surprises me enough that I turn to stare at her.

'After everything I've already put you through?' She asks as if she's actively tried to torture us. Not simply needed a little help.

'Yes. After everything.' I nod. Her eyes bore into mine looking for a lie. I keep my gaze steady and relaxed. I don't want to scare her off by showing her how desperate I am for her to stay. How desperate we all are.

It's clear she's enjoying our smells by the way she clutched our shirts before but I don't think she's had a chance to consider the implications of that. The thought of her, our omega, leaving, it causes me physical pain. And I know the other guys aren't doing much better. Mary suggested we should give her some space and try not to overwhelm her with our presence. Otherwise they would all be in here right now. As it was we'd agreed to shifts, it just so happened she woke up when it was my turn to sit with her.

If she really wants to leave we'll let her but I don't think she wants to go. I think she's just scared to let us take care of her.

'You really sure? You don't mind me staying here?' Her voice begs me to be telling the truth. I wrap my arm around her pulling her close to me so I can purr for her. I feel it, the way she instantly relaxes.

'Stay as long as you like.'

Chapter 32. Melanie

A girl could get used to this kind of water pressure. The showerhead is hot and hard as I hold it tight against my thigh and let it pummel my muscles. I was in a cocoon of heat with another shower head above me raining down soft fat drops of water.

George sat with me a while longer. I could feel the stress and the guilt pulling at the edges of my brain but I couldn't help but relax. Tucked against the warmth of his side, his rumbling chest vibrating through me. It felt amazing. Eventually my stomach grumbled and he jumped up apologising for not offering anything sooner. I kind of wanted to demand he get back down on the floor. And this time let me lie on top of him while he purred. But I had manners.

That being said, I did practically demand to take a shower before any food. I know the nurses had done their best to clean all the soot and ash off me at the hospital but nothing was quite the same as a proper shower.

This shower was amazing. I really didn't want to get out. But it was time. It had already easily been ten minutes. A shower this decadent had to be burning through the water. If I was going to be staying here one thing I would not be doing was running any of their bills sky high.

I turn off the shower sadly. Not only was it probably the nicest shower I'd ever been in but it also had some of the best smelling bath products in the world. I don't know what this fancy stuff was but my hair feels like silk and my skin smells like heaven. A kind of clean musk that didn't really smell like anything but was soothing. I stand in front of the mirror as I dry off in my towel.

I'd need help changing the dressing on my leg. But otherwise I truly was unscathed. It was more than a minor miracle. My memories of the fire were stronger now that I'd been awake awhile. And as a result I hadn't been surprised when I'd hacked up more grey phlegm in the shower. My throat and nose still felt stuffy but my chest felt better from the steam. I honestly felt okay. Not myself but okay.

I'd cried actual tears for the first time in a decade and it honestly didn't surprise me. It was like everything was just closer to the surface. When George handed me the fluffy towel and told me there were already toiletries for me in the bathroom I'd almost cried again.

I use the toiletries now, surprised, and yet not, to realise they were all brand new tubes of what I usually use. The small bag in front of me had my favourite vanilla hair oil, my cinnamon toothpaste, my nighttime and daytime moisturisers along with my cleanser of choice and some fancy mud mask I'd never seen before. There was even a bottle of the lavender oil I often put on before bed. The only thing missing was my descenter. I guess that didn't matter now that they all knew. I wasn't going to miss the horrible metallic taste of it in my mouth when I accidentally inhaled it.

I grab the hair oil and run some through. I really should take the time to brush it through properly and then set my curls but my arms are tired. I brush my teeth and put on some of the night time cream.

I look okay all things considered. I had dark circles under my eyes from the stress and the lack of quality sleep. And my pallor was a little ashen but otherwise I was okay. That being said I still longed for some make up.

I'd never worn a lot, just a touch of tinted moisturiser and some mascara most days but right now I'd kill for it. Because I was about to head out to the kitchen where four extremely hot sexy alphas were waiting for me. Four lovely guys who I had embarrassed myself in front of in more ways than I could count. Thus my vanity was kicking in and I wanted to look like less of a mess. But that was only half my problem.

Now that I was clean I could smell the hint of smoke and hospital on the pajamas I'd worn in here and I didn't want to put them back on again. There was no robe in here which meant my only option was to walk out in a towel. And while the guys seemed to have the big blanket thing covered that did not extend to their towels. This thing only just wrapped around me with maybe an inch to spare.

I dash across the hallway to my room and head over to the dresser. I open the first drawer. Empty. Second drawer, empty. In fact all of the drawers are empty. Not even a mystery sock. The wardrobe is the same. A few coathangers with nothing on them.

The only clothes in the entire room were the four men's t-shirts currently in the mess that I had left the bed. I lift them up to examine and can't resist pulling the whole pile towards me to breathe deep. Goddess they smell so good. Each of them alone smells amazing but all together they were like bliss. But underneath they also had the trace of smoke and hospital making me not want to put any of them on. Besides, walking out there in one of their shirts would be kind of weird. Walking out in a towel wasn't much better but I didn't have another choice.

I slide out the door again turning left and begin sneaking down the hall. The rest of the house is more colourful, with dark timber floors and soft dark walls. Next to the bathroom is another door leading to an office with bookcases on every wall. Off to the left is a large arch that leads to the living room with the world's most giant dark blue sectional and a massive TV. But the voices are coming from further down on the right.

I step through the next arch to see a long wooden table. Further around the corner is a big beautiful kitchen. It has a large stove, a giant fridge and a huge kitchen island. It looks like the front cover of a home decor magazine. Except for the four big guys currently having a whispered but very vehement argument.

John keeps pacing away and running his fingers through his curls to the point that his hair was starting to look less stylish, unruly and more chaotic frayed mop. Sam has his hands on the counter and keeps bending over at the waist and stretching like he has a pain in his stomach or maybe gas. Mick is standing next to the stove, his arms folded as he contemplates the floor. George's back is to me but I can tell he is speaking even if I can't hear what he 's saying. Whatever it is, the others are not happy.

The sight of all four of them, all riled up, all together. It looks good. Their scents mixing in the air create a more dynamic and brilliant version of the t-shirts. It's not as balanced, one second there are whiffs of whiskey with stronger notes of vanilla, a hint of lavender. And then one of them huffs out a breath and it shifts and all I can smell is cinnamon before the whiskey creeps back in again. I close my eyes so I can focus on the blend, it's like listening to music. It's like being in a whirlpool of the best things in the world and I hum to myself in contentment.

Then I perfume.

I feel it. The rush of heat to my skin. The burst of scent suddenly radiating off my neck and my wrists. Wherever my blood is close to the surface. And then I can smell it. The strong sickly sweet flavour of my strawberry scent. And I'm not the only one.

'Sweetness.' Mick calls from his position beside the stove. I open my eyes to find all four of them staring at me. In my towel. Oh yeah.

'Um, sorry to interrupt.' I mumble and George growls. 'I mean not sorry. Sorry. I was just wondering if I could borrow some other clothes?'

KNOT FOR REAL

Chapter 33. Mick

I think I just swallowed my tongue. Based on the scents swirling in the room I'm not the only one reacting to Melanie either. All four of our scents darken once we smell her. My mouth watering at the rich sweetness of her strawberry perfection. And if that wasn't enough she's also practically naked. All her lush deliciousness on display. The top of her breasts peeking over the top of the towel. A sliver of her pale hip poking through the gap in the fabric. Her thick thighs nervously stepping side to side.

Shit, she's uncomfortable.

'One second sweetness.' I call as I round the kitchen island toward her, trying not to growl at the bandage on her calf. 'I have more clothes for you, they're in the dryer.'

'Oh?' She seems confused.

'I was warming them up, I didn't hear you get out of the shower.' I brush my lips to her forehead as I pass without consciously planning to do it.

I jog down the hall to the laundry. It's just past her bedroom and across from the bathroom, which is currently airing her scent into the hallway like that's its job. My god, how is anyone supposed to get used to that scent? I feel like I can taste candy on my tongue when I smell it.

I duck into the laundry and rip open the dryer. In it is a collection of loungewear and pajamas I had delivered this afternoon. All in the dark rich tones I'd seen throughout her apartment. When we got home this afternoon and I helped her to her room, she didn't seem to care what she put on so long as she could go back to sleep. I left the red ones out because they were the colour I liked best and then I'd left her alone to change. By the time I came back she was buried under the swathe of blankets and deeply asleep and I was lamenting that I'd never seen that dark wine colour against her skin.

I grab the warm pile of clothes from the dryer and toss them into a basket. Pulling our old shirts out of the mix, I quickly jog back to the kitchen. Everyone is exactly where I left them. The three guys standing around the kitchen, their mouths hanging open like broken puppets. Melanie standing towards the dining table shifting her weight back and forth.

'Here.' I say as I put the basket down on the table and gesture for her to help herself. 'It's all yours.'

'Thanks.' She mumbles, shifting over toward me. Her movement seems to rouse the other guys from their stupor and they get back into action.

We'd been trying to figure out what she might want for dinner when George had come storming in announcing she was in the shower and that none of us were to touch her. This had sparked an immediate argument. It had taken a few minutes for us to sort through it but eventually what we realised George meant was sexually. He didn't want any of us to touch her sexually.

In the end he didn't need to come barking at us. We all agreed. Although Sam was visibly reluctant.

If she had a heat spike and she needed us to ease her, that was one thing. But none of us were to touch her unless she actually asked us. Not that any of us would ever touch her or anyone without their permission but more that we weren't going to initiate. I asked George what had brought him in here barking mad and so set on this point and all he'd said in response was, 'No one has ever been good to her.'

We all felt that. She smelled like heaven and was one of the sweetest, most hard working and kindest people I'd ever met. And

I'd only known her for three days. The least we could do is show her some kindness.

I'd spent the day reading up on touch starvation and how to treat it. I'd also read just about everything I could find on omegas, what made them happy, how to take care of them. I even called my sister to ask for tips. We didn't speak often, maybe once a month. But she was the only omega I knew and I had to start somewhere. She seemed thrilled by the idea that we had found someone and her giddy energy had turned her into a wealth of knowledge. In fact it had been her suggestion to put the clothes in the dryer. She said that warm dry soft clothes after a shower was one of the best feelings in the world and it seemed Melanie agreed.

'Hmm.' She sighed, searching through the clothes. 'What do you think of these?'

'Perfect.' I smile at her as she holds the turquoise crop top and gypsy pants in front of her. Descriptions I now knew thanks to an embarrassingly large amount of time spent on Pinterest to give me ideas.

'Wait.' Melanie pulls the clothes to her nose. 'They smell like you. Like all of you?'

'Yeah I put them in the dryer with some of our things. The smells won't be strong but it will stop them from smelling new.'

'They smell amazing.' She murmurs in awe. Thank you Pinterest.

'I may have added extra lavender. Since it seems to be your favourite.' I tease. Her cheeks redden with a pretty blush and I have to tense my muscles not to groan. It seems if she blushes she perfumes. But just as I close my eyes to savour the taste of her scent in my mouth it changes. Her strawberry taste becomes too ripe, too sweet, like the fruit about to rot.

'I'm so sorry about yesterday.' I start racking my brains trying to figure out what she's apologising for. Yesterday when I saw her at the store? Or did she mean yesterday as in this morning at the hospital.

Either way I couldn't think of anything she needed to apologise for. 'I didn't mean to.'

Her whispered words and the drop in her gaze and I realise what she's referencing. She's apologising for her arousal. And I'm confused. No, not confused. Upset. I'm upset and angry. Why the hell is she apologising for that? My hand darts out to grab her chin so I can look her in the eye.

'Sweetness, what are you apologising for?' I grunt out. I don't know why I want her to say it. But I need her to say it. I need to know her exact words so I can fight them.

'For... using you.' Her words are whispered. The others are still busy arguing over who's making what for dinner and I know they didn't hear her. Because if they did they'd be just as frustrated as I am right now.

'Sweetness. I don't want you to apologise for your needs to me ever again. Do you hear me?' I demand and she nods into my grip. 'If you need me, I'll be there. Whatever it is, do you understand?'

'Yes, but...' Her eyes lower and so I tilt her chin higher so I can see them again. With our height difference I've got her neck fully extended as I crane my own to stare down at her. '... I didn't ask.'

'Darling you were in a heat. You didn't have words. But your body asked me and I said yes. I promise. I wanted to be there for you. So did Sam.'

She nods but her teeth are worrying her lower lip and I can tell she's still bothered. I sigh. This beautiful creature is apologising to me for coming apart in my arms like a goddess and I want to rage. I pull her against me instead. I don't have words but with her in my arms I feel her relax a little. I want to go on holding her all night but she shivers. Her hair is damp against my chest and our house isn't exactly toasty.

'Quick sweetness. Go get your clothes on and then we'll see if these other idiots have figured out some dinner, okay?' She nods as she hurries back off in her towel, the fabric gaping dangerously as she moves, flashing me the cleft of her bum. God damn it.

'George is right.' I grumble as I come back to the guys gathered around the kitchen island. 'Hands off.'

'Yeah I get it.' Sam snaps back. He was definitely the least fond of this plan but I didn't doubt that he would abide.

'So what did you guys decide on for dinner?' I ask.

'I want to make fried chicken.' John grumbles.

'I think burgers would be better.' Sam grunts.

'I'm pushing for pasta, comfort food.' George adds. They all sounded good to me. But I'd seen what kind of foods Melanie reached for when we'd been painting together and I had a feeling they were all wrong.

'I think she's going to want eggs.' I chime in. They all stare at me like I'm batshit but just then Melanie comes back in. I sense her rather than see her and I can't help the smirk that crosses my face when she speaks.

'Is someone making eggs?' Her voice sounds so hopeful. 'Can I have some?'

KNOT FOR REAL

Chapter 34. Melanie

Mick and Sam are currently both doing my hair and I can not stop giggling.

Dinner consisted of boiled, still runny eggs with buttery toast cut into thin slices for dipping. They didn't have proper egg holders but it turns out a shot glass works in a pinch. I'd tried to help with cleaning up, but I had been forced bodily from the dining room and deposited onto the couch. I'd then suggested to John that if he grabbed my hair oil I could fix his curls. When I'd explained to Mick and Sam that I wasn't doing my own because my arms hurt when I held them above my head, they swung into action.

Which is why I now had two great big men sitting behind me debating the correct way to finger tighten my damp curls while John sat between my legs and let me play with his hair. Surrounded as I was on all sides I was practically bathing in their smells. Mick's lavender was coating my right shoulder. Sam was the vanilla on my left. And John was cinnamon. I hadn't expected that. He was always so sweet and so corny. But as I played with his hair I began to realise it quite suited him. Sweet but spicy.

'That's wrong.' Sam huffs. 'She said you had to twist then loop.'

'At least mine aren't all different sizes.' Mick grumbles and I laugh again.

'Guys watch me again.' I say as I rake my hands through John's hair and grab another section. 'Gentle twist to create the clump, then loop de loop to make it plump.'

I repeat the rhyme my grandmother had taught me when I was young.

'My side's better.' Sam crows.

'In your dreams.' Mick snaps back.

'What are we watching?' George asks as he enters the room. 'Or should I ask, what are we doing?'

'Melanie needed help with her hair.' Mick explains while gesturing dramatically behind me. I've been watching their efforts this whole time on the blacked out television.

'Help is a strong word.' George mutters while contemplating the outcome.

'They tried, and I appreciate it.' I smile at him. He gazes down at me but his eyes wander to the group. Taking John's position between my knees, Mick and Sam at my back as they fiddle with my hair, elbowing each other in the process.

'Catch.' He calls out, tossing something as he flops down on the couch to our left.

'Marshmallows?' I contemplate the bag in awe.

'According to Charlotte there was an unholy number of those in your kitchen.' Sam chuckles. 'I hope you don't mind. We had her check what you like to eat.'

'No that's lovely. They're my favourite heat snack.' I smile as I pop the bag open.

'Heat snack?' Mick asks. I pause with a marshmallow in my mouth. I'm not old fashioned enough to think that talking about things to do with your heat is rude. Heats happen. They don't often happen to me but I try not to get caught up in the whole puritanical don't talk about it shit. But at the same time I never talk about it.

Other than Sandra who's a beta I don't have that many close friends. I did try and talk to my sister about it when I was coming up on my first heat. I thought she could tell me what to expect. She acted like I had asked her to divulge state secrets or defuse a bomb. So I just never got in the habit of talking about these things.

'Yeah, you know foods that are easy to eat and full of energy.' I shrug. 'The cramps and everything can be exhausting to the point you don't want to eat, but you need energy. So it's good to have things that you can just shove in your mouth.'

'Noted.' Sam's voice hints at innuendo and I reach back behind me to slap at him playfully. But I appreciate the humour. For a second there the room started to feel tense.

'So, what's the plan?' George asks our little grouping. 'Are we still playing at the hair salon or do we want to do something else?'

'Do you want a turn?' I ask him. His coppery hair is more wavy than curl but it would still benefit from some attention.

'No thanks.' He chuckles.

'Was that a yes?' Sam asks, his tone mocking.

'I think so.' Mick agrees as I feel them both shift their legs out from beside me. 'I think the bossman wants his hair played with too.'

'You two better stay right where you are.' George warns holding up his finger to signal them to stay back.

'Oh come on boss.' Sam mocks. 'Her hair oil smells like vanilla, don't you wanna smell like me? Might help you with the ladies.'

'I don't need help.' George mutters and I feel a pang of displeasure in my stomach. I'm sure none of these guys had trouble getting dates. I watch as Sam and Mick close in on him from two sides.

'I dunno.' Mick taunts. 'I think you need all the help you can get.'

There's a pause while George maintains his position lying down on the couch. Sam and Mick leering from above him. Then Sam dives for George's head but it isn't there anymore. Mick aimed for his legs but is now clutching a couch cushion. George throws his arms around Sam's torso then drags his arms back behind him and essentially sits on Sam's hands. Then he reaches out towards Mick who's still digging himself out of the cushions and wraps his arms around his neck in a choke hold.

The whole scene takes about five seconds and then there's George smiling while the other two wriggle under his control. My mouth is hanging open.

'Wow.' I stutter. George smirks at me and releases his two packmates. They both snarl at him as they rub at their sore spots, shuffling away back to their positions by my side. I can't stop staring at George. 'You're good.'

'He knows.' Sam grumbles.

'He literally wrestled at the Olympics, so he has an unfair advantage.' Mick's tone is cranky but there's a touch of pride.

'You did?' I don't know why it surprises me so much considering the display I just saw but this lovely tempered exacting man being into wrestling did not compute.

'I did.' He nods.

'Will you teach me?' George's eyes darken. My own scent warms in response. Sam groans beside me, making Mick laugh while he continues to play with my hair.

'I'll teach you.' He nods. 'Once you're better.'

'That reminds me,' I almost slap my forehead at my own stupidity. 'Do you guys have bandages anywhere?'

'Why do you need a bandage?' Mick grumbles, his fingers stilling in my hair.

'My leg, I got it wet in the shower.' I lift my foot up onto the couch so I can pull up my pant leg and show them. It's not bad but the edges of the waterproof bandage are damp and it's almost certainly not sterile anymore. Mick stands beside me.

'Up you go.' He grunts as he reaches down and lifts me over his shoulder. I squeal, as my face lands in the center of his back, my bum in the air.

'This seems unnecessary.' I grumble into Mick's back as he walks.

'Beg to differ.' Mick mutters as he deposits me on the kitchen island. He brushes his lips against my forehead just like he did before he went to grab me the clothes. And just like then I feel myself blush as a warmth settles in my belly. 'He'll take care of you.'

Mick leaves. Mick leaves?

I hear a container open behind me and I turn to find John, opening a big plastic container full of bandages. Beside it is a small paper bag from a chemist. John opens it and pulls out two tubes of cream and a pill bottle as well.

'We should have had you take these straight after dinner.' He mutters to himself. He moves to the sink, grabbing a glass and fills it with water. He shakes out two pills into his hand and passes them to me. 'Take these.'

I don't answer him, I just let him drop the pills in my hand and then put them straight in my mouth. I take a sip of the water and then put the glass to the side. He pulls a stool up between my legs and his head is bent towards my shin. I can't see his face but I can tell he's upset. He's been upset all night.

I know because I've known John for a year now. If it wasn't for him I wouldn't have agreed to be here. He's the one I know. The one I trust. The other guys were great but John was my friend. Except right now he isn't looking at me.

Well he is, he's looking at my ankle as he slowly rolls up my pant leg. He slides it up over my knee, his hands then caressing my skin on the way back down to my bandage. Carefully he picks at the edge, pulling back the adhesive. He's so careful, trying to pull it gently. But it's barely moving. I reach down to cover his hand with my own. I still his motion and he freezes. I see his deep breath lift his shoulders as he continues to stare at my leg.

'It's okay.' I murmur. His eyes shoot up to clash with my own.

'It's going to hurt.' He breathes.

'I know.' I nod as I bite my lip. His fingers grip the edge of the bandage and he pulls. I can't help the whimper that leaves my mouth. It hurts, but only for a second.

Chapter 35. John

Her soft cry breaks me. I lean forward to bury my face against the thigh of her uninjured leg and try not to groan. She whimpers like a goddess.

'Are you okay?' She asks her fingers running through my hair like when I rested my head back between her legs and wondered if this is what heaven was like.

'I'm supposed to ask you that.' I grumble as I lift my face from her perfect pillowy thigh to look at her.

'I'm fine.' She shrugs, pushing me back from my space nestled between her legs so that she can contemplate her calf. There's a patch of angry red skin. 'Ew.'

'It could be worse.' I offer as I begin reaching for the antiseptic spray. It was a shallow burn. I spray the area with disinfectant as quickly as I can but she still winces. 'Sometimes it's better if you don't know it's coming.'

'No time to brace for the pain.' She agrees. I reach for the analgesic cream next, temporary pain was one thing, the thought of her constant pain would drive me mad.

'This should make it feel better.' I murmur as I gently swab the pale cream across her skin. She sighs her relief and I know I'm right. 'I'm going to put it on thick, and then put a bandage on top so it slowly sinks in all night'

'You're good at this.' She gestures to the medical supplies along the bench.

'Once upon a time, I thought I wanted to be a doctor.' I shrug.

'Really?' Her tone of surprise is fair. It was hard to imagine that I'd wanted to do anything other than coding. Especially not something that dealt with people.

'I even applied to med school.'

'Did you get in?'

'Everywhere I applied.' I'm boasting but I don't care. The other guys might be taller and stronger but I'm smarter.

'What changed your mind?' She asks as she watches me place the new bandage over the cream making sure it covers the entire wound.

'My dad died.' I hear her intake of breath, I don't know if it's because of what I said or my touch but I rush on. 'As soon as he was gone, I realised the only reason I'd considered med school was because he had wanted to be a doctor.'

'How did he die?' Her voice is curious as well as concerned.

'A car accident. I'd just finished high school.' She scoots forward on the bench so that her legs hang down more as she pulls me into the circle of her arms.

'Mum?' Her mumbled question is tentative.

'Took off after I was born. Never met her and never want to.' I shrug with my arms around her. Most people think it must be a sore spot but I genuinely never missed the woman I didn't know. My dad and I had been close and he'd had a huge network of friends so I'd never wanted for company or support.

'I'm sorry John.' She mumbles into my shirt.

'It's old news.' I give into my urge to stroke her hair.

'I'm still sorry.' She mumbles again. I can feel her hot breath between my pecs.

'Can I ask you something?' I speak into her hair, inhaling deeply. Her hair might be covered in vanilla oil but all I can smell is strawberries and my mouth waters.

'You can ask.' She hedges. George would be proud. Never commit till you know what it's to, he would say.

'I know that designation doesn't really matter but... were you hiding it from me on purpose?' I feel her stiffening beneath me and I start to purr automatically.

'I wasn't hiding it from you specifically.' She speaks slowly. 'More everyone. It was just easier if no one knew. '

'I get it.' I say. The problem is I feel so bad. All those times I'd asked her about gifts for omegas and she'd answered so insightfully and I'd never clued in? Oh god! All those times I asked about gifts for other omegas. I groan.

'What's wrong?' She asks, pulling back.

'You must hate me.' I moan.

'What? No! You must hate me?'

'Why would I hate you?' I demand.

'Because I hid that I was an omega from you.'

'But not because you don't trust me?' I clarify.

'Of course not!' She practically yells in her fervor.

'Then why would I be mad. Even if you did hide it from me on purpose I wouldn't be mad. I was a strange alpha to you. Keeping your designation private was safer. If anything I'm proud of you for taking care of yourself.' Even if I hated that she had to.

'Oh.' She grumbles. 'Well then why do I hate you?'

'Because I came in there time and time again asking for help getting gifts for omegas.' I lament.

'That's literally what the store is for?' She says it like I've missed the point.

'Yes but I should have been getting gifts for you.' I explain.

'For me?' Her note of surprise should probably make me laugh. But instead it makes me want to break something. 'Why would you buy presents for me?'

The complete look of confusion on her face is what makes me realise.

She hasn't figured it out. I want to tell her. That we're scent sensitive, that she's ours. I want to point out that the way we're all responding to her, the way I've obsessed over her for a year even before I scented her, it means something. Even how quickly she's becoming comfortable in our home, amongst us. This is special. But I can't.

'Everyone deserves gifts.' I defer. We'd all agreed not to overwhelm her. So I distract her. 'So what movie do you want to watch?'

'We're watching a movie?'

'It's Friday night, if we're not out that's what we usually do.' At least it's what I normally did. George was often at a work function. Sam had his fair share of those too, otherwise he was at a bar or a club. Mick would often head out as well. And I would be alone on the couch. But tonight they weren't going anywhere.

'What would you guys normally watch?' She asks.

'Oh, no you don't.' I tut. 'Guest picks the movie. And no trying to guess what we'd enjoy. We want to watch something you love. If that involves finally forcing George to watch a Disney movie, so be it.'

'He's never seen a Disney movie? Not even when he was a kid.' Her face is as appalled as I was when he'd first told me.

'I know right, it explains a lot.' I shake my head in mock disapproval.

'He's not so bad.' She shoves gently against me and I catch her hand to my chest so I can push her fingers deeper into my skin.

'You say that now.' I let my voice trail off implying she would change her mind. She wouldn't. If you worked opposite George you would think he was a tyrant. If you worked for George you'd call him exacting but fair. If you knew George you'd call him a big old softie. 'So what movie? Has to be a favourite of yours or something you really want to watch?'

'Have you guys ever watched The Fifth Element?'

'I think I could do it line for line.' I nod.

'I'll pick something else then.' She shakes her head.

'No it's perfect, go tell the guys to tee it up and I'll be in to join you in a minute.' I speak as I step away to start cleaning up the mess.

'You sure?' She checks again.

'Yep. Now do you think you can bravely limp back to the living room while I tidy this up or should I call for Mick?' I threaten with a smile.

'I can limp.' She chimes as I help her slide down from the counter. My hands linger on her waist while I steady her. With her feet on the ground her head just brushes under my chin and I feel the urge to kiss her crown. But she tugs me down and places a kiss on my cheek first. 'Thanks.'

She heads off toward the living room, a surprising amount of bounce in her step for someone who was in hospital earlier today. I assumed we'd be bringing her dinner in bed and that she'd be straight back to sleep. But this? This was the girl I knew before the fire. Back when she was just Melanie. Tough and kind and beautiful.

This was the girl I was falling for even before she was our omega. And I was growing more obsessed by the minute.

Chapter 36. Melanie

I fell asleep maybe ten minutes into the movie. Tucked up between two large warm bodies, I'd felt so relaxed I'd simply drifted off. But now someone was waking me.

'I'm so sorry baby.' George's voice whispers from just above my ear. 'But I have to wake you up. Mary is only a few minutes away.'

'Omf- kay.' I mumble into my pillow.

'John's taking Whisper for a walk and Mick is making you a coffee and food. Just start trying to wake up.' George keeps his voice low.

'You need help waking up?' I hear Sam from the doorway and then the whole bed rocks as I feel his body bounce on the end.

'Garumph.' I grumble trying to kick him through the blankets. Unfortunately my legs are twisted and bound in the sheets and so I can't actually reach him.

'I thought you were helping Mick?' George demands. He's sitting next to my head, running his fingers through my hair.

'He wasn't helping.' Mick's smokier tone drifts over me as the smell of coffee reaches my nose. I reach my arm out in search of the coffee.

'There she is.' Sam chuckles. My searching hand does not encounter coffee but rather a ridiculously large hand.

'Noooo.' I moan as I'm gently lifted up by Mick's tug on my hand. He releases me and I flop back, but instead of landing on my pile of pillows I collide with George's chest. He's shuffled in behind me to prop me up. 'What time is it?'

'Seven thirty.' Sam nods. Damn normally I'd be awake and working by now.

'Mary wanted to come and see you before she went into her practice today.' George explains. 'Tomorrow we'll have her come later so you can sleep in.'

The rumble of his words behind me feels nice as Mick slides a breakfast tray over my lap and sits on my other side. There's coffee, which I reach for immediately. But also a muffin, some yoghurt, sliced fruit and toast.

'Who's eating all this?' I gesture at the smorgasbord.

'You need to keep your strength up.' Mick chides.

'And I'm here to help.' Sam grins as he steals a piece of the toast.

'I didn't make that for you.' Mick scolds him.

'I'll try not to be offended.' Sam rolls his eyes. I pick up a piece of fruit and dip it into the yoghurt before biting into the peach with a moan, it's so good. 'Do that again!'

'Sam.' George growls his name in warning as I perfume and soak the room in strawberries.

'Sorry.' I mumble.

'I'm going to keep a count of how many times you say 'sorry'.' George grumbles.

'Why?' I ask, eating another piece of yoghurt covered fruit.

'Because it's a habit I want to help you break.' George explains.

'And how are you going to do that?'

'I don't know yet. Punishment isn't my thing. But as a team we'll figure it out.' The other two smirk in agreement at George and I feel another flush come over me.

'What's going on in here?' A woman's voice drifts through the door. It's familiar but in a far off way. Like something you remember from a dream.

'She was pulling up as I came back in.' John explains from beside the woman, as Whisper wanders straight to his new bed in the corner and settles in to go back to sleep.

'Hi Mary.' George greets the lady without removing his arm from around my shoulder. 'We were just making sure Melanie was up. But we'll leave you to it.'

As he speaks he stands, propping pillows behind me to keep me upright. Sam leaps from the bed, loops his arm around John's shoulders and heads for the door. Mick grabs the pale blue armchair from the corner and brings it closer to the bed before dropping a kiss to my head and turning to go.

Should I get up? I should do something. Am I meant to sit in the chair? I try to shift under the breakfast tray and almost topple the whole thing over.

'Don't get up.' Mary stops me as she approaches and takes a seat in the armchair Mick moved closer. Yeah that makes more sense. 'How are you feeling?'

'Fine.' I shrug.

'You seem a lot more yourself today?' She enquires.

'Yeah. I mean, I know we met yesterday but it's all kind of blurry.'

'That's the combination of the pain killers and the heat haze but also withdrawal.'

'The suppressants.' I grumble.

'That's right. How are you feeling without them?'

'I had some cramps in the night but nothing bad.'

'I'm sorry to say those will continue and probably get worse. Although I do have a list of stretches I printed out which will help immensely. They'll be a bit like contractions, getting stronger and closer together until you go back into your heat.' She explains.

'What about taking something else? Something other than Shiffalix?' I ask.

'If you had seen me before this all began I would have had a few options but with your body already in withdrawal introducing anything else now would cause more severe hormone fluctuations that could do you damage.'

'What if I hurt someone during my heat?' I ask, fear lacing my tone.

'Has that happened before?' Mary asks calmly.

'No but... I tried to.' I remember my first heat, in the clinic, trying to kick people.

'You don't have to tell me any of the details. If you become a danger to anyone, even yourself, I have confidence that George and the others will be able to subdue you.' After the wrestling demo I'd seen last night I didn't doubt that. 'How is it going here?'

'They're so nice.' I smile at her. It's the truth.

'I'm glad to hear it.' She nods. 'Now I want to just talk you through a couple of things today, now that you're more yourself. Then I need to give you a short exam, check your temperature. And then that's it. I'll be back tomorrow for the same thing.'

'What do we need to talk about?' I ask.

'You mentioned cramps and those will continue. But you'll also have heat spikes, like mini heats that last for twenty minutes or so.'

'Okay.' I'd heard of heat spikes. Many omegas got them in the days or even a week before their full heat but I'd never had one, when you came off suppressants you just went straight into heat. 'What do I need to do?'

'Heat spikes are like a full heat. Your body will need easing however you are comfortable doing that, with yourself, or toys or others. Your omega will come to the surface. Whatever she wants or needs, will be right for you and your body. Do you have everything you need?' Her tone tells me she isn't referring to food or clothes.

'I'll pick up what I need.' I hedge.

'Okay then. Let's put that breakfast tray to the side for a minute, though it would be a good idea to eat as much of it as you can.' I nod as I let her help me slide the tray to the end of the bed. 'I mostly just want to take your temperature and check your lungs. You inhaled quite a lot of smoke.'

I nod as she moves in closer. She slides the stethoscope all over my back asking for deep breaths over and over again. Then she slips the thermometer beneath my tongue and waits. My temperature is standard for an omega, higher than betas or alphas but today it's even a little warmer still.

'All done.' She announces as she repacks her bag.

'Free to go?' I tease.

'Almost.' She smiles as she retakes her seat. 'The suppressants you're coming off have a tranquilising effect, without them you might feel a little intense.'

'That's for sure.' I sigh. 'Everything feels more. Bigger, closer and louder.'

'That's an accurate description. But the combination of coming off them and now being with your scent sensitive pack is an extra complication.'

'My what?' In my shock I yell the question loud enough to have Whisper lifting his head. My scent sensitive pack? Oh god. Oh no.

I just thought they smelled good. That without the suppressants in my system I was able to enjoy scents again. But scent sensitive?

It explained so much. Why I felt so comfortable around them. I didn't trust people easily but with these four it had never been in question. And oh god their smells. Their perfect combination of scents that had me dizzy whenever they were in the room.

'Shit.' Mary spits the oath that was ringing in my head. 'I'm sorry Melanie. I assumed you realised. That was incredibly unprofessional of me.'

'No, makes sense. I keep breathing them in like a cocaine addict. I should have figured it out by now.' I shrug as I feel my insides crush me. Shit, shit, shit. If I was scent sensitive to them. That meant they were sensitive to me. Which meant it didn't matter if they liked me. They didn't have a choice. They were stuck with me.

Fuck.

KNOT FOR REAL

Chapter 37. Sam

Fuck this was doing my head in. After the doctor left, Melanie wandered out in a trance. George insisted on taking her on a tour of the house, which was fair but I'd seen her walk off and it was like watching a zombie. He skipped the top floor with the omega suite claiming he didn't want to put pressure on her but I disagree.

I may not have wanted an omega but I wanted Melanie.

She'd been in the house for nineteen hours. I'd known her for six days. Was it insane to want someone in your life, in your home, forever, after knowing them for a week. Yeah. But I was happy to plead insanity and have her move in tomorrow.

The guys still want to hold back. I get it. I do. I don't want to overwhelm her. But I also don't agree with the hands off approach. Not letting her know we're hot for her is not right. I want to tell her how crazy she's making me. How every day since I've met her I've woken up hard because she's sauntered through my dreams making me crazy.

And now that I've held her in my arms and watched her come apart, sometimes when I'm near her I feel like I can't breathe. Except I have to breathe because it's the only way of pulling her scent deep inside my lungs where it belongs. I daydream about licking the flavour straight from the source and drowning in her sweet cream.

Am I a pig for having these unsavoury thoughts about our houseguest who's currently still wading through a personal crisis? Maybe. But I can't help my thoughts.

At least I'm pretending I'm a gentleman like the other guys want. Hence currently pummeling the punching bag to burn off my energy. I close my eyes, resting my hands on the punching bag and leaning back into my hips to stretch out the muscles tensing there. My alpha knows where he wants to be.

'Um.' A sweet voice calls. I spin to look at the woman of my fantasies standing in the doorway of our gym. Damn but she looks hot in those skin tight black leggings and some sort of sports bra top thing. I'm going to need to buy a present for Mick to thank him for all the clothes he's bought her. With everything she owns soaked in smoke and ash it was necessary but I don't think any of us would have done such a good job.

'You okay?' She's loitering by the door staring at the room like it might hurt her.

'Can you share?' She asks.

'I like sharing.' I shrug. I have no idea what she's referring to but my mind drifts back to that moment in front of her building. When she shattered in my arms like a goddess while I watched her writhe against Mick. Sharing was great.

'The room. Can I share the room with you?' Okay I'd take what I can get.

'Of course.' I gesture for her to come in.

'Mary gave me some stretches to do, but if it's a problem or I'm interrupting I can just do them up in my room.' Still she doesn't enter. 'Sorry, I'll just go.'

'No you don't.' I growl dashing across the room to haul her back to me. I wrap my arms around her and lift her up to carry her back into the space. I'm a hot mess and I can feel the sweat of my chest soaking into the back of her sports top. I love it.

'I don't want to get in the way.' She complains as I release her gently.

'You're not. And how many sorrys are we up to?' I demand.

'Four.' She mumbles.

'Five now.' I correct.

'I disturbed you.' She gestures at me and the room.

'You came into a shared space. No apology necessary. It's five. And if you fight me I'll join in on the brainstorming team for how to punish you. And you don't want that.'

'I don't?' She asks, confused.

'Nope, I'm a lawyer. I know crime and punishment. I'll come up with something evil.' I tease, leaning forward to tap my knuckles against her chin.

'Like what?' She challenges me. I know what she's thinking from the way she winces. She thinks her punishment will be painful. But not if I had my way.

'Like having to wear a crown all day and make us wait on you, hand and foot.'

'Who are you punishing again?' She grumbles in surprise.

'And you have to tell us what to do to make you come.' Her eyes darken as her breath catches. Her strawberry scent bursts around us and I close my eyes as I try not to groan.

I turn away towards the free weights and pick up the two largest dumbbells within reach and place them on the bench. Then remembering she was here for stretches I grab a yoga mat from the side and place that in the space next to me.

'Here you go.' I announce, gesturing to the set up.

'Thanks.' She mumbles and sits on her mat. Yep I made it awkward. She rolls out some printed pages in front of her and then stretches her legs out each side and leans forward. Damn. Those leggings are clinging to her like a second skin.

'Do you like yoga and stretching?' I ask as I sit on my bench and try to face forward and not stare at her ass as I do a set of bicep curls.

'No, Mary gave them to me, she said they'll help with the cramps.' I have another suggestion for what will help with the cramps and it's not stretches.

'Have they been bad?' My voice is neutral but if she tells me she's in pain, pain that I could replace with bliss and pleasure. Well I think I might actually go insane.

'No, not bad. Just uncomfortable. They might get worse though. I was actually going to ask...' Her voice trails off. She's changed positions now, so that she's lying on her back with her pelvis in the air because I deserve to be tortured.

'What were you going to ask?' I prod.

'It's nothing.'

'Tell me, please.' I ask calmly.

'George said that the police had closed off my building till Monday but do you think I could go back and just grab a couple of things?'

'Like what?' What did she need that we hadn't thought of? I know John was currently at a bookstore to make sure she had stuff to read. I'd seen Mick ordering even more clothes today, and not just loungewear, dresses and jeans and a ridiculous amount of frilly underwear. Apparently he'd asked this morning and she preferred soft lacy things. It was one of the many reasons I'd been pummeling the punching bag.

'Just a couple of things.' She doesn't elaborate. Tossing my weights to the side I hop off my bench to kneel in front of her where she's now sitting on her knees.

'There's no way to get into your place until Monday. But whatever you need, tell me and we'll get it. Or if it's sentimental I'll make sure George knows to have someone fetch it the second it's possible. Okay?'

'Okay.' She nods and I feel my shoulders relax.

'What do you need?' I ask again.

'A vibrator.' Fuck. I can't. I close my eyes to stare at the ceiling as I make sure I have control of myself. 'Just because of my heat symptoms, you know.'

'Of course.' I mumble. Of course she needs one. And yet none of us even thought of the one thing she might need most. We are assholes.

I am a double asshole because her request is not only making me question our ability to take care of her but also filling my brain with images. I can see her lying back in bed, her eyes closed as she holds the vibrator between her legs until she cries out.

'It can wait.' I open my eyes and see her gaze has fallen to the floor.

'No. Pick something online, and if they don't do same day delivery I'll go get it.'

'No seriously. It can wait. I can always just...' Her voice trails off. The same image as before fills my mind but now it's her hand between her legs. The other hand pinching her nipples as she makes herself cum. '...use the shower.'

Nope. No. Too much. The thought of her in the shower, hot water flowing down her luscious body, the head of the shower massager between her thighs. Her gasping for air in the steam, the cold press of tiles against her back. Nope I'm actually dying.

'I'll get you what you need.' I growl out. 'Excuse me.'

I stand and walk away from her because the only other thing I can think to do is push her back onto her yoga mat, tear those stupid leggings off her, starting with the crotch and bury myself so deep inside her she never wants a toy or anything that isn't one of us, between her legs again. I walk out into the courtyard, straight past the sauna and jump into the plunge pool, my sneakers still on.

The freezing cold water snaps me back from my thoughts. I can do this. I can control myself. Even if my every instinct is screaming that she needs me. That her body needs me to turn pain into pleasure. I will control myself.

Chapter 38. Melanie

Why can't I control myself better? I should have just gone online myself to order something or made do. But no, I had to ask. Why the fuck did I ask him about a bloody vibrator?

I know why. I resolved to ask one of them what the chances were of getting access to my stuff because I was loath to spend money on something I already owned. What I hadn't thought through was his reaction. It was all my fault.

All morning I've been reeling from what Mary told me. Scent sensitive. That's what we were. That was why everything felt right. That's why I wanted them around me all the time. Why I felt like I couldn't get enough of their company. Although to be fair I'd felt that way before I could scent them.

The longer the suppressants were out of my system the more I felt these new instincts emerging. The desire to breathe deep every time one of them was near me. The need to be in their arms and bury myself into their chest until they purred. And other desires were also making themselves known.

When Mick asked about more clothes this morning I'd been embarrassed to ask for underwear. But I needed it, my boobs did not do well without proper restraint. This crop top sports bra thing was comfortable but if I tried jogging right now I think I'd knock myself out. And without my slick-proof underwear I was going to keep making messes. When he'd asked me what I liked to wear and I mentioned my favourite brand he agreed to buy some of the 'padded monstrosities'. His words not mine. But then he asked what I would like to wear if I wasn't worried about my slick or my scent and I admitted that I like lace. He smiled in approval before kissing my forehead and lingering to whisper against my ear.

'I'd like to see you in lace.' And that was it, I had to go change out of the pajama pants I was wearing. Which was when I switched to these leggings and the sports top knowing I'd eventually make my way down here to do the stretches Mary suggested.

First I tidied my room and made the bed, even as I wished I could just climb back in and go to sleep. I took Whisper out for a break in the backyard and then I'd looked for something to do. I wanted to be helpful. Maybe clean or cook something for them. But the house was immaculate and John was already in the kitchen working on something. I tried to help but he insisted I relax instead.

So I was here in the basement, trying to do the stretches and just stay out of everyone's way and instead I was making everything worse.

I know scent sensitivity wasn't anyone's fault. It was just something that happened. No one really knew why, although every month it felt like another scientist was claiming they had solved it. But if we were scent sensitive, that meant they were stuck with me.

Their alpha instincts would take over and no matter how they felt about Melanie the person my omega would call them and they'd have to put up with me. My too sweet smell. My lumpy curves. And my shitty omega instincts. I could only hope that she didn't do anything to embarrass me. Or try to hurt them.

I could feel a whine building in my throat as I watched Sam walk away into the courtyard. Here I was, perfuming all over him because he said he'd get me what I need. That was it, that was all it took. His eyes full of concern and his deep voice asking me what I needed and promising to get it for me and I was a puddle of need again. And hot. So hot I was sweating from stretching which made me pathetically unfit.

I watch through the glass wall to the courtyard as he jumps into the pool fully dressed and I let my whine escape.

It was too much. I wanted them. I wanted all of them. And because our other natures were compatible they were going to be stuck with me while I craved them. They were going to have to muddle through my crazy with me just because of a trick of biology. I didn't just want to whine. I wanted to cry.

'Melanie?' I look up from contemplating my yoga mat to find Sam standing in the doorway to the courtyard. His shoes and socks are gone, bare torso in nothing but exercise shorts and he's dripping wet. Like actually dripping all over the floor.

'Hmm?' I try to swallow the whine of longing pushing up my throat. I want to lick the water from his abs. I want to grab his hair and hold his wet cold face against my heated skin.

'Can you toss me a towel from that shelf there?' He gestures to the cabinets behind me filled with jump ropes, more mats and towels. I stand in slow motion. I must have stretched too hard because everything is aching. I move slowly as I go toward the shelves. They're high but I can just reach.

I pull down a towel and cross towards Sam. It's too hot down here. They should put in a fan. I hold out the towel to him as the room begins to spin.

'Melanie, are you okay?' Sam's voice is full of concern. But I'm fine. I'm just hot. Too hot. And I'm sore. And I want a hug. I try to tell him that. That I'm fine, not that I want a hug. But I can't get my mouth to work right. My lips are fuzzy, like they're not really there. 'Melanie?'

'Dizzy.' I mumble the words as I feel my knees give out.

Chapter 39. George

I have been over this documentation three times and I still can't wrap my head around it. Only two thirds of what Melanie paid to the bank went to her mortgage. The other chunk just disappeared. And whatever charlatan had put this contract together was a downright imbecile. They counted the business loan twice. Giving her a laughably low credit score which was completely false. She had no other debt, steady income and more in savings than I would have managed at her salary level. She shouldn't be in such a bad position.

Tomorrow I was taking Melanie out. We needed to go to her place, check on the new window and I had a meeting I couldn't get out of. But now I was also headed to her bank to figure out what was going on and who I could yell at.

'HELP!' Sam's voice ricochets through the house.

I'm down the stairs before I realise that I'm moving. Only one thing would make Sam sound scared like that. Melanie in Danger. I'm careening toward the gym a few feet in front of Mick who's also running like his life depends on it. Sam's on the floor with Melanie limp in his arms.

'She just passed out.' He moans as I slam onto the ground beside him.

'When?'

'Just now, we were talking and I stepped out to cool down. When I came back, she was handing me a towel and she collapsed.' Her face is cradled against his chest. She's breathing deeply but her eyes are closed, her face slack.

'I'll call Mary.' I reach for my phone and remember it's upstairs. 'Shit.'

'Don't bother.' Mick's voice calls across the room as the lights go out plunging the room into a soft glow. 'She's in a heat spike, the darkness will help.'

He kneels beside me as he runs his fingers along her cheek and her face turns towards his touch. Her eyes open and I can see it. Her pupils are blown, barely any of the crystal blue left. And she's whimpering. Whining.

'Oh baby.' I moan as she looks up at me. 'Are you okay?'

'She needs easing.' Mick's voice is steady but I can feel him vibrating beside me. 'Sweetness. What do you want?'

Melanie shakes her head, her eyes darting around our little circle. She looks scared, nervous. I remember what Mary said about her omega not being able to speak.

'Do you trust me?' She nods, her hand reaching out to touch my chest. 'Tell me.'

She still doesn't speak but she pulls my arm the way she did the other day and curls into my chest. I sit back, stretching my legs out in front of me so that she can sit between them more easily.

'Lay back against me babygirl. I'll hold you.' She turns away from me resting her back against my chest. 'Good girl.'

'You got a plan here boss?' Mick asks as he sits beside me, Sam kneels in front of us. I nod. I don't have a plan. But I'm going to act like I do.

'Babygirl.' She looks up at me, her head tilted back against my chest. 'Give me your hands, I'm going to hold you, okay?'

She holds her hands out in offering. I cross my arms in front of her so I can grip her hands. My arms band around her letting her heat sink into me. She sighs and snuggles deeper into my hold. Her hips twitch as she gets comfy.

'Do you need more sweetness?' Mick mumbles, pushing the hair off her face.

'Kisses.' She mumbles, I could cry with happiness that she's finally speaking. Mick leans forward, his kiss gentle and sweet and she squirms within my embrace.

'More?' Mick asks as he pulls back from her lips.

'More.' She murmurs. I drop my lips to hers from above and sip the sweet strawberry flavour off her lips. As soon as I pull back for breath Sam is there kissing her as well and when she begins to pant he slides his lips to her collar bone and begins kissing down her body. Her hips buck.

'Sam.' I only say his name but he knows what I'm telling him. He pauses in his descent groaning into her abdomen as he sits back onto his heels.

'No.' She grumps. 'More.'

'What is more?' Mick asks her. 'Use your words.'

'More kisses. Lower. More hold.' She pushes against me and I adjust my grip to hold her more firmly. Sam dives back to her lips but quickly diverts to her collar bone, between her breasts, her stomach. Descending further this time.

'Babygirl.' I whisper in her ear as I watch Sam's lips graze the edge of her leggings. 'Did you want Sam to eat you?'

Her eyes lock on mine even as her hips flail trying to get closer to Sam's lips. She nods and I sigh with happiness.

'Use your words.' Mick mumbles from next to my shoulder.

'Eat me.' She mumbles. Sam grips the waistband of her leggings and pulls them down slowly, revealing her flesh inch by inch. She has nothing underneath. I groan.

'Please never buy her underwear.' Sam tells Mick as he strips the leggings away from her and we take in the sight of our girl naked between us. Her slick is coating the inside of her thighs and the smell is sweeter than syrup, the sight unbearably hot.

'Hungry?' I ask Sam.

'Starving.' He responds before lowering his head to her center.

She moans as she pulls against my restraint, not fighting it but testing it. Assuring herself that I have her, she's safe in my arms. I'm not letting her go anywhere.

Melanie spasms in my arms. Her legs flail trying to get closer to Sam and so I shift my weight, tucking my ankles around hers. I pull wider, opening her further, making Sam moan.

'How does she taste?' I ask.

'Try for yourself.' He pulls back just far enough to run his fingers through her slick Then he dives back in with his tongue as he places his fingers within my reach. Melanie surprises both of us when she leans forward to tentatively lick his fingers. Our matching groans of approval encourage her and she pulls his finger into her mouth causing him to groan into her as he snatches back his hand.

The second his hand is gone my lips crash down on hers. The flavour of her mouth combines with the flavour of her slick and I moan into her as I try and capture more with my tongue. It's heaven.

'More.' I demand. Sam lifts his head, replaces his mouth with his fingers again.

'I think she likes that.' Mick mumbles in awe as Melanie bucks. Sam lifts his hand and she presses her mouth to his fingers, painting her own lips with her scent. We all stare transfixed until she whimpers, her hips thrusting without Sam attending to her. Sam responds to her call and slips his other hand back between her thighs. I can see him working two fingers into her over and over again. I can't look away.

'Mick, taste.' I snap. Mick slides forwards to grip Melanie's head in his hands and gently tilts her face toward him so that he can sip at her lips. I can tell he intends to be gentle but one taste and he's plundering her mouth. Sam's fingers slide faster inside her and as I watch he adds a third and lets his thumb start grazing her clit.

She bucks, still restrained in my arms, held open for her pleasure. Mick kisses her as Sam drops back down to lick at her bud while his fingers saw in and out of her.

'Come for us babygirl.' I growl in her ear. 'We want you to come all over us.'

My words are her undoing as she tears her face away from Mick to cry out. Sam growls his satisfaction, his tongue lapping at her as she shudders through her pleasure. Mick pulls her face back to him so he can keep sipping from her lips.

Sam eventually pulls back, a smirk on his face showing how proud he is of himself. Mick pulls back as well, dropping kisses onto her cheeks and brow as I slowly release her legs and her arms. She's limp in my lap, but not like before. She's relaxed and her eyes are returning to normal even as they drift close.

'Fuck.' Mick's low oath echoes the one in my mind. We all stare at her as she curls up between us all completely unbothered and satiated. She's still naked from the waist down and the sight of her thick thighs, so ready to be grabbed and squeezed, the dip of her hip, the curve of her ass. I'm drooling. I want it to be my turn to eat her.

'We should get her to bed.' Sam mumbles and I nod. She'll get cold down here.

'Mick?' I ask but he's already reaching down to lift her into a fireman's carry. Sam picks up her discarded pants and a towel.

'Sam, why are you drenched?' I ask.

'Jumped in the pool.' He doesn't elaborate. I raise my brow in question but he just nods at the girl now cradled against Mick's chest as explanation.

'Fair.' I nod as we all turn to leave the gym. John is standing in the doorway.

'I'm going to go out on a limb and say that I missed something.' He mutters taking in Sam in his wet shorts, me in my disheveled button down and trousers and a half naked Melanie cradled against Mick's chest.

'You missed a lot.' Sam shrugs as he leads the way. We've all been missing out on a lot.

Chapter 40. Melanie

I am never leaving this room again. Not until the day someone tells me I can move back into my old apartment and I never have to look any of these men in the eye ever again. Alternatively someone needs to tell me this has all been a dream.

A really really good dream.

I never really remember much from my heats but whether it was because it was just a heat spike or simply because it was so good, the feel of Sam eating me while I was held tight in George's arms and kissed by Mick was probably going to replay in my mind on my deathbed. I'd come so hard I'd fallen asleep instantly.

I could guess how I ended up tucked back into my bed. Mick. It could have been any of them but I had a feeling it was Mick. He seemed to have a thing for picking me up and throwing me over his shoulder.

Now I was tucked up in bed alone. The blankets pulled up over my head. And I was never leaving again. Ever. Could I be any more of a psycho?

Sam had been trying to do a workout and the sight of him and all his rippling muscles, his smell, his words assuring me he'd take care of me, it was too much. I'd dipped over into one of the heat spikes Mary had warned me about. I was gone. I was a writhing pool of need that the poor guys had to attend to. They didn't deserve this.

They didn't deserve being stuck with me by some stupid trick of biology. When Mary had told me this morning that we were scent sensitive it had sent me for a loop. But I'd been determined to make the best of it, for them. For eight years I'd been on my own, taking care of myself and I'd been fine. The way I figured it, I could just keep doing that but be here. Then the fact that I was foisted upon this lovely pack wouldn't be a problem.

Despite today's earlier meltdown I was still resolved to that plan. Once I got through this heat I'd get back on the suppressants, different ones the doctor approved of and then I would even be able to avoid situations like today.

In the meantime I needed food. I checked the time on the phone George had given me on the bedside table. Nearly midnight. Pathetic. I'd headed down to the gym a little before lunchtime which meant I'd been sleeping for close to twelve hours. I guess that at least explained why I was so hungry.

Climbing out of bed I appreciate the soft wine red pajamas I do not remember putting on. They were the same ones I'd woken up in yesterday. Someone must have helped dress me. Yet another horrifying thought.

I pad out into the hall followed by Whisper who immediately turns the opposite direction and taps at the backdoor.

'You need to go out buddy?' I whisper as I open the door for him. Whisper charges off to the right where the stairs to the backyard and grass are.

'Tap the door when you want back in.' I call after his retreating wiggling figure as I gently close the door and then walk quietly down the hall and into the kitchen. It's the middle of the night and I don't want to wake anyone but I'm starving. Leaving the light off, I navigate to the fridge using the glow that comes in from the street lights outside. Inside there are tons of containers that I'm guessing are leftovers. There's a covered plate and behind it is some small tubs of yoghurt. Not wanting to eat anything intended for someone else I snag one of the yoghurts and sit at the kitchen bench.

I peel off the lid and lick it clean of thick creamy goodness and hum to myself. I was even more hungry than I realised. Using my finger I scoop some of the yoghurt out of the container and into my mouth.

'I know we have spoons.' Mick's smokey voice drifts into the room and I jump.

'You scared me.' I chastise him as I place my yoghurt down to cover my heart with my hand. 'What are you doing up?'

'I heard you let Whisper out and I wanted to come check on you.'

'Oh, sorry. I didn't mean to wake you.' I apologise then wince when I see him lift his eyebrow.

'How many sorry's is that now?' He asks, leaning onto the counter next to me.

'I woke you.' I defend.

'Actually I was already awake. So no need to apologise. And even if I was sleeping, it still wouldn't be apology worthy, in my opinion. So how many is that?'

'Six.' I sigh.

'That's quite the bill you're wracking up.' He teases, nudging me with his shoulder. 'Did Whisper wake you up?'

'No that would be my stomach.' I lament as Mick rounds the bench to locate me a spoon and hands it over. I feel embarrassed to be caught eating with my fingers but I didn't want to go searching through drawers making unnecessary noise.

'We did debate waking you for dinner but decided we should let you sleep in the end. Don't you want something more proper though?'

'Yoghurts fine.' I say as I scoop a mouthful out of the little cup.

'John left you a plate in the fridge.'

'Oh, I saw that.' I nod.

'You don't want fried chicken? I'm loath to admit it but it's really good, even reheated. No one here could claim to be a great cook but John's fried chicken is probably the best thing any of us make.'

'I didn't think it was for me and I didn't want to eat someone else's leftovers.' I shrug.

'They were intended for you. John wanted to wake you, to impress you with his cooking prowess. He even took the plate to your room hoping the smell of it would wake you but all it got him was Whisper's attention. John ended up taking him for a long walk.'

'He didn't have to do that.' I grumble.

'He wanted to.' Mick states a hint of censure in his voice.

'Oh. Okay.' I finish my yoghurt

'Still hungry?' Mick asks.

'I'm fine.' My stomach gurgles as the yoghurt reaches it.

'You sure?'

KNOT FOR REAL

Chapter 41. Mick

Clearly she's still hungry. My alpha is growling at me to hold her down and force feed her a three course meal. I'd settle for just a few more mouthfuls.

'I could make you some eggs?'

'No don't go to any trouble.' She seems aghast at the very thought.

'At least eat some of the food John left for you. It would make him happy.' I offer.

'Okay.' She nods. I retrieve the plate from the fridge, and turn the light on over the stove as I remove the wrap. I could turn on the overhead lights but I'm kind of enjoying the feeling of secrecy the darkness is giving us.

I lean back on the kitchen counter to contemplate her while the food spins in the microwave. She's fiddling with the spoon in her now empty yoghurt tub. Her hair is a wild mess of curls. And I was right, the red looks utterly decadent against her pale skin. Like she really is made of strawberries and cream. I could easily eat her up.

Flashes from this afternoon flick through my mind. The taste of her slick on her lips as I plundered her mouth. The sight of Sam buried between her thighs held open by George. She was stunning, splayed out between us.

A gentle tap sounds down the hall.

'That will be Whisper.' She mumbles, jumping down from her stool and skittering away. I can hear her as she lets him in and as always he puts himself back to bed.

I was hoping that this afternoon would have brought her out of whatever funk she was in this morning but if anything she seems even more uncomfortable.

I wish we could just tell her that we're a scent match. That we all wanted her before we even knew she was an omega. I want to show her to the omega suite. I want to bite her, and let our souls entwine so she can feel it. So she can feel how much we want her and so I can get inside that head of hers. But I'll settle for getting her fed.

'I'm back.' She mumbles from her seat at the kitchen bench behind me. I realise the microwave has stopped and now I'm simply staring at a black door. I yank it open, test her food and then spin around and place the plate in front of her.

'You don't have to eat all of it, but as much as you can. You had a big day.'

'Hardly.' She snorts as she starts on her food. 'I let the doctor prod me, made an arse out of myself and then slept for twelve hours. That's not a hard day in my book. Twelve plus hours of slinging coffees is a hard day. Today was just pathetic.'

'Pathetic?' I know she works hard but thinking of her on her feet for twelve hours in that coffee shop makes me flinch. She needs a foot massage.

'Yeah, all I've done since I've got here is sleep and let you guys feed me. I'd say that's pretty pathetic. Even before you take into consideration the other thing.' I slide onto the stool one over from her. She's sitting with her left leg hanging down and her right leg resting on the stool between us.

'May I?' I gesture to her foot where it hangs on the edge of the second stool.

'May you? What?' She asks, her face full of genuine confusion as she picks apart the fried chicken with her fingers between mouthfuls of green beans and carrots.

'Foot massage?' I offer.

'You don't have to.' She grumbles, pulling her foot down so that she's perched on the stool properly again.

'I know. Indulge me.' I ask. She hesitates and I'm about a second away from falling to the floor and crawling under the bench to massage her feet from below when she slowly lifts her leg again and extends it back towards me.

'I haven't had a pedicure lately, they might be gross.'

'Do you like pedicures?' I ask. Instead of screaming to the heavens that even if her feet were calloused potatoes I wouldn't give a shit.

'Yes. Mostly I just do mine myself but every now and then when the store was having a good month I'd treat myself to a pedicure. I don't know what it is about those big massage chairs, coffee in hand, feet in water, but it makes me feel like a princess.' Noted. Tomorrow I would have to find out what was the best pedicure place in the area.

'I've never had a pedicure. I've been to the podiatrist but I have a feeling it's different.' She smiles at me but then her eyes close and she moans as my thumb digs into the arch of her foot. 'Good?'

'Amazing.' She mumbles, shoveling more food into her mouth. 'What did you go to the podiatrist for?'

'Ingrown toenail. Sexy right?' I tease.

'Reassuring actually, it's nice to know at least one of you four are actually human.' She groans as my fingers continue to push through the arch of her foot.

'What do you mean?' I ask.

'Just that you all seem so perfect and put together. It's nice to know that you have flaws. It's less intimidating. Makes you seem human.' She murmurs.

'We're very human.' I offer, surprised she feels that way.

'You're sure?' She teases.

'Definitely.' I nod dramatically.

'So you get sick?' She quizzes me, her dimples flashing as she indicates her pointer finger like she's counting.

'Yep and George turns into a giant snivelling baby, it's horrible.' I offer.

'You get in accidents?' She holds up a second finger.

'John does. I've seen him legitimately just walk into a door.' I chuckle at the memory. He wasn't even texting or on his phone, just lost in thought.

'And you have the toenail so that just leaves Sam. What's his flaw?' She holds up a fourth finger.

'I think I should let you figure that out for yourself. But I'll give you a hint...' I pause dramatically. '... follow your nose.'

'What?'

'That's all you get. Other foot please.' She spins on her stool to give me her other foot. 'So does that help you to relax around all of us?'

'A little. My human is always showing, it's nice to think you're not all perfect all the time. Just most of the time.'

'Far from it. Are we intimidating you?' The question slides off my tongue easily but I feel it choke me.

'A little. Not like I find you scary. Just the four of you... it's a lot.' I nod. We were a lot and she'd been through a lot which is why we were going slow. 'I mean, I come out of nowhere and end up shacking up in your house. It's hard not to feel like an intruder.'

'You know we were looking for an omega. George had us on this terrible dating app thing.' I want her to know we were ready. That we wanted someone.

'Yeah, I know. John got courting gifts from my store all the time. And Sam said something about it the other day. How you were taking a break from that?'

'Yeah, it became a bit much.' I offer. That was the polite way of saying we'd lost hope and the energy to keep going.

'Too much, I get that.' Her shoulder slumps dramatically. I don't like it.

'What's wrong?' I ask as I reach for her chin to bring her eyes back to mine.

'Nothing. I just... I worry.' She exhales.

'About?' I let go of her chin to focus my attention back on her foot. I can't keep staring into her eyes or I'll kiss her.

'You guys were looking for something. And you couldn't find it. I guess I just worry about what you were looking for. In an omega. You know?' I sigh with relief. If she's thinking like this, maybe she's thinking about being ours.

'I don't think we knew what we were looking for. But if I had to give it a word I guess I'd say we were looking for the perfect fit.' And we couldn't find it because we hadn't found her.

'Perfect fit?' She asks.

'Yeah. Someone who could fit in with all of us in our different ways. You know what they say, there's no such thing as perfect, but there's a perfect for you.' She laughs at my recitation of the make up brand's famous slogan.

'Perfect for you.' She mumbles at me.

'Yeah.' I smile at her. She's definitely perfect for me.

KNOT FOR REAL

Chapter 42. Melanie

I wake up with a new determination. I set an early alarm to do what I do best, make coffee and food. The guys stumble into the kitchen not long after I start, and they find me.

Not the house troll I had become. I was as put together as I could be in another pair of leggings and the nicest of the shirts. I had my hair pulled back. And thanks to the additions to Mick's grocery order yesterday I even had some make up on. I looked more myself than I had since I'd arrived. I was determined.

I served them each their favourite coffee along with some of my sweet potato hashbrowns with eggs and bacon. When everyone was fed I cleared the table and did the dishes. I put on a load of laundry, some of my things along with household stuff. Then I took Whisper out on a long walk so John wouldn't get stuck doing it again.

They wanted someone perfect, well that wasn't me. But I could make myself better. They were matched with me thanks to biology or fate or whatever you wanted to call it and I was going to be the best damn omega I could for them. My mother's voice was already echoing through my mind and I was weirdly grateful for it. She always had a long list of ways I could improve and it gave me somewhere to start.

I tracked down some paper and a pen and was now sitting in the corner of my room brainstorming with Whisper. John was in the living room playing video games, George had disappeared to wherever it was he disappeared to. Sam was upstairs in his room, reading I think. And Mick had told me he was headed to his workshop in the garage. That last one made me curious and I'd wanted to invite myself down and see the space but that would have violated rule number one I'd thought of.

Never insert myself. I was going to stay out of the way and unless they specifically asked me to go somewhere or do something with them. My goal was to be as unintrusive as possible. Which led perfectly to rule number two.

Don't be needy. This one felt harder. I knew I didn't actually need them. I'd been getting by fine without them for years. But off the suppressants and surrounded by their smells my omega instincts were waking up. I was loath to walk past John where he was gaming and not dive into his lap for a cuddle. Sam smiled at me earlier and I wanted to climb him like a tree. I'd even felt the urge to ask if Mick could wear me like a backpack all day so I didn't have to be alone. And that would have conflicted with rule three.

Be as helpful as possible. I was going to make sure that I cooked and made their favourite coffees. And anything else that sprang to mind that felt like it was making their lives easier. That way I wouldn't be a mooch. And that was rule number four.

Don't let them waste money on me. I'd pay them back for the clothes and other things that they'd had to buy me. I had money. Sure I wasn't rolling in it right now but I would find a way. But this is where I had gotten stuck. What else could I do?

Four rules didn't feel like enough. It had to be five. Five rules made it feel real and important. I reached over to scratch Whisper behind the ears.

'You got any ideas bud?' He lifted his head from his bed and shook. 'I'll take that as a no.'

I knew what my mother would say and I knew she was probably right. These were four of the fittest men I'd ever met so with a dramatic sigh I added rule five.

Lose weight.

I slipped the paper and pen into the weird stretchy pocket on the side of my pants and headed downstairs.

I wanted to take a nap. But I could hear my mother's voice in my head teasing me, her 'sleepy Mellon' she used to call me, like that was a thing. Well not anymore. I was going to resist my urge to nap and I was going to work on the whole Mellon thing.

I may have learned to be comfortable in my body but the thought of these four regretting being matched with me was more than I could handle. It might take awhile but I knew how to do it, I'd done it before. Cut out all the dairy, no carbs, stick to lean protein and leafy greens. I'd make sure the guys never had to be ashamed of me. I'd never be skinny but I could be leaner. And so I head to the gym.

I jump on the treadmill as soon as I walk through the door. A light run to burn some calories, then I'd stretch out to keep the cramps at bay like Mary had said. Until I got my toys and made sure I could take care of myself I had to make sure I at least didn't show I was in pain. Hopefully if I could get through all of that I could even do some light weights. Build some muscle.

'What are you doing?' Sam's voice calls from behind me. By the time I grip the machine and turn to look at him he's in front of me turning the machine off. 'You already took Whisper out.'

'A little extra cardio never hurt anyone.' I offer.

'It could hurt you. Mary made it clear you are meant to be resting. Your body needs to heal and prepare for your heat to return. You need snacks and naps, not whatever this is.' He gestures at the machine.

'I'm fine.' I shrug.

'Melanie.' I love the way he says my name, making each syllable clear. Mel- ah-knee. The only problem is it seems to mean that he's angry at me.

'What?' There's a tremble in my voice as I suppress my whine. I can handle anything, but alpha anger always makes me nervous. And without my suppressants I can feel my thighs vibrate with the desire to kneel. To fall down in front of him and just start apologising for everything I could have ever done that was wrong.

'Why are you down here?' He asks the question like it's causing him pain .

'To work out.' I offer. It seems pretty obvious.

'Why?' He repeats his question

'Why do you work out?' I hedge.

'Because I have a lot of frustration and repressed rage. You?' I wasn't expecting such an honest answer.

'Ah...' My voice trails off. How do I explain?

'Tell me.' He growls.

'I just want to make sure I'm the best I can be.' There that's the truth.

'Say more.' He grunts out.

'Just, you know. I guess I wasn't worried before. But now. With you guys...' I gesture at him by way of explanation but clearly I'm failing as confusion stitches his eyebrow. So I push on. 'Last night, when I was eating dinner, Mick joined me, he was saying how you guys had been looking for someone perfect. So I just figured I'd try and make myself better.'

'He said WHAT?' Sam yells. I want to drop to the floor and whine.

'He was helping me. I get it. It will take time but... where are you going?' Sam marches away from me towards the stairs but he doesn't go up them. Instead he turns right down the tiny hallway I've yet to explore and disappears from sight.

I run after him as I hear a door crash open and a loud bang. I race through the gap, ignoring the door hanging off its hinges in time to see Sam punch Mick in the face. We're in what is clearly his workshop with tools, computers and whiteboards in every direction. But I don't have time to appreciate the fullness of the space because as Mick falls to the ground Sam climbs on top of him.

Sam swings again but Mick blocks it and then they're gripping each other's arms and rolling from side to side. Mick ends up on top pushing Sam down into the floor.

'Calm down.' Mick screams at Sam, spit flying from his mouth.

'Fuck you.' Sam yells up at him as he wiggles his legs in a weird kind of kick and flings Mick to the side.

'What is wrong with you?' Mick yells as Sam spins around and tries to hit him again. Mick springs to his feet and dodges out of the way.

'What the fuck did you say to her?' Sam demands.

'What?' Mick's confused eyes swing to me in the doorway. Sam doesn't repeat his question. He lunges again and tackles Mick at the waist bringing him to the floor.

'What the hell?' George yells pushing past me and diving onto the other men. 'Break it up.'

'What's happening?' It's John at my side in the doorway. I look at him as I feel my eyes fill with tears. The anger radiating off the wrestling men is making me dizzy.

'It's all my fault.' I whine as my vision blurs.

Chapter 43. John

The image replays in my mind again. Melanie's eyes filled with tears, her skin pale as she fell into my arms.

It's all my fault. She'd whined as she passed out.

But it wasn't. It was ours.

Things calmed down quickly once she collapsed. The guys abandoning their testosterone fueled pissing match to make sure she was okay. Once we started talking instead of the guys swinging at each other it had all been sorted out in a few seconds.

Last night while Mick made sure she had some proper food he'd tried to convince her she was already perfect for us. And failed. Because according to the list we found in her pocket she was trying to lose weight, and not be a burden and something else. I didn't get to finish reading before George ripped it up and threw the pieces away with a growl.

All morning she had smelled wrong. She was so bubbly and energetic none of us wanted to get in her way but I don't think any of us believed she was happy. Now we knew what she was thinking, we just didn't know why.

And we weren't going to get any clarity until Melanie was Melanie again.

Right now she was her omega. And while she was possibly the sweetest cutest thing in the world she was also clearly terrified.

Mary came by for her scheduled lunchtime check in just as Melanie had started to come to. The only problem was, it wasn't her. And it wasn't a heat spike. It was like Melanie was gone, her omega had taken over and the only thing she wanted to do was run and hide. She'd settled in her room with the doctor but when any one of us came in she dived under the blankets and refused to come out.

Which is why I was now sitting on the floor opposite her door with a pile of books. I had Emma, her dedicated reread of the month and a bunch of other titles that were newer. I had no idea what she may or may not have already read. The plan had been to give them to her at dinner but that hadn't happened. And then she'd been so bouncy and busy this morning I figured it could wait.

I also had a tea tray with a mocha, just the way she liked them and some cookies I'd just finished baking when the fight broke out.

'You can go in now.' Mary speaks from above me as she exits Melanie's room.

'She's scared of us, isn't she?' I ask, defeat etched in my voice.

'It's more just that she's scared. Her omega has definitely been poorly treated in the past and as a result anger seems to be a trigger for protection.'

'I don't understand.' I groan.

'Our second natures, our animalistic selves, they protect us. Those instincts aren't just there to give us entertainment value, they're an evolutionary strategy to help us stay safe and find community. And make more of us. But everyone focuses on that last one a little too much.'

'It's a pretty important part.' I shrug.

'But it's not all of it. Melanie got scared today and so her omega forced her way out to try and protect her. In this case that meant hiding.'

'What do we do?' George calls out, coming down the hall towards the doctor.

'Make her feel safe. I'd suggest no more fighting in front of her. Get her talking more. Telling you what she wants. And no more over exercising. Fifteen minute walk in the morning and afternoon and the stretches, that's the upper limit.'

'We can handle that.' I nod as I stand.

'Good, now point me in the direction of the other two so I can patch them up. John, you can go in. She's mostly her again. Kind of slipping in and out. But she did ask for you.' She practically shoves me toward the door as she heads towards the kitchen with George where Sam and Mick are waiting with a bloody nose and a swollen lip.

I pick up my tea tray with the books in a bag on my shoulder and knock on her door. There's a harumph sound which I take to mean come in. I can't actually see her but the pile of blankets moves slightly. I put down the tray, place the books on her bedside table and take a seat in the blue armchair still next to the bed.

'Melanie?'

'Yes?' Her voice sounds strong even though it's muffled by the pile of blankets.

'I have cookies and a mocha.'

'Okay.'

'Do you want to come out of there?'

'Not really.'

'Do you want me to come in?' She doesn't answer. I wish we were bonded so I could hear what she's thinking. 'Melanie?'

'Yes.'

'Is that yes you want me to come in or yes you heard me ask that question.'

'In.' Her voice is so high I have a feeling it's her omega instincts answering. I carefully lift one side of the blanket and lay down on the bed. Then I shuffle forward, pulling more blanket over me until I find her. Barely any light gets through so I can't make out her face, only her shape.

'You okay?' I ask.

'Better.' She whispers as her hand reaches out to rest on my chest.

'Sorry about their fighting.'

'I'm the one who should be sorry.' She moans rolling away from me.

'Who did you sucker punch?' I ask in confusion. Sam was the only one who needed to apologise in my eyes.

'It was something I said that made them fight.' Technically true but not the truth.

'Those two were fighting each other long before you came along.' I offer. I reach out gently and slide my arms around her so that I can pull her against my chest. I can barely breathe under here but I'm not complaining because not only is the bed soaked in her perfectly sweet strawberries there's also hints of all of us in here.

'They shouldn't fight over me.' She harumphs as I hold her.

'What should they fight over?' I ask.

'Nothing.' She sighs dramatically against my chest and I can feel the fabric ruffle with her breath.

'Say more.' I prod her to keep talking.

'Sam says that too. *Say more.*' She imitates Sam's voice, making me laugh.

'We all do. It's something George started. When we were first pack we were getting in lots of fights. Not always fist fights like today but arguing all the time. George realised that a lot of it was just misunderstandings. Often we'd fight and eventually we'd realise we were on the same side and didn't actually disagree. So he came up with this idea, or rule or whatever. Whenever one of us feels like we are upset or confused, before we start yelling we say 'say more'.'

'You want to yell?' Of course she would focus on that.

'No I'm just confused.'

'Oh.' She seems confused as well. 'Can I smell chocolate?'

'Yes cookies and a mocha, you want?' I feel it as she nods tentatively and I gently peel back some of the blankets and slide out the top of the bed to prop myself on the pillows. She does the same beside me. I reach over and carefully lift the drink from her bed side and hand it to her.

'Thanks.' She smiles up at me as she sips. She's very much Melanie now but I can see what Mary meant about her omega lingering. I feel like I'm being watched by her as well. One wrong move and Melanie will be gone again.

'Cookie as well?'

'In a little bit.' She turns to put the mocha on her other side table before turning back to me. 'Are they still mad?'

'Sam and Mick?' She nods. 'Nah, they've taken plenty of swings at each other in the past, they get over it pretty quickly.'

'I mean at me?' She grumbles.

'At you?' I'm confused.

'Yeah, are they still mad at me?' She mumbles

'No one was ever mad at you.' I almost yell but manage to keep control. 'Not even a little bit. Worried about you, yes. Sick over fighting in front of you, yes. Embarrassed by our pack antics, big yes for me. But no one is or was ever mad at you.'

'I upset Sam.' I try not to roll my eyes.

'Sam upset himself.' I point out.

'It won't happen again.' She shakes her head as she nestles into her pillow.

'It probably will. Sam's a hot head. We tease him about being full of hot air all the time for more reasons than one.' I try to tease.

'I was just trying to be better.' Her voice is imploring me to understand.

'Yeah I know, we may have found your list.' I feel her embarrassment as her strawberry scent rots.

'Oh.' Her soft word makes me want to scream. She felt a need to write a list of rules so as not to bother us when literally all any of us wanted was to be needed by her. We all need to have a proper talk, and soon.

'I went to the bookstore yesterday.' Is it tacky to distract someone from their sadness with material possessions, yes. But watching her eyes light up is so worth it. I reach for the bag before dumping out the books on the bed. 'I got a selection so you can pick based on your mood.'

'Good choices.' She coos, turning over the books in her hand.

'I even got you another copy of Emma.' I say as I dig through the pile for the book in question and hold it up to show her. 'Which I'm embarrassed to say I've never read.'

'Really? It's my favourite.'

'I remember.' I smile as I push some hair back from her face. 'Shall we read it together?'

'That will never work, I'm a fast reader, waiting for you to finish each page will kill me.' Her eyes widen in mock horror although I sense some of it is real.

'I'm pretty fast myself. But how about I read it to you.' I offer.

'Really?'

'Get comfy.' I say as I hand her a cookie and then settle back against the pillows. She curls into my side resting her head on my shoulder as I find the first page. 'Ready?'

'Yes.' She mumbles around a mouth full of cookie.

'Okay then.' I think I'm in heaven. The comfortable bed, drenched in her scent, with her warmth pressed up against me and my food in her mouth. Yeah this is perfect. 'Emma Woodhouse, handsome, clever and rich, with a comfortable home and happy disposition seemed to unite some of the best blessings of existence...'

KNOT FOR REAL

Chapter 44. Melanie

My shop is a disaster. And this was it cleaned up. When George had asked me to come out with him today I'd assumed we'd go straight to the store. But first we stopped by to check on the new glass window at Brian and Dan's recyclable art studio. It was lovely to see them and incredible to see how far they'd come on the window so quickly. Then George had to have a meeting so I went with him and waited in his office reading one of the books John got me. Then we had lunch which George seemed to manage to make last for two hours and so it was close to three by the time we got to the bookstore. Which I now realise was George's tactic to let the cleaning crew go through first. But it was unnecessary because my shop is still a disaster.

The giant burnt hole in the middle of the floorboards draws my attention. While much of it has been cleaned there's still ash and soot hanging all around the space. And all the books are ruined. Some are water damaged from where the fire department sprayed. Others are simply so soaked in smoke and ash they would never be sellable. I'd salvage what I could but it wouldn't be a lot. Maybe I could do a fire damage sale and everything smokey was half off.

'I wish you'd seen it when it was whole.' I murmur to George. He's still standing by the door, his eyebrows stitched together in concentration.

'I can see what it's supposed to be.' He states firmly.

'Not the same.' I shrug as I move behind the counter and head upstairs to my apartment. The smokey smell is stronger up here even if all the damage was only to the shop. I brace myself as I reach the top of the stairs and take a deep breath as I open the door. The whine that slips out of my throat is one of pure distress.

'Sh, it's okay.' George's voice rumbles against my back as he presses himself into me and begins to purr. 'We'll fix it, I promise.'

I nod my agreement and try not to get distracted by the sheer emptiness of my space. Someone has been through and taken all the soft furnishing to get washed, the counters have been wiped down, every window is open to let out the smell but it's still strong. All of my art is gone, I assume to be cleaned and the barrenness of the walls kills me. I head to my room. My main goal in coming here today was to pick up a few of my personal items. Some of my toys for obvious reasons but also some of my own clothes. I am once again in leggings and a t-shirt and while it's comfortable I long for my dresses, and jeans.

I head into my room and get to work. Grabbing my bag out of the closet, flipping it open and filling it up. I grab clothes from my previously clean pile on the chair in the corner, knowing that everything will have to be washed again. Which reminds me, I still have clothes in the washing machine. I go to head that way but George is blocking my path in the doorway.

'Are you okay?' He asks.

'Fine.' I smile as I push past him. I'm not fine. I'm devastated. I feel like my insides are trying to squirm out of me and I want to scream and cry but I've had plenty of experience squashing those feelings.

I dump my laundry out of the machine which, thankfully, I never turned on. Despite being my dirty laundry they are now the cleanest thing I own since the smoke smell apparently didn't penetrate the machine. I head back to my room and dump the pile of dirty clothes straight into my suitcase. Gross yes, but efficient.

George is sitting on my bed looking around the space. It's completely stripped of my linens meaning it's just a bare mattress in my old four-poster frame. It looks naked and barren without my many colourful pillows. Old and gross when compared to the gorgeous perfectly dressed man sitting on it, staring at me.

'I can send someone for all your other things.' George states calmly.

'That's okay, I don't have a lot I need to bring. Just want some of my clothes and my personal things.'

'Okay.'

'Actually do you mind if I have some privacy?'

'Of course. I'll wait in the living room?' He offers and I nod. He immediately stands. But he doesn't leave. Instead he walks straight to me sliding his hand along my neck to the back of my head. 'Anything you need.'

His whispered words caress my forehead but he doesn't kiss my crown like Mick does. He just breathes in my hair as he tucks me beneath his chin for a moment before he departs.

I hear his footsteps echo down the hall. And I shove my hands over my mouth to muffle the cry that comes out of me. Forcing the tears back I head over to my drawers, throw my personal items into the mix of my suitcase, throw some more clothes on top and then zip the damn thing shut.

That's it, that's my whole world. Yes I have books and records out in the living room I'll want with me eventually but I don't need any of it now. The guys have better everything anyway. Better kitchenware, better furniture, better art.

I steady myself, take a deep breath and push my bag out into the hall and into the living room where I find George inspecting my little balcony over the courtyard.

'Ready.' I say. Originally I planned to spend longer here, organising and cleaning but since so much of that was already done and seeing the space empty was making me feel hideous all I really want to do is go back to their pack house and take a nap.

'You built a beautiful life here.' George murmurs from the open door.

'Thanks.' I shrug. I thought it was beautiful. And most important to me it was all mine. But it's gone now. I knew I'd fix the store eventually and all my possessions would be cleaned and returned but I didn't think it would ever feel the same.

'What do you want to do now?' He questions gently. I know he had contractors through today and I should ask about those and make plans but it's all too much. I don't want to do anymore today. I'm too tired.

'Go back to your place.' I shrug. What else was there to do? They were stuck with me after all. But George seems to ruffle at the assumption and I quickly amend. 'Unless you need to go somewhere else. Whatever you need.'

'No!' It isn't a bark but there's power in his voice. 'What do you need?'

'Nothing.' I shrug.

'You're telling me you can just walk through this space, see all the damage downstairs and be fine?' His breath is becoming ragged.

'No but it's going to be fine.' I step forward to place my hand on his chest. 'Right?'

'Yes.' He grunts out.

'Then I trust you.' I smile up at him. It's the truth. I'm sad and I'm hurting but I do actually trust that he'll help me.

'Fuck.' He groans, stroking my neck again as his hand slides to the back of my head, his fingers threading through my hair. But this time he doesn't rest his head against mine or pull me to his chest. His fingers grip the roots of my hair as he tugs my head backwards and his lips descend till his open mouth is resting just a millimeter above my own. 'Say that again.'

My brain is scrambling as my body reacts. I feel my slick pouring out of me, my perfume explodes around us and he groans. My breaths come in soft pants pushing my chest against his creating delicious friction. I can't remember what I said before. What does he want me to say? I think hard.

'I trust you.' I mumble, my lips bumping into his as I say the words.

'Good girl.'

KNOT FOR REAL

Chapter 45. George

I shouldn't be doing this. We'd all agreed to keep our desire for this woman on the backburner while she healed and rested. But I can't.

All day I've been with her, inhaling her scent, receiving her smiles. And now this.

Her sad strength as she walks through her space that someone else destroyed is killing me. I can see what the space was. How beautiful and colourful and bold it would have been. But the cleaning crew has taken all of her things away and the space is bare, empty and I can feel how it's cutting her open.

I can feel the tears she's holding back and it's killing me. I want to take away her hurt. I want to fill her with so much pleasure she can't even think.

'Melanie.' I whisper her name against her lips as I let myself crash into her. I know I've tasted her lips before but not like this. This is not just about her needs but about desire. I want her. And I want her to want me. I let my lips brush against hers gently as her strawberry flavour burst across my tongue. I tug against the hair in my grip, pulling her head back as my other hand pulls like a vice against her waist sealing our bodies together. I can't get close enough.

I plunder her mouth, breathing deep the smell we make together. Whiskey and strawberries. Bitter and sweet. My fingers dig into the fleshy give of her hips as I move to push her against the wall. I need her captive, to feel like I can reach every part of her and she can't stop me.

With her sandwiched between me and the wall I release my hand from her hair and the other from her waist so that I can glide my hands gently down her arms. Gripping her hands I lift them above her head, holding her gaze as my thigh pushes between hers.

'Okay?' I ask. She nods at me sweetly, her eyes confused and clouded with desire. She's still here but I can see her omega pushing forward, her pupils growing. But I want her. I want my Melanie. I need her omega to trust me with her. 'Stay with me. I won't hurt her. Let her stay.'

I don't know how I knew those would be the right words but it works. She nods at me and her pupils contract, bringing forth the bold blue I have come to love. I move so that both her hands are held in my left grip as I glide my other hand down her arm, along her ribcage and to her hips. I let my fingers dig into the thick flesh as I slide my grip to her back side and pull her up. Pulling her against me. Forcing her to widen her stance till I can feel her heat on my thigh. Her feet lift off the ground as the weight of her settles against my thigh.

'Good girl.' I murmur as I feel her hips rock against me. She's riding my thigh, all of her weight pushing her heat against me and it feels like heaven. I slide my hand up till my thumb can brush against her nipple through her thin shirt and bra, leaning down to press my forehead to hers as she whimpers. 'You feel so good.'

'Thank you Daddy.' I freeze. All the blood in my body instantly boils as my eyes close and my jaw snaps shut. I try and take a breath as I feel my alpha thrash against me. He wants me to lose control so he can take his woman, his omega. But not today. The rut blockers allow me to shove him back. I breathe roughly as I open my eyes.

I'm so hot right now I want to rip these stupid leggings off her body and bury myself so deep inside her I can't tell where my body ends and hers begins. I want to pleasure her till she screams. And then I want to keep going till she can't scream anymore. Her voice and her body, worn out and spent on my dick.

My gaze crashes into hers so I can begin to tell her all the filthy things I want to do but I freeze. Melanie has unshed tears in her eyes.

'Babygirl, no, what's wrong?' I plead even as I lean in to kiss her so that she can't answer me. I need her softness, her flavour to ground me. Her lips move against mine but they're tentative and slow. 'Tell me.'

I pull back to stare into her eyes. The tears are gone but she's nervous, I can feel it. She's tight and tense where moments ago she was soft hot butter.

'I didn't mean to.' She mumbles. Her eyes pleading with me to understand. But I don't understand.

'What didn't you mean to do?' I ask leaning in to press gentle kisses to each of her cheeks as my free hand plays with the dip of her waist. Her hands are still held above her in my grip and I feel her fingers twist with uncertainty.

'Call you... that.' Her gaze drops from mine as she speaks and I can feel it. The shame. It's radiating off her, her sweet strawberry smell is bitter like burnt fruit. All the heat leaves my system.

'You're apologising for calling me daddy?' Her face tips forward to bury in my chest as I ask the question and so I feel rather than see her nod. 'Why?'

'I know it's gross.' She speaks into my shirt. And I growl. I can't hold it back. I see the vibration of my chest ripple across her skin. It's fascinating to watch. I want to growl against her and watch the sounds I make flutter the skin of her breasts and shake her hips.

'I like it.' I whisper into her hair. 'When you called me, I almost lost it.'

Her head pulls back from my chest finally and I look into her eyes. I see confusion and surprise.

'Oh.' She mumbles. 'I thought you were going to get mad.'

'Mad?' Why would I get mad?

'Or make fun of me.' She continues like I didn't speak.

'What?' Now I'm confused.

'Well that's what happened...' Her voice trails off as her eyes widen with fear. I don't blame her. I don't need her to finish the sentence. I understand what she's telling me. Someone has mocked her for a perfectly innocent honorific during sex.

'When?' I demand.

'A long time ago.' She whispers gently, like that makes it better.

'Who?' She doesn't answer me and I think I know why. But I need her to say it. 'Who told you it was gross?'

'My pack.' I stiffen at her referring to anyone but us as her pack.

'Assholes.' I grumble as I lean back from her, letting her feet slide down to the ground again. I release her hip so I can reach up and take both her hands in mine as I lower them and step back. Her hair is mussed, her lips red from my savage kisses, her sleeve is pushed to the side and hanging off her shoulder. I gently lift it back into place, letting my fingers graze her collar bones as I do.

'Thanks.' She mumbles towards my fingers not looking at me. 'Sorry.'

'For what?' I ask.

'Just sorry.' She mumbles.

'Well then how many does that make?' I ask.

'Seven.' She sighs. Her shoulders slump as she continues to stare at the center of my chest. I want her eyes but I don't want to lift her chin. I need her to want to look at me.

'Come on, we need to go.' I grumble as I pull away and tug her to follow.

'Back to your place?' She asks and I sigh. Our place, I want to correct her but we're still trying not to rush her.

'Yes. We need to talk.' I grunt out as I grab her suitcase and tug it along with us.

'That sounds bad.'

'It's not. I just have some questions that I think the other guys are going to want to hear the answers to as well.'

KNOT FOR REAL

Chapter 46. Melanie

'What are you two doing home already?' Mick demands as we come in the front door. He's holding a cardboard box and wearing what appears to be sweatpants and nothing else. My god his arms are wider than my head.

'Need to talk.' George bites out behind me. He's angry. The whole drive here he kept twisting his hands against the steering wheel like he was trying to strangle it.

'Pack meeting?' Mick asks and George must nod because Mick hurries off. George steers me towards the dining table and seats me at the head before taking a seat on my right. I don't have time to ask him what's going on before Mick, Sam and John all file in behind us. Mick has put on a shirt but I notice all the guys are wearing ratty clothes. It's only just past four in the afternoon, why are they home?

'What's going on?' Mick asks as he leans in to kiss my head and takes the seat opposite George. John's sitting next to him on my left. Sam beside George on my right. Everyone is silent and it makes me tense. This feels like a business meeting. One I'm not prepared for.

'I kissed Melanie.' George says it like he's committed a crime. And judging by the other guys' expressions he has.

'It was your rule.' Sam slaps the back of his hand against George's shoulder.

'I know.' George sighs. 'It was a mistake.'

I visibly flinch. A mistake? It was a mistake to kiss me. Damn. Well I guess I know how he feels about being scent sensitive to me. I didn't know I was still holding out hope but I feel the last ember of it die in my chest.

'No, sweetness.' Mick's voice pulls my attention as his hand reaches out and clasps mine where it sits on the table. 'Not like that.'

I nod. I don't know what he means. And I don't really care. George regrets kissing me. Just like they probably all regret being matched with me. It's just one big, 'wish this wasn't happening' party. And I get it. No one wants to be bound to someone without choice. Particularly if that someone is me.

'So what does this mean going forward?' John's question is directed to George.

'That's not why we're talking.' George shrugs. 'Melanie said something and I wanted to ask her about it but I realised you would all want to know as well.'

'What did she say?' Mick questions, his hand now massaging mine. He does stuff like this whenever he's near, so I've gotten used to it but right now it's almost distracting. George may not have enjoyed it but my hormones had run riot when he kissed me. And they hadn't settled. And Mick pushing all the tension out of my hand with his gentle calloused fingers was not helping my body calm down.

'Daddy.' I whisper the word. 'I called George Daddy. It just slipped out.'

Their soft smells explode around me. Where a moment ago they were faint, maybe a little bitter with concern, suddenly they're strong. I feel like I'm taking a bath in their scents and I whimper.

'Say it again.' Sam growls and I glance up from the table to see his eyes dilate and his breath shaking his chest.

'Don't.' George barks as I open my mouth to do as I was told. 'Please.'

I nod as he softens his command. He doesn't want to hear me say it again.

'Why?' Mick demands. His fingers have stilled against my hand mid massage.

'We need to talk.' George grunts, I can feel his alpha radiating off him, forcing the others to settle. 'She apologised.'

'She does that a lot.' Sam shrugs.

'She apologised for calling me Daddy.' George explains and I feel myself sink lower in my chair. Maybe I could turn into water and puddle under the table. 'That's what we need to talk about. Melanie darling?'

My eyes bounce to his as he calls for my attention. His eyes are soft, a concerned smile on his face as I look up at him. I can feel the others' eyes on me. Are they disgusted? Or just embarrassed by me? Sam seemed to like it before but now he's tense with anger. Maybe I imagined it.

'Yes?' I ask.

'Can you tell us what happened with... your other pack?' I can't imagine what he wants to know, it was so long ago.

'They died.' I explain. 'Before we could bond.'

'How?' John's voice drifts from the end of the table and I turn to look at him.

'Car accident, on the way to our bonding ceremony.'

'Fuck.' Sam swears his head falling into his hands.

'But before that?' George prompts.

'Before that what?'

'You said you were sorry because you knew it was gross, you said they'd told you that.' I'm already nodding as he speaks.

'Yes, during my heat, apparently I kept asking for things they didn't like.'

'Like what?' Mick's usually smokey voice is like gravel.

'I kept referring to them as Daddy or Sir instead of their names. And I asked...' My voice trails off. I know they need to know but I don't want to say it. 'I asked them to spank me, and hold me... tight.'

'And they told you that was wrong?' Sam's voice is incredulous.

'They said it was an omega's job to present and take what they gave, not make demands and be gross.'

'Anything else?' George asks.

'No.'

'Anyone else?' Mick asks.

'No just them. And the heat clinic.'

'You used heat clinics?' John's shock is almost comical.

'Not regularly. Just once.' I shudder a little at the thought. 'I don't remember it.'

'Any of it?' Mick urges me on.

'I...' Words fail me. No one ever wants the details. In the past when I say I don't remember, people just leave it at that. 'I didn't enjoy it.'

'Why not?' Mick prompts gently.

'I wasn't enjoying myself. I wasn't... wet. I kept running from the volunteers until one of them grabbed me, accidentally spanked me, when he was trying to get me to hold still. Then I perfumed and they realised I liked that.'

'That's not abnormal.' Mick's voice reassures me. I nod. There's more but I don't want to say it. But I feel like I have to.

'So they kept hitting me.' I feel the growls more than I hear them. Their vibrations come at me from every direction. 'They realised I liked it so they kept hitting me until it hurt. A lot. And they started calling me names. Said that I would like that as well. But I didn't. I started crying and they just kept going.'

'What the fuck?' John's voice is distant and my eyes stay locked with Mick as he nods at me. His eyes look glassy and sad.

'When was this?' George's voice washes over my shoulder.

'It was my first heat, I was eighteen.' I mumble, my eyes still locked on Mick.

'That would have been before the regulations and vetting programs.' George states matter of factly.

'I can't.' Sam shouts as he stands to leave the table.

'I'm sorry.' All four of them groan and Sam stills in the doorway.

'That's eight.' George grunts out. There's so much tension in the room but I don't understand it. I can tell they're angry but why? Because I fucked up my heats years ago? Are they worried about having to deal with me now? Should I offer to leave again?

I want to apologise again. More. I want them to know how sorry I am that they scent matched with such a disaster. But I can't find my words. My throat is tight. I feel the sting in my eyes. I'm about to cry. I try to run from the room but I don't make it out of my seat before I'm captured. I feel two giant arms wrap around me and haul me into his chest and I wrap my legs around him instinctively as the tears begin to fall.

'I'm so sorry.' I sob into his shirt.

'That's nine, sweetness.' Mick whispers into my hair.

KNOT FOR REAL

Chapter 47. Mick

I have never felt this angry before in my life. Melanie, my sweetness, has been treated worse than I could ever have imagined and she doesn't even seem to understand. I can tell from the confusion in her eyes she isn't aware that all of us are considering murder as she speaks.

Her old pack, the ones she was going to bond with, how dare they? No one should ever tell anyone what they are supposed to do with their bodies. What's supposed to turn them on or bring them pleasure. But doing that to an omega during their heat, never. I wouldn't care if my omega asked to cover me in glitter and moo like a cow if that's what they wanted. What they did was cruel. I'm glad they're dead. Even as a sadistic part of myself wishes they were still alive just so I could hurt them.

And what she's describing. Wanting us to take control, protect her, hold her down, spank her. These were all so normal to us. These were the things we wanted as well. The fact that she wanted them as well just proved to me she was ours.

'It's okay.' I whisper into her hair as I retake my seat with her in my lap. She clings tighter as her face buries into my chest. She's breaking my heart with her gentle tears. I want to squeeze so tight all her broken pieces get stitched back together and she never wants to cry again. I know that's not possible. I know tears are inevitable and that sadness is not the enemy. But still I hate it.

'Shhh. Babygirl, it's okay.' George whispers from across the table.

'You're going to be okay, sweetness.' I murmur against her head.

'How can we help?' Sam's voice is pleading as he comes back into the room. Normally if he's angry he's downstairs pummelling the punching bag till he bleeds. But he can't leave her, so instead he takes her abandoned seat.

'I... I... I don't...' She hiccoughs as she continues crying under my chin. John pulls his chair closer so he can reach out and stroke her arm. George leans back in his chair, his head tilted back in contemplation. Like he's trying to solve a problem. She wriggles in my arms and I realise she's pulling back to wipe her eyes, so I let her.

'I'm sor...' She stops herself when she feels us all brace.

'Good girl.' George rumbles, catching her attention. She looks over her shoulder to him and then around at all of us.

'I'm such a mess.' She laments. 'And you're all being so lovely. I know I'm not allowed to say it but I do feel bad.'

'I'd rather you didn't feel it than just not say it.' I grumble leaning forward to kiss her forehead.

'Agreed.' Sam chuffs, I feel him reach to push the hair off her face. John has his fingers tangled in hers. Her strawberry sweetness that had grown too strong, like overripe fruit, softens and becomes warm like syrup again and I can feel us relax.

'Turn around babygirl.' George doesn't bark, but the alpha in his voice is unmistakeable. George keeps his other nature leashed more than anyone I've ever met and he never lets the energy show without good reason. So I'm not used to the strange urge to lower my gaze and agree with him.

Melanie turns within my arms so that she's sitting on my lap facing outwards across the table. I loop my hands gently across her stomach to keep her in place and to stop the wiggling before it makes me an arsehole. John takes her hand again while Sam reaches out to place his hand on her knee.

'Can you explain?' George asks her.

'Explain?' She asks in return.

'I don't want you to apologise again. In fact it would make me very happy to never hear the word sorry on your lips ever again. But can you tell me what you think you're apologising for.' George asks calmly.

'Um...' She looks from John to Sam, her eyes sliding between them like they might have the answer. I lean forward and bury my nose in the back of her hair so she knows I'm here with her as well. We're all here with her. 'For being a mess.'

'What does that mean?' George presses which would not have been my response. I want to shout that she's not a mess, she's perfect. But George's power is keeping me leashed.

'Well, just that I'm not very good at being an omega.' Again I want to protest. 'I wish you guys weren't stuck with me.'

'Why do you say that?' George snips and I feel her tense. Does she know? Does she know that she's ours? 'Why do you say we're stuck with you?'

'Um... yesterday... no, the day before, when Mary was here, she mentioned...' Her voice trails off and I feel us all sigh with relief. She knows. Of course she does. Even if Mary hadn't mentioned it she would have figured it out with the way we're all hanging all over her all the time.

'We're scent sensitive.' George's grumble soothes me. It's out in the open now. My brain skips ahead to weekend adventures, holidays, shopping trips and sleeping in together. I crave it. I didn't know how much I wanted her until I met her.

Even before any of us realised she was our omega we'd been crazy for her. That first day when she'd climbed into my lap on her kitchen floor, I'd felt the pull of our other natures and knew it. Even if I didn't know that I knew it. And now she was all ours. Together we would worship her. Love her. I feel so elated I could actually float. Her strawberry scent wafts around me making me feel like I can breathe deeply for the first time in my life. And her soft curves wrapped up in my arms makes me want things in a way I didn't know I could. It isn't just that I want this woman's body. I crave her. Just the thought of her pillowy breasts, her soft belly, her thick thighs. I feel myself stiffening in my pants.

'We're scent sensitive.' Her soft voice echoes George's words. It feels like a balm to my soul. She knows. We can start worshipping her and touching her the way we always should have been. We can test her limits. Teach her that everything her body wants is good. Help her find her pleasure.

'Sweetness.' I mumble with reverence into the back of her hair as I press a kiss to the back of her neck. She flinches and I pause.

'I feel so bad.' She grumbles.

'Why?' George asks the question in my mind.

'Because you're stuck with me.' She deadpans like it's obvious.

'Why do you keep saying that?' Sam's tone of confusion from beside me reflects what I feel.

'Well I know you don't actually want me.' She shrugs in my arms.

'WHAT?' George demands as John groans and Sam swears.

Chapter 48. Melanie

Have you ever been in the same room as four incredibly angry alphas? No? Well I don't suggest it. The power flowing off all of them is intoxicating. It's making me want to climb under the table and hide. Or maybe climb on the table and try to make them laugh. Running was always an option? Anything to stop the waves of disapproval I can feel radiating through me.

'Explain!' George demands. I want to but I can't. I'm scared. I'm not scared of him. But his anger is scaring me. No wait. It's scaring my omega. She's the one that wants me to hide. It's weird. I've never felt her so present before. Or maybe I have but not since I was a teenager. Normally when I'm in heat or when she takes over I'm just gone, but this is different. She feels awake. And angry as well as scared. But she seems to know what she wants. And she wants the big alpha with his arms around her. I turn my face from George and bury it in Mick's neck.

'Cool it.' Mick snaps above my head. I feel my omega ruffle her own feathers in pride. She likes that Mick defended her. She likes him. I can feel it now. She likes all of them. How Mick always feels like safety. How Sam wakes her up with his teasing and flirting. How John makes her laugh with all of his banter and jokes. She even likes George and his demanding nature. Just not right this minute.

'Melanie?' It's John's voice beside me and I open my eyes. 'George isn't going to bark again. But can you try and explain what you mean.'

‘Take your time.’ Mick’s voice radiates from above me. I pause and take a breath. I can explain, of course I can. It’s not hard. I just don’t want to.

‘I know... I know I’m not anyone’s first choice.’ I stutter out as four growls reverberate around me and I shudder.

‘Sorry sweetness.’ Mick is the first to recover. ‘Go on.’

I shake my head. I don’t want to. I can hear my mother’s voice in my head reminding me that I wasn’t attractive enough to be so annoying. I can hear my old pack explaining to other people that I was a friend of the family. I remember realising that was all they ever described me as. Never as someone they wanted.

It still hurts to think of them. We’d met at one of my dad’s work functions and I was instantly smitten with all of them. I was just twenty two when we met and they’d seemed so mature and sophisticated being in their thirties. They’d courted me. I’d spent my heat with them, and although it hadn’t gone well, they assured me they didn’t mind. It hadn’t been long before they’d asked to bond me and I’d said yes.

I would have been happy with a private ceremony. Exchanging our bites in private. Letting our souls entwine and then luxuriating in the feeling of just being together. But my mum had wanted the whole formal ceremony. And since it was one of dad’s business partners sons that headed the pack a huge party had been planned at his golf club.

I had been there for hours already, getting smothered in makeup and hair spray when we’d gotten the news. The limousine that had been bringing them to the ceremony had been t-boned by a truck. They had all died instantly. They were all gone. I was all alone again.

I’d broken down crying on the spot. To me joining their pack had meant leaving behind my family. Making my own start. They were picking me and I was picking them. It had been the best kind of life I could see ahead for myself. A life of freedom and love.

The ceremony planner had taken me home while my mother went to help my dad commiserate with his colleague. They got me out of my ridiculously ornate dress and I climbed into my bed and there I stayed. For three days. I drank the water and tea mum left for me. I picked at the plates of food she brought. But mostly I just sat and stared around my room. I'd been so close to happiness, so close to freedom and then it had all been gone.

By the end of the third day my mum had enough. She was forcing me out of bed and into the shower when I'd fallen to the floor begging her to just leave me alone. That's when she snapped.

'I don't know why you're carrying on like this. They were only bonding with you because your dad and Frank's dad had a business merger in the works. Seriously you're carrying on like a toddler who lost their favourite toy. It's embarrassing.' And then she'd left me on the floor.

I stopped crying.

We planned our ceremony so that it was only a few days before when my heat was supposed to hit again. When it did come I'd gone insane. I tore down the cream floral curtains. I threw every blanket and sheet out into the hall. I even ripped up some of mum's plush golden carpet to reveal the old wooden floors underneath. Two days later, when I came to, I found my room shredded and my walls painted with whatever I'd been able to find in my old art supplies box. It was a disaster.

I'd gone to the doctors with mum the next day and he'd prescribed me Shiffalix. That was ten years ago. It had been awhile till I had started to feel kind of okay again. Once I was up on my feet, mum had pushed me to get back to dating. I'd refused. In fact I'd refused to do a lot of things. I wouldn't go out with them or eat with them. By that point Lucy was dating her pack who were also friends of my father's colleagues and just being around them made me feel hollow.

I don't want to be in these memories. I hate that they're coming up now. I can feel the tears coming back and I don't want them. Fuck I want my suppressants back. I want the drugs that made all of this quieter so I never had to deal with any of it. I whimper as my omega thrashes against the thought.

Don't bind me again. I hear the words in my mind but they're not my voice. Well it is my voice but deeper and richer. I like it. The words in my mind silence the thoughts and I feel calmer. Mick is purring beneath me and I feel her drag my attention to it.

Focus on the feeling. My omega speaks to me again. She guides my mind to focus on the warmth of the hand in mine. The softness of Mick's shirt at my back. The vibration of his purr relaxing something deep inside me I didn't know was wound so tight. And nothing feels that scary anymore.

'They didn't actually want me.' The words spring from my mouth. I'm the one talking but I can feel my omega's presence in my voice. I think the others can as well because suddenly I feel their attention. It's like they're listening to me in a deeper way.

'Who didn't?' It's George who asks the question.

'My pack. The ones who were going to bond me. They didn't actually want me. It was a business deal with my father. That's why they'd agreed.'

'Fuck.' Sam's voice drifts from my other side and I realise he hasn't spoken for a while, hasn't touched me. I turn my face to him now as he speaks. 'I'm sorry.'

'You're not allowed to say that.' I tease.

'This is different.' He groans, reaching forward to push the curls away from my face. 'I'm not apologising for being somewhere or needing something. I'm saying sorry because no one should ever feel like they're not wanted.'

'Okay.' I nod at him. The vehemence in his voice tells me he knows the feeling well himself. I understand the pain in his eyes.

'Those guys were arseholes.' He grumbles, reaching out to tap my nose.

'Agreed.' John's voice comes from the other direction as I feel Mick nod his agreement into the top of my head.

'Babygirl?' George calls for my attention and I look over. I'm sitting in Mick's lap, the other two pressed close to each side. But George is sitting away from me and I don't like it. I need them all closer.

'Closer.' I demand, my omega's desire clearly ringing in my voice. George reaches across the table to touch my hand. My omega beams inside me.

'Babygirl, those guys were arseholes. And that was about them, not you.' I nod. I know what he's saying. I've heard it before from Sandra and my therapist. But it wasn't just them. I haven't been on a date in eight years. No one ever wanted me. Even these guys wouldn't want me if it wasn't for stupid scent sensitivity.

'I know.' I sigh.

'Do you really?' George asks. I want to nod but I feel my omega shake my head no instead. *Tell them.* She demands of me.

'No one wants me though.' I whisper.

'We do.' George grunts and I feel more than see the other three nod their heads.

'Not really.' I murmur.

'What do you mean?' George demands.

'You don't touch me.' I shrug.

'That's not strictly true.' Sam's tone is grumbly as he turns to George with a scowl.

'I told you it was a mistake.' George snaps at Sam and I flinch.

'I know.' I sigh, collapsing my weight back against the soft chest behind me.

'What do you know?' Mick asks.

'George regrets kissing me.' I mumble.

'What? NO!' George looks horrified.

'You just said it was a mistake.' I point out.

'Not like that!' He yells.

'It's okay.' I rush to soothe him. I don't want to make him angry again.

'I want you. We all do. We all kissed you the other day.'

'I didn't.' John sulks beside me.

'You respond to me when I'm in heat. But I mean me, me. You don't actually want me.' My words don't really make sense but I think they get it as George flops back in his seat away from me, horror still etched in his face.

'You think we don't want you?' George mumbles.

'Well I mean I know you want me but only because we're scent sensitive. You're not actually attracted to me.' I feel Mick groan and John freeze. Sam laughs. Loudly. I turn to him in confusion.

'You just made me so happy.' He chuckles as his hand reaches out to cradle my cheek.

'I did?' The other three are furious and yet Sam seems genuinely overjoyed.

'You did. Melanie, we all want you. We were all crazy about you before we even scented you. I have wanted to bend you over and fuck you till you scream since the first moment I met you. Long before I knew you were an omega. But these other arseholes are under the impression that we need to go slow. So can you please tell them that they're wrong so I can start gloating.' The image he paints makes my cheeks warm and it takes me a second to realise that the others are waiting.

'I just figured you weren't attracted to me.' I tell them.

'You're killing me.' George groans.

'Sorry.' I mumble without thinking. I'm expecting the growl when I realise what I've said. But not for the loudest growl to come from beside me. I turn to John and watch as his eyes dilate and he bares his teeth in anger.

'That's ten.'

Chapter 49. John

Something inside me snaps. This beautiful woman I was obsessed with for a year seems to think that I don't want her. But I do. I want her mind. I want her kindness. I want her sense of humour. I want all of her. But I especially want her body.

'Hands on the table.' I growl out. It's not a bark. She doesn't have to listen to me. But I want her to. I want her to do as I say so that I can show her the pleasure we've all been holding back, thinking she needs time and space. Why didn't we just ask her? Fuck we're arseholes. She's spent all this time thinking we didn't want her while I know for a fact I am not the only one that's had to take matters into my own hands while she's been in this house.

She doesn't move. Sitting in Mick's lap her eyes trained on mine in confusion. I want to show her how much I want her but I need her to want it to. To agree to this exchange. I keep my gaze steady as I let all my desire for her flow through my body.

Slowly she lifts her hands from her sides and places them gently on the table. I growl my appreciation and it echoes around us as the other three see her compliance.

Her gaze darts around our little group taking in our expressions and I see the moment she starts to believe we want her. I can feel the energy shift as her omega preens under our gaze because my alpha wants off his leash. But this isn't about them. We'll get to that later. This is about us.

Slowly she leans forward out of Mick's embrace, putting her weight onto her hands on the table and stepping forward. She keeps going till her hips bump the edge of the table. It's her, it's my Melanie. But in the arch of her back and the tilt of her smile I also see her omega. Her omega that's goading the darkest parts of myself. And I'm going to show her.

'John?' George calls my name, checking I'm okay. That I'm in control. I am very much in control and I'm about to show this sweet girl how badly I want her.

'Pull down her leggings.' I don't know who I'm commanding but it's Mick that moves forward to slide her pants down, his hands caressing her as he goes. Her bare bottom in the sky, I smile at her creamy white skin.

'No panties.' Sam mutters and I make the mental note to join in Sam's campaign to stop Mick from buying her underwear if it means she's going to be bare beneath her clothes in this house.

'They won't get here till tomorrow.' Mick mumbles entranced by her creamy white skin. I move forward and he automatically steps to the side so I can stand behind her. Sam is sitting beside her, reaching out his hand, raking it over her arms and her shoulders. Mick takes my place and sits on her other side, copying Sam's movements. Stirring her. George keeps his seat opposite Melanie and leans forward to tilt her chin up and capture her gaze.

'Babygirl, are you okay if John punishes you for what you did?' She nods. 'Good girl. Tell us why are you in trouble?'

'I said sorry too much.' She squirms.

'That's right, you apologised unnecessarily. Are you going to hold still for John?' George asks as his hand strokes the hair away from her face.

'Yes.' She whispers.

'Yes what?' George asks. I feel Melanie tense, we all do.

'Yes Daddy.' She murmurs. George's approval at the title radiates off him.

'Good girl.' He leans forward and kisses her lips fiercely. 'Now focus on John.'

'Yes Daddy.' She says with more confidence as she wiggles her ass in the air making my palm tingle. The other two are still stroking along her arms and shoulders as I step up closer behind her and let my hand trail over her cheek.

'George is going to count for you.' I tell her. 'After every spank I want to hear you say 'thank you'. Okay?'

She nods into the table, her hips wriggling in earnest. I haven't even touched her but the smell soaking the room tells me that she's enjoying this even more than we are.

'We're going to use the traffic light system. If you feel yourself getting overwhelmed and you need us to slow down or let us know you're close to your limit you say yellow. If you want us to stop, you say red.'

'Yes sir.' So George was Daddy and I was Sir. Works for me.

'Are you ready?'

'Yes sir.' I nod at Mick and Sam, and they pause in their strokes along her arms as they nod back. Their hands become soft weights holding her down against the table. George leans forward gripping both her hands as he drops his eyes to hers.

I lift my hand and pull it down through the air until I collide with her soft skin. The ripple of my smack rocks her and she wiggles into it. I pull my hand back and see the soft red glow on her skin left behind by my touch. I caress it immediately, soothing the sting till she moans.

'One.' George counts.

'Thank you.' She whispers. All four of us tense. Her thank you rings through us with the voice of her omega and our alphas preen with pride and pleasure. I raise my other hand bringing it down on her unmarked cheek.

'Two.'

'Thank you.' Her response comes quicker this time. Her scent thicker. Her slick glistening at the top of her thighs. I bring my second hand down again quickly, surprising her and she moans.

'Three.' George grunts.

'Thank you.' She groans, her thighs quivering. I lift both hands and bring them down one on each cheek, one after the other, spanking her twice in quick succession.

'That's five.' George's tone is soothing. His gaze is on hers but I can see his excitement in the way his muscles tense, his shoulders around his ears, his jaw clenched tight.

'Thank you.' Melanie sighs. I want to draw this out but I can't. I need to do this. I need to go faster and harder. I bring my first hand down again while the other hand draws a pattern through the red rose that's blooming on her butt.

'Six.'

'Thank you.' Melanie murmurs, her voice becoming languid.

'I think she's enjoying herself too much.' Sam groans. She could never enjoy herself too much as far as I was concerned.

'Do you like this?' Mick leans forward to whisper in her ear.

'Yes.' She breathes out, her ass wiggling for more.

'What do you like?' Mick asks as I drop my hand onto her ass again and she flinches.

'Seven.' George's voice is barely a whisper.

'Thank you.' She gasps.

'Answer me?' Mick asks sweetly, gently stroking the hair away from her face.

'It feels good. It feels like... like you want me. Like you care.' Her admission robs me of breath. That was what was making her so wet, so hot. The thought that we cared about her. We did more than that. I bring my hand down again.

'Eight.'

'Thank you.' She moans with delight as I trace my fingers across the pink stains on her cheeks. God she's gorgeous. Her rounded reddened bum thrust high in the air, her thick thighs wiggling with need. I was ready to finish.

Rather than bringing my hand down again I pull my arm back and swing forward to catch the cleft where her thighs meet her bum and watch with delight as ripples flow across her skin and her back arches in pleasure.

'Nine.'

'Thank you.' She moans sweetly. I pull back my other hand and slap it forward into her other cheek. Then both my hands are tracing light patterns on her bright red skin. She moans so loudly I almost think she's coming as she shudders in delight.

'Ten.' George grunts.

'Thank you.' She whispers.

Chapter 50. Melanie

They want me. I can feel it, and it's making me crazy. All this time I felt like they were stuck with me. I felt guilty that I wasn't better for them. But now with all of their gazes fixed on me as John punishes me I feel desired and wanted. It's addictive. It feels like I'm in heat. There is so much pleasure running through my body. But rather than drifting away to a different place in my mind I'm still here. So is my omega but she's content to let me be in charge.

I want them. They want me. They don't think I'm gross. They like it and it's making me so hot. I can feel the slick sliding down the inside of my thighs as I try to hold still. I need more. Now that the spanking is over I need someone to take me but I don't know how to ask.

'Babygirl?' I look up to see George's kind eyes boring into mine. 'What do you want?'

'Um...'

'Tell Daddy.' His tone is warning. The way he says it makes my knees weaken. If I wasn't lying across the table I would have fallen. I know what I want. But am I brave enough to say it? I feel fear trickle down my spine. What if what I ask for is wrong?

I look into George's eyes, his gaze locked on mine. He wants me. He wants me to tell him what I want.

'Cock.' I mumble.

'Say it properly.' His tone holds a hint of teasing.

'Please daddy, can I have a cock?'

'Good girl.' He leans down to kiss my cheek where I'm still splayed out on the table. 'Who do you want first?'

First? As in more than one?

That's right, all of them. My omega is thrilled and impatient and I'm overwhelmed. What if I choose wrong? Or do something wrong.

'Babygirl.' George barks and my attention snaps back to him.

'Yes Daddy.' Just saying it makes my thighs clench together. And he smiles.

'Tell us who you want.' He demands.

'John.' I'm still laying across the table my arse in the air and I can feel him move in to press against me. I moan with delight. I feel the hard length of him through his clothes.

'Hold still.' John whispers over me as he pulls back for a second. I can hear him sliding out of his clothes. The fact that I can't see him, only feel him is making this more intense. His hand slides across the angry red bloom of my bum and his gentle caress against the sensitized skin has me shuddering. 'You ready?'

I nod. I feel the head of him press gently into my folds. He rubs himself up and down, getting himself wet with my slick. Then he's pressing forward and I can feel his head find it's home. I gasp as he begins to slide in. Opening me. It feels like heaven to be stretched. He slides in an inch as he strokes his hand down my back.

'That's a good girl.' George leans over me and kisses my cheek. 'Take his cock.'

I whimper as John begins sliding in and out. Pressing deeper each time. The friction forces pleasure up my spine. He pulls all the way out and I want to protest but then he pushes forward hard and fast and I barely swallow my scream. It feels so good. I'm so hot and wet every little movement sends lightning through my veins. My hips start twitching, seeking more.

'Fuck me.' Sam groans. I turn my head towards him as he strokes the hair away from my face.

'Next.' I murmur as I nod at him. He smiles as he drops a kiss to my cheek.

John pulls back and then thrusts into me so hard we rock the table and my eyes slam closed with pleasure as my face turns automatically into the wood beneath me. I feel the press of his knot against my opening and I want him to keep pressing. But he pulls back instead. Then he pushes down on my hips as he does it again, pulling out so slowly I think I might scream and then slamming back into me with so much force I see stars.

'Let me help you there, sweetness.' Mick's voice floats above me. I don't know what he means until John pulls back on my hips, leveraging me away from the table and pushing into me harder and faster than before. Then I feel Mick's distinct touch, his giant hand caressing my stomach. Moving lower and lower until his fingers find my hidden nub.

I moan. It's too much. George is still gripping my hands, Sam's fingers in my hair combine with John's pounding into me and Mick's touch. I'm coming. My body shakes and clenches as I ride out my pleasure. I feel John's hips still as he groans at the way I clench him and then he's spilling inside me. A new spark of pleasure starts deep inside me as he leans over to press himself into my back.

'Next time we do this, I'm going to knot you so deep that you'll have to sit on my lap through dinner. And everyone will know my cock is inside you. ' He drops a kiss behind my ear as he pulls back.

There are hands everywhere. Stroking me. Massaging my hand. Caressing my face. Rubbing against the tender skin on my backside. I almost can't take it. It's too much, the feeling of comfort pressing in on me.

'Did you want more?' John's voice is teasing. I nod into the table. I want this feeling forever.

'Who did you want next, babygirl?' George asks as I try to breathe and think.

'I think she wanted me.' Sam's voice reaches me through my stupor and I nod. 'Come here, love. I want to watch you bounce.'

I nod at him as I lift my gaze to his. The thought is kind of scary. That he will see all of me wobbling above him. But the look in his eyes tells me that's what he wants, to see all of me.

He's leaning back in the chair I was sitting in before and he looks like a god. I don't know when he got undressed but I'm thrilled at all his exposed skin. I want to rub myself against him. I watch as he grips his dick and strokes himself.

'Come here.'

KNOT FOR REAL

Chapter 51. Sam

Melanie is a goddess. I watch as she slowly lifts herself up from the table and steps towards me. She's nervous. I can tell by the way she bites her lip but she doesn't need to be. I have been obsessed with getting inside this woman since the first moment I met her. And after watching her come on John's dick I'm so ready for her I could cry.

She hesitates in front of me, so I pull her forward, slipping my thighs between hers as I drag her to sit in my lap. George and Mick shift to stand at her sides as she settles onto me. John leans back against the table, still trying to bring himself back under control as he watches her.

'Lift up.' I tell her and watch as George and Mick each clasp an arm and help her rise so I can slide the head of my erection along her folds. 'So wet.'

'She's a good girl.' George mutters into her hair above me. I push myself till I'm aligned with her entrance, my head barely pressing into her and she moans. Slowly she begins to lower herself, her weight gently pressing down into me as I pierce her and slide into her heat. I don't move. I barely breathe as she uses George and Mick's hands on her to control her descent.

My hands clasp at her waist. I want to push her down, hard. I want to slam up into her. She's barely taking half of me. I want to be buried in her. I want to push her down onto my knot so I never have to let her go. But she's panting as she rides me, not letting me all the way in, just sliding up and down, controlling the pace. I let her. I'll let her do anything she wants.

She tilts forward and the angle changes and she shudders. It is so much sweeter than I ever imagined being with her. Her small movements. Her breathy pants. I feel crazed. I'm too harsh. Too hard. As she twitches around me her eyes open and lock with mine. Her crystal blue gaze is clouded with pleasure. But there's something more, some uncertainty. Something she's asking for.

I hold her gaze as I grip her hips, letting my fingers dig into her flesh till I'm sure she will bruise. And I see her relax. Her lips part. I know what she wants.

I pull down on her hips as I thrust up, seating myself all the way inside her. Her swollen clit collides with my stomach and I watch her eyes flutter close. I rock her against me as she shudders. She's the sweetest thing in the universe and she's mine. She's all of ours. But right now she's mine.

I sit forward in my seat, tilting her till her feet leave the ground. She's still holding onto George and Mick as I push her back, my arm banding around her waist until she's bent backwards towards the table. With one arm locked around her, my other reaching out to brace on the table behind her I kiss her deeply.

It's not tentative, my mouth is open over hers as our tongues tangle. I drink her sweet flavour, so different coming from her mouth, than when I tasted her in the gym. Softer but more addictive.

'Can you take more?' I whisper against her lips. She doesn't say anything, she just nods. I lean back away from her where she's bent over my arm, so I can adjust my angle. Then I slide out of her and slam home again rolling my hips as I do.

Her moan is so loud I imagine the neighbours could hear it. It makes me proud. She's been so quiet. Moaning softly. And I know I'm not the only one who enjoys her noises. Mick and George still grip her arms and they seem just as lost as I am.

'Help me.' I grunt out, standing roughly, with her in my arms. They help me take her weight and lay her down on the table, her hips hanging over the edge. John moves to make space for us and then reaches down to pull her shirt up and expose her breasts to our gaze. His fingers graze her nipples and I watch in awe.

George pins her hand down beside her head and Mick copies him. Then he lets one hand slide down along her waist and her hip, gripping her thigh. Slowly he pulls her leg back towards himself where he stands at her shoulder. I feel George copy his movement so that our girl is balanced between us. Spread wide by their hands on her thighs, holding her open and pinning her to the table.

'You ready?' I ask and she nods enthusiastically, her eyes wide with delight.

'Yes.' She whispers. I smile down at her as I pull out and slam into her again. The table shakes as she calls out with the force of my thrust. John strokes her hair and her nipple with the same reverence as the other two tighten their grips on her, squeezing her hands and her thighs so that she knows we're all her for her. My knot is pressing against her but not into her and I can feel her fluttering trying to pull me inside.

I pull out and push back harder and faster than before. Now that she's moaning she can't seem to stop as her head begins twisting side to side with pleasure. I give one more deep hard thrust and I feel her clench hard around me before her back bows off the table and she shudders into her release.

I pause. I didn't expect her to come so fast. But the combination of us holding her between us, stretched out and safe and my knot slamming against where she needed it most must have pushed her over.

I want to keep going. But I feel like she needs a minute. We all do. This morning George reminded us all that we weren't to touch her. That she needed time. I am so happy he was wrong.

I knew it all along. She needs our desire. To feel wanted. The others might know how to take care of her, and help her and read to her but this is what I knew. Pleasure. And she needs more. I want to drown her in it.

I reach down between us and gently pinch her clit to watch her shudder. Her eyes spring open and connect with mine. And she smiles. It's a wicked smile, full of dirty thoughts and I feel myself falling harder. I never wanted an omega. But I want her. I would put everything on the line for Melanie.

'You okay?' John whispers as he noses into her temple, stroking her hair that's resting along the table. She nods at him, her eyes still on me.

'Do you want more?' I ask, already suspecting my little minx is still feeling needy. She nods again but more shyly this time. I hate that she feels shy about her needs and her pleasure. Not for long. If there's one thing I will dedicate myself to in this lifetime it's making this girl proud of her body and the things it can do. Especially how well she takes my dick.

'Hold tight.' I tell her as I nod at the grip she still has on George and Mick's hands. I see her fingers clench and hips fall just a little more open as George and Mick pull her wider for me.

I pull back and slam into her again but this time with less force. I don't hold myself deep inside her, I pull out and slam home again and again. Faster and faster. My knot bumping against her each time is making me crazy.

As I piston myself into her, her tits bounce up and down hypnotically. I want to lean down and suck on them, squeeze them but I'm too busy gripping her arse to hold her right where I want to as I push faster.

John is either a mind reader or has the same idea because he leans over her chest from above her and her moans get louder. I can't see what he's doing but her hips begin to shudder and rock. I feel myself almost ready to burst.

I look down to where I'm disappearing inside of her. Her slick has made us both so wet we're glistening as the smell of strawberries and vanilla combines to make me feel like I'm inhaling ice cream. There's whiskey and lavender and cinnamon floating around the room but when I look down into the beautiful mess we're making together all I can smell is us and I want to drown in it.

I reach out my hand so that my thumb is pressing against her clit and begin rotating it through our wetness. She clamps down on me but I keep going. Not letting her body suck me in. I know I'm about to be spent but I want her to go so far over the edge she doesn't come straight back down.

John pulls back, her breasts now wet from his mouth and whispers something in her ear. Her head bounces up and down with an obvious yes. I watch as his hands reach out and clearly pinch her nipples in unison. And her back bows off the table so sharply I'm worried her spine will break.

I push harder as I feel her orgasm begin. Her flutters keep growing and I slide my thumb from her clit and down inside her to push into the space my knot would go. And she screams.

This isn't like the sounds she made before. There's no grace. No beautiful soft sound. This is the scream of someone who can't hold it in and I love it. I spill myself inside her as she shudders so hard she vibrates.

She falls back on to the table, her limbs loose as her eyes close.

Chapter 52. Melanie

Oh my goddess. I think I just left my body.

In fact I know I left my body or at least fell asleep because I'm no longer in the kitchen. I'm on the couch. Behind me I can feel soft cushions and in front of me is a person who is half naked at least. I know because my fingers are dug into his fleshy chest and the light smattering of hair. And I am drenched in warm lavender.

Mick.

I open my eyes slowly and stare into the warm rich skin in front of my face. We're on the couch and Mick has me tucked against it, blocking the world out with his frame.

'What happened to your shirt?' I ask continuing to slide my fingers through the short curly hairs on his chest.

'You removed it.'

'I did?'

'Yep.' He kisses my forehead.

'And how did we end up on the couch?'

'You went into a heat spike toward the end and your omega took over. She was feeling needy, and wanted cuddles. So I carried you in here and laid down with you while the others... they're working on something.'

'How long have I been out?'

'Only an hour.' He kisses my head and snuggles me in closer. He seems content to hold me and I really do need a minute. I like being in his arms.

The last thing I clearly remember was realising that these guys wanted me. Like wanted me, wanted me. They weren't disappointed we were scent sensitive. That the fear I'd been carrying around that they were ashamed of me and didn't want me wasn't even remotely close to the truth. And they wanted the same things I wanted.

It wasn't just that they could put up with me, like my old pack did. They wanted it to. The powerplay. The tension. It was so hot. I was so hot. Still. I'd called John Sir and he'd groaned. I'd called George Daddy and he'd loved it.

I wiggle with joy without meaning to.

'Happy about something?' Mick chuckles into my hair.

'Everything.' I whisper into his chest. It was sappy but it was true. This was more than I had ever imagined I would have. I didn't realise there would be joy in being scent sensitive. I thought it was only a prison sentence. But it was like inhaling fairy floss scented crack. And they wanted me. Like physically. They'd left no room for doubt on that. I felt almost guilty now for having assumed that they didn't.

I could feel the dark thoughts still hanging in the back of my mind. Thoughts of what other people might say. Thoughts of my family and how they were going to react when I eventually told them about this pack. Maybe my pack.

I mean if we were scent sensitive and they like me that was where this was going. Right?

'I can feel you overthinking. Try to relax, sweetness.' He kisses the top of my head as he starts to purr. I want to meld with his chest till the vibrations soak into my bones. They feel so good. I wiggle again realising that my feet barely pass his knees and I'm once again amused by the giantness of this man.

'You comfortable?' I ask. I was snuggled between him and cushions so I was fine but he was balanced against the edge of the couch.

'Beyond. I love having you here like this.'

'Imprisoned?' I tease as his arms flex tighter around me pulling me even harder into his frame.

'Yes. But also just here. In my arms. I like it.'

'May I ask who's shirt I'm wearing. And who's boxers for that matter?' Both were stretchy and comfy but I don't remember putting them on.

'The shirt is Johns, the underwear is Sams. I would have happily left you naked.'

'They wanted me dressed?'

'No we were unanimous on the naked plan. You seemed to want to be covered in their scents.'

'Well that's embarrassing.' His purr rumbles with his chuckle. I'm glad he can't see me, tucked beneath his chin as I am.

'Actually it was hot. Once you had their clothes on you jumped into my arms and demanded 'snuggles'. I've never been so honoured in my life.' I pull back to glance up at him.

'Are you teasing me?' I demand.

'No.' It's on the tip of my tongue to call him a liar but his gaze is too sincere.

'You were honoured to have me demand snuggles?' I ask, incredulous.

'You had four of us to choose from and it was me you wanted for comfort. I was thrilled. I can assure you the others were jealous. George seemed particularly put out.' He chuckles at the memory tucking me back against his chest and his purr.

'Is he mad?' I whisper.

'No.' I feel him shake his head above me. 'He wishes he was me right now but he's not mad.'

'Should we get up and go find him?' I don't want to move a muscle but I will.

'No, he'll find us in a little bit. You just snuggle back in here and we'll make sure your omega is completely happy.'

'I've never felt her like this before.' I mumble into his skin.

'What do you mean?'

'I mean, like, I can feel her thoughts. Like she's a whole other person inside of me.' Even as I speak I feel her preening inside me at the attention she's receiving.

'That's what my alpha's like. Actually, he's a lot more talkative than I am.'

'So he talks to you?' I felt like I was going crazy when I first heard my omega's voice inside my own head.

'Yeah. He tells me things that he wants me to do or pay attention to. Mostly that's you.' He nuzzles against my hair again.

'Tell him thanks.' I smile against his chest.

'He can hear you. Just like your omega can hear me when I say, hello beautiful. Is there anything else you need?'

I like this one.

'She likes you.' I say the thought out loud and my omega practically dances inside me at being able to communicate. I want to ask her so many questions. Like where has she been? If this is normal, why haven't I heard her before?

'What about you? Do you like me?' Mick asks.

'Yeah.' I sigh.

'Not the enthusiasm I was hoping for.' He teases me.

'No, it's just... Why haven't I heard her before?'

'It was the suppressants. The ones you were on are strong, they not only lower your hormonal levels but also act upon your brain chemistry. They stop the pathways where her thoughts flow alongside yours, so you can't hear her. It's like being put in separate rooms.'

'You sound like Doctor Mary.'

'She suggested some articles for me to read.' He shrugs around me.

'What else did they say?' I ask out of curiosity.

'That as your omega surfaces we'll need to show both of you lots of affection. Support you two while you learn to work together. And if you're comfortable with it, lots of skin to skin contact.'

'I'm comfortable with it.' I tell him, dragging my hands more firmly against his chest where they've been drawing lazy patterns. 'Can't you tell?'

'I'd guessed.' He shrugs. I bury my nose in his chest and rub my cheek against it. A scent mark. I didn't really plan to do it. And god only knows if I did it right but I tried.

I feel him freeze as his purr suddenly stops. All his muscles locking around me. Then I'm on my back, his face above mine, wild with joy.

'Sweetness, did you just mark me?'

'Did I do it wrong?'

'No sweetness. It was perfect. But I'm going to have to kiss you now. Okay?'

'Okay.' I nod before his lips crash down on mine. He tastes like sweet lavender. I never thought I'd enjoy such a floral taste but it soothes me as it stirs me.

I try to push him to kiss me harder, faster. But he keeps his pace slow, almost gentle. But his kisses are so passionate and deep I feel drugged. I still want more. I nip at his lip with my teeth to try and get him to kiss me harder.

'Ouch.' He teases me like I really hurt him.

'Sorry.' I mumble against his lips. His weight pushes me into the couch as his hands drag my arms above me.

I'm stretched out beneath him as he pins my hands above me on the cushion. Clasping both my wrists in one hand, his free hand slides slowly down my side. Grazing his fingers along my arm, down past my elbow, diverting to my ribs.

'That's one.' He mumbles into our kiss. His fingers dance along my ribs as he tickles me. I try to slide away, squirming as I laugh. But I can't escape his grasp.

'I promise I won't say it again.' I beg through my giggles as I twist beneath him.

'Good.' He smirks, leaning back in to kiss me and sliding his hand up to clasp my jaw and pull me deeper into the kiss.

My hips buck up against him without my permission and he groans into my mouth with pleasure. His hand abandons my cheek to dive straight to my ass and pull me firmly up into him. I can feel his length hard against my thigh and I shudder.

'More.' I whisper against his lips as I let my body roll against his. He shakes his head as he kisses me.

'Sweetness, I think you need rest.' He seems unhappy about his conclusion and it makes me downright mad. More importantly it makes my omega mad. I can feel her stomping her foot and swearing at him inside of me. It almost distracts me from the way his lips are pressing against my jaw as his teeth find the sensitive skin behind my ear.

'I thought you wanted to make my omega happy?'

'I do.' He groans into my neck. 'What does she want?'

Okay girly, what do you want? I think to her and she freezes. It's the shock of being asked. Of getting to answer. But she recovers quickly.

Tell him to fuck us. Slow and firm.

'Um.' She might be comfortable with that language but I wasn't sure I could say it. 'She wants...'

'Sweetness. Whatever it is, I am going to say yes.' I hesitate. 'She needs you to speak for her. Trust her. Let her trust you.'

I know he's right. I can feel her hesitancy to tell me, to talk to me at all. She doesn't trust me and I don't trust her. She's the reason we got hit. She's the reason my pack didn't like me. She was why I had been alone. Or maybe not. Talking to the guys tonight had made me realise, maybe she was trying to get me away from the wrong people. Unsafe people. And now that we were safe it was time to be brave.

'Fuck me. Slow and firm.'

Chapter 53. Mick

I'm in heaven. Because the thick delicious angel below me, who I was already trying to convince myself was real, just asked me to fuck her. Slow and firm. Was I dead? Because this was better than any heaven I'd imagined.

'Anything you want sweetness.' I whisper into her neck, surprised I still have the power of speech. This woman. Fuck.

Watching her before with John and Sam had felt like a religious experience. It almost washed away the pain of realising that she felt unwanted. That we had contributed to that. By hiding our desire we'd let her doubt how much we wanted her. Well that wasn't going to be a problem again.

'Open your legs for me sweetness.' I grumble into her hair as I pull back. I should take the time to undress her but I'm enjoying her being smothered in the scent of my brothers too much.

I push up so I'm staring down at her as her delectable soft creamy thighs fall open. I sink back on to my knees sliding down the couch till I line my face up with her sweet center. I can smell her thick strawberry candied perfume. Amongst it is hints of cinnamon and vanilla so rich she smells like pastry.

'Fuck me.' I mumble as I lean down, pushing John's boxer shorts roughly to the side. She's stunning. Slick and so hot I can feel it on my face. Still swollen from before, she's so sensitive, the shallow breaths shaking my lungs seem to rattle her as well. I could stare at her for hours but I'm too hungry to wait.

I dive forward, sliding my tongue straight between her sweet soaked lips and diving into her core. Her fingers grip my scalp, pulling me closer. She tastes even better than she smells and so I lap at her to drink my fill.

Burying my face firmly against her, I nose against her clit as my tongue thrusts into her again and again. She's already moaning, her hips writhing up against me. I feel like a god.

'More.' She pants. Well, I won't deny my omega anything. I slide my face up to wrap my lips firmly around her clit as I slide my hand up her thigh. Gently I place my finger against her heat and push. Finding the soft bulge just inside her, I flick my finger quickly.

'Oh goddess.' She moans, her hands abandoning my head to tangle in her own hair. She tenses suddenly, her thighs slamming tight against my ears as she comes. I don't remember hauling her thighs over my shoulders or my other hand coming up to grab her hips and hold her still so I could devour her. But as she shakes against me and comes back down to earth, so do I.

She's still swathed in my packmates clothes, pushed haphazardly to the side so that I can reach her. She deserves more. She should be in her nest. Surrounded by everything she finds beautiful. Bathed in warmth and golden light.

'Hey.' Her fingers grab my jaw, pulling my face from her stomach where I laid my head. 'What did I do wrong?'

'Nothing.' I spit emphatically, coming to my knees so I can lean down over her dropping kisses on her face, her shoulder, everywhere I can reach. 'You. Are. Perfect.'

'Then why'd you go so still?' I hate that she assumes that she is the one who did something wrong almost as much as I hate that I let my annoyance at myself affect her.

'I was just thinking that I should be taking better care of you, is all.' I explain as I tuck myself into the crook of her neck. I'm careful to keep my weight off her as I cage her against the couch, hoping my body heat keeps her warm. We need more fluffy blankets in this room.

'I feel very taken care of.' She whispers against my head. Her fingers are playing in the short hairs at my neck. 'Just one little note? From my omega, not me.'

'What's that?'

'Pretty sure I said, fuck me, not eat me.' She giggles and I feel her laughter ripple through me.

'I'm so sorry. What a dreadful mistake.' I grumble into her hair. Keeping her against me I slide one hand down to push my sweatpants out of the way. My cock springs free already bouncing around trying to find where it belongs. I push the boxers to the side again as I gently align my head against her. 'Let me fix that.'

Still holding her tight in my arms I tilt my hips till the tip of me notches inside of her. She gasps as I groan. She's so tight and I am bigger than my brothers. I push up as I slowly flex my hips in gentle rolls, pushing into her barely a millimeter at a time.

'Big.' She moans and my alpha preens with pride. It's hardly relevant but knowing that I'm stretching her, fills me with an animalistic joy I should probably be ashamed of. But I'm not.

'You can take it sweetness. Just hold on to my shoulders and relax.' Her body does as I say, gripping the thick muscles beside my neck and letting her legs fall back against the couch. 'Good girl.'

A fresh flood of wetness surrounds me at those words and I have to resist slamming myself deep inside her. But my omega wanted slow and firm and I live to serve. Gently grasping her thigh I pull it up, and open her so I can press deeper. Rolling my hips as I slowly thrust in and out.

'You're taking me so well.' I grumble, pulling back to look down at her. She nods slowly, her eyes wide as they stare up at me. 'You ready for more?'

She nods again, biting her lip. The shirt she wears is bunched up under her chin, her breasts swaying freely, her face red with blush and to me she is perfect. Sweet as she is filthy. I lean down to press a firm kiss against her mouth, the slight pain of my bruised lip reminding me how much more we owe this woman. I pull back, lifting her leg higher as I reach down with my other hand and roll her clit between my fingers.

Her hips thrust up uncontrollably and I lean forward, stealing another centimeter inside her. She gasps from the feeling. Over and over, I do it. Pulling out a little, rolling her till she gasps then plunging forward. Slowly she takes me all in. It's sweet torture watching as I slowly disappear insider her. Till finally I feel my knot pressing against her wet folds and I know I'm as deep as I can go.

I collapse down, sliding my arms around her head to cradle her neck and hold her into my chest. Her arms cling to my waist pulling me down against her. We're as close as we can be and yet I want more. But I can't take it, not here, not yet.

'Can't knot you sweetness.' I whisper into her hair and she whines, her disagreement. I can't help but smile at the needy keenness of her voice. 'Don't worry, I will, I want to.'

I kiss her cheek as I rock my hips back and then roll them into her. Holding her as tight as I can, I thrust in short little hip rolls, pressing my knot against her clit. Rocking harder but never letting her out of my hold so that she bounces within my arms.

'Please, please.' She groans before her mouth latches onto my shoulder. Her lips suction as her teeth graze my skin and I can't take it. It's too much like the bite I want to give her.

'Come for me sweetness.' I demand and she nods her head. She wants to. But I feel her shake and quiver, I can tell she can't get there on her own. 'I'm going to count down from five, and when I say, you come.'

She nods dramatically against my chest and I feel her twitch closer to her release with just the rule.

'Five.' I start my count. 'Oh my god you're such a good girl.' I groan as I pull her in tight against me as I let my hips thrust forward, rutting against her.

'Four. Feel how wet you are for me, sweetness.' I grunt out trying to go harder but unwilling to pull back and let her out of my arms.

'Three.' I choke out as I feel her pulse around me, her orgasm ready to take her.

'Two. Sweetness you're killing me, you're so tight.' I swallow the word in a growl into her ear, her caged in my arms, my hips slapping against her thighs.

'One.' I groan against her ear pushing myself hard into her clit so she can feel the pressure she needs without my knot. 'Now come for me sweetness.'

She screams her release into my ear, her body shaking in my arms. As I feel her spasm and grip me I let go of my own pleasure. It's like lighting up my spine as my orgasm crashes down upon me. Spilling myself inside her, I shudder like I'm vibrating.

I pull her tightly against me as I slide to the side, pulling her with me, so I don't crush her as I fall into the couch. I'd never given much thought to what it would be like to be with my omega but even if I had, I never could have imagined this.

Chapter 54. Melanie

I'm hungry. I have no idea what time it is. But my stomach is growling like I've missed a whole day's worth of food. Mick left himself inside me and I feel so full, so content. If it wasn't for my grumbling stomach, I think I'd be happy to stay here all night.

'What are you thinking about?' He asks, pushing a stray lock of hair away from my face. My instinct is to lie and make up something romantic or at least more normal but my omega demands I tell the truth. I sigh.

'I was just thinking if I didn't have to eat I would quite happily stay here with you inside me all night.' He laughs softly leaning forward to kiss my forehead.

'Me too sweetness, me too.' I can feel him smiling into my hair and I want to preen with joy. His arms tighten around me as he rolls, pulling me on top of him so that I'm straddling his lap. His back is pressed into the couch cushions and the change in position makes me aware that he's no longer completely spent. In fact if I rocked my hips I bet I could...

'Fuck. You're trying to kill me.' He groans, his arm flopping against his face to cover his eyes. I look down at where we're joined and feel the urge to laugh. We're still dressed. Mostly. His pants are tucked down but not off. My shirt has fallen back down and the boxer shorts I'm wearing have slid mostly back into place around where we are joined. I look like I'm just sitting on him. I rock my hips to assure myself he's still inside.

'Sweetness. If you keep doing that we're going to start this all over again.' He groans from under his arm. His hips flexing up into me.

'And that would be bad?' I ask.

'No but you need to take a break babygirl.' My eyes snap to the voice in the corner. George is walking into the living room with a cocky grin I've never seen before. I feel myself melting under his gaze. He's changed at some point so he too is wearing loose sweatpants and a rather old worn looking shirt that gapes around his neck.

'Yes. Daddy.' I'm still cautious but he nods his approval as he reaches down to wrap his hand gently around my throat and guide my lips to his. His kiss is short and firm and I find myself swaying into it.

'Good girl.' He murmurs against my lips.

'Not helping.' Mick grumbles from beneath me and I realise I'm still sitting on him. He's in me. While his packmate leans over the back of the couch and kisses me. Fuck that's hot. Slick flows from me as I feel my perfume burst around me. 'Shit. I don't know what just happened but she liked it.'

I pull away from George, reaching up to cover my face with my hands.

'No hiding baby girl.' George's grip switches to the back of my neck pulling my gaze up to him. 'We love it. Promise.'

I nod as his fingers trace small circles on the side of my neck. Mick's hands stroking up and down my thighs from below. I am never going to calm down if they keep this up. I rock my hips with need and Mick reaches out to still them.

'Either we stop now or I'm not stopping.' Mick growls.

'Just a pause.' George mutters.

'Okay.' I nod. George smiles at me and it lights up his whole face. I bask in the warmth of it. Mick's hands that had been stilling my hips grip them tighter as he lifts me off him. The space inside me quivers and I whimper without meaning too.

'Just a pause.' George reminds me as he lifts me off his packmate, over the couch and straight into his arms. I wrap myself around him nuzzling deep into the crook of his neck. 'Good girl.'

'I'm hungry.' I grumble into his muscles.

'I figured. We have a picnic set up in your room'

'Everything ready?' Mick asks as he comes to stand behind me. I lost track of him for a moment and in the process he found a shirt. My omega doesn't like it.

'Yeah it's all good.' George assures.

'No!' I grumble.

'What's wrong?' They ask in unison and it would be comical if my omega wasn't so upset. I'm not used to feeling her this intensely. Nor am I used to feeling so strongly about anything, let alone this. But I don't want this, I need it. 'Shirts off!'

It's not a request, it's a demand. I feel like a petulant child and I brace for them to tell me off. Tell me to behave. Tell me to stop being a brat. But instead I feel Mick move behind me and then his shirt is being placed against my chest as George shuffles me into his packmates hold and removes his shirt as well. Handing it to me so that I'm clutching both their shirts to my chest, my legs still wrapped around George, my upper body pressed back into Mick, his arms around me.

'Better?' George asks and I nod. 'You keep those.'

Mick shifts me back into George's grip and he carries me down the hall into my room. I'm so content I almost don't notice the smell. It can only be wet paint.

I squirm in George's arms and jump down to the ground turning to face my room. I barely recognise it.

All the plain furniture, gone. The white bedding, gone. Even the curtains are gone. And where there were boring cream walls is now a blue so dark it's almost black. But they haven't left the walls blank, some of my artwork from home is hanging on the wall. In fact many of my missing possessions are here, clean and perfect.

In the center of the room is now a massive four-poster bed, bigger than my one at home. The bedding is dark blue, with extra pillows in dark green and gold. It's everything. It's everything I said I wanted. And they gave it to me.

I spin back to George and jump. He catches me as my lips land on his. It's not a gentle kiss. Or even a passionate kiss. It is aggressive and soon my lips are abandoning his so I can kiss his cheeks, his shoulder, everything I can reach.

'Thank you.' I mumble between each kiss. 'Thank you, thank you, thank you.'

'You're welcome.' George smirks at me. 'But it really was a team effort.'

I turn to look at the three other men in the room and I'm overwhelmed by how each of their smiles transforms their faces. They beaming at me, proud and happy at how I'm responding.

'Thank you, all of you. You didn't have to do this but I love it.'

'Of course we didn't have to.' Sam rolls his eyes as he takes a seat on the floor. 'But after that reaction I hope you know we're all going to be competing to see who can spoil you the most.'

'Yeah I'm going to win that one.' Mick grumbles as he sits besides Sam on the floor. It's then that I notice the picnic. The room now also includes a dark blue rug, at least an inch thick. And in the center of it is a picnic of sorts. There's cheese and crackers and fruit. It looks amazing.

'We're going to eat in here?' I ask as I join them on the rug. It's ridiculously soft. John and George sit beside me till we're all gathered in a circle.

'So you can enjoy your present.' George nods at me and I smile so wide it hurts.

I pull Melanie's shirt over her head, throwing it away like it offends me. Which it does now that I can see her beautiful breasts heaving in front of me. They should never be covered in this bed. The boxers are next as I place kisses all along her skin and gently peel them down her legs before they join the shirt on the floor.

She's gloriously naked, her creamy skin contrasting against the dark blue pillows. Her thick thighs clenching together hiding from me what I want most. I grip her knees gently and pull them apart so I can settle my face between her thighs. I slide my hands underneath her to hold her where I want her. Letting my breath caress her folds as I wait. Staring up at her, waiting till her eyes land on mine.

'Good girl.' I whisper against her clit before I let my mouth descend and pull the swollen bud between my lips. She moans as her back arches pushing her into my mouth. She tastes like heaven. And she smells like us.

I groan with pleasure as I take long languid licks along her slit. Sliding my hands from her ass, I let one snake up to wrap around her hips and hold her down as the other finds its way to her hot wet center. I let my fingers dance along her opening, stretching her, teasing her, testing her. I need her begging.

I keep my assault against her clit going as I slowly dip my fingers inside her, curling them up and back towards me again and again. Her fingers reach down into my hair to push me away but I don't let her. I need her to coat my tongue. I set a rhythm with my fingers as I let my lips close and suck her inside my mouth, letting my tongue flick against her.

Her cry of pleasure as she comes against my face soothes something deep inside me, where my alpha lives. I feel him rumble with pride like I never have before. And he settles. All my life I've had to fight to keep him calm, to hold him back. But her flavour on my tongue as she screams is everything to him.

Chapter 56. Melanie

That was intense. In the last twenty four hours I'd thought I was getting used to the sensations these men could steal from my body but that was different. It wasn't the same as when I submitted for John or took Sam. It was vastly different to Mick's love making. They all felt incredible in different ways. But this...

I feel settled. It's the best word I can think of to describe it. Like everything is going to be okay now. Not because things wouldn't happen but because I won't be alone. There's a part of me that almost feels weepy.

Then his tongue darts out for another taste and I forget everything but the feel of his mouth on me. He dropped his head to my thigh and snuggled against my softness as I came down but it seems he is now done waiting.

'Sensitive.' I eek out as he rolls me between his lips.

'Good.' He snaps, his cocky grin flashing up at me as he begins dragging hot open mouthed kisses against my skin. His tongue and lips drag against me leaving a hot path that quickly cools as he moves higher. Without pause he pulls my nipple into his mouth. The pressure and the heat are delicious as his hand finds my other breast and squeezes.

'Ahh.' I moan.

'Too much?' He whispers on my skin.

'No.' I shake my head as I stare down at him. 'But a lot.'

'You remember your safe words?' He questions with a raised eyebrow.

'Will I need them?' I tease.

'I don't know. But, I can only do the things to you that I want to if I know you will be honest with me. If it's too much, at any time, you tell me.' I nod. His sincerity has chased away my words and so instead I pull him down to my lips.

He groans into our kiss before pulling back to rearrange himself so that his hips are held in the cradle of my thighs. Gently he pulls his length through my wet folds coating himself in me. It's the most delicate of touches right where I want it, but so far from what I need that it makes me feel crazy.

'I need you.' He groans. I feel the same way as his head presses forward and notches inside me. I kiss him as he applies pressure and he slowly slips inside. He's so thick, and it turns out I was wrong, I am sore. But it's a gorgeous kind of ache as he stretches me again.

'More.' I try raising my hips to force him deeper faster but he continues his slow and steady pace.

'Greedy girl.' He whispers into my hair while he keeps up his mind numbingly slow pace. I'm so done with his sweet torture, I speak without thinking.

'Fuck me Daddy.' George freezes above me. Then he growls in my ear and slams home so hard I lose my breath. With him buried deep within, his knot already pressing against my entrance I shiver, it's not an orgasm but something close. Like it was too much pleasure all at once but not enough. George's hips pull back and slam forward again and I see stars. My body quakes.

'Do you like that babygirl?' I whimper as I nod. I can't form words. I can't do anything but cling to him as my fingers claw at his shoulder blades and beg him to continue. 'Do you want more?'

I nod. Every slide of him inside me feels like electricity rolling through my spine. I feel wanton and delicious with my legs thrown open.

One of his hands clutches my thigh and lifts my knee back towards me. He slips deeper still, a feat I didn't think possible and the change in the angle puts more pressure on my clit as I begin to shudder.

'I can't.' I don't know what I'm saying but suddenly I'm mumbling. 'I can't. It's too much. I can't.'

'Yes you can babygirl. Say your safe word and I will stop but you are mine. And you can take it. Let me give you this. Please. Let me do this.'

I nod. I feel tears on my cheeks and I don't know why. I'm not scared. I'm not sad.

You're happy. The voice inside me explains. *Now let go. He'll catch us.*

I listen to the voice. I stop trying to hold onto anything but the man in my arms and let the feelings inside me take over.

When George pushes firmly against me, I feel his knot slide inside. I explode. His lips suck on my collar bone as he shudders through his own climax. I scream so loud it's embarrassing as my whole body pulls taut. It's almost too much, it feels too good. But I let it take me. And I let myself fall.

His knot expands inside me, locking us together and every muscle in my body relaxes as the pleasure rolls through me.

I thought I remembered what this felt like. To be full and held. But this is so much better than my memories. We lie together panting into each other's skin. His whiskey scent tickles my nose. He's never smelled this strong before, it makes me feel drunk.

His forehead rests against my chest as he holds himself above me. There's not a bit of space between us but I feel none of his weight. We're stuck together. Literally and figuratively. And I love it.

I tilt my head to kiss him. It's a gentle rolling kiss, sweet and innocent. Which feels strange considering he's buried deep inside me, sweat still dripping off both our bodies.

Chapter 55. George

I have been wasting my life. Because nothing I have ever done has felt as good as getting this room painted for Melanie. Watching my brothers laugh and tell stories on each other. Taking it in turns building combinations of crackers, cheese and fruit and feeding them to her. It was a perfect evening.

Eventually Melanie climbed up in her big new bed, remarking on how it felt perfect and almost passed out. We'd worn her out.

I'd chosen the bed specifically for its size and we all piled in around her. Sam and Mick on the edges. John and I closest to her. I'd say I didn't care where I was as long as I was in her bed but that's not true. When in her sleep it was me she curled into, I knew I'd fight my brothers to stay here.

But now it was Tuesday morning and they all scurried off. John and Sam had work, Mick merely mumbled the word 'project' before wandering off, leaving me alone in bed with Melanie. With her pressed into my side, the room soaked in all of our scents, I had a feeling it would be awhile before I willingly headed back to work.

'Coffee?' She mumbles into my chest.

'No good morning?' I tease, kissing her forehead.

'Good morning.' She smiles up at me without opening her eyes. 'Coffee?'

'Mick made you one, it's right here.' When Mick had brought me a long black earlier he'd also left her a latte in an insulated mug so it wouldn't get cold. The man truly was a genius.

Melanie sits up on the pillows next to me as she takes the mug in both hands and sips. She lets out a small sigh of pleasure before turning her gaze on me.

'How are you feeling?' I ask. She blushes in response but her eyes don't leave mine.

'Good.' Her dimples pop as she smiles. 'Really good.'

'Good.' I tease as I drop a kiss to her cheek and swap the phone in my hand for my own mug of lukewarm coffee and snuggle into the pillows with her.

'Who were you texting?' She gestures at the abandoned phone.

'Emailing actually. I had to write out a list of follow up things for my secretary.'

'What time do you have to go in today?' She sighs as she pushes the blankets away from her and kicks them down the bed. She's still in John's shirt and Sam's boxers and they cling to her softness, outlining her thick hips and hinting at her hard nipples.

'I don't.' I tell her, my gaze now glued to her chest as I lick my lips.

'You don't?' She sounds surprised.

'Nope, I just cancelled everything.' I shrug, tearing my eyes from her breasts so I can look her in the eye. 'There's a few emails I should deal with later but nothing important enough to warrant leaving you.'

'Bet you say that to all the girls.' She wiggles her eyebrows with the innuendo.

'Never.' I state emphatically. 'Normally I'm more a work first, play never guy.'

'What changed?' She asks slightly confused.

'You.' It's the truth. She changed everything. Before her I may have wanted an omega but not in the way I wanted Melanie. Having an omega was about doing the next right thing for our pack. Having Melanie was everything.

'Woah.' She whispers up at me, her eyes wide at whatever she sees on my face.

'Yep. We had a chat while you were asleep.' I offer, trying to lighten the mood.

'About?' She questions while sipping her coffee.

'You. And how we're not going to hold back anymore.' I shrug like it's no big deal.. It was actually a huge discussion. She'd been out like a light and so we'd all taken the chance to chat. Well, Sam had taken the chance to gloat really. But we'd all discussed it. The fact that we had been complete alphaholes in assuming we knew what was best for her. And how going forward we'd all just put our cards on the table. Still we didn't want to pressure her but we planned to trust her to make those boundaries.

'Why were you holding back to begin with?' Curiosity laces her voice.

'It was my dumb idea.' I shrug. 'Mary said we should be careful not to overwhelm you and I decided that meant we all had to keep our hands to ourselves and not scare you with how head over heels we all were for you from the second we met.'

'The second we met huh?' She rolls her eyes like I'm exaggerating.

'Technically, for me, it was from the moment I first heard your voice.' I put as much sincerity into my voice as I can. I need her to know it's the truth.

'I liked your voice too.' She murmurs and a moment of silence presses in on us.

'I didn't realise that us holding back from you was hurting you. I'm really really sorry. We were all so crazy about you it never occurred to me, or any of us, that you would think that we didn't want you.'

'Well...' She murmurs leaning into kiss my shoulder. 'I don't think that anymore.'

'Good girl.' I kiss her forehead again. I can't help it. I just want to leave my lips on her skin permanently.

'Do you get in trouble for saying sorry or is that just me?' She pokes me in the shoulder. I capture her hand and lift the coffee away to the bedside table.

'You don't get in trouble for saying sorry.' I explain as I roll back towards her until I'm leaning over her. 'You get in trouble for saying sorry when you've done nothing wrong. At one point I think I heard you apologise to a chair.'

'I bumped into it.' She shrugs.

'It's inanimate.' I roll over some more until my hips are nestled between her thighs.

'You're inanimate.' She grumbles sarcastically.

'No, I'm not.' I press myself firmly between her legs and delight as she squirms beneath me. 'Are you sore?'

'What?' She mumbles as I begin kissing down her neck, rolling my hips against hers. She's already lifting her hips up to meet me and I smile into her skin.

'Are you sore? Do you need a break?'

'No.' She harumphs out as she pulls me to her lips. I let our tongues tangle as her fingers move to grip my shoulders and pull me down into her. 'Knot me?'

I growl. God do I want to knot her. To make her mine. The other guys resisted last night because she needed all of us. But they're all gone. It's just the two of us. And we have all day.

'Is that what you want?' I pull back to look at her face as I let my alpha ask the question. Melanie nods enthusiastically, a wicked smile crossing her lips.

'My omega says knot me and make me yours or she's going to start saying sorry all the time as well.' My smile feels like it's going to break my cheeks as I dive down to kiss her again. I will never know how we got so lucky but I'll never not be grateful.

I pull Melanie's shirt over her head, throwing it away like it offends me. Which it does now that I can see her beautiful breasts heaving in front of me. They should never be covered in this bed. The boxers are next as I place kisses all along her skin and gently peel them down her legs before they join the shirt on the floor.

She's gloriously naked, her creamy skin contrasting against the dark blue pillows. Her thick thighs clenching together hiding from me what I want most. I grip her knees gently and pull them apart so I can settle my face between her thighs. I slide my hands underneath her to hold her where I want her. Letting my breath caress her folds as I wait. Staring up at her, waiting till her eyes land on mine.

'Good girl.' I whisper against her clit before I let my mouth descend and pull the swollen bud between my lips. She moans as her back arches pushing her into my mouth. She tastes like heaven. And she smells like us.

I groan with pleasure as I take long languid licks along her slit. Sliding my hands from her ass, I let one snake up to wrap around her hips and hold her down as the other finds its way to her hot wet center. I let my fingers dance along her opening, stretching her, teasing her, testing her. I need her begging.

I keep my assault against her clit going as I slowly dip my fingers inside her, curling them up and back towards me again and again. Her fingers reach down into my hair to push me away but I don't let her. I need her to coat my tongue. I set a rhythm with my fingers as I let my lips close and suck her inside my mouth, letting my tongue flick against her.

Her cry of pleasure as she comes against my face soothes something deep inside me, where my alpha lives. I feel him rumble with pride like I never have before. And he settles. All my life I've had to fight to keep him calm, to hold him back. But her flavour on my tongue as she screams is everything to him.

Chapter 56. Melanie

That was intense. In the last twenty four hours I'd thought I was getting used to the sensations these men could steal from my body but that was different. It wasn't the same as when I submitted for John or took Sam. It was vastly different to Mick's love making. They all felt incredible in different ways. But this...

I feel settled. It's the best word I can think of to describe it. Like everything is going to be okay now. Not because things wouldn't happen but because I won't be alone. There's a part of me that almost feels weepy.

Then his tongue darts out for another taste and I forget everything but the feel of his mouth on me. He dropped his head to my thigh and snuggled against my softness as I came down but it seems he is now done waiting.

'Sensitive.' I eek out as he rolls me between his lips.

'Good.' He snaps, his cocky grin flashing up at me as he begins dragging hot open mouthed kisses against my skin. His tongue and lips drag against me leaving a hot path that quickly cools as he moves higher. Without pause he pulls my nipple into his mouth. The pressure and the heat are delicious as his hand finds my other breast and squeezes.

'Ahh.' I moan.

'Too much?' He whispers on my skin.

'No.' I shake my head as I stare down at him. 'But a lot.'

'You remember your safe words?' He questions with a raised eyebrow.

'Will I need them?' I tease.

'I don't know. But, I can only do the things to you that I want to if I know you will be honest with me. If it's too much, at any time, you tell me.' I nod. His sincerity has chased away my words and so instead I pull him down to my lips.

He groans into our kiss before pulling back to rearrange himself so that his hips are held in the cradle of my thighs. Gently he pulls his length through my wet folds coating himself in me. It's the most delicate of touches right where I want it, but so far from what I need that it makes me feel crazy.

'I need you.' He groans. I feel the same way as his head presses forward and notches inside me. I kiss him as he applies pressure and he slowly slips inside. He's so thick, and it turns out I was wrong, I am sore. But it's a gorgeous kind of ache as he stretches me again.

'More.' I try raising my hips to force him deeper faster but he continues his slow and steady pace.

'Greedy girl.' He whispers into my hair while he keeps up his mind numbingly slow pace. I'm so done with his sweet torture, I speak without thinking.

'Fuck me Daddy.' George freezes above me. Then he growls in my ear and slams home so hard I lose my breath. With him buried deep within, his knot already pressing against my entrance I shiver, it's not an orgasm but something close. Like it was too much pleasure all at once but not enough. George's hips pull back and slam forward again and I see stars. My body quakes.

'Do you like that babygirl?' I whimper as I nod. I can't form words. I can't do anything but cling to him as my fingers claw at his shoulder blades and beg him to continue. 'Do you want more?'

I nod. Every slide of him inside me feels like electricity rolling through my spine. I feel wanton and delicious with my legs thrown open.

One of his hands clutches my thigh and lifts my knee back towards me. He slips deeper still, a feat I didn't think possible and the change in the angle puts more pressure on my clit as I begin to shudder.

'I can't.' I don't know what I'm saying but suddenly I'm mumbling. 'I can't. It's too much. I can't.'

'Yes you can babygirl. Say your safe word and I will stop but you are mine. And you can take it. Let me give you this. Please. Let me do this.'

I nod. I feel tears on my cheeks and I don't know why. I'm not scared. I'm not sad.

You're happy. The voice inside me explains. *Now let go. He'll catch us.*

I listen to the voice. I stop trying to hold onto anything but the man in my arms and let the feelings inside me take over.

When George pushes firmly against me, I feel his knot slide inside. I explode. His lips suck on my collar bone as he shudders through his own climax. I scream so loud it's embarrassing as my whole body pulls taut. It's almost too much, it feels too good. But I let it take me. And I let myself fall.

His knot expands inside me, locking us together and every muscle in my body relaxes as the pleasure rolls through me.

I thought I remembered what this felt like. To be full and held. But this is so much better than my memories. We lie together panting into each other's skin. His whiskey scent tickles my nose. He's never smelled this strong before, it makes me feel drunk.

His forehead rests against my chest as he holds himself above me. There's not a bit of space between us but I feel none of his weight. We're stuck together. Literally and figuratively. And I love it.

I tilt my head to kiss him. It's a gentle rolling kiss, sweet and innocent. Which feels strange considering he's buried deep inside me, sweat still dripping off both our bodies.

His hands slide beneath my shoulders pulling me up as he rolls us onto our sides, pulling my thigh up over his hip to accommodate the way we are still joined.

'I love you.' He whispers.

'What?'

'I know, I know. Too soon, not the right moment, all that. But remember I'm not holding back from you anymore. And it just occurred to me, I love you.'

'You do?'

'Yep.' He smiles at me as he tucks my hair behind my ear so he can hold my cheek. 'I love your tentative smiles and your sweet concern. I love how incredibly smart you clearly are. Not just because you read more than anyone I've ever met but also because you run your own business, and take care of yourself. Although that last one you're going to have to bend on a little. I want to have a starring role in the taking care of you thing.'

'It's too... I can't...' I mutter, overwhelmed by everything he's saying and everything I'm feeling.

'I know. You don't have to. It's an offer. Not an obligation.' He kisses my forehead as he tucks me below his chin.

'I really do want to, it's just a lot.'

'I know. Do you need to use your safe word?'

'Not yet.' I chuckle.

'What about if I ask to show you the omega suite?'

'You have an omega suite?' I'm surprised. I thought I'd seen the whole house.

'Yep, it's most of the top floor. I didn't show you because I thought it might be too much and I dumbly decided to make the decision for you. But now I'm offering. Say no if you don't want to see it. But the decision is yours, not mine.'

'I guess I should probably at least look at the nest. I mean my heat is due to restart any day now.' I mumble.

'Okay.' He shrugs. But something feels off.

'What's wrong?' I ask. His dramatic sigh ruffles my hair.

'Nothing. With you in my arms, nothing could ever be wrong. My alpha just wishes that you wanted to see the nest, not out of practicality but because you're excited. Because you want to be here with us.'

Tell him. My omega demands.

'I do want to see it. But there's a part of me that worries that I'll see it and love it. And then you'll change your mind. Or get sick of me. And I'll be attached but you won't want me anymore.' I speak quickly to get it all out.

'I wish there was something I could say to convince you, that is never going to happen. But I think I'm just going to have to show you. With time you're going to realise exactly how crazy for you we all are.' I blush at his words.

'I've never had an actual nest before.' His growl quickly transforms into a purr.

'From now on you'll have everything.' He grumbles as I sigh with contentment. Right now I feel like I already do.

KNOT FOR REAL

Chapter 57. John

Nervous and angry is a weird combination but it was what I was feeling.

Last night I'd come home to find Melanie teaching George and Mick to make gnocchi. She was standing between them laughing as she showed them how to roll out the little balls of potato goodness and I fell even deeper for this girl.

I rushed forward for a kiss, surprised when George growled at me and snatched her up into his arms. I paused in confusion as Melanie started stroking George's arms telling him everything was okay and Mick laughed.

'Same thing happened to me.' Mick shrugged. 'It seems the bossman here is suffering some alpha territory issues.'

I watched as Melanie blushed at his explanation and realised that meant George must have knotted her. It was common for alphas to become territorial after, even more so if they were scent sensitive. I was actually impressed that George was letting us in the same room, even if we were pack.

'Can I just give her a kiss on the cheek?' I'd asked and he'd nodded without releasing her so I'd settled for dropping a peck on her cheek and whispering in her ear. 'I missed you.'

I'd then joined in on the gnocchi making and had the joy of the whole scene repeating again when Sam finally made it home from work and made the mistake of trying to snare Melanie into a hug.

The night had been going so well and I'd had plans about what we would all be doing later that got completely derailed when

Melanie's phone rang during dinner. And kept ringing. With a sigh worthy of a walk to the gallows she'd excused herself to answer it and then came back moments later looking like she wished she'd died.

'What's wrong?' We'd all chorused together unintentionally.

'That was my mum, I don't know how but she heard that I was here, about you guys.' The way she spoke was like she'd handed us a death sentence.

'So?' Mick questioned, opening his arms to her. She'd climbed into his lap so willingly that I felt all of us sigh with relief. Melanie didn't answer the question though, she just played with the collar of his shirt.

'She wants us all to come over for dinner tomorrow night.'

'So we go.' I shrug. She nodded into Mick's chest but didn't say anything. We all shared concerned glances with each other and returned to our food. But the energy changed because it was clear Melanie was upset.

We spent the evening cuddling on the couch and eventually Mick carried her to bed and once again we all climbed in around her. George insisted on holding her against his chest while she slept.

I'm not sure any of us slept well. I know I didn't. I knew Melanie had a somewhat difficult relationship with her parents. Their decision not to take her in when her heat was coming on and the fact that they hadn't checked in on her except to make this demand for us to all come for dinner made me pretty certain that they weren't people I was going to respect. But the way she went from light and laughter to small and sad in the space of one phone call had me wondering how I was going to stand these people.

A question I asked myself again as I watched her fret over what to wear. As if she could get it right or wrong. Eventually she settled on a simple sheath dress she had brought with her that she looked stunning in. George insisted we all wear suits and look our best so as to make a good impression.

We agreed we wanted to make a good impression, hence why I was nervous. But anger pushes to the forefront as I watch Melanie fidget and step side to side with nerves as we wait on her parent's doorstep.

It was weird. My dad had been gone not long after I moved out but I could never imagine not having a key to his house or him getting me to wait for him to open the door instead of me just wandering in.

The stress radiating off Melanie reminds me of the time I had to tell my dad that I'd lost his lucky baseball cap. I'd borrowed it without asking and then somehow lost it down by the river with my friends. I was sure he was going to be furious but he'd just said that I knew better than to take without asking and that in the future I should try and do better.

He wasn't even mad that I'd lost it. He just shrugged and said that these things happen, the part I needed to work on was my fear of asking and being told no. He said a real man knew how to hear no and be proud he asked instead of disappointed he didn't get the answer he wanted.

Even growing up I knew I'd won the father lottery. A fact that had become even more apparent when my brothers shared stories from their childhood. George was mostly abandoned by his beta parents who were more interested in making money than his existence. Mick had grown up in the foster system, something he never spoke about. And Sam, well Sam didn't speak about his upbringing much either but many years ago he drunkenly divulged his story which was somehow the worst of Sam's and George's stories combined.

I was glad my brothers were also here tonight, I didn't have a frame of reference for how to support Melanie but they did.

'Should we ring the doorbell again?' I ask.

'No, we should just wait.' As she speaks the door finally opens to reveal the horrible woman who came into Melanie's cafe, what felt like a month ago but was actually only last week.

'Hey big sis.' She snarks. I feel the urge to steal Melanie away and we haven't even entered the house. This is not going to go well.

'Hey Lucy.' Melanie smiles as she steps inside. We all crowd around and follow her in, not so subtly competing to see who can be closer to her. 'Where's your pack?'

'At home. They had other things they needed to do tonight.' Lucy shrugs before walking off down the hall. Melanie takes off her shoes so we all do the same and pad after her down the hallway.

I can't imagine Melanie growing up here. It's all varying shades of cream and so sterile. It's the opposite of everything I know her to love. We enter the dining room to find an older couple sitting at the head of the table. They stand and George steps forward to greet them.

'You must be Maxwell and Irene. I'm George, and this is my pack. That's Mick, Sam and John.' He points to us each in turn but none of us step forward to greet the couple as he did. We agreed we should try and impress them but being civil was still going to be a stretch. Some of us felt that meant not murdering anyone this evening.

'This is such a surprise.' Irene remarks, her hand on her chest. 'When Melanie's friend mentioned that she was spending time with a pack we just didn't believe it.'

'We're very taken with your daughter.' George remarks quickly, and loudly to cover the growls that emanate from myself and Sam next to me. Mick seems to have tuned out from the room entirely, simply playing with a strand of Melanie's hair as he stands behind her.

'You're all so tall and handsome, not what I would have expected.' Irene remarks, unaware of our ire. I watch as Melanie's gaze drops to her feet and I barely resist the urge to bark at her mum to shut up. 'Though I suppose any omega is appealing when they're close to their heat.'

Melanie blanches and it's only her fingers gripping mine that stop me from lunging at the woman. How dare she insinuate that we'd only want Melanie for her heat. I was obsessed with her for a bloody year before I even knew she was an omega. I'm sure I'm about to start yelling when George speaks again.

'Actually we're courting your daughter with the intention to bond. If she chooses us that is.' I smile and barely resist punching the air. Take that bitchy mum. Not only do we want your daughter, we plan to keep her forever.

There's an awkward tension in the room. Her parents are unsure as to what to do now that George has made our intentions so clear.

'Well, you should all sit down.' Maxwell gestures to the seats around the table. George pulls the bottle of wine out of its bag as a gift to them and they make a horrible fuss over it being such a nice bottle as we all take our seats. Maxwell sits at the head of the table, his wife and his other daughter next to him. Without consciously planning we all seem to agree to seating Melanie at the other end with all of us in between.

'I hope you all like fish. I don't know what Melanie's eating habits are like around you but we did try and teach her how to eat healthy. She never quite got it though.' Irene murmurs the last into her glass. She casts a sideways glance at Melanie and I watch as she shrinks down further in her chair.

Yep I was going to consider tonight a success if we didn't murder anyone.

Chapter 58. Melanie

This is somehow ten times worse than I'd ever imagined it could be. And yet not nearly as bad as it could be at the same time. After George's declaration the room was tense. My parents seemed unsure of what to do in the face of these men who wouldn't laugh with them when they made jokes about my weight or my cafe. So now it seemed they were trying to figure out what was wrong with the guys since they liked me. And as such my father started grilling them about their professions.

John explained what he did as a programmer and my dad made a joke about technology being the death of real business. Sam talked about being a lawyer and my mum had chimed in with a story about a lawyer who had cheated one of her friends. Mick went next talking about how he worked as an innovator and my sister had gone on a rant about how her pack had come across so many people who called themselves that but never really did anything.

That was when I excused myself to the bathroom.

These poor guys, they didn't deserve the crap my parents were trying to put on them. I'm sure if my parents had met them in any other setting, a work function or at the club, they would have been considered great guys. But because they came here with me it seemed my parents were set on making them out to be nothing.

Too bad because they were four of the kindest, smartest, most charming men I'd ever met. And I was pretty sure that wasn't just the scent sensitivity talking. But hell even if this was all just hormones I was going to run with it because damn did they make me happy.

Listening to George declare his intentions to bond with me had a light waking up inside me I didn't think could even shine in my parents' presence. However it was also the first I knew of this plan. I wasn't really surprised though.

George may not have told me outright that they wanted me to be their omega and bond with me but he had told me he loved me. And he'd taken me on a tour of the omega suite asking me how I wanted it decorated and heavily implied that I would move in there. Bonding was the next logical step.

As a child I'd dreamed of taking the bond. Connecting myself and my soul to the person or people I loved. The thought that you would always be able to feel the people who loved you. That you could connect your souls and share your emotions, your thoughts. It was the greatest gift you could give.

But after everything that had happened with my old pack I'd just kind of assumed that it would never happen for me. But now? Now I had some things to think about.

I washed and dried my hands and then fixed my hair before leaving the bathroom. I knew my mother wasn't happy with the way I was dressed tonight but the guys had all loved my simple dress and my loose curls. And it was for them I wanted to look good anyway.

I step out into the hallway ready to reenter the fray only to be stopped by my sister lounging against the opposite wall.

'Hey big sis.' She snarks

'Do you have to start?' I sigh.

'What?' She shrugs all innocence and surprise.

'The big sis thing. I'm younger than you.'

'But you're bigger.' She points at my stomach as if I'm not a hundred per cent aware of what she means.

'So? Who cares? Doesn't make me less than you.'

'Never said it did.' She pastes a fake sweet smile on her face.

'Don't start that crap.' I groan. This is what my family was best at, spinning things around and making me feel crazy, like all their harsh words were figments of my imagination.

'You think you're just going to wander off into the sunset with those men? You don't think they're going to get bored of you?' I don't respond. Because I had wondered the same thing myself. What would happen if they got sick of me?

'Look, we've only just started courting. Nothing's set in stone yet.' I hedge.

'Please, if they want to bite you, you're going to let them. You'll take what you can get.' She snaps as she steps off the wall, standing right in front of me. 'And then one day you'll start hearing all their real thoughts. About how your ass is going flat. Your boobs aren't as perky as they used to be. That you're not as funny or interesting as they thought you were. And you can't escape it. You can put up a wall but it doesn't do much.'

'Lucy, what are you talking about?'

'Just you wait. Wait till they bark you into submission because you disagree with them, or bark at you to suck them off because they're in the mood and you're not. Then you'll understand.' And suddenly I did.

I understood why my sister was the way she was. She'd been raised in the same house as me. And on the surface she had it easier because she was a good girl. The one who looked right and dressed right and got good grades. But she was just as controlled by our parents as I was.

And then when she finally had her escape, she finally got a pack, they turned out to be just as shitty as our parents. It made sense now. Why she'd become so much crueler after she'd bonded with them. It made sense, but it didn't make it better.

'That's not what it's going to be like for me.' I say it with conviction because even though it's only been a few days I know the guys would never say those kinds of horrible things to me, or do the disgusting things she's describing. They'd never take away my choice or try to make me feel small. In fact it seemed they all lived just to try and make me feel better.

'Whatever.' Lucy rolls her eyes as she pushes past me into the bathroom.

I stride away with a certainty I hadn't felt before I came here tonight. That these men are what I want. I get back to the dining room and take my seat at the opposite end of the table to my parents. From here they look small. Small people who I'd let have far too much control over my life.

'So George, you still haven't told me what it is you do?' My father drawls. He looks oily. Slimy almost.

'Have you heard of Jamieson enterprises?' George asks.

'Of course, great company. I would love to do business with them. You work there as a sales rep or something?' My dad's interest piqued. And it annoys me. I know what George is about to say, that actually, it's his company.

That it had been a small family business when he'd taken it over and that almost out of spite for his parents he'd grown it into the empire it was today. They'd basically abandoned him so that they could build the company and never actually managed to do so. So he'd made it the multi-billion dollar company it was, with its charitable wings, environmental principles and fair employment strategy to prove to them that you didn't have to screw people over to make something successful.

I know all this because we discussed it in bed. While we were locked together. And I told him all about my cafe. He listened like I too had built an empire. Asking questions and praising my effort. And I thought about all the times my parents had mocked my ambition for no reason other than they didn't understand it and suddenly I was mad. I was mad at them in a way I'd never really let myself be before.

'Actually I don't work there, I...' George speaks but I don't want him to explain.

'I want dessert.' I cut him off.

'Excuse me?' My mother scolds me. 'You father and George were speaking.'

'I know.' I stutter. Years of acquiescing kicks in, making me want to back down. But I feel John squeeze my hand, Sam's squeezes my knee where I didn't realise he'd placed his hand. Mick and George are smiling at me. 'But I want dessert.'

'You know we don't keep sweets in the house.' My mother chides as Lucy wanders back into the room and takes her seat.

'That's okay.' George winks at me. 'We have plenty of desserts at home.'

'I guess we should get going, what our girl wants, she gets.' Sam shrugs as he stands and the other three follow suit.

'I think I need some more proper food as well. I'm still hungry.' Mick grunts.

'Me too.' John announces to the room at large before leaning in to whisper in my ear. 'And I'm not just hungry for food.'

I blush so violently it's embarrassing as the four of them lead me out of the dining room leaving my family sitting at the table in shock. They help me gather my coat and my shoes but just as we begin to exit George grabs my collar and pulls me close so he can speak into the crown of my head the way he loves and whispers into my hair.

'Good girl.'

Chapter 59. Sam

That was a hard dinner. Not only because Melanie's parents are clearly social climbing arsesholes. But because it reminded me of so many dinners before.

That house was just like my parent's. With its stark white on white design right down to the judgemental comments and obsession with perfection. The only difference is that Melanie's story doesn't have as dark a beginning as mine.

I wanted to take her straight home, maybe have some ice cream and then get into bed and follow it up with her sweet strawberry syrup straight from the source. But the others had a more important plan. Which is why we were now standing in the massive Nesting Co. store.

I'd never been in here before and it wasn't as bad as I'd envisioned. It was all soft lighting and sweet scents. Every pillow shape, density and texture you could imagine, they had. Every blanket size, thickness and fluffiness, they had. And all of it came in every colour from soft pastels to dark rich colours.

Which seemed to be what Melanie was drawn to. She was nervous when we first came in. But with George whispering in her ear, John squeezing her hand and Mick carrying her from place to place, she'd gotten over her nerves. She still tried to fight to return some velvet pillows when she'd spotted their price tag, but when George retaliated by turning to the shop attendant and doubling the order, she gave in.

So we wandered from room to room, from pillows and blankets, to candles and lighting and now into the pampering section. It was filled with robes and eye masks and every beauty product man had invented. I broke off from the group and went looking for bubble bath to clear my thoughts.

Being back in that kind of house, so similar to the one I had grown up in, brought back memories of my own childhood I didn't want to linger in. But it didn't seem I had a choice. My mind kept coming back to the worst thing I'd ever done.

'You smell like a burnt marshmallow.' A sweet voice chimes from behind me. I lift my arm still contemplating the shelves, and Melanie immediately slides underneath like I knew she would and I sigh with relief at the contact.

'I always smell like a marshmallow.' I shrug. As I point at the rose scented bubble bath and she scrunches her nose no.

'You don't normally smell like you're burning though.' She prods.

'Just old thoughts coming back, nothing for you to worry about.' I pull her in tighter so I can kiss her cheek.

'What if I want to know?'

'You don't.' I sigh as I reach for a cotton candy scented bubble bath, I show it to her and she nods and so I head back towards our cart dragging her with me.

'Do you want to know all the things on my mind?' She lilts from under my arm.

'Yes of course.' I sigh leaning against the trolley. It's close to overflowing but there's still so many things I want to get her.

'Even if they're not nice thoughts?'

'Yes.' I groan, giving up and turning to stare at her. She's still wearing the gorgeous sheath dress from the dinner and with her hair down, backlit by the soft lighting of this section she looks like an honest to god angel.

'So it goes both ways right?' She shrugs.

'I don't want to burden you...' Her growl cuts me off as she steps toward me grabbing onto the lapels of my jacket to look me in the eye. As soon as she realises what she's done, she's so surprised she snorts with laughter.

'Sorry, I've never done that before.' Her eyes soften. 'But I now understand George's fury at that word when I said it.'

She moves to stand next to me, her hand reaching out to take the tips of my fingers in her hand. She smiles sweetly up at me, waiting.

'You really want to know?' She nods. 'Your parents reminded me a lot of my own.'

'That doesn't sound good.' I smile at her candor.

'I also had a sister.'

'Had?'

'When we were little, I was maybe nine and she was five, there was an accident. We were at one of my dad's work functions, their colleagues' house. We were climbing trees and she fell. I ran to the house for help but it was too late.' The words come out stilted and soft. I don't really want to talk about it.

'You were so young.' Her voice matches my own in volume but in hers there is shock.

'But I was older. I should have been taking care of her and...' I heft out a deep breath I didn't realise I was holding. 'My parents never let me forget it.'

'Was that why you didn't want an omega?' I can't help but tilt my head down onto her shoulder and groan.

'I can't believe I said all that stuff to you. I'm such an idiot.' I think back to our earliest meeting, when I thought she was a beta when I tried to flirt with her by assuring her I didn't want an omega.

'You were honest.' She shrugs.

'I was wrong.' I growl, placing my hands either side of her on the shopping cart, caging her in. 'I thought having an omega would be like that. Would be like the pressure that was always on me to take care of her. After she was gone, the way my parents always blamed me, it was like I owed them my life because I hadn't saved her.'

'Sam, you didn't...' She lifts her hand to my cheek but I can't let her speak.

'I know they were wrong and are full of crap. I know. But I was scared to have someone who needed me again. She needed me and I failed her.' My eyes implore her to understand. I failed the most precious thing in the world to me. And now she was it. The most precious thing in the entire world. I needed her to understand I could fail her like I failed before.

'You didn't fail her. Your parents did. And then they failed you.' I close my eyes as she shudders through a breath. 'You can't fail me. It's not possible. Not if you keep trying. That's the only thing I ask, keep trying to share. And as long as you're trying you're making me feel like I'm worth fighting for. That's everything to me.'

'I love you. I do. I love you so much. You're so kind and hard working. And so loving and beautiful. I love you.' I kiss her firmly before pulling back. There's surprise in her eyes. 'You're incredible. As is your arse.'

She laughs as I break the tension between us. And I chuckle as well loving the way her dimples pop when she smiles like that.

'You know it was really sweet until that last thing.'

'I am who I am, and your arse is a masterpiece.' I kiss her again, slower. Sliding my hands down to grab her arse and haul her against me. I feel the others approach, knowing they overheard most of our conversation if not all of it. I've never really spoken to them about my sister before and something feels softer inside myself for having shared.

I pull back from Melanie reluctantly knowing the others are standing at my sides waiting. She's flushed pink from our kiss and her sweet strawberry smell is thicker than before. Almost like toffee. It's incredible. If this was what I was going to get for opening up I was going to be doing it a lot more.

'That's everything we need to get today.' George explains adding a few more things to our shopping cart. 'The attendant has already sent some stuff to our place along with a team to install.'

'Already?' Melanie asks in a daze.

'It was a part of our booking.'

'We had a booking?' John is as surprised as I am. I thought we'd just wandered in here.

'Yes an after hours booking.' George gestures to the shop around us. 'Did you not notice we had the whole store to ourselves?'

'I just thought we were the only ones insane enough to be doing their shopping at nine o'clock at night.' I shrug. Now that he pointed it out, the hovering attendant and the empty store, yeah it made sense.

'I organised it as a surprise for Melanie.' He smiles down at her in front of me. We've all cornered her against the shopping cart full of gifts. She's still blushing, even more than before.

'Melanie are you okay?' Mick reaches out to rest his hand against her forehead. And my pleasure in her soft blush evaporates instantly.

'Just warm.' She shudders at his touch.

'No sweetness.' Mick steps in between us, lifting her into his arms. 'We need to go home. Now.'

Chapter 60. Melanie

So warm. I'm so warm and tingly. Like there's a bubble bath under my skin. There are bubbles. And there is a bath. But it's not hot like me.

'Why am I in the bath?' I ask no one in particular.

'Just needed you to slow down for a second sweetness.' A big voice rumbles above me.

'Mick?' I turn confused, and there he is beside me. Or beside the bath. I'm in the bath and he's kneeling next to it.

'I'm right here.' He smiles at me as his big warm hand draws circles on my back and I lean towards it.

'Mmm. You feel good.' I sigh into his massage.

'So do you.' He smiles. It's a nice smile. Like he's got a good secret. I like secrets.

'What's the secret?' I whisper to him.

'There's a secret?' He asks, his face full of amusement.

'Yeah, look at that smile. You have a secret. What is it? I'll keep it. I'm good at keeping secrets.' I nod till my head hurts. I am the best at keeping secrets. So good.

'What secrets do you keep sweetness?' He asks, his warm hand tracing circles on my back trying to distract me. But I won't be distracted. Laser focus. Lasers are cool. Focus is hard. Wait. Secret.

'That I was me, an omega.' I tell him my secret. Look at me focusing. Nailed it.

'Yeah that was a big secret. I'm glad I know the truth now though.' He smiles at me and I reach out to put some bubbles on his nose. I'd put a bubble beard on him but he already has a real one. George is prone to stubble but Mick is the only one with a real beard. It's so soft. I like it. I like him.

'I'm glad you know too.' I assure him as I put bubbles on his eyebrows. 'It fixes the other secret.'

'What's the other secret?' He asks as I wipe off his bubbles so I can start again. I think he needs more on his cheeks.

'Come closer, I need to whisper.' He shuffles till his face is hanging on the edge of the bath staring up at me. He's so cute. When I first met the giant I thought he was scary. Not anymore. He's too sweet to be anything but cute.

'What's the secret?' He mumbles up at me while I pile more bubbles on his face, this time giving him puffy cheeks.

'I was lonely.' I tell him, making sure the bubbles are even.

'We were lonely too.' He tells me. His eyes so serious it hurts. I push the bubbles off his face and clean my hands so I can close his eyes. Too serious.

'That's not the secret.' I grumble before releasing his face and letting my hands flop back in the water.

'It's not?'

'No, the secret is, I'm not lonely anymore.'

'That's the secret?' He smiles at me. He definitely has a secret.

'Yeah.' I nod.

'And why is that a secret?' He asks.

'If I don't tell anyone it won't go away.' I shrug. My brain is so fuzzy and warm. Like nothing is really happening. So I can say it now. Now doesn't count.

'Sweetness, we're not going anywhere.' He tells me with a growl. It rattles the tub and puts patterns in the water.

'You can't promise that.' I explain. 'No one can promise. You could die.'

'True.' He bites out.

'You could get bored of me.'

'Never.'

'You could change your mind.'

'No. We want you. That's not going to change.' He shakes his head.

'For now.' I sigh. Sliding deeper in the bath. My hair is all piled on my head in some clip I don't remember putting in it so I let the water lap up around my shoulders. 'It's such a shame.'

'What's a shame?'

'I like you all so much.'

'We like you too.'

'I'm going to be very sad when you leave.'

'We're not going to leave you.'

'I know.' I sigh. I know he says that. They all say that. But they'll leave eventually. Argh. I don't like these thoughts. They're all slow and sad. Gross.

I'm too hot again. I try to get out of the bath so I can cool down but as soon as I stand out of the water I'm boiling. The water dripping down my body feels like it's evaporating as it sizzles against me.

'What's happening?' I demand.

'Your heat.' Mick explains wrapping me in a big fluffy towel. It feels nice. He lifts me from the tub like I weigh nothing. Never going to get used to that. How strong he is, he can just plop me where he wants me which is right next to the sink. He strokes the towel against my skin, drying the lingering damp before letting down my hair.

'Am I going to ruin it?' I ask him. But it's not me speaking. My omega shakes with fear inside me. She's scared. It's been so long since we did this for real. And she ruined everything. We ruined everything, together.

'No sweetness. The guys are almost finished setting up the nest and then I'll take you in there. And you can do whatever you want. If you want to stay in there by yourself we'll wait outside for whatever you need. It's whatever you want. Whatever you want is right. You can't ruin anything if you just tell us what is right for you.'

'And if I want you in there with me?'

'Then that's where we'll be.' I sigh as I lean forward burying my face in his chest. He's changed at some point and he's wearing a flannel top. I love it, it's so green and soft and it feels good. And it smells like him, like lavender. I rub my face against it again.

'Sweetness, can I carry you in there now?'

'You still have to tell me your secret.' I pull my head back to demand of him.

'I don't have one.' He shakes his head, eyes filled with confusion.

'Yes you do, when I was in the bath and you were all smiling, I could tell, you had a secret.' He tucks the hair behind my ear smiling down at me. Even sitting on the counter he's still so much taller than me. But I'm a couple inches taller than normal so I can pull on his ears and make him look me in the eye. 'What were you thinking about?'

'How much I love you.' He hefts out a breath. His lavender smell soaking into me.

'Oh.' I let my gaze drift to the ceiling as I contemplate that.

'Oh.' He chuckles, placing his forehead on my collar bone and rolling his face side to side against me. It feels nice. Like a weird massage.

'Is that a secret, that you love me?' I prod.

'Not anymore.' He chuckles into my skin.

'George and Sam said it too.' I sigh as my arms hold his head against me.

'Did they now?' His voice is muffled.

'Do you think it's true?' I ask the ceiling.

'Yes.'

'That's good.' I nod as I let him go and he pulls back to look down at me again.

'It is?' He smiles. I like his smile, it makes his beard move.

'Yeah. It would suck to love people who didn't love me.' I explain.

'Is that your way of saying you love us too?'

'Not yet.' I shake my head.

'We're ready.' George's voice calls softly from the doorway. I look over to him leaning his shoulder frame as he stares at me. I think he's been there awhile.

'Ready.' I nod. 'Up please?'

I reach my arms up and latch them around Mick's shoulders. He chuckles as he slides his hands from my knees up along my thighs, lifting me up into his arms.

I let him carry me from the pretty bathroom into a big bedroom I vaguely recognise. But it wasn't this pretty magenta colour when George showed it to me before. And none of this pretty furniture was here. He stops on the far side of the room gently setting me on the ground and opening the door behind me.

I turn and step inside the nest. My nest.

It's perfect.

Chapter 61. Mick

George had the painters here first thing this morning so there's still a faint smell of paint in the air I don't like but it was definitely worth it. I watch as Melanie wanders into her nest and spins around. There are soft sconce lights along the edges casting soft golden flickering light along the dark red walls. The pit's covered in black plush material and then filled with every shade of pillow and blanket you could imagine, all of them bright jewel tones.

'It looks perfect.' Melanie whines, her tone devastated. I want to lurch at her through the door but I don't. I find myself gripping the doorframe to hold myself and my brothers back as they try and push past me to get to her.

'She has to invite us in.' I grit out through my teeth.

'She's upset.' John growls at my shoulder.

'Melanie, Sweetness.' I call and her watery eyes lock on mine. 'Would you like any of us in there with you.'

Her head tilts to one side and then the other as she contemplates us. We must look intensely strange, all of us bare chested, in our sweats crowded in the doorway just to be an inch closer to her.

'I need you to fix it.' She nods.

'Fix what?'

'It smells wrong.' She scowls at the room like it offends her.

'Okay.' I nod still, holding my brothers back I whisper at them. 'That's not an invitation, you alphaholes. She needs the space to be right before we can go in.'

'But she needs us to fix it!' George snaps.

'I know.' I growl at him. 'So stop trying to push past me so I can get what she needs.'

They immediately relent and I cross the room and grab one of the three laundry baskets and carry it over.

'Grab the other ones.' I nod towards the baskets and the guys jump to help. Since there's only two more I watch as Sam and John take each end of one of the baskets even though it's light as. It's so comical I make a note to replay the image for Melanie when we bond. Because we need to bond.

If there is one thing that has become wildly apparent to me it's that I will follow this girl around like a lost puppy the rest of my life. I don't care if she bonds me or not. But I hear her doubts. I look at her family. And I want nothing more than to bite this girl and make sure she knows that she is it for me.

'Melanie, Sweetness.' I call into the room again. She's kneeling in the center, her gaze darting around the space, confused. 'These will help.'

I push the basket into the room and she launches for it, immediately pulling out two items and dashing to the other side of the room to bury them amongst some pillows. The guys put the other two baskets next to me in the doorway and I push them into the room as Melanie comes racing back.

We watch in silence as she flits about the room with our old clothes and the linens from our rooms. She stuffs them amongst the pillows, constantly rearranging them, patting at them, trying to get them to stay exactly where she wants them.

She's beyond sweet like this, all instinct and candor. She growls at pillows when they tilt and snaps at blankets that don't stay as she laid them. She's a natural. The nest takes shape quickly and I feel honoured to even watch her do this. The thought that she is doing this for us is almost too much.

Suddenly she sits in the middle of the room, looking side to side, sniffing the air. She shuffles a few pillows on her left and then sniffs the air again. She must finally be satisfied because her eyes close as she takes a deep breath.

'Mick, come here.' She demands as her eyes snap open and land on mine. I don't pause to think as I throw myself into the space kneeling in front of her. She smiles and reaches out to run her fingers through my beard.

'Can we come in too?' One of my brothers calls into the room but I don't turn, I don't care, because Melanie is smiling sweetly at me as she scratches my chin through my beard.

'You can all come in.' She calls over my head, her eyes not leaving mine. I hear rather than watch my brothers launch themselves into the space and spread out around Melanie. I pray they remember my earlier lecture about kneeling out of respect for her and her space when they come in. And letting her make all the initial decisions. It was common we'd eventually take over but at first all the decisions needed to be hers.

'What now?' John whispers from beside me and I hold back my chuckle. He's been the most concerned about us getting this just right. As far as I know he's never participated in a heat before.

'Be patient. She'll tell us what she wants. Won't you, sweetness?' I direct the last to Melanie, nodding to encourage her and she nods back.

'Tell you what I want?' She says it like a question and I nod again.

'That's what we want.' George growls nearby.

'Whatever you want.' Sam chimes in.

Melanie kneels in the center of the room looking at each of us in turn. There's no confusion in her gaze but she seems unsure. Like she's trying to figure something out. I want to assure her that whatever it is we will solve it for her. But I wait. I know my brothers are taking my lead and I know she needs space to feel how much control she has here.

'John.' She calls her left hand reaching out for him. He moves forward on his knees and takes the hand she's offered. She guides him to the side and pushes on his chest to get him to lay down in some pillows.

'Sam.' She calls next, he rushes forward but she puts her hand on his chest and then points to the other side of the nest. 'There.'

He moves away from her reluctantly but flops against the cushions she pointed at. She reaches for George next, pushing him into a blanket. Were all perfectly spaced around the nest. She sits between all four of us, closing her eyes as she inhales.

I can smell it too. The perfect balance she's created. She's piled the pillows in such a way that the room swims with our smells so perfectly even that it's now its own thing. She's balanced us. Perfectly.

She breathes one more deep breath as she opens her eyes. Her pupils are blown wide. Her eyes land on me and I feel the weight of her omega stare as it looks me up and down.

'Pants off.' She demands and we all rush to comply as she licks her lips spinning in a circle to take each of us in. All of us naked we simply stare at her. She's gorgeous. All of her lush curves, her swaying breasts, her thick thighs. She looks like all of my fantasies come to life as she tosses her dark hair over her shoulder and her gaze comes back to collide with mine.

I expect her to tell us what to do, what she wants. But instead she slides forward onto her hands and begins crawling towards me. I groan my desire as she slowly moves closer, climbing on top of me and straddling my lap.

'Big guy.' She mumbles as she caresses my face with the tips of her fingers.

'Yes sweetness?' I'm so hard between us I can barely think.

'Kiss me?' I don't respond, I capture her lips with mine. Leaning forward and pushing her till she's flat on her back in the center of the nest, with me hovering over her. Our tongues tangle as our lips glide against each other. It's raw and it's filthy. And I love it.

She moans into my mouth, her arms drifting from my shoulders, along my back, to pull me harder against her. I let my weight drop down onto her and she sighs into my mouth. I tear my lips from hers to place kisses along her collarbones and down her stomach.

'Sam.' She calls my brother forward to take my place on her lips as I kiss the inside of her thighs. I hear him as he groans into her kiss and I exhale into her folds. I let my tongue dart out and lap at her center. Her cry is so loud I lift my gaze and find Sam has latched onto her breast with his lips as he caresses the other with his hand.

'John.' She moans and he moves forward to kiss her as Sam and I continue to lathe her body. She's so hot, pulled tight between us, all of our scents in the room. It's too much. I can't stand it. I double my efforts against her clit, sliding my hand up so I can plunge my finger inside of her. I need her to cum. I need her to bathe us in her scent.

Sam seems to have the same idea because when I look up he's pulling her nipple between his teeth as he pinches the other one, making her back bow away from the blankets beneath. All the while John kisses her, running his hands along her face, whispering something I can't hear.

She's so close, I can taste it.

KNOT FOR REAL

Chapter 62. George

'Are you going to come for us babygirl?' I grumble as I watch my pack devour Melanie in front of me. I never thought I'd enjoy being left out as much as I was right now. But with our beautiful omega spread out in front of me as I watch all of my brothers make her moan with pleasure I have never been happier.

She tears her lips from Johns and he simply descends to her chest, pushing Sam's hand out of the way as he latches onto her nipple.

Her eyes turn to me. Her lips are red, cheeks flushed, eyes dark as she slides her hands along the back of each of their heads and holds them tighter to her breasts.

'Good Girl.' I murmur. She's so hot right now, commanding them, taking what she needs.

I thought I was proud of her earlier tonight when she asked for dessert and let us take her from her horrible parents' house. I thought I was proud of her when at the store I watched her choose the items she really wanted when at first I'd seen her keep turning to the sales rack. But seeing her like this, this took the cake.

I already knew I loved her but I didn't know how much until I realised that just seeing her happy, seeing her receive pleasure, even if it wasn't at my hand, was enough. One day I was going to bond this girl and she was going to be mine.

'Are you going to come for your pack?' I grumble. She nods, her eyes on me, her mouth open on a moan as she lets them bathe her in pleasure. I can't resist getting closer and I slide in next to her head, taking her chin between my fingers. 'Come for us.'

I whisper against her lips and her eyes close. I can see her whole body tremble around us but I can't take my gaze from her face. Her pleasure crests through her body as a blush spreads over her cheeks. I hear all my brothers groan around me as she moans and shudders.

No one comes as sweetly as this girl. I lean down and press my lips gently against hers. She overwhelms me with her sweet perfection.

'I love you so much.' I whisper against her lips as I pull back. She grabs my hand wrapped around her jaw and pulls my palm up to her mouth, kissing the center of my hand and I smile. Her lips nuzzle along my palm drifting towards my wrist, kissing along my arm till she's almost to my elbow. I smile at her as I feel her teeth press into my skin.

I realise what she's doing a moment too late as I feel her pierce my forearm and her energy spirals inside me. It's like being filled up with warm golden light. I feel it as she floods through my body, worming into the darkest crevices of myself.

Forgive me. I hear her voice inside me and I freeze as she reaches up to cradle my face. We haven't discussed this. I know I'd said we wanted to bond with her but we hadn't actually discussed it with her. I'm reeling as her words sink into me. Why would I need to forgive her?

I don't think as I grab her hand from my cheek and sink my lips through the skin of her wrist. The bond between us pulls taut as I feel myself slide into her. She's so soft and kind but so full of worry.

There's nothing to forgive. I think back at her, locking my eyes on to hers as a single tear drifts down her cheek. *You're mine.*

She nods, a smile touching her lips. She was mine and she knew it. She could feel it now and I've never been happier. I know I should have found a way to stop this but I'm so overjoyed to be inside her mind, to feel her soul, her energy.

'Holy shit!' Sam mumbles and I become aware of the room again. My brothers are all staring at me. Taking in the enormity of what I just did. I know they will all be with me but we still should have discussed it first and I feel a pang of concern for them.

'Don't.' Melanie grumbles below me. I bring my eyes back to hers as she begins sliding out from her spot on her back and begins pushing me down into the cushions. I let her soft pressure direct me where she wants me as she climbs on top of me.

I'm in a daze as she straddles my laps and then guides herself down onto me in one smooth movement.

'Fuck.' I groan as I feel her pleasure ricochet through our bond. I not only feel her heat and her warmth I feel how she feels, how much she loves having me inside her. How she feels adored and protected by me and it's all I even wanted.

'Fuck me Daddy.' She whispers against my lips and I don't need telling twice. I grip her hips as I thrust up into her, rocking her against me. It's fast and hard and rough and she loves it. Bouncing against me, listening to me grunt and groan because she feels so good. And I never want this to end.

She starts to flutter around me and I feel her pulling me in deeper as she gets closer to her orgasm. Grinding against my knot pushing me so close to the edge I think I'm going to lose my mind. She pushes against me, rolling her hips and my knot slips inside her, expanding instantly as I come deep within her.

As soon as I fill her up she's coming around me shaking so hard she practically vibrates on top of me. I wrap my arms around her, pulling her into my chest as she falls limp against me, my knot deep inside her.

Holy shit.

Her eyes close, she's not quite asleep, but resting against me, her breaths deep and even. I stare out over her at my brothers who are all staring at us in awe.

'What now?' Sam asks the room at large. I feel like I should answer but I don't know. Every discussion of us taking the bond, of having an omega, they were all theoretical but this, this was real.

'She bit you?' John asks and I nod.

'And you bit her?' Sam presses and I nod again. I know they all saw but they seem to need me to confirm.

'Then we all need to bond with her. Today.' Mick states.

'Today?' John seems daunted by the thought.

'If we all want to share the bond, to be able to hear each other and not just her, then we have to bond as close together as possible. If she doesn't want that then we'll just bond with her another day, but we'll never have the true bond, only with her.' He shrugs like it's no big deal. But it is.

Having a pack bond would mean everything to me, to all of the guys, I know it. But I'd never even for a second want to put pressure on Melanie for that if she didn't want it. If I never felt my brother's souls inside mine I could live. But if I ever did anything to hurt Melanie I'd want to die.

'When she's a bit more lucid we'll ask her if she wants to bond us all.'

'She wants that.' Melanie mumbles into my chest, just loud enough for us to hear. But it's not just Melanie, it's her omega. The distinct timber of her voice gives it away.

'Are you sure?' I ask, lifting her from my chest to stare into her eyes.

'Yes.' She smiles at me. 'She loves you so much. We love you so much. But she's so scared. I needed to... I had to... she didn't want to wait... but she was scared you'd say no.'

'Never.' I grumble as I wrap my hands around the back of her neck and kiss her. 'We love you too.'

'I know. But she needs to know, it was the only way.' Her eyes implore me to understand and I do. Melanie needed this. She needs the bond. But she was too scared to ask so her omega took it for her.

'I'm proud of you, babygirl.' I murmur.

'Thank you Daddy.' She smirks back at me. God do I love this woman.

'Who do you want next?'

Chapter 63. John

A year of waiting and I still don't feel like I'm ready for this woman. She's incredible, beautiful and apparently she wants to be ours. I watched as her teeth pierced George's skin and I couldn't even process what I was seeing.

From the first second I realised she was an omega I'd started fantasising about what it would be like to claim her. To let my teeth sink into her skin, let our souls and our energy entwine. To feel her thoughts and be able to send her ours. But I'd never imagined what it would be like to have her claim us.

Not only had she bitten George. He'd bitten her. The first bond was made. She was linked to our pack forever. Just the thought sent lightening through my veins.

I watch as she turns from George, still sitting on his lap and her gaze flits about the nest. Her crystal blue eyes are dark now but she's still my Melanie. Her smile, those dimples, her curls, she's always been mine.

Her gaze lands on mine and I lose my breath. Her smile becomes a smirk as she slides from George's lap. His knot releases her only because she's in heat. Any other time they'd be locked together for at least half an hour, but when an omega is in heat our bodies know and they adjust to make sure she has what she needs.

She crawls towards me but I can't wait, as soon as she is within my reach I tug her down onto some cushions pulling her beneath me.

'I love you.' I whisper, knowing the others can still hear me even if my words are just for her.

'She loves you too. She just can't say it yet.' Melanie's omega answers. I nod my understanding as my lips find hers. A part of me still worries about how much I hurt her. I didn't know she was ours, because of the suppressants, but our other natures still clearly called to each other.

Did she want me the way I wanted her? Did she suffer when I came in asking for gifts for other omegas? I cringe whenever I think about it.

'She can take as long as she wants.' I assure her as I swap to kissing her neck. She tilts her head to give me more access and I groan my delight as she moans with pleasure. I kiss every inch of her skin I can reach till she starts to whine.

'Knot, please.' I shiver at her words. Pulling back I line our bodies up, ready to plunge deep inside her. 'No.'

I freeze.

'What's wrong?'

'No, I want to...'

'What do you want, baby?' She doesn't answer me, just pushes on my chest so that I move away from her right to the edge of the nest. I'm confused but I will always do what she wants.

She moves around me so that she's between me and my brothers and the rest of the nest and then she drops forward. Her ass high in the air, her chest flat in the mattress as she presents.

'Fuck.' Sam grunts from the other side and I nod my agreement. He can't even see all of her the way I can right now, he can only see her lush ass thrust in the air. I watch as slick dribbles down the inside of her thighs and I lick my lips. I want to taste her. But my gorgeous girl has demanded a knot.

I slide forward running my hand over her ass before gripping her hips and rubbing myself against all her perfect wetness.

'You're dripping for us, baby.' She nods into the cushions beneath her before turning her head to look back at me.

'I need you.' She begs. I align myself with her entrance and push home in one smooth motion. She's so hot and wet I almost black out.

My fingers dig into her hips holding her still as I begin to thrust deep inside her. I feel her flutter around me already pulling at my knot which is more than ready for her. I push it inside and feel her squeeze it tight.

I've never knotted anyone before and nothing could have prepared me for the experience. It's perfect pressure, everywhere I need it, all at once. I know the second I come it's over so I hold on as I thrust into her, my knot preventing me from sliding in long strokes so I vibrate against her in tiny thrusts pushing her closer and closer to the edge. Her moans echo around the room as she comes but I keep going. I'm not done with her yet.

I raise my hand dropping it against the soft flesh of her arse with a resounding smack. She shudders around me as her orgasm begins to build again without the first one ever having ended. She's a mess of need and I love it.

I bring my hand down again on her other cheek and then repeat, again and again, till her skin glows red. She's shuddering into the cushions in front of me, sweat dripping from her skin as slick continues to pour into my lap.

'Mick, Sam, come closer.' George grunts out. I can't focus on him but I feel it as they all move closer. I feel my alpha instinct want to growl at them, to make them back away from what's mine. As I go to snap, Melanie's hand snakes back and grips my thigh, squeezing it and I remember. George can hear her now, this must be what she wants.

I let my brothers crowd in around us as Melanie's hand shifts from my thigh searching the air behind her. I reach out and grab her hand and she latches on, pulling herself up. I shift back on my knees so I'm still deep inside her as she practically sits back into my lap. She pulls my hand around holding it to her cheek for a moment before her teeth sink into the very center of the palm of my hand.

I come instantly, my knot inflating inside her, locking us together. I feel her bright light sliding beneath my skin, twisting through my body as it finds its home inside me.

Bite me. Her thought echoes inside me and I don't think, I push the hair from her shoulders and sink my teeth into the back of her neck. I feel myself, my energy pouring into her like it's finally found home. It's incredible, she's incredible.

Yes she is. George's thought appears in my mind and I smile, my teeth still buried in her skin.

Hello brother. I think back to him.

I need them too. Melanie's thoughts push into both our minds. It's strange to be able to feel them as a part of my own mind and yet they are separate. Like we're all in a hall together, able to speak to each other, know each other, but still individuals. Now I know what Melanie needs.

'Sam, Mick, closer.' I snap. Mick slides in so that he's right in front of her, George is on our left and Sam on our right. Melanie reaches for Mick first, pulling him down into a savage kiss and the giant of a man goes more than willingly.

Her lips slide from his down along his collar bone. Her lips land on his chest, above his heart and I watch as her teeth break the skin. Mick groans and I feel the first flicker of him in our bond. He sits back onto his knees to stare at Melanie but she isn't waiting anymore.

She turns to Sam and he's kissing her savagely when Mick slides forward, bowing before her and kissing her belly. His lips slide to the side and he sinks his teeth into her plush hip. The bond pulls tight and I feel my brother connect to all of us.

Wow. Mick's thought echoes into our bond and I couldn't agree more.

Melanie preens inside at the praise and so we all push more thoughts at her. I feel it as my brothers praise her kindness, how beautiful she is, how smart. And she takes it all in. But her focus isn't on us. It's on Sam.

Her lips pull from his and he tries to recapture them but she pushes his head to the side and bites straight into his neck. This bite is more vicious than the others and I can tell instantly it's going to scar worse than any of our gentle marks and I smirk. He's going to love that. I can already feel that he does.

She releases him and his hand reaches out, sliding down her back pushing her forward into Mick's grip who instantly captures her lips as she lands on all fours.

'Excuse me.' Sam smirks pushing me back as he slides forward so that he's hovering over the very center of her ass cheek. 'Naughty girls need reminders.'

He sinks his teeth into the red bloom left by my hands and smirks as he enters the bond. The piece of shit laughs into the connection as he licks the mark he just made.

'Now every time you spank her, she'll get double the pleasure.' I can feel his pride just as I can feel Mick's awe and George's gratitude. I'm still knotted deep inside Melanie and it's the most incredible feeling in the world.

Chapter 64. Sam

For three days now we've been in Melanie's nest with her, attending to her every need. I'd helped omegas through their heats before at the clinic but it had never felt like this. With her thoughts and the thoughts of my brothers inside of me, every single second was pure perfection.

We forced her to take breaks, to eat and drink water. Mick even carried her into the shower when she complained about her skin being too sticky. But every time we were as reluctant as she was to stop.

Sometimes she needed two or us or even three of us to attend to her. But more often than not she'd just pick one of us and demand our knot. And the rest of us were more than content to sit back and watch.

Melanie is currently passed out on Mick's chest, George lying next to them, stroking the hair back from her face, John running his hand up and down her calf. I not only feel peace but I feel all of their peace and it makes mine stronger.

She's cooler. Mick mumbles into the bond. And we all push back our agreement. About an hour ago her heat had started to break, her temperature was dropping and she felt less needy. Which was fine by me because I could still feel how much she wanted us.

Melanie, the sweet woman we all loved, would have wanted to talk about it and be sure that we'd discussed every ramification and every benefit. But her omega just knew what she wanted and took it. And I would forever be grateful for that.

I would have happily waited for eternity for her to be ready to take the bond but now that it was formed I had plans. I was going to use that connection to make sure she knew how much we all wanted her. Also to make sure she was getting as much pleasure as her body could take.

You know what we still haven't done? I send the question into the bond along with a mental image or all four of us with her at the same time. Mick snorts his approval, while George rolls his eyes at me.

You sure that wouldn't be too much? John thinks back.

I think she'd like it.

'I think you're right.' Melanie mumbles.

'Sorry honey, go back to sleep.' Mick croons as George strokes her hair.

'I'm awake.' She yawns, sitting up, astride Mick as she stretches. Holy shit.

'Melanie?' I ask. A blush warms her cheeks as she nods. We all rush forward at once, crowding around her.

'How do you feel?'

'Are you okay?'

'What do you need?'

'What can we get you?' Our questions all come out at once as we surround her.

'I'm fine. Tired. A little hungry. But I'm good.'

'I'll order some food.' George snaps out as he begins to pull away but she reaches out and stops him.

'Not yet. Just stay with me a moment.' He nods and moves back in on her right. John's sitting to the left with me at her back so that we surround her and we've all got our hands on her. Stroking her hair, clutching her hand, grazing her skin. She loves it.

The bond feels different with Melanie back in control. There's a shy feeling that wasn't there before. An adorable kind of sweetness but it's tinged with doubt.

'What is that?' I ask without meaning to. She can feel what I'm referring to as I poke at it in our connection and she sighs.

'Just worrying.'

'About what?' Mick asks. But she doesn't answer, she just shrugs. It doesn't matter that she doesn't have the words because we can feel it. She's worrying about us, about taking the bonds, about whether we still want her. About Whisper.

'He's with your friend Sandra.' George answers the easiest of the questions. 'She told me that you owe her brunch and details as soon as you're ready.'

Melanie nods.

'It wasn't just the heat.' I assure her. 'We want you, we want the bonds, you must feel how happy we are.'

We all shove our joy and happiness at her till she giggles.

'Yes I can feel that.'

'Then what's wrong?' Mick asks, pushing the hair from her face.

'It's hard for me to trust it.'

'Understandable.' I grumble into her shoulder blades. I do understand. Probably better than my brothers. When you're raised in criticism and doubt the better you feel the harder it is to relax. Some of my thoughts must drift into the bond because I feel Melanie's agreement inside me. I love that I understand her but I hate that she shares these feelings.

'I hate that you understand too.' She whispers to me.

I lean forward, tilting her head back so I can capture her lips. I need her. I need her taste on my tongue reminding me that this is real. And it's what she needs too.

'All of us?' I whisper into our kiss and she nods. God I love this girl.

Breaking the kiss I turn her back towards Mick who she's straddling and begin kissing along her shoulders as I push the mental image at my brothers again.

'She should rest.' Mick shakes his head.

'She's hungry.' George adds while I feel John trying to figure out exactly how it's going to work. I resist laughing as I shake my head at my brothers.

'She needs all of us first.' I explain. Melanie's perfume explodes around us confirming that I'm right. With all of us kissing every part of her we can reach she's already leaking slick so thick I can smell it in the air.

Mick sits forward lifting Melanie up onto his lap so that he can reposition himself at her entrance. Holding onto her waist he kisses her as he guides her down onto his shaft. She moans, throwing her head back, leaving space for John to slide forward and kiss her neck.

She leans forward into his kiss creating the perfect angle for me to dip my fingers between her cheeks and use her slick to coat her tight hole. Melanie shudders at the contact and George growls his delight. I slide a finger inside her and have to bite my lip to stop my noise.

Fuck but she's tight. I work my finger inside her slowly while she sits there kissing John with Mick inside her. George keeps caressing her skin and dropping kisses everywhere he can touch. She relaxes around me and I add another finger, flicking them inside her to make room.

'Please.' She moans into John's kiss. I pull my fingers out, shuffling forward to align myself and push forward. I barely slip inside her and I can feel her body vibrating with pleasure. I go slow, making tiny movements in and out. With all four of us caressing her, the pleasure building in her body, I keep stretching her till I'm seated deep within.

I knew it would feel good, I didn't know it would be this good. I can feel Mick inside her as well, the man is just laying back on the cushions staring up at all of us like we're his favourite show. I nod at him and he smirks as he slips his hands around her waist, lifting her from us both as we pull back and then pushing her down onto us again.

'Fuck.' Melanie screams with abandon. We can feel her pleasure echoing our own and it's so intense I feel dizzy.

George stands next to her and reaches out to push the hair from her face. She turns towards him immediately taking him into her mouth. He wraps his hand around her throat to guide her up and down his length.

She reaches out to take John in her hands. Sliding up and down his length, she matches the rhythm we all set together.

I feel wild, electric. Like there's fire under my skin and lightning in my spine. It's never felt like this before. We hurtle towards our peak together. Everyone's feelings flowing within the bond, pushing us higher and higher.

I can't hold on much longer. I'm not sure which one of us thinks it but we all agree. It's too much. Too much pleasure.

Melanie begins to shudder between us and I know she's about to tip over. I hear George growl as Mick calls out, 'now' and then she's coming. Her body spasming between us triggering all of us in turn. I feel Mick's knot expand inside her, almost pushing me out as I come deep in her ass. Melanie swallows George deep as he comes down her throat and John shoots his load against her stomach.

It's too much, all of us together. Too perfect. Too good.

I lean forward resting my head against Melanie's back as she folds forwards onto Mick. John and George collapse against us as well until we're just a pile of sweaty bodies trying to catch our breath.

Chapter 65. Melanie

'It looks incredible.' I tell Brian and Dan. As they step back from the masterpiece that is now my front window. It's hard to believe that they'd made this out of recycled beer bottles. The stained glass style window not only features my logo but has a beautiful pattern all around it that filtered light casting rainbows all over my shop.

You're incredible. Mick whispers in the bond as he comes up behind me and drops a kiss to the top of my head.

It's been two days since my heat broke.

I rested all day Sunday. Letting them feed me while bossing them around as they helped me arrange all of my stuff in the omega suite. That night we cuddled up in the attached living room and watched a movie in essentially a giant pile of cuddles.

I was tucked up against Mick, who was sketching in his notebook trying to design a doggy elevator to make it easier for Whisper to go outside and then come straight back up to me. George sat next to him playing with my hair, my hand, whatever he could reach as he dealt with the emails from the many people he had blown off in the last week to be with me. John had his head in my lap letting me run my fingers through his curls while Sam rested on my thighs a few inches lower tracing his fingers along my bare calves. I'd never felt so content.

I spent yesterday morning answering emails on the new laptop George got me alongside him in his home office. I was doing a grand reopening on Friday and I had a lot to organise but it wasn't a very effective work day. George kept reaching over to kiss me or hug me till eventually I just pulled my laptop across and sat in his lap while he made his phone calls.

I spent the afternoon with Mick in his workroom while he worked on his doggy elevator concept. He'd already installed a doggy door that morning that meant Whisper could now go outside whenever he wanted, which seemed like enough to me. But he was worried about Whisper going up and down the three flights of stairs all the time.

Monday night we all gathered for dinner, my first Monday night pack dinner. It was Sam's turn to cook which apparently meant steak and veggies. Apparently that was the only thing he knew how to cook. After dinner they pushed me to go straight to sleep but I had other ideas. Ideas Sam fully supported, that led to all of us being up late.

John walked me here to the cafe this morning, far earlier than he needed to be in the office and helped me tidy the place some more. The burnt floor had been replaced and every inch of my cafe was now spotless thanks to George's workmen. I don't know how they did it but you could barely smell a hint of smoke anywhere, or on anything.

John helped me lay out my stock and rearrange my counters till he had to go to work at which point I went home. I even took a nap with Mick before he brought me back to the shop to meet with Brian and Dan. Then I just sat back and watched as they installed my new window.

Three weeks. That was it, I had known these men for three weeks. John I'd technically known for a year but the rest of them, this, it all started only three weeks ago and I could barely wrap my head around that.

So much had changed with their mere presence in my life. And not just my living arrangements and my wardrobe which had doubled in size thanks to Mick's apparent love of online shopping.

It was everything inside me. Finding people who wanted to be in my life, who saw my accomplishments, cheered me on, it just made every second of every day feel better.

God I was such a sap now.

'You ready to go?' Mick asks from behind me, his arm wrapping around my waist.

'I don't want to.'

'Then we won't.' I feel him shrug. It's that simple to him. But it isn't to me. I don't want to do this but I feel like it needs to be done.

'Tonight I want a bubble bath with you in it.' I sigh and gather my things.

'Whatever my omega wants.' He nods. We decided I would move in with the guys pretty easily. It's only a couple of blocks to walk over here in the morning for work. And now that George sorted everything with the bank it turned out I had more than enough income to hire someone almost full time, so I would have help. But that thought led my brain back to the horrible situation I now had to go deal with.

'Remind me again why I'm doing this?' I ask Mick as he helps me into the passenger seat of his truck.

'Because they broke the law.' He shrugs before heading to his side.

I turn and stare out the window at the passing buildings. We're headed into the city to George's office. I'm excited to see it properly, last time I was too embarrassed to go upstairs in just leggings, no matter how much George had insisted it was fine.

The drive passes in silence, and Mick helps me out of the car at the other end and then shepherds me into the building. He waves at the receptionist and she in turns waves us through security. Within moments I'm being ushered into the conference room and I sigh my relief.

They're all here. I knew George would be here but Sam and John must have taken off early from work to make sure they could be here by five. The room is full of all of their scents, of our scent, the specific mixture that is all of us and it relaxes me even as other parts of me stir.

'You look hot.' Sam calls by way of greeting. He had to leave early this morning so this is the first he's seeing of my black jeans and blue sweater. It's a nice combo if I do say so myself.

'Thanks.' I smile at him.

'You also look very professional and beautiful.' George adds as he gestures at the seat next to him, which Mick helps me into.

'Well this is a business meeting.' I nod.

'I hate meetings.' John shudders as he sits next to me. 'That's why I like coding, very few meetings, lots of actually getting work done.'

'Are you mocking what I do?' George asks casually, letting his chair spin towards John and I on his left. George is sitting at the head of the large table, although he's pulled me closer to him so that we basically share the spot. John and Mick sit on my side, Sam on the other, all of us waiting.

'I mean do you actually do any work anymore?' Sam asks, his voice full of humour. 'I figure at this point you basically just delegate.'

'Some of us were just born to lead.' George shrugs. I can tell they're trying to relax me with their banter. I can feel their intent in the bond. It's fair. My shoulders are up around my ears as I think about what we're about to do.

'Sorry I'm late.' Detective Charlotte calls as she enters the room and takes the seat next to Sam. 'Getting tech to run confirmation on the CCTV footage was more complicated than I thought.'

'But it's sorted?' Mick asks her in his gruff voice. He's almost as worried as me. Not about what was about to happen. About me. If he had his way I'd be at home eating ice cream letting the others sort this. But I know deep down I needed to be a part of it.

'They're here.' Jamie's voice comes through the intercom.

'Send them in.' George calls out, his finger on the device. 'You ready?'

All eyes are on me and so I nod. I don't know if I'm ready but we're here and it's happening and nothing can go really wrong since they're all here with me. John puts his hand on my knee while George clasps my hand under the table and we wait.

The door opens and the parade of too tight suits begins as I watch the three ass-keteers file in. They're grins are wide as they take the other end of the table, their eyes on George. Apparently the big investor meeting that they were telling everyone about at lunch the other week was with my alpha.

It's Josh who spots me first, he was always the most observant, always the quickest to find something to insult. The other two are only moments behind him though and they all freeze and look at me.

'What are you doing here?' Mark asks, his face contorted in confusion. As head of their pack he's normally the most cocky and there's something about seeing him on his back foot and confused that makes me feel more settled. After everything I've learned about them they should be worried.

'I see you know my omega.' George's voice radiates with pride. He loves calling me that. He even managed to slip it into conversation with the food delivery guy.

'What's going on?' Frank stutters. 'We're here for a meeting.'

'Actually you're here to get arrested.' I explain.

Chapter 66. Mick

Watching Melanie's shoulders straighten as she tells these douche bags what's actually happening is such a turn on. I think Sam's rubbing off on me because I never used to be so easily aroused or so obsessed with sex. Then again maybe it was just Melanie. Her presence was inspiring.

Nah I'm rubbing off on you. I hear Sam smirk into the bond and I resist the urge to roll my eyes at him. This is a serious moment after all. One I am very close to ruining because I'm so proud of our girl I'm beaming at her like an asshole.

If any of you want me to be the one rubbing off on you, you'll cut out the internal chatter and let me focus. Melanie growls into our connection.

It's hot. The way she's gotten so much more comfortable telling us off, telling us what she wants. It honestly makes me hornier still but I tell my body to cool it, as we all pull back from the bond so she can focus on the room.

'Arrested?' Asshat number one stutters as his brain comes back on line. Honestly I'm not sure I could tell these guys apart if I tried and I'm not all that interested in exerting any effort on them.

'Yes.' Melanie nods.

'What are you talking about?' Ass two spits. 'We're here for a meeting with Mr Jamieson. He's interested in investing in our start-up.'

'No I'm not.' George shrugs. 'If you hadn't bribed my assistant Jamie you wouldn't have gotten this meeting.'

'We didn't... what are you...' Ass three stammers.

'Don't bother denying it. When I told Jamie about your impending arrest today he confessed everything. And now I know about his mother's medical bills, it's all being sorted. I just feel bad he didn't think he could ask for help.'

'Bribery isn't illegal.' Number one spits out.

'Actually, it is.' Charlotte cuts across the ass trying to defend himself. 'As a police officer I can assure you bribery in any form is illegal.'

'Police officer?' Three grumbles.

'Yes, the one who will be arresting you.' Sam smiles at his friend.

'You can't arrest us for slipping someone's assistant some cash.' One of the morons stutters out. But I'm losing interest in them quickly. Instead I turn to stare at Melanie who is blushing, eyes blazing as she stares down her brothers' in law.

'Actually the charges are...' Charlotte opens her phone to check her notes. 'Breaking and entering, arson and fraud. Along with half a dozen other things.'

'We don't have to sit here and listen to this.' One of them yells and turns to the exit. As if that was their cue, two uniformed police officers enter and block the doorway.

'There's another two units in the foyer.' The older of the two directs her comment to Charlotte who just nods.

'Please take your seats.' George grumbles at the three alphas floundering at the other end of the table. He doesn't even bother to bark at them, and he doesn't need to, they're so weak and pathetic they practically fall into their chairs. 'Now as my omega was saying, you're here to be arrested.'

I can feel the pride in his chest that radiates every time he gets to call Melanie his omega. Melanie blushes in response and I enjoy the soft glow in her cheeks that strengthens her scent.

She confessed to me last night when I was massaging her feet that she'd always felt her scent was too strong and too sweet. I had to agree. She was far too sweet and kind and wonderful and her scent matched her. She was also strong and bold beneath her occasionally shy exterior. And in that way too her scent was perfect for her. There were eight alphas in here, all with strong smells and the only thing I could smell was her. She was too much in the best possible way.

'What's all this about?' The smarmiest of the asshats demands.

'You vandalised my store.' Melanie answers.

'You can't prove that.'

'We can. The shop across the way installed security cameras a while back. They point across the road at my store. They caught everything.' She was not wrong, they caught everything. I'd made a copy of the tape from the night of the fire for my own personal collection. You couldn't see much of what happened between us. But the footage brought back great memories for me.

'You're full of shit.' One of the asses spits his words at Melanie and it takes a lot of self control on my part not to lean across the table and punch him in the face. I'm not the only one fighting that instinct. But Melanie is holding us all back in the bond.

'Actually it turns out you are, because when my alpha George was helping me with some banking details he discovered that my mortgage was set up incorrectly.' I know Melanie is still talking but I can barely hear her over George inside my brain.

Did you hear her call me her alpha? I never would have thought George could be as moony eyed and enthusiastic as John but here we were. He was practically beaming inside. Although you couldn't tell from his face. He still had the look of someone who would prefer to be committing murder rather than sitting in a boardroom. This is why he was so successful.

'What's your mortgage got to do with us?' One of the idiots gripes.

'Well according to the bank representative who was arrested earlier today, you guys convinced him to double down my interest to make me pay almost double all of these years. Then he siphoned off the excess and gave you guys half. Apparently it was all your idea.'

I enjoy watching the colour drain from all of their faces. It happens in unison, like someone turned off the colour on the tv. They blanch so suddenly I worry they'll faint.

'You can't prove that.' One of them mumbles.

'I can.' Charlotte chimes in. 'Turns out your friend at the bank never really trusted you three so he recorded all of your conversations and kept very detailed notes about the payments all of these years. He was almost excited to turn you lot in. Seems you basically blackmailed him to do it in the first place. Which is another crime we can add to the charges actually.'

She makes a note on her phone while we all sit and wait. The three idiots seem to be stunned into silence which is probably best. If I heard them trying to defend what they did to our sweet girl I'm not sure I'd be able to resist hitting them. For years they had siphoned away her hard earned money to pad their lifestyle. Then they'd broken in and smashed up her store because they had the shits that their business wasn't going well. And when that still wasn't enough they'd barked their omega into going back the next night and torching the place. Melanie's own sister had been forced to set fire to the building knowing she was inside.

Melanie went to talk to her this morning and she'd confessed everything. We hadn't actually had a clue about her involvement until she was sobbing. She would not be charged, not when she'd been forced to do it by her alphas. It boggled my mind that they could have treated their omega that way. I'd rather cut off my own fingers one by one than cause Melanie any harm. For now Lucy was in a clinic for abused omegas across town. There was still no love lost between the sisters but I could feel Melanie's relief that her sister was to be left out of this mess.

'Do you have anything you'd like to say?' Charlotte directs her question to Melanie, but she's already shaking her head no.

'Just take them away.' She shrugs.

The two uniformed cops step forward and two more enter behind them. I watch with more glee than is entirely appropriate as they're cuffed and dragged from the room. And I'm not the only one. George, Sam, John, we're all smiling. Charlotte says something to Sam and then she follows out the officers and we're all left alone again.

It was over. Our girl was safe. The assholes who had tried to hurt her were headed to jail. And we got to take her home.

'So what now?' Melanie asks us as we all sit in silence.

'Pizza?' Sam offers with a shrug.

'You sure that's a good idea?' John lifts his eyebrow at Sam.

'She has to find out eventually?' Sam shrugs.

'What?' Melanie demands

'You'll see.' We all chime in unison.

Chapter 67. Melanie

Tonight was a celebration. The guys drank beers while Mick procured my favourite soda. And together we demolished six full pizzas plus garlic bread. I watched with awe as Mick ate almost two whole pizzas by himself. The big guy needed fuel.

We hadn't even bothered to turn the TV on at first. We just sat around talking about everything and nothing as we unwound. The guys took particular pleasure in recounting how my asshole brothers' in law had squirmed and paled as they realised they were fucked.

When George had first shared his theories with me Monday morning I wish I could say I had trouble believing it. But I just nodded. He'd finally talked to the guy at my bank I had dealt with years ago and he'd been very quick to point the finger. From there it all just kind of unravelled. And when Charlotte called to tell us about the footage from the shop across the street I couldn't even feign surprise.

My sister's involvement hurt. I'd been raging at first but when I talked to her this morning and she confessed everything, I understood that she didn't have a choice. But it was still a lot to process that she had actually set fire to the building I was in.

When Mick suggested after our nap that I should probably talk to a professional about it I had immediately nodded my agreement into his chest. I reached out to my old therapist this afternoon and set an appointment for next week. I was strong and I could handle anything but I was going to need help processing this one.

With the pizza demolished we selected a movie. Much to my delight it was John's pick and he chose Mulan, forcing George to finally watch a Disney movie. He grumbled at first about it being for kids but by the time the rest of us were singing 'be a man' I could feel his enjoyment in the bond.

The bond had become a source of constant pleasure. A part of me had always worried about what it would be like to have someone else's energy wrapped up in my own like this. And there were moments that were hard. When I felt a sudden flash of anger and it took me a second to realise it wasn't mine but rather Sam across town learning about the fraud for the first time.

But the bond was still new. In time we would learn to control the leakage even when we were overcome. Even just in the few days we'd all learned how to open and close our paths into each other's minds with more ease than I would have thought possible. And we'd come to rely on it fast.

Yesterday, John kept using our connection to fire off random coding questions that he didn't actually need answers to but rather just needed to discuss. He kept telling me that I was better than a rubber duck. A joke he assured me would make sense if I ever learned to code.

Sam used the bond to get us all to chime in with opinions on a case he was unsure if he wanted to prosecute or not. Mick similarly got us all to weigh in on design options for the Whisper-vator 2000, his external dog operated dumbwaiter style elevator. Patent apparently pending.

George was the only one who stayed mostly silent in the bond. But he was the first one to respond. And every time it was with a giddy pleasure I couldn't really understand. Whenever we conversed in the bond he sent me a wave of gratitude. Every time I tried to ask him why he was thanking me he'd just smile and say, 'For being you.'

He was tucked up behind me now, as I laid across the couch with my feet in Mick's lap. What had started as a foot massage was now just him tracing lazy patterns into the skin of my ankle. Apparently tomorrow me and him were getting pedicures together and I was not only excited for the pampering but also the sight of this giant in one of those massage chairs, with his feet in the water.

Sam flopped down on the far end past Mick, his hand on his swollen belly declaring death by pizza long before the movie began. John was sitting on the floor in front of me, his head resting on the couch in front of my belly. He always found a way to sit with his head near enough my lap I could run my fingers through his hair.

With a belly full of food, surrounded by my men with peace and contentment pulsing through our bond I could feel my eyes starting to droop but I fought them. I was not missing the rest of this movie.

'Oh no.' Mick's voice startles me as he groans. 'Incoming.'

'Shit.' John pinches his nose in front of me.

'What's wrong?' I ask as I prop myself up on my elbows. Too late I realise I should have followed John's lead and blocked my nose as the smell reaches me. 'Oh god what is that?'

'That would be Sam.' George gags from above me.

'I call it his weapon of ass destruction.' John grumbles. I hear Sam's wicked laugh from the far end of the couch.

'You should see a doctor.' I gag. The smell is already fading but I feel it in my nose still.

'Every time the man eats more than one piece of cheese this happens.' George explains. 'Milk is fine, yoghurt fine, all dairy, fine. But cheese turns him into a deadly weapon.'

'Have you considered banning all cheese from the house?' I offer as I flop back into my position with my head in George's lap.

'Why should the rest of us suffer a cheeseless existence because he can't handle it.' John tilts his head back on the couch to catch my eye.

'We're suffering right now.' I point out.

'They fade quickly.' John shrugs.

'I did try to warn you.' Mick tickles the bottom of my foot and I pull it back on reflex as I turn my gaze to his.

'So did I.' John chimes in.

'I was too scared it would frighten you away.' George shrugs above me, his fingers once again running through my hair.

'No way I was filling you in on my dirty secret.' Sam calls out from the far end. 'I wanted you to find me hot for as long as possible.'

'You're still hot, now I'm just going to worry about what we feed you.' I grumble back to him.

'So you admit that you think I'm hot?' Sam demands and I roll my eyes as I focus back on the movie.

'I guess we're all not so perfect after all.' Mick teases me still playing with the skin of my ankle.

'I guess not.' I huff out before whispering under my breath, knowing that they will hear me anyway. 'But you're perfect for me.'

I feel them all flutter with joy in the bond and I know it's time.

'Oh by the way...' I pause, making sure that I have all of their complete attention. 'I love you.'

Content Warnings

Knot For Real contains the following:

Explicit sexual content throughout, including multiple partners, power exchange dynamics, consensual D/s elements including spanking, restraint, praise, and the use of honorifics.

Omegaverse biology including heat cycles, knotting, scent sensitivity, suppressants, and bonding/bite mechanics that are central to the plot.

A past non-consensual experience at a heat clinic, described in moderate detail. The character involved was an adult. This is not depicted approvingly and is addressed as harmful within the narrative.

Past emotional and sexual shaming by a prior romantic partner, including shaming of sexual preferences during a heat.

Grief and betrayal — the death of a prior pack in a car accident is a significant backstory element, compounded by the revelation that the relationship was not what the protagonist believed it to be.

Emotionally abusive family dynamics, including maternal criticism of body size and weight, conditional affection, withholding of emotional support, and use of a childhood bully nickname.

Disordered eating behaviours as a stress response, including meal restriction before family visits. This is not depicted approvingly.

Medical negligence, including long-term prescription of an inappropriate medication and dismissal of a patient's reported symptoms.

Anxiety, panic attacks, and dissociative episodes.

Property destruction and arson, including a fire that occurs while the protagonist is inside the building.

Brief depiction of domestic coercion within a secondary character's relationship. This character is not punished for actions taken under coercion.

KNOT FOR REAL

Touch starvation and its physical and psychological effects, depicted with care.

If any of these are difficult for you right now, it is okay to set this one aside.

Acknowledgements

I want to acknowledge my bestie who has listened to me fret over whether or not to publish this book. Your calm assurance that there are other people who will love my world as much as I do has meant so much to me.

I also want to acknowledge therapy for helping me push past my fear of publishing. Seriously, this is so scary. If anyone finds any spelling mistakes let me know. I tried my best but I'm dyslexic as shit.

To any other budding authors out there I say, don't wait. Don't let them tell you that self publishing is vanity based. If you've poured your heart into a story and you love it and you want to share, that is all that matters.

I'd also like to acknowledge my dog who has missed out on so many pats, so I could keep writing, because I do need both hands. I am so sorry I am yet to grow a third hand so I can be patting you at all times.

To my family, you inspired so much of this book and all that I write. And for that you should probably apologise.

About The Author

Anida Clarmen is a pen name. I promise you I am not ashamed of what I have written, it is hot and funny and emotional and I love it.

However, I keep having this vision of sitting across from someone at a dinner party and they mention they like my writing and then we both have to sit there knowing that I am the reason they masturbated. Or went and woke up their partner. And I'm just not sure I could handle that level of awkwardness.

But while I won't tell you my name let me tell you some things about me that are even truer.

I love love. The only thing I've wanted to be my entire life is loved. Sometimes I wanted to be a chef, or an actress or (obviously) a writer. Usually my latest whim was determined by whatever my favourite tv character of the moment's profession was. But underneath that what I always wanted was to be loved.

I think that's all any of us want. We pretend it's money or sex or fame but all of those things are just ways of pretending we are loved when we don't actually feel it.

So here is my offer to you. My goal is to always write characters who learn to be themselves or who are so wholly dedicated to being themselves they don't let anything get in the way. And I do this so we can all keep practicing the narrative of how we one day say, I am enough. I am loved.

Whomever convinced us all as children that in order to be loved we needed to alter ourselves, should really go to hell. You were, are and will always be lovable. You just need to find the right people. And if you don't feel loved, there is nothing wrong with you, those just aren't your people.

So go find your people, you delicious little pervert. By reading this book (and this about the author) you're already one of my favourite people.

Coming Soon

The Second Nature series will continue with Knot Happening.

Follow Me

AnidaClarmen.com[1]

1. http://anidaclarmen.com

www.ingramcontent.com/pod-product-compliance
Lightning Source LLC
LaVergne TN
LVHW050921080826
845145LV00001B/156

* 9 7 8 1 7 6 4 6 5 8 5 1 5 *